MONGOOSE
R.I.P.

MONGOOSE
R.I.P.

A BLACKFORD OAKES NOVEL

WILLIAM F. BUCKLEY, JR.

RANDOM HOUSE NEW YORK

Library of Congress Cataloging-in-Publication Data

Buckley, William F. (William Frank), 1925–
  Mongoose, R.I.P.

  I. Title.
PS3552.U344M6   1988   813'.54   87-28344
ISBN 0-394-55931-2

Manufactured in the United States of America

First Edition

For Samuel S. Vaughan
—Gratefully

We have found concrete evidence of at least eight plots in-volving the CIA to assassinate Fidel Castro from 1960 to 1965.

p. 71, 94th Congress, 1st Session, SEN-ATE, Report No. 94-465. Alleged Assassi-nation Plots Involving Foreign Leaders. An Interim Report of the Select Committee to Study Governmental Operations with Respect to Intelligence Activities. United States Senate together with Additional, Supplemental, and Separate Views. No-vember 20, 1975

SENATE SELECT COMMITTEE TO STUDY GOVERNMENTAL OPERATIONS WITH RESPECT TO INTELLIGENCE ACTIVITIES

FRANK CHURCH, Idaho, *Chairman*
JOHN G. TOWER, Texas, *Vice Chairman*

PHILIP A. HART, Michigan
WALTER F. MONDALE, Minnesota
WALTER D. HUDDLESTON, Kentucky
ROBERT MORGAN, North Carolina
GARY HART, Colorado

HOWARD H. BAKER, JR., Tennessee
BARRY GOLDWATER, Arizona
CHARLES McC. MATHIAS, JR., Maryland
RICHARD S. SCHWEIKER, Pennsylvania

"The attempted assassination of Sukarno has all the look of an 'operation' by the Central Intelligence Agency: everyone got killed except the appointed victim."

—Editorial Paragraph,
National Review
December 14, 1957

·Book I·

Rufus was always formally hospitable, but even the few who had experienced his extra-professional hospitality—Blackford Oakes, for all his youth, was conspicuous in that small and irregular company—could never quite be sure which Rufus it was they were now going to be exposed to. Today—a wintry January Sunday early in 1963—being simply another occasion in which two confederates had been summoned by Rufus to his country cottage in Maryland, they had no presentiment of the purpose of their visit.

There, at unpretentious "Lockton," many meetings had taken place over the years since Rufus came back from London after VE-Day. But if he had had to guess, Blackford would suppose that Rufus—in his sixties now and resisting the retirement he had sought so resolutely since his wife's sudden death—was wrestling with a special problem. Not unusual: Rufus was generally wrestling with problems, not excluding the dogged inclinations of his industriously cultivated roses, dormant now, in the chill, in the little greenhouse. But Blackford caught an intimation of gravity in Rufus's face when, after lunch, he distributed the material, telling Anthony Trust and Blackford Oakes to read it ("Read it thoroughly," were his actual words), that he would rejoin them later in the afternoon.

Slouched about in the sitting room in their sweaters and corduroy pants, they weren't in an entirely reflective frame of mind. The evening before, in Washington, they had disported in postcollegiate exuberance after a long and eventful professional separation, attending a college basketball game and celebrating their bachelorhood, Sally Partridge being so many

3

miles away in Mexico and Anthony's lady in London. Besides, the documents they were given to read were in many respects lurid, melodramatic—preposterous even, so their exchanges were not always in the diapasonal mode when, every ten or fifteen minutes, one of the young CIA agents would interrupt his reading to make a comment or ask a question. Though the root matter at hand was unquestionably grim.

"Oh no, *no!*" Anthony Trust said at one point, laying down his sheaf of papers. "A big cheese in the Mafia, the President of the United States, and the identical girlfriend!"

Blackford Oakes, seated in the armchair opposite, looked up from his own reading.

"What are you talking about?"

Trust read on a moment before replying. He then laughed—a touch of harshness, but mellowing into humor. Rufus had said he would be gone for two hours. When Rufus said he would be gone for two hours that did not mean that he would be gone for two hours and five minutes, or one hour and fifty-five minutes. He would be back at 7:15, a half hour away—Blackford glanced down to look at his wristwatch. He had a good half hour's reading yet to do, but he was enjoying Anthony's amusement.

"Do you remember Ashpriss at Greyburn? Or had he left by the time you got there? Yeah, I guess he had—you came as a third-former, and he had graduated. Well, when I was thirteen, I was . . . buggered . . . by Ashpriss."

"You—*what?*" Blackford looked up, genuinely arrested, curious, inquisitive. "I never even knew anyone it happened to."

"Yeah, well, at Greyburn by the time you got there you were almost sixteen. Too old. It didn't happen all the time, in every dormitory, the way the novels make you believe, or for that matter C. S. Lewis and Orwell; but it did happen to me, the bastard."

Blackford found it hard to link Anthony's current amusement with such an episode—was it twenty-one? Yes—twenty-one years ago when they had both left Greyburn "College," in the damp Leicestershire countryside, to return to America after Pearl Harbor.

"What makes you bring it up?"

Anthony leaned forward, got up to stir the log fire, and sat down again, his face radiant in what, under entirely different circumstances, Blackford had once referred to as "your lewd, voluptuarian smile."

"Well," Anthony said, "years later—I mean, hell, it was only year before last, in London—I went to one of those huge dinner parties at Rambley's. You've been there, must have been: he collects beautiful and preferably titled people. And what do you know, at that long, narrow table, sitting directly opposite me was—Ashpriss. Only now he is *Lord* Ashpriss, and sitting on my left was—Lady Ashpriss. Ever met her?"

"No."

"Well, she is a beauty all right, but also the most *fearful* left-wing bore. If she had known who my employer really is, I doubt she'd have talked to me. I should have told her. That would have been worth sacrificing early retirement. But she went on and on about how we *misunderstand* Khrushchev, and what *wonderful* things Castro is doing for Cuba, and why don't we take a more *aggressive* stand on disarmament? By now we had reached the dessert course, so I finally let her have it."

"What did you say?"

"Oh, something on the order of how much we missed Joe McCarthy back home, and what a pity we hadn't followed Bertie Russell's advice and marched into Moscow in 1945—that kind of thing. *Well,*" Anthony said, "she looked at me as if I had poured my champagne down her bosom—an excellent vintage—"

"You talking about the champagne?"

"I was not talking about the champagne. Anyway, at this point Ashpriss, sitting opposite, was staring at both of us. She then said with below-zero frost, 'Mr. Trust, I don't believe you and I have *anything* in common!' It was too good to be true—I mean, my polemical life might have ended just then—"

"What did you say?" Blackford asked, impatient.

"I said to her, staring at Ashpriss, '*Oh yes we do*, Lady Ashpriss.'"

Trust laughed. "I mean, you should have seen the expression on his face. La Pasionaria didn't know exactly what it was I had got off with, but she knew I was saying *two* things—one to her, harmless stuff, something quite different to milord . . .

"And now, and now . . ." Anthony Trust's lips suddenly strained. "And now a mobster called Sam Giancana can wink at his pals in Cosa Nostra and say that he has something in common with the President of the United States. They're plugging the same broad." Trust's lips formed distaste as he used the language of the streets.

Blackford made no comment. He resisted, whatever the circumstances, making light of JFK. He picked up his pile of papers. "Better get on with the reading. Rufus will be here soon."

A moment later Anthony interrupted again. "Ah," he said. "It's okay now, I see, according to file 203C. Apparently Hoover had a heart-to-heart last March with the Prez. Broke it up. But even so, it lasted"—he turned back two or three sheets in his folder—"over two years."

Again Blackford said nothing.

HE GOT THROUGH the material shortly after seven, and fifteen minutes later Rufus, dressed in his country clothes, came back into the room.

Rufus had only two outfits, his country outfit and his city outfit. In the city he wore a three-piece suit: navy blue (light wool), and, ever since the death of his Muriel two years earlier, a black tie. In the country he wore brown corduroy pants, a V-necked sleeveless sweater, and rubber-soled heavy garden shoes. Trust, anticipating Rufus's arrival, had removed himself from the rocking chair, sitting down in a straight-backed wooden chair directly opposite the fireplace. His folder was on the coffee table adjacent.

Rufus turned to Blackford. "The material you've now read brings you up to date on what we know—I had better correct that: brings you up to date on what *I* know about what has been going on involving the White House, the Agency, and Fidel Castro. What isn't in those files is what's scheduled to happen in the next week or two: a formal termination of the Agency's relationship with Rosselli and the Mafia people. But let's forget that for the moment and talk about the surround-

ing mess. Blackford, you're the youngest man in the room"—
Rufus had never got much closer than this to informality,
Blackford reflected—"Anthony is one year older, according to
the records—"

"Rufus," said Blackford, rising, "you mean I should attend
to the bar."

Blackford knew the simple (and spartan) routine. He had
spent four weeks with Rufus only a few weeks back, after
Blackford had returned, physically damaged, from Fidel Castro's prison. One whiskey before dinner.

Blackford had engaged in seven covert operations under
Rufus's guidance and in four of these Anthony had also been
involved. Since the death of his wife Rufus had become even
more reclusive, but between the two men—Blackford had
been twenty-six when, on his first assignment, in England, he
met the legendary spymaster—a special loyalty had developed. The basic social protocols established by the senior part-
ner were almost never violated. No profanity, no obscenity,
no gossip, with the important exception that professionally
fruitful gossip was always welcome, digested as carefully
as data on the inventory of nuclear missiles in Kazakhstan;
and, although they were colleagues in the service of the CIA,
Rufus was indisputably in charge. Blackford had been discreetly in Rufus's company at critical sessions with the head
of British Intelligence, and three times with the President of
the United States. There was no figure on earth who dealt
flippantly with Rufus, on whose judgment and skills General
Eisenhower had historically relied, beginning on the day
when, after consulting with Rufus, General Eisenhower gave
orders to launch the invasion of Normandy on June 6, while
cautiously protecting his resourceful counterintelligence men-
tor by vague references to auspicious weather ahead. It was
different with Trust—Rufus liked him, though there wasn't
the personal attachment. Rufus admired the tall, brainy,
bookish, fast-living, devoted enemy of the Communist effort
to control the world, the special, longtime friend of Blackford
Oakes. Anthony Trust had recruited Blackford in his senior
year at Yale.

"We need political perspective," Rufus lectured while Blackford, behind him at the bar, poured the three scotches and soda,

no ice for Rufus. "The principal *political* datum that affects us—affects the Agency—is the preoccupation of the President and the Attorney General with Fidel Castro."

"Can't hardly blame them," Trust interjected.

"I am not evaluating the Administration's position"—there was a touch of the reprimand in Rufus's voice. "I am seeking perspective for the sake of understanding—I won't say *mission*, not now; not yet; maybe not ever . . ." Rufus lapsed into one of his characteristic silences. They were generally brief, and always respected by all who knew him: one would as soon express surprise or impatience at an epileptic seizure. In a minute he resumed talking.

"Today, the newspapers published an interview with the Attorney General, you must have seen it. Robert Kennedy flatly denied that the White House had ever planned to provide air cover for the Bay of Pigs operation. That was a flat lie."

Rufus would never divulge the grounds he had for making such an assertion—except when he had to do so to retain analytical integrity. His job now was to press the offensive of the Kennedys against Castro. He could not do so by fabricating the history of their relationship. And Blackford and Trust, knowing him well, would have bet their lives, if necessary, on Rufus's word: The Attorney General had lied.

Rufus reached into his pocket and pulled out a clipping. He adjusted his glasses and read from it. "The Attorney General explained that despite the commitment of U.S. prestige in the Cuban invasion, the Administration could not get further involved. 'If'—I am quoting directly now, the Attorney General—'If it was just the Cuban problem alone . . . we would have ended it right there. But the Berlin issue was in a critical stage at the time. And there were difficulties in Vietnam and Laos, among other places. We just could not commit our forces in Cuba. Even in retrospect, I think this was the wisest decision.'

"But of course," Rufus put down the clipping, "neither he nor the President at this point thinks it *was* a wise decision. And then last October, a year and a half later, we discovered—thanks largely to you, Blackford—that the Soviet Union had deployed forty-two nuclear missiles in Cuba, and if two more weeks had gone by without our acting, the United States would have been hostage to the Soviet Union via Fidel Castro. Neither the President nor the Attorney General has been trained to endure that kind of thing.

"And every day there are new provocations. You saw last week—Castro's speech to the conference of Latin American women? Urging revolution everywhere in Latin America? And then, only two days ago, Castro murdered a defector right on the grounds of the Brazilian Embassy in Havana, and a second defector was beaten and died two days later in the hospital. The list is endless. Two thousand public executions, the largest political prisoner population, per capita, in the world. Ten percent of his own countrymen gone, mostly to America, the land he hates." He paused. "I am advised—I know it—that the Attorney General and the President are"—he hesitated, looking for the word, the right word—"they are ferocious on the subject of Fidel Castro. They view him not only as having been a frighteningly audacious threat to the United States—he had in place the nuclear armory to destroy us—they see him as a young Hitler, a young Stalin—fanatical, cruel, sadistic, mean, unreliable; a threat to any prospect of civilization in this part of the world."

Blackford, this time, interrupted. "Sounds to *me* like exactly the right way to think about Fidel Castro."

Again a rebuke was anticipated. But Rufus, feeling the need to make his point more explicit than he had done a moment earlier when reproaching Trust, was now the schoolmaster. "The point, Blackford, isn't whether Fidel Castro has outraged heaven and earth. He has. The point we need to evaluate is whether this loss of perspective by the White House is a critical professional disqualification. My ruptured appendix, Blackford, may be the first object of my concern, but there are certain things I would not do to my ruptured appendix. For instance, I would not hire a doctor who probed my stomach and, addressing my appendix, said, 'I'm going to get you, you sonofabitch.' " Blackford was astonished. He could not recall Rufus ever using that expletive, not ever. But when Rufus wished to explain something, he became above all things the teacher. Evidently he felt he needed now exactly to explain the distinctions he had summoned his two young colleagues to ponder.

"This morning I was asked to superintend an operation. Operation Mongoose has been operating since November of 1961. Mongoose has changed its name but not its purpose, so I still think of it as Operation Mongoose, and will continue to refer to it as such. I have been asked to effect the assassination of Fidel Castro."

There was silence. Rufus had not touched his glass. Now he did. He raised it to his lips and, eyelids lowered, touched his lips to it. He let the glass hover in front of his nose before putting it down again.

After a moment Blackford said in a whisper, "Asked by whom? The DCI?"

"No. Nobody in the Agency. Asked by the Attorney General." He paused. "The DCI does not even know—is not to know—the details of what has been designated as 'Executive Action.' "

There was nothing for Blackford or Trust to say at this point. Only Rufus could speak. He stood, as they waited without looking up at him to hear what he would say. He did not keep them waiting long. As if directly answering their question: "I said I would think about it. That I would need to deliberate the . . . assignment. That I would do so beginning today with two trusted associates, whose relative youth might give me a fresher perspective. And that"—Rufus turned and stared at the ebbing log fire—"I would need to devote time to consulting with someone else." Rufus used the word "someone" as though it were a proper name. Blackford knew that his old friend would consult his conscience, and pray for divine guidance.

Blackford and Trust waited. Rufus did not go on to say with whom else he would deliberate the question whether to accept the commission to kill Fidel Castro, the head of an independent country with which the United States was not at war. Rufus turned the subject quickly to the steak dinner he had ordered, which needed now to be cooked.

lthough it was a Monday—Tuesday, actually: Monday had ended at midnight, and it was after two—the scene at La Bruja Vieja on Flagler Street in Miami's Cuban sector was, as ever, spirited. The jukebox played "La Flor de la Canela." Antonio Soler, serving bar, wondered idly if this was the fifteenth or the twentieth time he had heard that song since coming to work at seven, relieving his younger brother who had worked beginning at noon when La Bruja opened for lunch. No food was served after eleven o'clock, just drinks, though there were always *chicharrones*, *maní*, and pretzels. The music could be heard, but so also could the conversation which, as usual, revolved around the center of the expatriates' cultural life. Antonio had been serving drinks to Alejandro Font (he was "Alex" now), and two companions, all three of them with special status earned by having been a part of that dismal operation that had collapsed at the Bay of Pigs almost two years earlier. The doomed anti-Castro counterrevolutionists were all released now—1,113 prisoners of Castro out of Cuba, most of them ransomed by efforts of the United States Government, specifically by efforts undertaken by the Attorney General. Robert Kennedy had browbeaten American pharmaceutical manufacturers into coming up with the $53 million in pharmaceutical drugs that Castro had much wanted, and sorely needed.

Oh, the stories they told of their experiences!—always to engrossed listeners. Antonio had by now heard those stories almost as often as he had heard "La Flor de la Canela," and it was getting late. But María didn't like to close the bar as long as there were six customers left, and Antonio could count six men and three women, drinking rum mostly, and beer. Alex was talking. "I don't care what you think, Gustavo, I say President Kennedy is going to engineer the liberation of Cuba. After all, didn't he say practically that when he gave his speech to us? His exact words were, 'I can assure you that this flag will be returned to this brigade in a free Havana.' "

"Ay, yayayaya." Gustavo drank deeply from his glass. "Kennedy is a politician, like all of them. He will do nothing."

Alex shook his head. "You are wrong, Gustavo. He cannot *tolerate* Castro. After all, just three months ago there was practically a nuclear war."

"There wouldn't have been a 'missile crisis' if Kennedy had given us air cover on the beach."

Alex groaned. "Not again, Gustavo, not again."

"All right all right all right. I agree to stop talking about the failure of April fifteenth, 1961, if you will stop talking about Kennedy's speech on December twenty-ninth, 1962. I say we let him off too easily."

"He got us out of Cuba, didn't he?"

"Yes, and the reason we were in Cuba in prison instead of in our homes was that he let us down in the first place."

Mario Hidalgo, silent up until then, raised his massive hand. "Stop! Stop! Enough! Both of you. Whatever happens in the future, we can't blame Castro on Kennedy. Castro, alas, is one of us—"

"One of *what*?" Gustavo banged his fist on the table. "*I* was never fooled by Castro. I knew *all along* he was a Communist snake."

Portly Niquita Oler, voluptuous in her tight-fitting yellow dress, reached over, snatched a half bottle of Budweiser beer from in front of Gustavo and poured it over his head. There were shouts—of anger from Gustavo, of hilarity from most of the others. Niquita had in their presence used this device before—to cool things off. Antonio judged that just the right moment had arrived to press the little button underneath the bar, whose tone sounded in the office of María Arguilla. Two buzzes meant that a disciplinary problem loomed. Three buzzes and she'd have called the police before coming into the lounge.

María Arguilla reached the landing alongside the bar. She stretched out her hand behind the hanging tapestry on which the old, crestfallen Cuban flag was embroidered. Her hand easily found the switch. With a single upward movement she flicked it off. The entire room was suddenly without light, the jukebox dead. A moment later, she flicked it back on. All eyes were now on her, but the silence continued. There was always silence when María Arguilla came on the scene. She commanded it.

She was what in Ireland they'd call a raven-haired beauty. In Cuba, they just said about her that she was "la huera bella," referring to the blondness of her skin. But her jet-black hair, worn in a bun at the nape of her neck, accentuated the light skin and the pale pink lipstick, the vivid eyelashes. At age twenty-eight, she was in total command: the manager of Santos Trafficante's Old Witch, *La Bruja Vieja*.

But she knew exactly when to change her posture. The room was silent, the sound from the jukebox aborted by the electrical blackout; she had accomplished what she wanted. In a moment she was once again the genial hostess.

"Antonio. Bring this gentleman a fresh bottle of beer on the house"—she pointed to Gustavo, who was drying his bushy hair with his shirt sleeve. "We are here, are we not, compañeros, to *enjoy* ourselves, to enjoy each other's company? Any cross word between us is a victory for—" she did not pronounce the name, pointing instead to the dart board opposite the pool table, on which was engraved a facsimile of the face of Fidel Castro, his nose the center of the target, awarding the successful dart thrower 100 points. "Give me ten cents," she reached out, palm up, imperiously over the table around which the commotion had begun. There was a race to be the first to put a dime into her outstretched hand. Mario got there first. María walked in even steps to the jukebox, inserted the coin, made her selection, and the lounge was filled with the voice of María Delores Pradera singing "La Flor de la Canela," the love song that for twenty years had brought tears to those prepared to shed them, and the eyes of Niquita Oler moistened as she leaned over the table and kissed Gustavo forgivingly square on the lips. Forgivingly, he in turn embraced her, and his companions cheered. María Arguilla looked at Antonio, who bowed his head ever so slightly in deference to her showmanship. María brought both hands to her lips and with a pantomimic kiss to her clients returned to her study, pausing at the bar to whisper to Antonio that he should close the bar in fifteen minutes no matter how many customers were still there.

BACK IN HER study she sat down at the desk and took out writing paper from the top drawer, taking a pen from the neat velvet holder upright in front of her. Ever since the books for 1962 had been completed by the accountant she had decided she was well situated to make the demand of Santos. He would be in his Chicago office for a week, he had told her over the telephone yesterday, so she addressed the letter to him there.

What she said to Santos Trafficante was that she had earned her ransom. She wanted back the 16-millimeter film Trafficante had had taken one night of his infamous show at La Gallinera on Calle M, in the riotous heyday of Batista's permissiveness. *Nowhere this side of Copenhagen can you see such an erotic spectacular!* was the word. The staff made a great show of pulling down a black shade over the single rose window high over the customers' heads. It wasn't that Trafficante was afraid of the police—he had taken ample care of them. Such good care that at that hour there was always a policeman outside; his assignment wasn't to come into the club to disturb the proceedings, but to prevent anyone else from coming into the club to disturb the proceedings—a holdup man, or even an angry wife or sweetheart. One of the waiters stood by the inside door of the club, conspicuously prepared to bolt it shut after those clients who wanted to leave could do so, whether out of scruple or merely to avoid paying the twenty-five-peso surcharge. But there were few of those. Most of the fifty-odd Americans and a few Cubans who had come to La Gallinera had come precisely to see Trafficante's notorious show.

And then that one night after the show, after all the customers had been ushered out, Trafficante had told his little troupe that they must go through it all again, as he was going to film it. They grumbled, until he pointed to the box with the envelopes—an extra week's pay for each of them. They laughed when he added that they could all have a drink or two while waiting to revive the, er, spirits of the principal actor. And, a half hour later, the tableau began again. Its climax, to appropriate musical accompaniment, featured the seduction of María Raja, as María Arguilla was then known, by the star stud of the season. When the customers were there the lighting was dim, but not so dim as to deprive the audience of all the detail they could wish for. But that night, María remembered as she wrote out her letter, the lighting was necessarily vivid to accommodate the camera. She remembered closing her eyes, not from the feigned fear and then rapture of the regular theatrical performance, but to protect them from the glaring brightness of the floodlights.

"I have worked for you for one full year at La Bruja Vieja," she wrote, "and you promised me that if I did well you would give me back that film. You made it to sell in Havana, but we both know it was never released after Batista appointed Salas Cañizares as police chief. And it is no good to you here. In America there is much competition for pornography, and anyway your cameraman was an amateur. I made you over one hundred and fifty thousand dollars last year. Tell me now that I can have it."

She completed the letter and closed her eyes, remembering the words of her lover in Havana a year earlier. "I saw that show in La Gallinera, and I've wanted you ever since. I quiver, even now, when I think about it. You were unforgettable—you have not changed. Someone told me there was a movie made of that show. I want a copy of that movie. Can you get it for me?"

"No, no, Fidel. The man who took it lives in Miami."

"*Qué lástima!*" he said, what a pity. "Well, I guess I will have to settle for all Cuba and you, María, live, instead of on celluloid."

3

Rolando Cubela was a medical intern in Havana at the time of the accident in Mexico. He had become accustomed to the sight of blood, following his father about, mostly around the bullrings of Mexico, before returning to their little farm in Placetas in Las Villas. His father was a farmer in the sense that he had inherited a couple of hectares. By trade he was a bullfighter—more particularly a picador, whose job, every Sunday in the arena, was to thrust his heavy, armored frame onto the wooden pole with the steel point at the end into the fighting bull, piercing the animal's tossing muscle, into which eventually the matador would thrust his lethal blade. The idea was to lower the bull's carriage of head, and hence his horns; and simultaneously to correct faults in the carriage of his head when the bull charged.

Rolando, from the age of six, excitedly accompanied his father around Mexico while his mother tended the little farm. Hand in hand they would go together to the bustling dressing room and from there to the *callejón*, the circular wooden partition that surrounds the bullrings, shielding the bullfighters. If there was an empty ringside seat—a *barrera* seat—above, Rolando was permitted to occupy it. Otherwise he would stand by the *ruedo*, peering out over it into the ring. He needed elevation—the *ruedo* is very high. Even so, some acrobatic bulls succeed in leaping over it when chasing their antagonists or when, in a seizure of cowardice, they charge forward to escape the torture, bounding over the *ruedo* into the *callejón*, quickly dispersing the bullfighters there into their reserve sanctuaries.

One such bull had knocked Rolando from his *contadero*

perch right into the ring, causing a great uproar in the crowd and a much greater uproar at home.

Either from his makeshift seat or hoisted by an idle and friendly peon, he had seen—he could count them—one hundred and sixteen fights before he was nine, and this means a great deal of butchery, including two dead *novilleros*, and a dozen horses impaled by the bull, never mind their mattress-thick carapaces. And there was blood at the farm where the Cubela family lived: it was Rolando who would kill the chicken when his mother decided to serve her *pollos fritos*. As a young student at the parochial school, Rolando was recognized by his classmates as a martial type: he boxed and he wrestled and often he picked fights, and there were often bloody noses.

But by age fifteen Rolando had decided he wished to go into an entirely different kind of life—bloody yes, but bloody-salutary, not bloody-destructive. He wished to become a doctor. If he was going to make it into the medical school, and be content as a doctor, he would need to make a major commitment, namely to protect life rather than mutilate it. He came to this decision rather solemnly, and during the week he let pass several schoolboy provocations which, a fortnight earlier, he'd have thought *casus belli*. That weekend when his mother told him to go out to the barnyard and kill a chicken, he announced to his stupefied parents that to do so was really a violation of the Hippocratic oath. They had never heard of this oath, but Rolando gave them an earnest reading of it, emphasizing what it permitted, what it did not, to medical doctors—which, he shrugged his shoulders, he would one day be. The father suppressed a smile and told Rolando's sister Elena to go kill the chicken, and Rolando to shut up about that doctor's oath, to remember that he was not yet a doctor and would never be one unless he maintained very high grades in school, and even then only if his father, forswearing the Hippocratic oath, could help kill enough bulls to pay Rolando's fees at medical school.

Rolando pursued his studies and, ten years later, after surviving the financial crisis brought on by his father's accident, was a devoted student of medicine, and a devoted revolutionary. His hot blood aligned him, as a first-year medical student, with the young men who were actively in opposition to the reigning Cuban dictator, Fulgencio Batista. Ernesto Sánchez, his roommate, was deeply read in Marxist literature and talked incessantly of the need to organize "at every level." Rolando managed to learn (as much as he wanted to learn) about the theory of class struggle while walking to Dr. Alvaro Nueces's class on hematology; Ernesto talked and thought more, even at the baseball games. As Rolando's indignation against President Batista, who had taken power by military coup four years earlier, heightened, his enthusiasm mounted to help overthrow him. Ernesto introduced him to members of the loose fraternity of young professionals—students of law, engineering, architecture, medicine—who felt the revolutionary bond. Their undisputed leader was Fidel Castro, at times wonderfully conspicuous, orating to captive audiences, at times furtive, exhorting carefully concealed little knots of fellow revolutionaries. And then one day Castro stormed into a radio station, seizing the microphone and inveighing against Batista and praising freedom and democracy and social justice and anti-imperialism for a full ten minutes while his companions kept watch for the police.

Again, at times Fidel was mysteriously gone—but never impalpable: he was "somewhere," fighting the noble fight. Mexico, maybe; Colombia; at the other end of the island; in the mountains; and of course there was the nineteen-month period when Castro was in prison, after the Moncada Barracks attack in Santiago de Cuba. But whatever Fidel Castro was doing, he was always a presence and Rolando, though temperamentally skeptical of authority and temperamentally assertive about his own rights, was greatly humbled at the thought of that singular presence in Cuba—in the Caribbean. Indeed, in the world— Rolando tended, after a great deal of Marx and Lenin, to think in planetary terms.

Rolando Cubela was assigned, on graduating, to Hospital Calixto García at Vedado in Havana, and was kept busy binding wounds in the Emergency Room and helping the doctors in surgery while studying their techniques. Every week he reported to Dr. Alvaro Nueces who, in addition to teaching, supervised the work of the interns at Calixto García. One night in August, after a very long day in surgery, Rolando arrived back in his quarters, shared still with Ernesto, and was given in breathless tones by Ernesto the message: Fidel Castro wished to confer with him. Rolando's brown eyes widened. Slowly, he let himself down on his cot.

"When? Where?"

With some exasperation Ernesto, the professional revolutionary theorist, said to him, "I did not *write down* where you were to go. One doesn't *do* that. I memorized it."

"Tell me, tell me," Rolando said, his whole face under his tousled hair pleading.

Ernesto lowered his voice. "Your instructions are to knock on the door of Calle O number 198 at exactly twelve minutes past midnight. Someone will open the door. You are to say, '*I am looking for my sister Ernestina. Is she here?*' You will then be led to Fidel."

Rolando Cubela gave thought to exactly how to dress appropriately. Fidel was of course hirsute, while Rolando had only the trace of a shadow. He wondered whether to shave, as he would do if he were going to a social engagement, or to leave his chin as it was. There was no way to accelerate the growth of his beard between nine o'clock at night and midnight, though as a doctor he knew enough about cosmetic techniques to darken his general appearance . . . No—that would be, well, foolish.

He decided he would go neatly dressed, but without a tie (just a hint of the proletarian disposition). He would wear a jacket, but his shirt sleeves would be rolled up, in the event Fidel should ask him to take off his coat. Would Fidel quiz him on any particular matter? Certainly he would not be asked the kind of theoretical-philosophical questions that Ernesto would be so much better qualified to handle . . . No—there was simply no guessing what it was Fidel wanted with him, Rolando Cubela, a medical intern.

The interval before he set out went slowly. But, relishing the coolness of the tropical evening and the balm it brought from the awful heat of August, he walked toward the meeting place, a matter of two kilometers or so. He had set his watch by the radio, and at exactly the designated time he crossed the street and knocked on the inconspicuous door, in a block crowded with two-story houses cheek to cheek.

When the door swung open, Rolando Cubela saw a stooped, skinny old man wearing a leather apron. Rolando spoke his lines metallically. The old man stared him in the face and asked to see Rolando's identification. Rolando handed over his intern's card, with his photograph. The old man, after an interval, said simply, "He is waiting for you. Number 257."

Flustered, Rolando asked, "On this same street?"

The old man nodded, and shut the door.

Number 257 was only two blocks away. The building was obviously an aging private house, probably built during the twenties: wooden, shuttered, the paint a flaky pastel blue, a hint of grass on the slender private land between the street and the slightly recessed entrance. Again he knocked.

He was greatly surprised. "Good evening, Rolando," said Alvaro Nueces, opening the door and quickly shutting it.

"Good evening, Doctor," Rolando replied, trying to suppress his surprise on learning that his famous teacher-scientist was a fellow revolutionary.

"You are to refer to me, when not in the hospital, only as 'Varo.'"

"Yes, Doctor. Yes—Varo." The doctor signaled to Rolando to follow him. They climbed one flight of stairs and, without knocking, Varo opened the rear door into a warmly lit room, comfortably large, the walls lined with books, window shades tightly drawn, an upright piano in one corner, a desk opposite, and, in the center, four upholstered chairs, two of them facing the other two, a knee-high table in between. Fidel Castro sat on the mammoth chair on the right, smoking a cigar.

Castro rose and Alvaro Nueces performed the introductions. The other two men in the room, one of them young and fair and wearing a sports shirt and slacks, the second middle-aged, dressed as a businessman might dress going out to dinner, were introduced simply as "Luís" and "Paco." Rolando had not got used to the brevity of revolutionary nomenclature and found it difficult to say *"Buenas noches,* Paco" to a man twice his age, and so said, with a little bow of his head, only *"Buenas noches."*

Castro asked his young guest if he would like a drink, and Rolando stammered out "Coca-Cola" before recognizing his error. He was wordlessly brought an Orange Crush, a sparkling orangeade bottled in Havana and paying no royalties to U.S. capitalists.

Castro motioned him down onto the vacant chair—Paco, after

shaking hands and informally saluting Castro, had walked out of the room, leaving the young man and Alvaro Nueces. Castro began to talk, and soon Rolando felt the hypnotic rush. As a medical student he had written a paper about that famous sensation for his anesthesia class. This must be like what the drug-taker feels, he thought: what I feel now, in the company of this giant, who will surely have a historic future.

Castro spoke at great length and with much passion about the need to liberate Cuba. A full hour went by before he shifted into the interrogatory mode: Was Rolando familiar with weapons? Oh yes, said Rolando eagerly. His father was—had been—a bullfighter, and as a young boy he had been trained to use all the weapons of the bullfighter. He even knew how to sharpen steel, had known how to do so before seeing his first scalpel; Rolando felt an impulse to boast about *something* to help accord in some way, in any way, for the distinction he was being paid.

Castro said he was not talking about "cutlery," but about firearms. Rolando said that he had been brought up in Placetas in Las Villas, in the open country his father farmed when not at the ring in Mexico. He had used his father's rifle from the age of twelve and had become an expert marksman, shooting rabbits regularly and even—Rolando became a little expressive—"a young deer, on one trek into Camagüey and also a wild pig—two pigs," he said self-effacingly. Though, he thought it fair to add, "I haven't used the rifle since I was fifteen." He added, lest he give the wrong impression, "Too busy becoming a doctor."

"Have you ever used a pistol?"

Yes, his father had a collection of which he was very proud, three pistols, one of them dating back to the Spanish-American War. "The imperialist war," he explained.

Castro came to the point. Varo—he motioned toward the senior doctor—had told him that Rolando had singular qualifications, and that he was eager to participate in the great struggle that lay ahead against the tyrant. Castro had in mind for Rolando a position of some responsibility. But he would need to be tested first.

Rolando nodded his head obsequiously. "Anything you direct me to do, señor."

"You are to carry out the orders of my revolutionary council. An execution."

Rolando could not entirely control his breathing. He could only think to ask, "Who, señor?"

Castro laughed. He laughed uproariously. Such a laugh as demands of subordinates sycophantic acquiescence. Luís joined in the laughter. Dr. Nueces joined in the laughter. Eventually Rolando found himself laughing. He reasoned quickly that he had asked a naïve question.

Suddenly Castro was silent. He rose. Luís and Alvaro instantly rose also, and Rolando.

"You will be told who at the proper time."

Castro extended his hand. To Alvaro, "Take our young friend to the door." And, to Rolando, "You will receive your instructions." There was no laughter left over; no levity in the room.

THERE WOULD BE—Rolando was given to reconstructing the events of that first night—the difficulty of coping with his roommate's fascinated questions (Ernesto had never met Castro). Walking as in a dream past Calle O, 198, up Avenida Infanta, and through the Eloy Alfaro park, back to his quarters, he prepared his answers. He concocted a story: Castro had recruited Rolando's cousin "at Oriente"—the far eastern end of Cuba he knew Ernesto had never visited and probably never would. That cousin had become close to Castro and had requested that, when back in Havana, Castro meet with Rolando Cubela, who had starred in his graduating class at medical school and whose sympathies were known to be revolutionary. Rolando (he would tell Ernesto) had spent an hour with the great man and was deeply impressed by his desire to liberate Cuba from the domestic tyrant and from foreign imperialism. Castro clearly had a towering perspective of what Cuba needed and, besides, was wonderfully informed on all matters—he had spoken "intimately" of the principal figures in Batista's entourage, his so-called Cabinet, and the fake assembly that Batista affected to consult about public policy. That, Rolando thought, ought to do it. He would improvise on details. Ernesto would ask whether Castro had made any mention of any further meetings, or of enrolling Rolando in any particular organization. Rolando would need to be vague.

It went plausibly, and the two young doctors had been up most of the night, talking animatedly of Castro and the future of Cuba.

Two days later, in the mailbox where Rolando generally found nothing more than his weekly paycheck, the schedule for the following week's activities at the hospital, and—occasionally—a brief note from his mother, he received the promised contact. A letter.

The following Saturday, at noon—the interns had off every other Saturday afternoon and Sunday; Rolando would need to arrange a substitute because, on the specified Saturday, he was on duty—he was to be at the Parque de la Fraternidad in Calle Prado, seated on a bench on the west side, reading a copy of *Hoy*, at 12:45. The letter was signed simply, *Luís*.

WHAT FOLLOWED THAT meeting, Rolando Cubela in later years had difficulty recalling in specific detail. Luís met him in the park and drove him to a remote farmhouse where a young couple took him in hand, Héctor and Amanda. He spent much of the afternoon in target practice with a 9-millimeter Luger. Ten years of inactivity with guns were quickly made up, given Rolando's training as a boy and his natural aptitude as a marksman. Within an hour he was hitting the bull's-eye at ten meters. "You will be much closer than ten meters to your target." Héctor smiled. "We hope."

The evening, he remembered through the mists that, so soon and for so long, descended on those surrealistic hours, had been greatly convivial. Neither Héctor nor Amanda, who tended their farm informally (that much was obvious to Rolando), knew very much about farming, but he was careful not to ask what it was that they otherwise did. Manifestly, they were college graduates, conversant with literature, philosophy, and, above all, politics. He was careful not even to ask when the—incident—would take place.

The next day, he remembered when taxing himself, as on occasion he did, to re-create the weekend, Amanda went into the city, and at that point Héctor, in the didactic manner of the schoolteacher, paced up and down the room, addressing Rolando but speaking as though a soliloquy.

Rolando's "target" always—"almost always—if he isn't there that particular day, why, we just postpone the operation"—attended the eight o'clock Mass at La Catedral de La Habana in La Habana Vieja. Most often he was alone—his wife and three older children regularly went to Mass at eleven.

Héctor pulled open a drawer and took from it four photographs, the first showing the entrance to the church, the second a picture of the building opposite, and pictures taken of the area from one side of the church, and from the other. Rolando was to sit in the front seat of a car with Héctor. They would park opposite the church, arriving at 8:35—"Mass usually ends between eight-forty and eight-fifty." Sometimes there were two or three cars parked opposite, cars belonging to "rich capitalists," but it would be easy to adjust to the situation. "Our car will be parked so that we can make a fast getaway."

The execution was to take place the following Sunday unless Luís got word to Rolando before then that for whatever reason the operation was postponed. When the congregation began to come out from the church, Héctor would point to the target. Rolando, wearing a ranchero's broad-brimmed hat and dark glasses, would wait until Héctor identified the target. He would then step out of the car, approach the target, fire the pistol at his face—"shoot three times at least, we do not want a wounded target"—return to the car—"don't run, there will be no need, and remember that the man who is calm, even if he is the assassin, is the man in psychological control of the crowd"—open the door, and Héctor would drive him away.

The following week, Rolando remembered, always in that haze, had been odd, both endless and stampede-speed fast. It required intense effort to concentrate on the work at hand, much of it delicate as he himself began to engage in the surgery for which he was being trained; but then, suddenly, he would find himself performing feats of extraordinary intricacy with the fluency of a Paganini going through a concerto, never mind that he had never practiced it. It was especially hard in the evening, when he had to chatter with Ernesto as though unpreoccupied. When, in their tiny little quarters—one room, two beds, two desks, a single window, a washbasin, the wheezy secondhand refrigerator his mother had given him as a graduation present stocked now with fruit and soft drinks and beer and bread and cheese—the overhead light was turned off, by common agreement at midnight, conversation would cease. Rolando lay fitfully on his bed, breathing the hot summer air. He thought of his Hippocratic oath, now not a child's affectation but a formal vow. He agonized, yet he did not waver in his determination to do what he had told Fidel he would do: Anything you direct me to do, señor.

It went flawlessly. They were strategically parked at 8:35 when, a minute later, a car drove up and parked in front of them, close enough to make a forward departure impossible without first having to maneuver. Héctor had reacted quickly, backed up his car, edged it out of the space he had occupied, and slowly reversed, double-parking alongside the car behind. "Nobody will complain," he whispered. "Sunday. We are obviously waiting to drive somebody home from church."

It was at that moment that, for the first time, Héctor showed him a picture of his target. He took it from a shirt pocket. A 3×5 photograph of a man in a colonel's uniform, glass in hand, trees in the background. A man in his late thirties, perhaps early forties; relaxed, smiling. Smiling warmly. A candid shot, taken presumably at a social function. He wore a trim mustache and had a full head of hair. Rolando discerned a small cross just below the neck, visible because the shirt was open, in the style of the Cuban military on all but the most official occasions.

Just before 8:45—Rolando had looked down at his watch, his heart pounding—the doors to the church opened and the worshipers began to file out. Héctor had trained a small set of binoculars on the entrance. A minute later he whispered hoarsely, "There! *There he is!* Quick! Quick!" His mouth dry, Rolando opened the door, his hand gripping the pistol in his pocket. Rolando walked a few paces in broad sunlight toward the chatting parishioners. He spotted the colonel without difficulty. He came out of the church his right hand holding his wife's, his left on the shoulder of a boy in his early teens; his family had accompanied him after all, Rolando thought in the blur. Rolando approached the colonel with a slight feint, turning him slightly to one side, as though he were bent on entering the emptying church. Ten paces away he stopped, pulled out the pistol, took aim, and fired three times.

He thought he heard the wail of a chorus of wailers—it sounded, in his memory, as if they had been trained to wail—and then the screams. Then he was back by the car. He opened the door, and Héctor sped off.

Clearly Héctor had rehearsed the escape route. They drove at an unprovocative speed, turning every few blocks in this direction and that. The license plate in the rear of the car had been smudged with mud. No one would be able to say more than that it was a Ford sedan; and yes, they might correctly guess that it was a 1953 model car; and yes, they would know it was dark blue, though no one would readily guess that the blue had been applied that morning from a bucket filled with watercolor. In an hour, back at the farm, the Ford's original old metallic gray would be easily restored.

Back at the farm. What had happened? Rolando could not remember, beyond the laundering of the car. He remembered only that at some point, later in the day, Luís had come by and driven Rolando off to within walking distance of his quarters, dropping him on Calle San Lázaro, near the hospital. He did not remember getting out of the car, did not remember where he went, remembered only returning to his room well after nightfall to find Ernesto jabbering. Jabbering about the assassination that morning of Colonel Blanco Rico.

On hearing that name Rolando asked Ernesto to repeat it. Then he lurched toward the washstand and vomited.

Blanco Rico! Blanco Rico! he repeated to himself.

Ernesto laughed, and asked whether Rolando had been out drinking. "It's not like you to throw up."

Then Ernesto had decided to be solicitous, asking Rolando whether he wished a thermometer. "Maybe you ate something. Where were you tonight?"

Rolando washed his face, and said he must indeed have eaten something.

He longed for privacy, and the thought crossed his mind to

go out and spend the night at a hotel. But he had only a few pesos. And then he thought of his medical kit. He walked over to the corner and opened it.

"What are you taking?" Ernesto asked, inquisitive.

"Fifteen milligrams of Compazine." His back was turned to Ernesto when Rolando discreetly opened the little red bottle and took out two Seconals, which he threw into his mouth, running the washbasin faucet, cupping his hands, and swallowing a handful of water. Without taking off his clothes, he went to his cot.

He dimly remembered in the course of the night Ernesto massaging his chest with Vicks, and that he had forced on him a sweater and socks.

"You are having one hell of a chill, Rolandito. If you're not better tomorrow, you'll be a patient at the hospital, not an intern."

The next day, during surgery, Dr. Nueces came by, doing his rounds. Rolando looked up from the open abdomen with the inflamed appendix. "I need to speak with you, Doctor," he said, in a voice as controlled as he could manage.

"Come to my office after the operation."

An hour later, the office door shut behind him, Rolando stood in front of the doctor who was leaning back at his desk, tense but prepared.

Rolando spit it out. *"Blanco Rico! Are you—are we—all mad?* Blanco Rico, the *one true, humane, patriotic* gentleman in Batista's entourage! He has performed more generously as head of military intelligence than anyone in memory! He is personally responsible for releasing over a hundred political prisoners. He is beloved even by people who hate Batista!"

"Yes," Dr. Nueces had said. "Yes. You are quite right about Colonel Blanco Rico."

"Then . . . ?"

"That is the point. Fidel doesn't want *anyone* around Batista whom the public admires. It's that simple. And Fidel is not our leader for nothing."

Rolando Cubela stared at the famous doctor, his teacher. He attempted to speak, but his mouth could not open, and three times he gagged. He turned, opened the door, arrested himself in the act of slamming it shut, closed it quietly, and walked down the hospital corridor, down the steps, the three blocks to his room. Ernesto would not return until well after dinnertime, and it was not yet noon. He lay on his bed, and wept.

4

Blackford took a taxi to the Fontainebleau Hotel where he would stay in the suite reserved year-round for the "XPando Corporation." It occurred to him as, driving down the throughway from the airport in mid-January, he looked about, eyeing a limited view of the ocean on his right, that for all that he had got about during the past twenty years, he had been only once before in Miami. That was in 1961, en route to Nicaragua, in the service of the Bay of Pigs operation. He knew intimately the streets of Havana. He had spent most of the preceding year there, on a personal mission for President Kennedy. He could get around in Berlin as readily as in Scarsdale, New York, where he had attended public school; and, for that matter, he could draw serviceable maps of Paris and London. He smiled grimly: he knew every corner of one cell in Lubyanka Prison in Moscow.

And now he must get to know Miami. Miami, the center of anti-Castro activity. Miami, to which an estimated 200,000 Cubans had come since New Year's Day of 1959, when Castro liberated the Cuban people. Oh, if only Velasco were here with him! For that matter, if only Velasco were—well, alive . . . anywhere. Blackford thought wistfully about the little chain-smoking Spaniard who had shared his adventure in Havana, dying there. For this mission a replacement had been assigned to help him, one Pano Iglesias—Salvador was his name at the baptismal font, Blackford had been briefed, but the man was known as Pano, even back when he served as a captain in Castro's Frank País Brigade. According to the dossier, a resourceful young man with an intimate knowledge of Castro's entourage and doings, and perhaps the only tie to the most important figure in Operation Mongoose. Moreover, Pano having defected two years earlier—shortly after the Bay of Pigs—he knew intimately not only the political scene in Havana but, by now, the whole scene here in Miami.

As the cab approached the hotel, Blackford's thoughts turned to the last hotel he had stayed at—with Sally. The brief visit in Acapulco over New Year's: he on convalescent leave, she on vacation from the University of Mexico, where she was teaching English literature.

He thought back on their first evening, after he had picked her up at the airport and taken her to the hotel, where he had reserved a suite of rooms. They went down quickly to the beach to swim in the ocean, returning to the suite only after the sun had set. Blackford showered in the second bathroom, entered the living room dressed in tennis shorts and a sports shirt and sat down while Sally, through the open door to the bedroom, chatted, with her wry blend of provocation and femininity. The champagne sat on the coffee table, and Blackford opened it.

"Blacky, dear, do you intend to tell me exactly what happened to you during the missile crisis? I appreciated your—occasional—letters, but you know, dear, you needn't have devoted as much time as you did to giving me the plot of Agatha Christie's detective stories."

"I was studying Spanish," Blackford said, smiling as he recalled the six *novelas policíacas* of Agatha Christie he had read during some of the long days in Havana. "You know, my Spanish is pretty good."

"I am glad to hear that, Blacky. And I, Professor Sally Partridge, am competent to test how good it is. I deliver three lectures per week at Filosfía y Artes *in Spanish.*" She appeared briefly in the doorway in her dressing gown, affecting her didactic posture at the lectern of the English literature class.

"How do you teach Jane Austen in Spanish?" Blackford asked after she had ducked back into the bedroom.

"Well, use your imagination. I assume you have a sharply developed imagination, Blacky, because you are always devising ingenious ways of killing people, are you not? *I know, I know,* I am not supposed to ask you direct questions. But we *can* agree that your Agency specializes in imaginative work? The Bay of Pigs operation, for instance. Now not *everybody* could have thought of that—right, Blacky? I imagine that if the entire operation had been planned by Castro himself, it could not have worked out better for him. He got a thousand prisoners, he humiliated America, and he mobilized the Cuban public on his side. You know, Blacky darling, I just thought of something—did I ever get around to congratulating you on that achievement?"

Blackford sipped the champagne, his eyes twinkling: Sally would never change. And that was fine with him, though there were . . . sensitive areas, and he hoped he would not need to labor to deflect her conversation sufficiently to stay away from the subject of Catalina.

Catalina! The bravest woman he had ever known. And, he allowed himself to muse on one of their first meetings, the best instructed in arts Sally herself was certainly . . . ingenious? (her word)—at. Sally was still talking, presumably from her dressing table, opposite the bed. Blackford couldn't see her, but her voice carried easily around the corner of the doorway to him.

Blackford said, "Oh, the Bay of Pigs was hardly our *greatest* triumph. Don't you think the Berlin Wall qualifies as Number One?"

"Ah yes, sorry. Of course. That was absolutely triumphant, the Berlin Wall. France, Great Britain, and the United States— all they had was a sound legal case giving them access to all of Berlin, plus a solid preponderance of nuclear weapons, and Khrushchev simply goes out and builds a wall down the center of Berlin. What I thought most magnificent about it all was that the United States Government did—nothing—about—it."

She was obviously manipulating her lipstick. Blackford thought back on the agonies of the Bruderschaft, and for a moment said, reverently, nothing by way of riposte. This quickly communicated a hint of resistance to her. He got back into his customary role, the succubus for her taunts.

"Mind you, Blackford, you did confide to me that you had had three meetings with John F. Kennedy and that you were mightily impressed with him. I'm glad of that, because that is yet another thing we have in common. I think his speech at the Berlin Wall where he said all Berliners would one day be able to say they were Berliners was one of the most moving I've ever heard. And then, and then"—Sally's spirits were, well, soaring a little higher than, arguably, the rules of the game called for—"that speech he gave a few days ago. Was it last month? Just after Christmas, to the returning Bay of Pigs soldiers, you know, where he said they would have their flag back over a free Cuba? Tell me, darling, are we going to invade Cuba? I do hope we can do that without losing any men."

"Awr . . . fuck you, Sally."

"Well goodness knows you have done enough of that, darling. Or is this a fresh romantic overture, dictated by the Agency? Oh my goodness, I never thought: Is our suite— wired?" She paused.

"Another thought, a worse thought: Are there cameras hidden about? You know, it would be terribly . . . *desconcertante*—that's Spanish for embarrassing, disconcerting—"

"I know what *desconcertante* means—"

"Terribly terribly *desconcertante* if a tape of us, engaging in intimacies, were to get out and make the rounds of the anti-American caucus at the University of Mexico. Oh, I can just see myself summoned to the office of the Rector. 'Señorita—Profesora—Partridge—he persists in speaking to me in English, in which he is very difficult to understand, but he is very proud of his English—'Profesora Partridge, I haff heer a tahp—eet is a tahp weeth yorr voiss on it an zee voiss of a jen-tle-man, an een it yoo arr makin ferry, ferry—extraordinaree souns—' "

"Sally. Enough. Are you jet-lagged?"

"Yes, dear. The Cold War has jet-lagged me for years now. Do you know that there are millions of people—I have met them all, all hundred million of them—who manage to live their lives away from the trenches? But me? I study English literature at Yale in the graduate school and am swept off my feet by a beautiful young senior—to be sure, he was two years older than I because he was delayed in his schooling by the great war to end all wars. My young Adonis is studying to be an engineer, and before you know it, he ends up being an engineer of the Cold War—"

Sally emerged from the bedroom, in pale blue cotton, with those pearls, and the radiant, amused, affectionate expression, the whole room dizzied by that special blend of her fragrance. She smiled, and sat down next to him. He handed her a glass, on second thought put it down and leaned over and kissed her, lightly massaging the sides of her face.

"You were saying?" he said hoarsely.

"I was saying, you are a *puerco guerrillero*, and how can we go on this way, you silly wretch, and don't think I didn't notice that scar on your shoulder when we were swimming. Oh, dear, Blacky—"

"Shall we talk about something else?"

He looked down at her dress, tight-fitting about her breasts and waist—"And do you need to visit me wearing an iron corset?" Suddenly he stopped, staring down at her brooch, a jeweled facsimile of the Mexican flag in small diamonds, emeralds, rubies.

"What's that?"

"Oh, a little present. From one of my students."

"Did he get an A?"

"He got an A for effort."

"Sally. That thing has got to be worth a couple of thousand dollars."

"You think so?"

"Who gave it to you?"

She replied teasingly. "A very wealthy student. His father has oil." Then, suddenly, a change in direction. The mockery was gone. "Why don't you come back with me to Mexico City? Just resign, it's that simple." She was pleading with him.

"It's not that simple, darling." Blackford's voice was of congruent gravity, respect, devotion. "One day, maybe. Besides"— he felt it safer to return to the familiar mode—"we're supposed to get married next year, remember? A solemn appointment we made at the hotel in Taxco?"

She was silent as he stroked her neck, turning her gently to one side and, with his teeth, nudging down the zipper behind her dress.

"Not here."

She rose, and they walked into the bedroom, where the lights were off. He closed the door to the living room. From the bed they could see through the open window the lights of the city. The air was warm, and there was the fragrance also of the sea.

Soon he was naked, and she was, and, his lips over her eyes, her head turned to one side, Blackford told her her eyes were more exciting than all the lights, all the sounds, all the pleasures of Acapulco. She moaned, and hugged him, and whispered that she loved him, would always love him, no matter what.

It had been so for three days. His last hotel stay. And now the Miami Fontainebleau.

THE TAXI STOPPED, the driver opened the door. Blackford roused himself, checked into the hotel, picked up two messages, and went up in the elevator to familiarize himself with the XPando Corporation's Suite 1202.

The living room was large and furnished as an office, with a desk and a typewriter and a couple of file boxes. Elsewhere there was the kind of thing one expects in hotel suites—the large sofa, the armchairs, the television set. Blackford opened the door out to the little lanai. He could see the waterway with the luxury yachts berthed, and, slightly farther east, the Atlantic Ocean. The view from the hotel at Acapulco a fortnight ago, he concluded, had been more glamorous. He closed his eyes and wondered whether he was truly engaged in an effort to relieve all those people, two hundred miles south, of their tyrant—or was it all about something else? He looked at his watch. Pano Iglesias was to come in, one of the messages had confirmed, at 5:30. It was 5:10. He would have a quick swim. Easy, down the elevator to the hotel lobby, and right to the beach. He swam vigorously.

Pano Iglesias was prompt. He wore neatly-ironed khaki pants, a narrow-striped cotton sports shirt, a trim dark blue blazer, and he carried a large briefcase. He was middle-sized, startlingly young in appearance (Blackford knew that Pano was thirty), his features were regular, his skin light tan, his nose aquiline. He was not wearing the mustache Blackford had seen in the picture he was shown in Washington.

"Pano," he announced himself. *"Para servirle."*

"I'm Blackford." Oakes returned the greeting, extending his hand.

In less than fifteen minutes, Blackford felt preternaturally at home with the young Cuban designated by Rufus to be his right hand. His English, though accented, was fluent. Rather than interrupt his rhythms he would sometimes simply use the Spanish word, and sometimes they would both lapse into Spanish, with which Blackford was by now fluent.

His specialty, Pano said, pulling a cigarette from his pocket—his blazer was quickly doffed and put back on one of the chairs against the wall—was the political situation in Cuba. Seated in an armchair he asked, Had he—"Blackforrd"—seen the morning papers?

"Only in Washington."

"Have you seen the report of Castro's speech?"

"No."

"Alas, not all of Washington cares very much about what is going on in Cuba. Fortunately, they care very much—that is my impression—in the White House."

Pano sprang up and dived for the inside pocket of his blazer. "The speech yesterday by Castro." He looked up. "I will maybe be telling you some things you know. I know you have been in Havana for many months. I don't know if you know how *enojado* Castro is with Khrushchev?"

Yes, said Blackford, he knew that Castro was mad at Khrushchev.

"It has cost Castro a lot of face, and he likes face a great deal. That pulling out of the missiles by the Soviets in October—he is crying *tears* about it. My contacts tell me he spends almost as much time swearing at the Kremlin as he does at the White House. Listen." Pano picked up the clipping and began to read. " 'In his speech, Fidel Castro made clear his decision to act independently of the U.S.S.R. regardless of the Soviet Union's agreements with the U.S. to remove its missiles from Cuba.' Ahh, nice that, no, Blackforrd? Huh? *Independent* of the U.S.S.R.? If he were independent of the U.S.S.R. he would just be another *caudillo* who calls himself a Communist and is especially practiced in *sadismo.*"

"I know from personal experience that he is a sadist."

"Yes, well listen. The paper then quotes Castro directly: *'The Soviet Government has reached certain accords with the American Government. But this does not mean that we have renounced the right to have the weapons we deem convenient and to take steps in international policy that we deem convenient as a sovereign country.' "*

Pano looked up again. " *'The weapons we deem convenient.'* Concentrate on that, Blackforrd. We know what weapons he finds convenient, do we not? Nuclear missiles. But they are gone now. Where else is he going to get nuclear missiles, if he wants them? I continue the story:

" 'Castro hinted that Cuba inclined toward China in the Moscow-Peking ideological split. Cuba planned to "set an example . . . to the socialist family," he said, in its reaction to the "public discrepancies that have emerged between the great forces of the socialist camp." ' "

Pano put the clipping down. "Fidel is angry with the Soviet Union, but he is suggesting how important it is that the Kremlin pursue him to stay on their side of the Sino-Soviet split."

Over a simple dinner, brought in by room service, Blackford listened to a description of the lesser-known figures around Castro. Pano ate heartily, the chicken and mashed potatoes and peas, the red wine and fruit and cheese, though he managed without apparent difficulty both to eat and to speak, and sometimes also to smoke, at the same time.

Blackford did not need to be told anything about Raúl Castro, the Stakhanovite Communist urging more and more orthodoxy and repression on his older brother; or, God knows, Che Guevara—Blackford reflected that he probably knew as much about that strange figure as any man alive. He had, after all, spent significant parts of the preceding spring, summer, and fall bargaining with him on behalf of President Kennedy. Operation Caimán, they had called that abortive attempt to bring off a deal. Or Osvaldo Dorticós, formally the President of Cuba: Blackford had known him as a member of a military tribunal that had sentenced him—and Catalina—to death. Blackford had read all the files in Washington, and most of the names were familiar to him: Faure Chomón, Carlos Rafael Rodríguez, Blás Roca, Major Juan Almeida, Armando Hart, Manuel Piñeiro. But some were not; and Pano's knowledge was encyclopedic.

"Who is Ingenio Tamayo?"

Pano loved such questions.

"Ingenio and I were at the Managua Escuela Militar together. His father was a big sugar baron. Thousands, tens of thousands of hectares. Pure Spanish blood. Ah, the Spanish-Cubans, how they missed out on Castro. You see—I am telling you much that you know; I know, I know, but all of it very very *importantísimo*. The Spanish, that special breed—Bacardí, Aspuru, Arrechabala, Aróstegui—always they kept their hands away from Cuban politics. *Manos fuera de Cuba!* Hands off Cuba, that was their slogan. They were like the English Vicar of Bray—"

Blackford could not abort the suddenly raised eyebrow. He wondered that Pano, while at military school in Havana, had run across the colorful eighteenth-century British tergiversator. He could hear Professor Curtis at Yale intoning the famous lines: "And this is law, I will maintain, / Unto my dying day, sir, / That whatsoever king shall reign, / I will be the Vicar of Bray, sir!"

"—whoever was king in Havana, that was quite all right by them, and when they felt that Castro was about to topple Batista, they went along, even helped Castro. Don Leandro Tamayo decided early in 1958 that Batista had had it, so he wasn't a bit sorry that he had used his influence to get Ingenio into the Managua Escuela Militar since he knew his strange son was pro-Castro even before his father decided to play the political odds. You see, Ingenio is very nearly blind, cannot see a thing—I am exaggerating, but he needs eyeglasses that look like the bottom of Coca-Cola bottles. Don Leandro spoke to the right person and *whishh*, Ingenio was in the elite military school. The rest of us had to have twenty-twenty vision.

"Ingenio was always a queer duck. Studious, and physically very fit except for his vision. He cheated on the marksmanship—I helped him. If he had a pistol and aimed it at Florida, he would hit Maine. Ingenio is a great hater. He hated most people, just for *conveniencia*. It was his temperament. But some people he hated especially. He hated our platoon leader, and one day during military exercises our platoon leader was at breakfast and, after eating his porridge, fell over in a convulsion and died. Big investigation. Poison in his porridge. But Ingenio was not identified. He is very clever in these matters. By this time I suspected him, but at least there was one less person in the academy that Ingenio hated, though he began then to hate the substitute. Fortunately for the substitute, we graduated.

"Ingenio Tamayo," Pano went on, "by the time he was twenty-six, had been promoted to captain and decided to join Castro, and approached a contact. A family friend, a scholarly graduate student who was being sent by his father to Oxford for postgraduate work, whose family and Castro's had always been friends. His name is Jesús Ferrer, and Jesús is becoming now an important figure in the resistance—he is another one of those pure Spaniards, skin *blanco*, *blanco*, like Marilyn Monroe. Jesús got Ingenio to Sierra Maestra, and he became very close to Fidel, very close to Fidel. Fidel uses him now for his most delicate *operaciones*. Ingenio's specialty is to dispose of people Fidel does not like but does not want to try to execute. Fidel has two execution *baterías*—he has his firing squads, and he has Ingenio. After Fidel arrived in Havana and expropriated the sugar industry, then the Cuban Spaniards began to howl, and one of the loudest howls came from Don Leandro. Fidel one morning read in *La Revolución* a story on a public *manifiesta* by Don Leandro urging Castro to get on with the restoration of the democracy he had promised. So? He calls Ingenio, and a week later Don Leandro is getting into his car to drive to his ranch house after dinner at the Vedado Tennis Club and—he never arrives home. No trace of him, or of his Cadillac. One day a diver will find a rusty Cadillac in the Almendares River. That was on a Monday. On Friday I ran into Ingenio at the Instituto Nacional de Reforma Agraria and I said to him how sad about the disappearance of his father. And you know, Blackforrd, you know, he just *smiled*?"

IT WAS NEARLY 10 P.M. when in midsentence Pano said suddenly, "Blackforrd, shall we swim?"

Blackford's answer was instantaneous. "Sure. Can I assume you brought your own trunks, or do I assume you guessed I would have more than one pair?"

"*El último.*"

They went down the elevator, Blackford in a dressing gown and trunks, Pano with his slacks over his trunks and a bath towel over his naked shoulders. They went to the bathers' exit on the basement floor and made their way out to the beach, empty though wonderfully inviting, with the low half-moon on the horizon. A few feet from high water, Pano stripped off his pants and dove into the gentle surf. Blackford followed, and they swam out together. Blackford wondered whether Pano would succeed in talking while he swam, was relieved he did not attempt to do so. Pano swam exultantly, and Blackford felt the competitive emanation and quickened his strokes. They were racing now, and Blackford felt the satisfaction of a totally mended shoulder as, little by little, he drew ahead of Pano. He stopped and waited when they were a half mile out. Pano spoke: "You swim well, Blackforrd, like a Cuban."

"You swim pretty well, like most Americans."

Blackford could see the grin, the teeth pearled by moonlight. Pano laughed. "Shall we?" He started back, and Blackford swam lazily this time, both of them at ease.

They dried themselves and walked back to the elevator. Pano said happily, "I think perhaps a beer. No, perhaps three beers."

In their suite they discarded their trunks and showered in separate bathrooms, and by the time they were back at their upholstered stations the beer had arrived. Blackford spoke directly.

"We need to know who might be the central figure in a cabal that could stage a coup."

"Yes, of course, that is the theoretical *cuestión*. But is it now the actual question? Who? I know who. And"—Pano smiled as he inhaled his cigarette smoke—"I know that you know who."

Blackford paused. Rufus had not been explicit on just how much Pano could be expected to know about the central figure. "By what name do you know him?" Blackford asked, cautiously.

Pano laughed. "Yes, of course. But at this point we do not mention names, do we, Blackforrd? What do *you* call him?"

Blackford paused. But only for a moment. "We call him AM/ LASH. A-M-slash-L-A-S-H."

"AM/LASH. *Ele A Ese Hache?*"

"Yes. LASH."

"Clumsy, no?"

"I did not give him that designation."

Pano paused. "If he—if AM/LASH—succeeds, he will be called AM/LASH *El Libertador.*"

"That could be arranged. It is a part of Operation Mongoose, as you have been informed, Pano, that the liberator must be plausible, that the Cuban people will welcome him."

"The Cuban people will require a little coaxing. Many of them think Fidel is God."

"Many Russians thought Stalin was God."

"Are we supposed to talk tonight about how to approach AM/LASH?" Pano asked.

"Are you in a position to make contact?"

"Yes."

"Shall we talk about those arrangements?"

Pano drank deeply from his glass. "Security is very important, Blackforrd. The identity of Mr. LASH is the . . . ultimate secret. Miami is full of Fidel's agents."

"I know. And both of us know who some of them are. And I must suppose you know more of them than I do."

"Yes. Yes. And there is one less of them tonight than at this time last night."

"I am aware that there is—interaction—between the two camps even here, in Miami."

"The one we—*eliminamos*—last night had been a trusted friend of mine for four months. It was very difficult, but duty is duty, and although I am sentenced in absentia to die by a Cuban military court, I still think of me as a Cuban soldier—" he reached into his back pocket and with something close to a flourish took out his wallet. From it he drew out a plastic identification card and handed it to Blackford.

"We received these when we were commissioned at the Managua Escuela Militar."

Blackford inspected the card. Pano, in solemn pose, looked like a seventeen-year-old, the lieutenant's bars pinned to his shirt collar. Blackford sensed the prickly question he had several times before sensed between strangers-in-arms. He laughed, and drank from his own glass: "You wonder about me, Pano?"

"I need to wonder about *todo el mundo*, the whole world. My professional *puntillo*— how do you say that, my friend?"

"Punctilio. Okay, Pano, but it is only right, then, that we should wonder about each other. Whom do you want to hear from about me?"

"The Attorney General."

Blackford whistled. "I have only once met the Attorney General, and I'm not certain he would even remember me."

"That does not matter. I trust Robert Kennedy. He is on our side."

"But if he does not know me personally, how could an assurance even from him satisfy you?"

"I trust that he would not give that *seguro* without first being absolutely certain."

"Very well," said Blackford, thinking quickly. "I will get you word from him. And from whom should I expect to hear about you?"

"Well," Pano looked at his watch. "Exactly twenty-four hours ago, you could have heard from my . . . late companion."

"We have a logical problem, Pano. Because suppose your late companion, as you describe him, actually was on our side? Theoretically he might have been disposed of because he discovered . . . your true allegiance."

"Ah, Blackforrd, you have a fine *punto*." Pano's smile was clearly genuine. "But before you came to me, you must have seen the order by the Supreme Military Court pronouncing me a condemned traitor, to be shot on sight?"

"Yes. And of course that is kindergarten cover."

"What do you want? Confirmation from, from—AM/LASH?"

"That would do nicely."

Pano spoke now more slowly. "That must mean that you have your own channels to AM/LASH."

"Yes, that is what I mean. One of the things I mean." He got up and stretched his arms. "Let us agree to work together as we have been doing, but to put off any communication by your channels to—LASH, let's call him—until I deliver the Attorney General, and you deliver—LASH. I guess both these operations will take a few days. Meanwhile," he picked up the tray with the empty bottles, walked to the door which he opened, setting the tray on the floor outside, "meanwhile, you can acquaint me with the Miami scene. But before you do that," he smiled, "we can both get some sleep."

Pano had risen and reached for his blazer and large briefcase. "My great pleasure to be with you, Blackforrd. We will go forward as brothers—provided you are not Cain!" He laughed, gripped Blackford's outstretched hand and went cheerfully to the door. *"Muy buenas,* Blackforrd. *Hasta mañana."*

5

It had been a pretty heavy day—the routine stuff plus the meeting with the congressional leaders, plus the new Canadian ambassador, plus the Farmers' Bureau speech, and ahead lay the state dinner, with all the movie stars coming in because Lollabrigida was getting the medal . . . But he had a few minutes, and went to his rocking chair.

Hmm. Heavy day. Well, has it ever been different? Arthur was telling me the other day about those long naps of Coolidge. Well, Professor Schlesinger, I take naps. He stretched out his hands, yawning.

They help. Good old Churchill. What a mind for detail. Told me a nap didn't count unless you got undressed. When he told me that at first I thought he had something else in mind, but no: Churchill was never that way. At least, not that I know of. Certainly not now, poor guy. Maybe I should ask Macmillan. God, Super Mac knows everything. When he told me that Philip II had naps even when he went off to the monastery, I had, goddamnit, to think real hard who Philip II was. But I remembered, just in time. Should ask Macmillan—Harold—about the younger Churchill. Poor guy, nap is what he does now most of the time. Must remember to drop him a note. He reached up and brought the pad from the coffee table to his lap, pulled out a pen, and scribbled.

Damn if I didn't dream of that Cuban bastard even during my forty-five-minute nap. When Mac Bundy brought me that paragraph from his speech I was tempted to tell him about Mongoose, but Bobby is right—nobody. Nobody is to know except Hicock. Even McCone doesn't know. At least Bobby

43

tells *me he doesn't know. Beats me how the goddamn Director of CIA doesn't know about Mongoose, a CIA operation. When the subject did come up—real theoretical—the day Tad Szulc came in here and plop I ask him, like I was asking about the World Series, what about assassinating Castro? He was shocked. Just hypothetical, I said.*

I could have been an actor. Come to think of it, lots of people've said I could have rivaled Clark Gable. Would rather have rivaled Joe DiMaggio, ho ho, though you can't slight Carole Lombard. Anyway, I said all the right things and then McCone, my Number One Papist, blurts out that assassination is a mortal sin. *Can't remember whether I got around to dissociating myself from mortal sin when I gave the Baptists that speech in Houston. "And what's more, gentlemen, not only do I believe in the separation of church and state, I believe in separating myself from the Ten Commandments." No—* he smiled. *No. I think even Nixon would have picked that up. "What's more, the Democratic candidate for President of the United States in Houston yesterday said he was in favor of dishonoring your father and mother, lying, murdering, coveting your neighbor's goods and your neighbors' wives . . ." Well, I mean, I don't think that would have been the time publicly to challenge Tricky Dick to a polygraph test.* He had a little chuckle.

Now that would blow up our democratic system. Polygraph tests for all presidential candidates after every speech. Instead of a debate. Maybe I'll shoot a memo to John Bailey on that, just to see the expression on Arthur's face the next day. Would be worth it. "Dear John. I know it may be early to think about the election campaign in 1964, but what do you think of the idea of challenging the Republican candidate to take joint truth tests in mid-October? We could agree to one question each from Larry Spivak, James Reston, David Lawrence, and Arthur Krock. Let me have your thoughts on this . . ."

He began to rock evenly, studiedly, in his chair. *Castro said—I won't forget his exact words—after my talk to the Cubans in Miami: "President Kennedy is a vulgar pirate chief. He has degraded the dignity of his position." Then he* said I had "probably had too much to drink." Dumb bastard doesn't even know I don't drink. Except every now and then a Ballantine. Correction: I had that vodka in Vienna toasting to Soviet–U.S. relations with Khrushchev. No wonder I don't drink more. If it had been two drinks maybe Khrushchev would have built his Berlin Wall a hundred miles west.

Hmm. Sometimes I think that first idea of Rusk's and Bundy's during the missile crisis—letting Havana have it in October with all our military might—was the right one.

We let him get away with it in October and he's the cock of the walk. Now he's even kissing Chinese ass! Well, no more, no more, and tomorrow I'll say yes to Bobby. He is right. Can't let that fucker stay around, and no more of the half-ass stuff we've been up to since 1961, got to do it right.

Bobby's right on the organizational level too. Two operations. Hicock will be in charge of Mongoose where there isn't any political involvement—a falling star lands on Castro during a parade, that kind of thing, whadyaknow. The other, what Bobby is primarily counting on and he's right—that will be for Rufus. Rufus will go along with a coup, but not with the Mickey Mouse.

Talk about Mickey Mouse.

They've tried everything except an overdose of poison ivy. I like the one that involved the cigar that would make Castro lose his hair. Arthur would call Hicock "a humorist." That and some of the other things were crazy, though who knows, one of them might have worked. But no Mickey-Mousing with Rufus. The LASH fellow, that's our ace. Good, clean, vintage South American coup. After all, they've been practicing coups since the Spanish left. Rich Goodwin has an interesting thesis, got it from some Chilean scholar. Up until the Spaniards left the hemisphere, you couldn't double-park in Latin America without the Spanish colonial governor sending a boat off to Madrid or to the Vatican to ask what was the appropriate penalty. They still haven't learned how to govern themselves. I'm all for the Alliance for Progress, but somebody told me they have had forty-three coups in Bolivia during this century. So what is one more?

And so what if this LASH fellow, after the coup, ap-

proaches us—real suspicious-like, like he was not going to have American imperialism substitute for Soviet imperialism, the whole bit—to decompress the Castro loyalists. Hell, Dick Goodwin could write the speech for him. He'd sound real tough about us the day after the coup. Then, a month later, just a few sensible overtures. After all, LASH can tell them—wonder if LASH is a speech-making type? If he gives three-hour speeches, I'm going to suggest a coup against LASH—he can tell them in his next speech that there isn't any point in continuing "mutually damaging economic hostilities"—something like that—with the United States. He can get U Thant to appoint a committee full of U.N. people etc., etc., to suggest "mutual concessions."

And by the time November 1964 comes around, maybe we will be up to a state visit over here for LASH. No. I'll go there first. Big concession. The Colossus of the North travels to little Cuba. I'll say some real pretty things about Cuban independence, and Cuban pride, and Cuban patriotism.

Would I say anything about Castro? Hell no, Stupid. LASH's big number is how he saved Cuba from Castro. No, no mention of Castro, but a whole lot of the other stuff.

He looked out at the Rose Garden. The muted lights showed the remaining flecks of the recent snowfall. He resumed his slow, rhythmic rocking.

Gotta keep it secret. Bobby says JM WAVE in Miami is making a lot of noise, but everybody puts that station's activities down to psy-war, which is fine, perfect cover for Mongoose. We got to clean up that business down there on that island, and there's no other way to do it, Bobby is right, no o-t-h-e-r way. Damned convenient, having your brother as AG. He tells me even Hoover doesn't know. Wish I knew that was so. But I can handle Hoover. Come to think of it, I can handle just about anybody. Wish Castro was a she, would be easier. As I told Bill Manchester when he asked me how come I make out all the time when he doesn't, I said, Bill, some people have it, some people don't . . . Not my fault, is it? Gotta have confidence. And the CIA is a hell of a lot more useful than I thought it was back after the Bay of Pigs. Only you got to remember the CIA is a big machine made up of little CIAs. And they don't always work with—what did Acheson say?—

"reciprocating gears." So tomorrow, just me and Bobby, and go with Mongoose. Period. Period, end Castro.

There was a knock on the door.

"Mr. President, the First Lady asked me to remind you it's almost seven."

6

It was inevitable, Larry Fillmore ruminated, walking home in the January chill from the safe house at the Hamilton Arms on Thirty-first Street where Operation Mongoose, or at least one part of it, had its headquarters. Anyone baptized "William Hicock" was going to be called Wild Bill somewhere along the line. Granted, if the baby William grew up acting like Caspar Milquetoast, or Donald Meek, or Adlai Stevenson perhaps, he might have got through life without anyone's being tempted.

But not this Hicock. Larry shook his head. He hadn't known much about Wild Bill's background—colleagues' bios don't get passed around in the Agency, not in the covert encampments. Obviously he had grown up in the West. Larry could only guess that Wild Bill (at the office the senior colleagues referred to him as "WB"—"as in Yeats," Hicock had said to his deputy on first meeting him) must have been captain of the hazing committee at his fraternity at college. He looked and dressed as one might expect a Wild Bill Hicock to look and dress. He wore cowboy boots, though the heel was not fag-high, just a stocky little nipple there, and then the conventional embroidery on the leather halfway up to his knee. Larry had never seen him with his shirt buttoned, but then Larry had never seen WB at any function, come to think of it, at which a superior official was present. WB was the boss at the safe house, boss of the four men and two Cuban-American women who worked there. And if anybody from Operation Mongoose field operations came into the safe house, why should WB put on coat and tie? After all, he was paying them, not the other way around.

And although WB had now five consecutive failures, he was

always cheerful and optimistic. "Next time, next time," he would say. And perhaps it would be so; no one at the shop doubted that they were dealing with an experienced and resourceful field official. Still, details were in short supply.

Looking about for a memo he had written for WB a few weeks earlier, one day when WB was out of town, Larry absent-mindedly thought he might have left it on WB's desk. He went in, didn't see it, and began opening the central drawer. Perhaps Conchita, who did cryptography for WB, had put it there. He didn't find the memo (which all the time was sitting in one of the baskets on Larry's own desk). But he did stumble on a picture of a younger WB. He was being decorated. Larry turned the picture over. Taped to the back was a faded *Stars & Stripes* clipping with the headline, "General Roy S. Geiger Decorates 1st Lieutenant Hicock." The picture caption read, "Major General Roy S. Geiger today hung a second Silver Star on 1st Lieutenant William Hicock for conspicuous gallantry in action in Okinawa. Lt. Hicock, from Laramie, Wyoming, received his first Silver Star, also for conspicuous gallantry, in Tarawa."

As he walked to the parking lot, Larry Fillmore paused at the corner of Thirty-first and M, waiting for the light. He wondered vaguely what exactly WB had done in the field. He never doubted that WB had earned his medals, but Larry would like to have known the details. He had to suppose that Wild Bill had emerged from the Japanese concentration camp before breakfast, shot a half dozen, and taken the rest prisoner. Or maybe he had hung down from a helicopter and lassoed a Japanese intelligence officer, whisking him off behind U.S. lines for interrogation. That was the kind of thing Wild Bill went in for.

Four such incidents, designed to consummate Mongoose—the elimination of Castro—in 1962. Sure, any one of them *might* have worked. Larry wondered if the world would ever know about Wild Bill's idea of staging the Second Coming of Christ, causing a great religious upheaval and the consequent overthrow of the anti-Christ Castro. And then there was the seashell that was going to explode where Castro went swimming.

He shook his head. WB was a bright guy. Certainly he was inventive—and his instructions were very plain: whatever happened to Castro, it mustn't be traceable to the United States.

But this new idea of the wet suit . . . All Larry Fillmore could do was to shake his head, again, though to do so interfered with his upstream concentration, at the traffic light, on the one-way traffic.

The next morning WB called Larry and Elihu and Conchita into his office. They sat down on folding chairs. WB was smoking a cigar.

"It's done," he announced to his little staff. "Got a call from TSD"—TSD was the CIA's Technical Services Division "—you remember, they said they'd try to come up with that wet suit according to my specifications? They've done it. It exists. What we have to do now is some thinking about how to manage Jim Donovan. Elihu, do you have the details on Donovan's trip?"

"Yes," Elihu said. Elihu wore tie and jacket and glasses. Clean-cut and clerical in manner, he spoke from notes, but notes that would mean nothing even if the chief cryptographer of the KGB happened on them—that was a part of the covert agent activities' training. When notes are necessary, devise a means of making them unintelligible save to yourself.

"Mr. Donovan is scheduled to leave on Saturday morning. He'll fly out of Andrews Air Force Base in a DC-4. The aircraft has Red Cross markings and its identification number is Z-997703—"

"Elihu, might we save a little time if you just said it was the same plane as on Donovan's other two trips?"

"Yes sir. Yes, WB."

WB did not like to be sirred. ("Wrong for this kind of unit. No chickenshit in Mongoose. We're not at Parris Island or administering a Marine division.")

"It's the same plane, it is scheduled to lift off at nine A.M. One hundred miles north of Havana, it will radio on 124 MHz, and will give out the code 'Donovan Z-997.' The signal will be met with 'Proceed on course blank'—probably about 194 degrees. Ten minutes later, the pilot will expect to see two Cuban fighter jets. They'll U-turn in front of Donovan's plane, and escort him into José Martí Airport."

"Where will Castro first see him?"

(Wild Bill wants to get on with this, Larry mused.)

"The Swiss consul didn't have that detail. All he said of any interest was that the Prime Minister has planned 'a little lunch' for Donovan, to 'commemorate the successful conclusion of their business.'"

"Good!" WB clapped his hands together with great force, and Larry imagined what little would be left of a small, thin Japanese soldier if he had mistakenly been standing between Wild Bill Hicock's hands.

"That's what we need, a little festivity. Makes gift giving appropriate. *Now.* The Bay of Pigs prisoners are of course back, and most of the $53 million of drugs went down there with Donovan on trip number two. He is taking with him the balance, some of the stuff we couldn't put our hands on in December. We have all studied Castro's habits at these social affairs, and even though we are the enemy, he and Donovan have always got along just fine. Hell, Donovan is used to trading with the enemy. After all, he got our U-2 pilot back, trading with Khrushchev. Anybody here ever met him?"

No hand was raised.

"Well, I managed to have a little talk with Mr. Donovan, Negotiator, U.S.–Cuba. Told him I was from Protocol, had instructions to check on the operation, and that Protocol thought that Castro might make a gift to Donovan. As you know"—he pointed to Larry—"I already told this to Larry—I planted the seed. The rest of you can now know that I told him that Castro has been observed scuba-diving regularly. He's taken a real shine to it. Swims usually off the beach at Jaimanitas over the reefs. I told Donovan that the only kind of wet suits the Soviet Union has are those made for KGB types. Frogman stuff. The suits left over from the pre-Castro tourist trade are pretty creaky. Nothing like the new sports models you pick up at Abercrombie and Fitch. I was going to suggest it if he didn't, but he did: 'Why don't we give him a wet suit?' So I said I would see to it that Mr. Donovan had a wet suit, nicely wrapped for Castro, and he said thanks. How you like that for planning!" WB beamed.

"So, really, it's just that simple. I'll do it myself. I'll be at Andrews on Saturday an hour before flight time, and I'll personally stow the wet suit package, neatly labeled, alongside Donovan's personal gear before he even boards the plane."

Larry felt he had to interrupt. "WB, these toxic materials the suit is impregnated with—"

"Don't ask me what they are. I didn't study chemistry. But they will work, that's the point."

"Yes. Well, when Castro puts his wet suit on, and a couple of hours later, back from swimming, begins to develop this strange fever which heads him straight into a coma and then—death—what makes you think that nobody is going to get around to examining the wet suit?"

"Larry, you made that point, as you obviously have forgotten, three weeks ago when I first had the idea. I told you then, and I repeat now, the TSD people I talked to said if the wet suit was in salt water long enough—and they *have* washed it out in salt water—there will be nothing that makes the suit look any different, smell different, nothing. So someone goes out diving, comes back. And not less than two hours later—remember that, not any sooner: at least two hours—the diver begins to feel sick. Vomits, fever, the whole bit. Now who in his right mind is going to think he got a disease from a lousy wet suit? I mean, the medical team at autopsy time will know he was poisoned, but they'll think in terms of what he ate, and what he ate is the responsibility of the cook at the luncheon, and if they want to question the hell out of him, that's *their* business."

Elihu cleared his throat. "Suppose, WB, that after Castro is dead, buried, etc., people start looking around at what he, well, left behind. Somebody's going to say, 'Gee, that's a nice wet suit. I think I'll pick that up for my son. He really likes to dive.' And then the next day the son dies of the same poison."

"*Because,*" WB explained, conspicuously slowing the tempo of his speech, as if speaking to a slightly retarded student, "because, Elihu, the people over at TSD tell me the toxicity of the chemicals will last only five or six days. The biggest risk we run is that Castro won't want to go swimming for a week or so, but I doubt that, because the suit will look real inviting by comparison with the stuff he's been using. So anyway, by the time your friend's son gets that suit, it will be safe as Johnson's baby powder."

Elihu nodded.

"Okay? Larry, you pick up the suit from TSD, you know the contact. Meet me here at seven, and we'll drive to Andrews with it. Check which departure lounge, and let me know. Conchita, you check every day with Donovan's office, in case there are any changes in plans. Elihu, keep your eye on the weather forecasts. We don't want to find out there's going to be a hurricane or a monsoon or whatever that will keep Castro from wanting to swim. I don't know what we'll do if that happens, but we'll have to be prepared to act fast on alternatives. Okay?" he rose. "Okay, team, that's it."

ON SATURDAY MORNING the weather in Washington was chilly but bright, and at eight, flashing a card from State Department Protocol identifying one "William Livingston," Hicock left his aide waiting in the officers' boarding lounge and climbed up the gangway of Z-997703. He was shown the private cabin where Donovan would ride. Hicock plunked his parcel down right on the table, neatly marked "For James Donovan, wet suit, gift for FC."

He returned to the lounge, picked up Larry, and they drove off, back to Washington.

WB was exhilarated. "Damned if I don't feel like a drink. What you say? It's Saturday."

"Sure," Larry Fillmore said, though instinctively queasy at the thought of a drink at 8:30 in the morning. They stopped at a bar where, without consulting him, WB ordered two bloody Marys. "Or," he winked at Larry, "do you think a rum and Coke would be more appropriate?"

Larry managed a smile.

THAT AFTERNOON, LARRY was playing tennis with his son at the Washington Golf and Country Club in Arlington when a club steward called out his name. Racquet in hand, he moved to the entrance of the court.

"Wanted on the phone, sir."

It was WB.

"Larry, been thinking. Donovan's due back at seven, maybe a little after, depends a little how long the—the gift-exchange party lasts. I think I'll just be a member of the little greeting party. I'll say to him, Protocol wants to know, did, er, the present, was the present . . . appreciated? Got to be thorough, right?"

"Right, WB."

"Well, I thought you might want to come along."

Larry knew WB's ways. He wanted company.

"Sure."

"Where do you want me to pick you up?"

WB could be that way. Others Larry had worked for would tell Larry where to be at what time.

"You talking about—six?"

"Yup."

"I'll be home. That convenient?"

"You bet. I'll honk twice. Honk honk."

"I'll be ready."

WB was full of talk on the way out. He was describing the consequences of their very long mission. "Needless to say, we're hardly going to get a parade in our honor. Maybe fifty years from now the historians will dig it out. But it makes you—well, kind of proud, doesn't it?"

"It sure does, WB. It was quite an idea you had."

"Don't count your chickens until they're hatched. Wonder who invented that expression? Useful. Wonder who *did* invent that?"

"Mother Goose, maybe."

WB laughed, almost cackled. They drove in, parked, and walked into the Operations Building. WB flashed his card. "We're here to meet Mr. Donovan on Z-997703. Any word from the aircraft?"

The lieutenant turned to the radio operator. "Any word from 703?"

Lifting the earphone from his right ear: "Expect to land seven one four," the young radio man said.

"Good. Thanks, Lieutenant. We'll go down to the lounge. Same one—Lounge C, right? There'll be a few other people there."

"They've already checked in, sir. Yes, Lounge C."

One of the three men was from the State Department, a second from Defense, a third probably CIA. WB nodded. "Protocol," he said, and sat down, picking up a copy of *Life* magazine. "Hmm." He turned to Larry. "Last week's. Typical."

"Typical of what, WB?"

"Typical of bureaucracy. All the same. Last week's *Life* mag, last week's everything. No forward thinking. Typical." WB fell silent. The only things he wanted to talk about he couldn't, not in a small lounge with outsiders.

Fifteen minutes later the little loudspeaker in the corner of the lounge wheezed on. There was static, then the voice from Operations.

"Z-997703, Mr. Donovan, coming in, taxi to Gate 6 in a couple of minutes."

The official greeters went out to the apron, and in two minutes the DC-4 wheeled up and the propellers stopped. The gangway was rolled up, the door opened, and Donovan walked out, a briefcase in his left hand, a large shopping bag in his right.

The State Department official greeted him. "Everything go all right, sir?"

"Fine," Donovan smiled briskly. "Nothing unanticipated." Donovan spotted WB. "Oh—Mr. Livingston. I have this wet suit back for you. Had dinner a couple of nights ago with a friend, big diver. I told him about our plans, and he gave me the absolutely latest model, not in the stores yet. Castro was tickled to death."

7

More often than not Fidel Castro was indulgent quite beyond the understanding of his closest colleagues whenever it was his brother, Raúl, who went off the deep end. But not that night. When Raúl made his impulsive suggestion, Fidel Castro denounced it as "ridiculous."

He then added, "Stupid!"

He followed this by "Asinine!"

And yet, his companions could tell, he had been strangely fetched up by it. The energetic suggestion had affected Fidel perhaps in part because of the sheer fatigue of listening for so long to so long and so depressing an account of what the imperialists and counterrevolutionaries were up to in Miami. Moreover, Alejandro, their informant, was not a specialist in the brisk intelligence summary, though it was hardly his fault. Everyone, Fidel included, kept interrupting him, asking for more details about this operation, that agent. Alejandro, as he was called—"I don't give a damn what his real name is," Castro had told his brother, who had gone to rather melodramatic lengths, in presenting him to the inner council, to explain why he would be called merely "Alejandro" during the afternoon's session—was hardly in a position to compress his answers, when he was being questioned by Fidel Castro, Raúl Castro, Ramíro Valdés, and Osvaldo Dorticós.

The news was dismaying. Station JM WAVE in Miami (Alejandro told them) was by now the largest CIA station in the entire world. There were no fewer than "hundreds—I would say between four and five hundred" operatives attached to

Station JM WAVE, Alejandro reported. "One third of them are trained CIA agents. The others are Cuban traitors."

Castro interrupted him. "Alejandro, *you* know they are traitors, *I* know they are traitors, *Raúl* knows they are traitors, *Valdés* knows they are traitors, *Dorticós* knows they are traitors. It would perhaps save time if from now on you simply refer to them as Cubans. We will know that you are talking about Cuban traitors."

"Yes, Comandante."

"You may proceed."

Alejandro did so. He said that Station JM WAVE, the CIA's code name for their Miami station, was planning, coordinating, and preparing to execute, direct assaults "of every kind, Comandante" against the Castro regime. Such operations, described in startling detail by Alejandro, included commando raids on Cuba itself; the smuggling of arms to be used inside Cuba by agents in place; the infiltration by Cubans in Miami into Cuba to fortify the rebel resistance. There were plans to commit acts of sabotage against critical facilities in Cuba, "including our power plants, our radio stations, our refinery, and even some of our sugar plants. And as you know, Comandante"— Alejandro turned to Fidel, who leaned back, cigar in mouth, in the huge easy chair—"there have been clumsy attempts on your life during the past two years. The missile crisis of October caused the CIA to suspend its dealings with the Mafia group—Rosselli, Trafficante, and others. They have been discharged. But the CIA has not withdrawn its offer of $150,000 as a reward to the underworld for your assassination."

How did he know this? Dorticós wanted to know.

Alejandro replied just a little stiffly that all his informants were subject to checks by his superior, Comandante Raúl . . .

"And though I cannot put my finger on it, I have the distinct impression that a separate echelon of CIA is now in charge of a direct assassination attempt. I have established that the agent Blackford Oakes, prominently involved with what they called Operation Caimán and with Che Guevara all last year, and whom you"—Alejandro paused for a moment, turning to Valdés for safe conduct—"whom Comandante Castro ordered executed last October, is a central figure."

"It's all right, Alejandro. Fidel knows that I gave you a full briefing on the events of October. Go ahead."

"The agent Oakes is in Miami. He is staying at the Fontainebleau Hotel. He has been there, in Suite 1202, for two weeks, and I would suppose he is there for the duration of the current operation. He does not travel ever—we have traced his movements—to the University of Miami South Campus, where Station JM WAVE is situated. It is possible that the people at WAVE do not even know that Oakes is in Miami. Or, for that matter, it is possible that they do not even know who he is. But it is not likely that he is in Miami on a mission unconnected with the mission of station JM WAVE. His exact mission we have not been able to ascertain."

Alejandro was able to identify some of the Cuban principals involved with WAVE—everyone in the room asked about one or more Cubans, in many cases sometime companions-in-arms, but hardly all. He had given his information in detail earlier in the day to Raúl. Efforts were being made to penetrate the inner council of WAVE. "I think we will be successful, but we don't know when the raids will begin, or which targets will come first. We do know that the agenda is as comprehensive as I have described."

Castro had listened, and his mood had blackened. Toward the end of the second hour, Raul and Valdés were questioning Alejandro on details while Castro sat, silent. But after a while he picked up a book from his desk, slammed it down and complained that the conference had degenerated into sheer speculation. *"Basta!"*

Alejandro froze at attention. Exercising great self-control, Fidel modified the tone of his voice, addressing Alejandro. "Yes, enough. You are doing good work, Alejandro, and you will be rewarded. You may go now. You will receive instructions tomorrow from Comandante Valdés."

The four men remained in Castro's office, scattered about the large oak table in the windowless room. It was one of the four offices Castro used, its address unknown to the diplomatic community, unknown, even, to the broader echelon of Castro's administration. Castro was not talking. After Alejandro left, he walked over to the shortwave radio, looked at his huge wristwatch, and played with the dial, in search of a station. "Mexico," he muttered. "Don't get any news of any interest from *our* stations." He was sitting almost absentmindedly by the radio when supper was brought in, separate trays on stands placed in front of Raúl, Valdés, and Dorticós. Fidel's own tray was placed directly on his desk, in obedience to his hand signal.

Raúl's rage was more expressive than his older brother's, and uncontained. He swore at the Kennedy administration, reminded the room that he had predicted their troubles would only be beginning with the end of the missile crisis and the pledge by President Kennedy made to Khrushchev. That pledge—that the U.S. would not invade Cuba nor seek to overthrow Castro's regime—was not to be trusted. Something dramatic had to be done. It was only after he was pressed to suggest just what might be done that he had said it, said it in sepulchral tones designed to enhance the drama he wished to invest in his proposal:

"We should commission the assassination of the mayor of Miami."

There was silence. Raúl took advantage of it. "I know Mayor Robert Tinhigh is not involved with the CIA operation, and he is not even of Cuban descent. But he is the mayor of the city that is becoming a garrison for aggressive operations against our country. He is a symbol, and he is responsible for what goes on in his own city. His assassination, with just enough of a trail to make unmistakable the motives of the people who ordered his death, would suddenly register with the Kennedy administration that we simply will not—*not*"—Raúl's voice was by now high-pitched, *"tolerate* what the Kennedy people are sponsoring."

It was at this point that Castro exploded. "A ridiculous idea! Stupid! Asinine!"

There was silence. Raúl did not reply.

"What is the point in shooting someone completely unattached to the anti-Cuban enterprise? I don't care if the sharks *eat* Mayor Tinhigh tomorrow morning. But I care about the political significance of an assassination that traces to me. If it does not trace to me, it accomplishes absolutely nothing. The mayor might have been killed by his wife's lover, for all that that would prove. But if it is traceable to us, then we have reached out and killed an elected American public official. Terrorism is a useful weapon, but it is not useful unless it accomplishes a political purpose. If it is traced to my government, the United States then has in its hands a weapon it can publicly use to justify counteraggression. Kennedy is always complaining that we are attempting to spread the Communist message throughout Latin America. Let him complain. Spreading the revolution is *our* business. But to reach *within* the United States and assassinate a mayor—that is the beginning of wholesale terrorist warfare. Algeria versus France, all over again, but we do not have the advantages that Algeria had in its quarrel with France. No. Stupid. Childish."

There was discussion, after a diplomatic interval, of alternatives. "For instance," Valdés said, "we could track down as many relatives as we can of the Cubans Alejandro has identified, and he will be identifying many more. Arrest relatives, charge them with complicity, execute a few, maybe quite a few, send the rest to prison camps—that would pour a little cold water on the movement, no, Fidel?"

Fidel merely nodded his head. Not the executive nod, always distinctive with Castro. Rather, the nod that signified that he had heard the proposal and would weigh it.

Dorticós suggested the possibility of a dramatic arrival in New York by Fidel himself. A speech before the Security Council denouncing the aggressive plans of the United States government via the CIA station in Miami.

Again Castro listened, giving the same nod.

"Or if your own presence would lend more weight than we want in this situation, we could have Carlos Lechuga—as our U.N. ambassador, he is on the spot in New York—summon the Security Council and let him give the speech, exposing the activities of JM WAVE."

"What exactly would he use for documentation?" Fidel asked. "Alejandro has told us what is going on, what is planned, but we do not have the kind of documentation that would make it clear that this is a U.S. operation, not merely an operation by Cuban traitors."

THE TALK CONTINUED, and Castro ordered beer and fruit and rum brought in. He poured rum into a glass—unusual for Castro, who although he drank occasionally, seldom drank in tense situations in which his leadership was critical. After downing half his glass, he addressed his brother with some calmness.

"I do agree with you that a gesture of some kind is important. The complaining public gesture we cannot make without documentation. Random terrorism is not useful at this moment. Something else."

"Why not," Dorticós suggested, "assassinate one of the CIA leaders involved in the operation? There are a half-dozen prominent CIA-affiliated people attached to JM WAVE, if Alejandro is correct. We could pick off one of those. No?"

"Why not," Fidel said suddenly, "Blackford Oakes?"

His eyes brightened, and he took another swig of his rum. "Oakes is *very close* to the President. I released him last October as the result of a *direct appeal* from the President."

Castro did not rehearse the details of the episode—the telegram that had come in from the Attorney General. A telegram that had been less an appeal than a threat of dire retaliation if Oakes was harmed.

Castro continued, "We let him go because it is true that he came to Cuba originally at the invitation of Che Guevara, authorized by me. But the point is that Kennedy took a personal interest in him. When the agent Oakes left Cuba, he had been sentenced to execution by a Cuban military court for acts of subversive interference in Cuban internal affairs. To carry out that sentence now would certainly be a way of saying to the President: You had your chance to live up to your promises during the missile crisis, and you have not lived up to those terms." Castro rose. He was giving a speech now.

"You have planned secretly to make war against my government. Well, the gesture of conciliation that I made to you in October is now *null and void!*" Fidel's right hand was outstretched, his fingers tightly closed—except for his middle finger, stiff in the international sign of challenge and mockery. "This to you, Mr. President!" Fidel Castro's facial muscles were white, and he was sweating. He sat down.

"That"—his voice was changed; he was the legal scholar, lecturing to his students—"what Kennedy is doing in Miami is the unilateral nullification of a contract, which leaves the other contracting party free to proceed unencumbered by the terms of the original contract." He turned his head triumphantly to Dorticós. "I find that very appealing; what do you think, Osvaldo?"

"I like it, Fidel. But there is of course a problem. If Oakes were here, convicted of violating Cuban laws, he would be subject to Cuban justice. But there is this problem: He is in Miami, where United States law applies."

"There is no point, Osvaldo, in being legalistic, just because I introduced a few legal principles into our discussion. True, Miami does not operate under Cuban law. But Miami—and this would be our larger point in executing Oakes—is engaged in plans to aggress against Cuba, so that there is a sense in which hitting back would be a form of . . . hot pursuit, no?"

Fidel very much liked his metaphor, and used it several times. "Hot pursuit," he lectured, "defines the right of the power being aggressed against to pursue the aggressor into his own country. Only last week, Senator—what's his name? The militarist from Georgia?—Senator Richard Russell, the Southern warmonger, asked President Kennedy to exercise the right of hot pursuit against our MIGs when they fire on vessels in international waters. Well, there is a sense in which that is what we would be doing. Blackford Oakes leaves Cuba and resumes aggression, so we visit Cuban justice on him as though we were pursuing him in retaliation against *his* act of aggression."

Dorticós said that was true, but that the events of the past year—the random attempts on Castro himself, mostly designed by the Mafia though commissioned by the CIA—were perhaps a part of history, not a part of the contemporary problem. "Perhaps we should wait until JM WAVE stages its first assault. According to Alejandro these assaults will begin any day now. Then, after the first such assault, we could take the position that a fresh war of aggression has begun, and that we intend to take symbolic recognition of this by carrying out last year's sentence against an agent obviously involved in that aggression."

"I like that," Fidel said. "Yes, Osvaldo, I think you reason well." He turned to Valdés.

"Tell Alejandro to spare no pains in attempting to discover exactly what the agent Oakes is doing. See that he is very well observed, so that when I give the order to execute sentence, we can strike quickly. Quickly. Neatly. And I will give thought to what kind of . . . coincidental communications we would make to the U.S. government following our . . . reciprocal gesture."

Raúl began asking a question, but Fidel raised his hand. "Enough. Enough on this subject. I wish to discuss now another item on the agenda, the length to which our initiatives toward Mao Tse-tung will go forward. For that we want two or three people who are waiting below. You, Valdés, are excused. Raúl, call in Roa and Rodríguez."

8

Nikita Sergeyevich Khrushchev tapped on his desk with impatience. "Aleksei, you are driving me crazy. But you would drive anyone crazy. How it is that you have not already driven crazy my beloved Rada? I cannot understand. You call me about this 'explosive interview' Castro has given to the French journalist, I tell you to come here to read it to me, and for one hour now—"

"I have been here only for ten minutes, Nikita Sergeyevich—"

"Well it *feels* like one hour, mother of God. You want to show off that you can read French? Well I *know* that you can read French. I know big assholes who can read French. Like De Gaulle. Yes. He is the best example of an asshole who can read French. But what *I* want is not the French, I want the *Russian*, and at the rate at which you are translating it, Castro will die of old age before I learn what it is that he told the French reporter. Why did you not have it translated before you came?"

"The newspaper came by pouch only this morning, an early edition secured by our correspondent in Paris. And you told me to come immediately with it. I could have had it translated first, and if you wish, Nikita Sergeyevich, I will leave here now and have it translated for you and come back in an hour or two—"

"An hour or two!" Khrushchev screamed. "An hour or two! That bearded madman in Cuba is making fun of me in front of the entire world, is misrepresenting me before the entire world, is—don't deny this, Aleksei—is making a mockery of the mother country of socialism which saved his Cuban ass just three months ago and which has been feeding his miserable little island for three years now, and you want to postpone telling me exactly what he said! Mother of God."

Khrushchev picked up his telephone. "Ring Kosygin."

Aleksei Adzhubei said nothing. Khrushchev tapped his fingers on the desk, stopped, wrested the newspaper from Aleksei's hand, and stared at the pictures of Castro in various heroic poses. The phone rang and he picked it up. "Aleksei Nikolaevich. Have you heard of the *Le Monde* Castro interview? . . . You know nothing about it? . . . Don't your embassies keep you informed? Never mind. Kindly send to my office *immediately* a simultaneous translator, French-Russian." He slammed the phone down.

He turned to his son-in-law. "You may go. I will call and tell you how to handle this in *Izvestia.*"

"Thank you, Nikita Sergeyevich." Aleksei reached for the issue of *Le Monde.* His hand flattened under the crashing force of Khrushchev's right hand.

"You idiot! You heard me call for a translator. What is he going to translate from? This morning's edition of *Izvestia*? Not that you don't need a good translator to understand the manure you manage to put into that paper. How do you *manage*, Aleksei, to cram so much shit into such little space? Maybe I should cut your paper allowance. No, you would leave out, then, the few things that are interesting."

Khrushchev sighed at his son-in-law. "Please go away, Aleksei."

Khrushchev sat in stony silence while the young bilingual clerk from the foreign office read from the interview in *Le Monde.*

Castro had said that Khrushchev "should not have removed his missiles without consulting us." Castro had said that "Cuba does not want to be a pawn on the world's chessboard." Castro had said, "Cuban sovereignty is a reality." Castro had said, "I cannot agree with Khrushchev promising Kennedy to pull out his rockets without the slightest regard to the indispensable approval of the Cuban Government." And Castro had said that although the Soviet missiles were not under direct Cuban control, they were "on Cuban territory and nothing should have been decided without consulting us. We are not a Soviet satellite."

He dismissed the clerk. Then he summoned a meeting for two that afternoon with Foreign Minister Kosygin, Defense Minister Rodion Malinovsky, and Vladimir Semichastny, Chairman of the KGB.

IT WAS A LONG afternoon, but in the end Kosygin had his way. There is no point, he had stressed and restressed, in permitting the alienation of Fidel Castro. He had, yes, been very provocative, first with his public gestures toward Mao Tse-tung, his public references to him as the true follower of Lenin and Marx—"Yes yes, the meaning of that was unmistakable, Nikita Sergeyevich"—but the Cuban revolution remained, notwithstanding the missile fiasco of last October. (This reference was artfully used. The idea of the missiles had been Khrushchev's; Kosygin had always been skeptical; but now Khrushchev took inward solace from what Kosygin did not know about the missile crisis.)

Kosygin went on. Cuba was an outpost of incredible value to the Soviet offensive in Latin America and it would be folly to run the least risk of simply handing Castro over to Mao Tse-tung.

Khrushchev had argued that Castro was hardly in a position to spurn Moscow for very long. "Who is going to give him his jets and his guns, and, for that matter, his bread?" Kosygin replied that there were two possibilities there, both to be avoided. One was that China would take on the economic and military responsibilities of feeding and caring for such a geopolitically valuable satellite, never mind the strain on China's economy. "After all, Nikita Sergeyevich, China is spending *billions* in Africa already." And then—and this, really, was the argument that conclusively won the day—"And then there is the third possibility. A détente between Castro and Kennedy."

Obviously to be avoided at all costs, said Malinovsky. Semichastny added his voice to the small chorus. "Obviously to be avoided. At all costs."

The decision was made.

Fidel Castro would be personally invited by Khrushchev to come to the Soviet Union on a state visit. It would coincide with the May Day celebrations. He would be lionized. "He will go back a tame donkey," Kosygin assured Khrushchev.

Khrushchev, though he had begun the session steaming against Castro, was captured by the very idea of taming the Cuban tiger, and when he rose he was in a good mood. "Good day, Aleksei Nikolaevich. Good day, Vladimir Yefimovich." To Malinovsky he said, "Rodion, kindly stay for a minute. I have one or two items . . ." He saw his other two consultants fraternally to the door, smiled, and closed it.

He returned to his desk. "My Tass digest reports, I read them this morning—I was interrupted by the *Le Monde* business— bring me this." Khrushchev shuffled through the papers on his desk. He put on his glasses and began to read: " 'Washington. Cuban refugee reports that some Soviet missiles are still in Cuba denied today. Major General Alva R. Fitch of U.S. Army Intelligence testified before a Senate Armed Services Subcommittee and said, "It is our belief that the Soviets did in fact remove all strategic weapons systems that were in Cuba at the time the U.S. quarantine was imposed." But Fitch conceded that thousands of Cuban caves probably were stocked with Soviet "ammunition, supplies, vehicles, and even aircraft." ' "

Khrushchev put down his glasses. "Rodion, do you know anything about this Cuban refugee report that claims we still have missiles in Cuba?"

Malinovsky leaned back in his easy chair and lit a cigarette. Yes, he said. He had the story. Still missing a few details, but essentially it was this. "I had the coded message from Major Kirov only last night."

What happened, he explained to the General Secretary, was as follows. As Khrushchev knew, the arrangements, to which maximum secrecy had been attached, were for the hidden missile to rest under one of those vast caves described by the U.S. Army Intelligence officer. The cave itself was filled with Soviet equipment designed for Cuban use: trucks, ammunition, three tanks, and six MIGs in various stages of assembly. The missile beneath it, Kirov reported, needs its regular maintenance. "In order to accomplish this, it is necessary—I can imagine it, can you not, Nikita Sergeyevich?—to make one's way through all that stored equipment, to a manhole cover which is kept locked with a padlock. There is nothing suspicious about it, Kirov assures me: it is simply assumed by the Cuban military that it leads to a ventilating device or whatever the engineers installed under the steel flooring.

"Well, Kirov went down there for his January check, with his flashlight and his electrical and radioactivity kit, and when an hour later he came up, he found someone staring at him, even though it was after midnight. He flashed his light on him and it turned out to be a very drunk Cuban soldier who, wandering home from La Cuesta—a bar—to the garrison, decided to have a look inside the cave. He came in through the door in the aluminum siding that covers the entrance to the cave at night. Kirov admits he left the door open; often it is open. It should of course have been locked. The soldier had his own flashlight and had begun snooping around the stored military equipment, which is not, of course, a secret. The Cuban garrison at the other end of the field is substantially maintained by what we continue to pour into that depot. The soldier was quite drunk and even had trouble speaking, Kirov reported, and he laughed a great deal. But he did say, 'I swear, comrade, that looked like a fucking missile you were fussing with down there.' Kirov just laughed, and said that underground ventilators made in Kiev tend to look not unlike the cone of a missile. He had just gone down to check it, Kirov told the Cuban, because it had not been working properly. He found that it was merely a matter of needing a little extra oil.

"Without alarming the Cuban, Kirov thought it would be prudent to ascertain his name and military address. He invited the soldier to have a shot of vodka in Kirov's private office at the end of the cave, the soldier gratefully accepted, and during drinks they exchanged names. Ramón Luminante, the soldier, instead of just giving his name, handed over his identification card, and Kirov quickly memorized its details.

"The trouble, Nikita Sergeyevich, came when a few weeks later Kirov read a denunciation in the Cuban press of a captain who had stolen a Cuban patrol boat and taken six soldiers and their wives to Miami."

"What trouble?"

"One of the soldiers was Luminante.

"Now, Kirov should have told us about this at the time, and he did not, and I shall reprimand him. But clearly Luminante is not taken seriously. Although obviously he made the allegation, it has received no attention in the Cuban press, and only over-night attention in the Cuban refugee press, and apparently General Fitch has completely reassured Congress."

"I don't much like it, Rodion."

"I would rather it had not happened, Nikita Sergeyevich. But I am not overly concerned. Kirov is a good man. And he is the custodian of a very important asset. We will tighten security at that depot.

"And always remember, among other things, that only Kirov and his small crew know how to fire that missile. He and his men are there as general matériel maintenance experts, along with the twenty, thirty Soviet technicians who look after the tanks, planes, etc. Kirov has asked when he can come home to his wife. He would need to be replaced with another nuclear technician. I am inclined instead to send his wife to Cuba. That would quiet him down. Anything else, Nikita Sergeyevich?"

Khrushchev clenched his jaw shut. He never raised his voice with Malinovsky. They were old Bolsheviks. And they had a secret.

·Book II·

9

Every few days Blackford heard from Anthony, sometimes by long distance, three or four times a week by mail. Trust was touring critical Latin American capitals, taking careful political measurements. Rufus had charged him to explore two questions, without ever touching directly on either in the course of conducting his investigation. The first was: How would individual Latin American governments probably react to a hypothetical assassination of Castro by a disillusioned follower? Would they (mostly) simply sigh with relief? Would there be left-wing demonstrations? If so, seeking what? A boycott of the new Cuba, ruled by the party of the assassin?

And the most important question. What if such an assassination, as the result of a catastrophic accident, were somehow traced to the United States?

Rufus and Trust agreed that "traced to the United States" could mean one of two things, and Anthony was to bear the distinction in mind. The first (and worst) contingency envisioned something that propelled the conclusion—or, if less than that, engendered hard suspicion—that the United States had conceived and expedited the assassination. The second sequence would reveal that the United States had indirectly expedited the assassination, for instance by making available critical weapons to resistance leaders, including the assassin. Rufus would be influenced in the guidance he gave to Mongoose by these reports, and the pace of Blackford's work in Miami would be affected by Trust's reports.

Anthony's telephone calls were informally, but carefully, coded. It was hardly necessary for him to communicate his news in detail. Blackford, on the other hand, needed to be more careful about keeping Anthony as much informed as was thought vital to his continuing exploration. During the first ten days Blackford had gone no further in talking with Trust than to say about Mongoose-Miami something on the order of, "Things are pretty interesting down here, but then I guess things are pretty interesting everywhere—right, Anthony?" As often as not Anthony would take the opportunity to hew to the lewd, low road; for instance, by attaching to "things" a meaning not intended. He would interpret a comment by Blackford to the effect that "things" were "interesting"—or "hot," or "exciting"—a meaning Blackford did not intend. Blackford remonstrated every now and then, when Anthony's lubricity got out of hand. "You are like a lot of Englishmen," Blackford once told Anthony. "They learn about sex later than we do and freeze into a Freudian first gear whenever anything remotely suggestive comes up." Anthony had replied solemnly that Blackford's observation reminded him of fucking. Blackford told him to do so to himself, to go to hell, to grow up; Anthony replied that he could not attend to all Blackford's commissions, he was simply too busy.

Tonight, though, something was different. It was in Trust's tone of voice. The call came from Mexico City, and Trust reported matter-of-factly that the teachers' union had that morning passed a resolution urging the government of President Adolfo López Mateos not to join the Organization of American States in the general economic boycott against Fidel Castro. Blackford waited to hear whether there was more of what he would call commercial traffic, but there was none, leaving him to wonder whether Anthony had spoken with or visited Sally, and so when Anthony was about to hang up he raised the question directly. He did not expect his best friend to visit a foreign capital in which his fiancée lived without calling her. So he said, "Anthony. Have you called Sally?"

There was just that hint of a pause. Very unlike Anthony, whose reactions tended to be instantaneous.

". . . Yes, of course I did. I mean . . . well, if you stopped in in London, would you fail to call the Queen of England?"

Blackford found the attempt at humor lame. "Have you made a date to see her?"

"Actually—you know, I've only been here two days, and I'm staying only a couple of days more. She's busy as hell—exams, papers, usual stuff—so we're going to try to connect up tomorrow, or Tuesday maybe. But for sure before I leave."

"Anthony. Sally would see you even if she had a thousand papers to correct. Can't understand it. Oh well, tell her I know I'm behind in my mail, but for sure I'll write her tomorrow. Maybe tonight. Give her my love."

Anthony said something or other, lapsing into badinage, and they signed off.

THE FOLLOWING MORNING the special delivery letter came. Blackford was absentmindedly eating a banana, his cereal and toast yet to go, while reading the *Miami Herald*. He nodded his thanks to the messenger, slipping him a coin. He finished the lead story in the paper. It detailed the two-year trade pact signed between Cuba and China, which included a long-term interest-free loan. He was thinking, goddamnit, Castro is a sly, effective bastard, when he picked up his fruit knife and sliced open Anthony's letter, which he expected would enclose a clipping or two of interest from a Latin American paper, as with his last few letters.

It was written on the stationery of the Hotel Geneve.

"BLACK: YOU SHOULD be getting this a day or two after we talk tonight on the phone. Maybe even tomorrow. I'd better get to the point.

"I phoned Sally Friday afternoon, after I got in. She sounded funny. She didn't say, 'Where are you staying?' 'When can we meet for lunch, dinner?'—that kind of thing. She said she couldn't talk right now because there was a car waiting for her outside to meet an appointment, and could she call me later? I gave her my number, but there wasn't any message from her that afternoon or that night, and when I called her on Saturday morning there was no answer.

"Saturday night I took Emily Hastings—don't think you know her, Legal Department, Embassy—to El Tecalí, puttin' on the dawg, Black. The steward led us past the Tecalí's banquette and I passed—Sally. She was seated with a Mexican guy. She looked very surprised, flustered. She introduced me to her date, one Antonio Morales. I said hello, and introduced Emily. Emily reached over to shake hands with Sally and knocked over a little flower vase. I dove down to pick it up and Sally's left hand reached there about the same time.

"Black, she was wearing a wedding ring.

"After I stood up, all I could do was say, you know, 'Good to see you Sally, Señor Morales'—and I went on to our table. When I spotted Sally and her guy leaving the restaurant, I asked the maître d' who my old friend's escort was, and he said they were recently married. I wasn't very good company for Emily on Saturday night. What can I say, Black? Maybe Sally was just pretending?

"Ever, A."

BLACKFORD FELT THE BLOOD drain from his head. He leaned over a full minute, waiting for the renewal of sensation. Then he rose and went to the telephone. He dialed the operator. But when the operator answered, he could not speak. He hung up, looked at the breakfast tray, lifted the glass of water to his lips, and walked back to the telephone. He drank and, carefully monitoring the movements of his mouth, dialed again.

"I want to speak to Mr. Trust in Mexico City. T-r-u-s-t. The telephone"—Blackford glanced down at the letterhead of the Geneve—"is 25-15-00."

Anthony answered the Hotel Geneve's telephone operator.

"I got your letter. I'm going to Mexico—"

"*Black.* She called me last night. She sounded, well, kind of drained. But she said I should know that she had written you a letter to the Fontainebleau, that she had meant to write it earlier, but that she 'couldn't.' But she had driven to the airport—right to the post office there, she said, about midnight last night. One of her students works at Pan Am and promised Sally she'd get the letter to Miami today. You should have it this afternoon or tomorrow morning. I think you should see that letter before you come."

Blackford experienced a strange sensation. He could easily

hear Anthony's words; he could evaluate them; but he could not do the normal thing, which was to formulate an appropriate—or, for that matter, even an inappropriate—reply.

Anthony was alarmed. "Black. Black! You hearing me?"

Blackford brought the telephone as close as possible to his lips.

"Yes," he managed to say. "Yes . . . I'll wait. Thanks."

He hung up the telephone.

He sat down and wondered, childlike, what to do. Without knowing why, he began a round of physical exercises. Deep knee bends. Push-ups. Sit-ups. Squat thrusts. He did these with no conscious attention to what he was doing, or to what lengths he was going. He worked out with a rigor that became inordinate. He was reaching for pain. When he had begun a third cycle of push-ups he became dizzy again, collapsing into a carpet moist from his own sweat.

He didn't know how long he had lain there when the telephone's insistent ringing roused him. On his knees he reached for it.

"Yes."

"It's Pano, *patrón*. Downstairs. Okay to come on up?"

"No," Blackford managed to say, in a relatively controlled voice. "I . . . can't meet with you today. I will explain later. I will call you." He hung up, raised himself back on the chair, and reread Anthony's letter.

Ten minutes later, dressed in khaki slacks, beach shoes, and a red light cotton crewneck sweater, he took the elevator down to the garage and gave his ticket to the attendant. Five minutes later he was driving. For reasons he did not seek to explore, he drove toward Key West. He drove at a moderate, detached speed, about fifty miles per hour. He invited to accost him, to occupy his mind, geometric and trigonometric problems of the kind, long ago at college, he had been professionally trained to grapple with, and back then there were no calculators, only slide rules. He was headed from Miami to Key West, a driving distance of 125 miles. He guessed—not a wild guess, an informed guess—that he was headed south southwest, or at an azimuth of about 195 degrees. He knew exactly the location of Key West. He would never forget it after his experience of only three months before, struggling to head there to escape in the little fishing boat before Castro's plane spotted him. *Come on, Key West, 24-24 North, 81-48 West,* as he wrestled desperately below at the navigator's station, with the Radio Direction Finder.

All right then. Now where exactly is Mexico City?

On the 100th meridian. He didn't need to join the CIA to know that. Third-form geography. But what was its latitude?

He remembered from one of the dozens of books he had read about Castro's epic voyage from Mexico to the Playa de los Colorados the heroic couplet in Spanish:

> *Viajando directo, directo al este,*
> *Vino Fidel, deshaciendo el oeste*
> (Voyaging straight, straight to the east,
> Fidel came, undoing the West)

Was the poet who put such stress on a direct easterly course being accurate, or merely poetic? Because Cuba lies between the Tropic of Cancer—the northern tip, where Havana sits— and Latitude 20, the southern tip at Santiago de Cuba, Castro's home town, directly west of which, at Los Colorados, he had landed his ship, the *Granma*. So, directly east from Mexico City to Santiago would mean Mexico City was at 20 degrees North. Longitude 100, Latitude 20. What is the distance between Key West and Mexico City? You drop down—he would round off the coordinates for Key West to 25 North, 82 West. To go to Mexico City, drop down five degrees, go west eighteen degrees. Down five degrees of latitude is easy, five times sixty means 300 miles.

But what distance can you assign to eighteen degrees of westward longitude at Latitude 20 North? Well—his mind now began to throb—the circumference of the globe is 25,000 miles at Latitude 0, the Equator. At the North Pole, the circumference of the globe is—nothing. Since from the Pole to the Equator is ninety degrees, then at twenty degrees you are seventy-ninetieths of an arc that goes from zero to 25,000 miles. Seven over nine.

Doing to his mind what he had done that morning to his body, he knew that with a pencil it would have been a matter of a minute to run through the figures. He would on no account have stopped the car to take that minute. Blackford dug the nails of his thumbs into his index finger to maintain focus.—Now, the distance around the globe is 360 degrees, so that eighteen degrees of that would mean—360 divided by eighteen.

A dividend, that one! An easy twenty. One twentieth of the distance around the world. One twentieth of twenty-five thousand miles is . . . Two into twenty-five, obviously, is 12.5. So that eighteen degrees of longitude at the Equator equals 1,250 miles. Now back to the other: seven ninths, of that, that's the number I want. Seven ninths of 1250 . . . Seven times 125 equals eight seven five and however many zeros, doesn't matter. Now 875 divided by nine. Well, nine times nine is eighty-one, leaving you with seventy-five left over, nine into seventy-five—8; 8.3. 972 miles.

He found himself driving past the city limits of Key West. He kept on. He assumed the road would lead to the commercial wharf, which it did, after winding through the commercial center.

There were boats there of all kinds for charter, which he had also assumed. He selected a 36-foot yawl, signed the paper, and paid in cash. He was about to board when suddenly he paused.

"Any provisions aboard?" he asked the old man with the large straw hat and no teeth who had written out the charter document.

He removed the pipe from his mouth. "Just water." He pointed to a supply store at the end of the dock. "You can get anything you want there."

Blackford went into the store and bought a handful of the first things he came on: two boxes of cookies, an apple, two bunches of celery, two bottles of tomato ketchup, two cans of soup. At the bar next door he bought six cans of beer and a bottle of gin.

He tossed his provisions onto the pipe berth, opened the navigator's desk, and pulled out the harbor chart. He looked then at the larger chart, and knew what he would do. He would sail out into the Gulf Stream, up to Miami. The enterprise engaged him fully. He worked with his dividers and his parallel rules, laying out the course. He returned now to the dock and walked back to the office where the old man sat.

"I'll want the boat for longer than a day."

"It's two hundred and seventy-five for one week."

Blackford gave him a credit card.

"And another two seventy-five deposit."

Blackford nodded. When the old man was done, Blackford put the two vouchers in his pocket.

"We tear up the deposit when the boat gets back," the old man said.

By sundown, Blackford was thirty-five miles out to sea, heading north by east. The wind was a vigorous sou'wester. With the help of the Gulf Stream he was probably doing over nine knots, he figured. He loosened the mainsail slightly, letting it luff just a bit, to spill a little wind. He would need pretty soon to reef it, the way things were going. He opened the box of cookies and ate one, and opened a can of warm beer to sip. He projected the seas and his own strength four or five hours from now. What he would do would be drop the main and experiment with the wheel, see how steady a course he could keep with a becket fastening the wheel at a good position. Then he would experiment with the genoa and the mizzen sail behind him, easing the little yawl toward its heading, in case he fell asleep.

AT SOME POINT he was sailing away from her, he knew. Tomorrow he would arrive, some time in the afternoon. Her letter should be there. The night was clear but dark, not a trace of the moon. The brisk wind was still warm, but getting less so, and it brought in a smell of faintly acrid foliage: mangroves along the waterway. He picked a star to sail by. The star would be good for a half hour. Then the revolving heavens would offer him another one, allowing him to keep his compass course at about 025 degrees. He opened the bottle of gin, stared at the ketchup—why ketchup?—took a bite from the apple and a slug from the bottle, and thought back on the quarrel they had had in Washington that summer five years earlier, when she so ostentatiously had gone out with the architect, whatever his name was, while Blackford looked about feverishly for consolation. He had found it, he supposed, in the struggle, the endless struggle, but one without any prospects for him now, even if the whole world were to become, tomorrow, a free and fair city. He had not enjoyed the first drink of gin and wondered whether he should take a second. He decided listlessly against it, reaching in the cockpit instead for a can of beer. He looked up, focusing on the constellations he had been so familiar with as an army pilot. They were still there. But, turning his head abeam, the one his eyes fixed on had splashes of starry hair that shimmered, and eyes to steer by, and lips set in a pensive, seductive mode. He felt a luff in the sail, snapped his head forward to the mast, and quickly located his navigational star. He had wandered high on his course, while looking back at that chimera over Mexico.

When he arrived at Miami's Miamarina, whose facilities he had read about in the *Florida Cruising Guide*, one fifth of the rented yawl's library, the burly dockmaster indicated an empty slip, took the spring line tossed to him, and then the bow line, and Blackford proceeded to make the boat fast. He stepped over the safety lines to the dock, his face red from the sun, his chin stubbled with a day's growth.

His first impulse was to leave everything and go to the hotel to read the letter. But he realized that nothing in the letter could, really, help; on the contrary. It would seek to make plausible what she had apparently done, which could not be undone.

So instead he attended there and then to necessary arrangements. He located, with the help of the dockmaster, an idle captain of a 50-foot yawl whose owner would be gone the balance of the month. They made the deal: a straightforward delivery, back to Key West, of the yawl, plus bringing Blackford's car back to Miami: a hundred bucks plus expenses. The captain wouldn't be going outside, into the Florida Straits and against the Gulf Stream. He would sail and power down the inland waterway, stopping one night, probably in the vicinity of Marathon. Blackford told him there were a couple of beers and nearly a full bottle of gin in the boat, "nothing else."

"I'll bring my own provisions," he said. "My boat's full of stuff. Don't worry."

Blackford noted, and memorized, the skipper's name and the name of his yacht, and gave him the two vouchers from the Key West marina. He told him exactly where his car was parked, wrote out the license number, handed him the keys, and said he would expect to see him, and Blackford's car, at the Fontainebleau Hotel "in a couple of days. If I'm not in, you can leave the car with the doorman, and leave your bill for expenses with the desk, Room 1202."

There was nothing now to do except to go and read the letter.

"Got a ride?" the captain called out, as Blackford began walking toward the main office.

"I'll call a taxi."

"No. I'll drive you. I've got my car up there."

The captain, a heavy man of about fifty, chatted that he was happy to have the diversion. "Gets boring as hell sitting in a boat, doing nothing." His wife was away, visiting her parents in Arkansas, and wouldn't be back for a week. Would Oakes mind if he took a companion with him to Key West, "just for the ride?"

Blackford said he wouldn't mind.

"She just loves to sail, and she can do the cooking," the captain said, driving into the Fontainebleau Hotel. They shook hands.

The letter was in his box. He took it up to his room and decided he would shave and shower before reading it. Half dry, he sat down in his shorts and opened the letter.

It wasn't long, though Sally, with her fine hand, could crowd more words onto a sheet of paper than a typewriter with an elite type.

"DEAR BLACKY: You will have heard from Anthony that I tried, but failed, to write this letter earlier.

"What you now know I have done is, really, the central message: I decided to marry another man. You will ask yourself (why shouldn't you? I did): If you had asked me some time during the last ten years to marry you, would I have done so? Answer: Yes—yes, provided it hadn't been during those special years, off and on, when I was concentrating so hard on my work.

"And if I had asked you the same thing, you'd have said Yes—except when this mission, or that one, simply required postponement. We did decide, that night in Taxco, on an actual date, which is little more than a year ahead, and I just don't know whether something would have happened to postpone a June 1964 wedding. We'll never know. What did happen was that six weeks ago I met Antonio Morales.

"I'm not going to describe him, I don't think you'd want that. All I can say is that when he asked me to marry him, I found myself saying, Yes—to a whole other world, a world I knew only in literature. Suddenly my whole nature moved me in that direction. I decided I'd give that Yes the supreme test, by weekending with you in Acapulco. My agreement to marry him survived that test.

"And yet what I said to you in Acapulco—don't think it was just post-coital hyperbole—remains true. I do love you, and I will always love you. But I have selected another man to be my husband. It's that simple, and that complicated.

"In order to know what kind of pain you are experiencing, I have only to ask myself what kind of pain would I be experiencing if it had been the other way around, and I had heard that you had got married? You will tell yourself that The Other Way Around couldn't have happened. I thought the same thing. I was wrong. Maybe you will find, sooner rather than later, that it's so with you; and I know that when you find her, you will also continue to love me. But I think it only prudent (ah, what would my beloved J. Austen have done without that word?) to say goodbye. I don't expect to hear from you.

"Blacky, my darling, I don't *want* to hear from you."

SHE SIGNED IT just her ornate, tiny "S."

IN MEXICO CITY, Señora Antonio Morales de Guzmán sat in the patio of the house in Coyoacán, the verdant district south of the center of the city which at the time of Porfirio Díaz had been countryside but was now an elegant residential pocket in the tight city sprawl that stretched beyond Coyoacán to University City, on the road to Cuernavaca, Taxco, and Acapulco. Antonio had inherited the mansion when his mother and father were killed, nine months earlier, in an airplane crash in Venezuela.

It was a quiet but elegant wedding reception, here in the

patio and outside in the garden. Antonio (he was still officially in mourning) had invited fewer than a hundred friends, Sally only two or three of her professional colleagues and M'Lou Weeks, her roommate at Vassar, together with her husband, who was attached to the Embassy. Antonio's best man, Pedrito Alzada, had participated too zestfully in too many champagne toasts, and now he escorted Sally to the large garden, intending—he said—to show her the remains of the treehouse he and "your husband" had built as playmates.

At the end of the garden, by the large oak tree, he confided to her that the previous owners of this lovely estate, dead so recently and prematurely, in their fifties, had been the victims of an awful delinquency. "As you know," Pedrito bent over her, looking down on her floral head wreath, "I am Tony's"—they called Antonio "Tony," and apparently had done so even before he went off to school in America—"lawyer, and it fell to me to do the investigation. I flew to Caracas. What I discovered was—that the airplane had run out of gas!" Pedrito choked his own throat with his right hand, in melodramatic horror. "While flying high over the mountains, on the way to Angel Falls. I was in Caracas when I discovered the company's dirty little secret—the newspapers didn't have it. By that time the company flying the plane had declared bankruptcy. There was no possibility of collecting damages. So I had to decide: Shall I tell Tony? Or isn't he better off thinking that his mother and his father died in an unavoidable crash? I think I did the right thing. Do you?"

Sally looked at the party-dressed, self-assured, animated young lawyer, like Antonio in his early thirties; probably—no, manifestly—more than merely a lawyer to Antonio. (Would she ever get around to calling him Tony? She doubted it.) She knew the answer his friend wanted to hear. "I'm sure, Pedrito, that your judgment was sound. You know—Tony—very well, you grew up with him. If for whatever reason sometime in the future you think—we think"—Sally reminded herself that she was now the primary consultant in respect of anything that bore on Antonio Morales de Guzmán—"that he ought to be told what really happened, we can do so, and give the reasons for not having told him earlier."

Pedrito nodded his head vigorously, in extravagant recognition of her sagacity, and they strolled back toward the little knots of Mexican family friends, bejeweled socialites, university dons, matronly aunts, childhood servants. And, also, the recently retired triumphant Spanish matador whose Mexican investments Antonio Morales, now the principal figure in the firm of Morales y Durango (there were no Durangos left), handled. Luís Miguel Dominguín, slim, handsome, bright-toothed, sensual, was a splendid figure, whose historical renown was guaranteed by the single act of having fought with Manolete *mano a mano* at Linares in 1947 when Manolete—Manolete the Great—was killed by a Miura bull which, while mortally wounding Manolete, was mortally wounded by Manolete, talk about two scorpions in a bottle. The bull died before the matador, but not by much: Manolete lived only ten hours. Dominguín had gone on to establish that his light did not shine only on that one successful afternoon. His luster, almost unique, was finally overshadowed by young Antonio Ordóñez, but there were those who believed that no one in memory would ever outshine the brilliant young Luís Miguel, dressed now like an Italian movie star, with a a tiny palette of colors below his handkerchief pocket, the flora and fauna of Latin American honorifics. He approached Sally, and said in modestly fluent English, "I hope you will be happy here, Señora—"

"Sally."

He bowed. "Sally.—Luís Miguel. And, if I may ask, where are you going on your wedding trip?"

"We are postponing a trip. Antonio has urgent business in the office, and I have another six weeks before midterm break." She laughed. "Obviously we did not plan our marriage months ahead."

He smiled, and said he was certain that if this "felicitous event" had been planned years ago, it could not have been "a more auspicious union." And, lowering his voice: "Tony is mad for you, *loco* mad."

Pause.

"I can see why."

The way he said it . . . Of course, Luís Miguel was renowned for his habits, the ribald *taurino* street-question being, Had Luís Miguel gored more bulls than women? To which the conventional reply was, *¿Quién sabe?* He had just now said what he said with a smile of which sensuality was the principal constituent. Sally came very near to saying, "Antonio has not yet seen what you call 'why.' "

And indeed Antonio had not lain with Sally. It wasn't only that the Spanish tradition was so firm on the subject, it was that Antonio believed so wholeheartedly in that socio-religious tradition, among others—so many others—and would never have made a prenuptial advance. Tonight would be the first time she saw . . . Tony . . . unclothed. She assumed that, for a while at least, all the initiatives would be his; and she was, in the anticipation, acquiescent. It was inconceivable that in bed his nature would be—transformed. She looked past the head of Dominguín at her husband, kissing the hand of an exiting matron, and her eyes involuntarily stripped him of his clothes, and she felt a surprising thrill of anticipation. Even as she had, at New Haven, the night she decided to surrender her virginity to Blackford.

11

Sally Partridge always associated her early childhood with the lake in Connecticut by which her family lived, in the little cottage designed, during the twenties, for summer use, but used by the Partridge family year-round. Sally remembered when first she began to wonder, at an early age, whether the cottage belonged to them, or to the Phoenix State Bank & Trust Company in Hartford. "They must hire that fella full-time to come collect my payments," Hal Partridge said one summer afternoon, closing the front door on the bank clerk—it did no good to try to reach Hal Partridge over the telephone, because Southern New England Telephone had cut off service owing to a delinquent bill. Moreover, during the summer there was no income from Sally's mother, Faith, who taught English at Indian Mountain School, the little preparatory day school down the road from the boys' prep school, Hotchkiss, which lay grandly on the opposite side of the lake. But indigence wasn't Sally's concern as a young girl. Nothing troubled Sally except the mood of Ronnie, her brother, older by two years. If Ronnie was sad, Sally was despondent. If he was exuberant, she was elated. If he was reprimanded or chastised by his father, Sally felt the pain.

Ronnie's interest, above all things, was a 16-foot sailboat. In August of 1938, his father had sold a long piece to the *Reader's Digest*, and had received in payment one of those prodigious checks. That check made him for a full day feel and act like J. P. Morgan. He caught up six back-due months with the Phoenix Bank; the telephone was put back in service, and he brought home a steak for dinner. It was at that complacent dinner that

Ronnie, who at age fourteen had been serving as a counselor at the little boys' summer camp half a mile up the lake, asked his father if he could borrow ninety-five dollars. It had been a very long time since anyone had thought to go to Hal Partridge in pursuit of a loan, but, feeling flush with his success, the father had asked his freckled son, with the volatile face that registered the nuance of every mood, what it was he wished to do with ninety-five dollars.

The words came tumbling out. Jack Fisher, the senior counselor, was leaving the camp. He was going off to work at Sun Valley, a budding ski resort out West. Obviously there would be no point in taking his boat to Idaho, so he had decided to sell it. At lunch yesterday he mentioned at the counselors' table that he was going that afternoon to place an ad in the *Lakeville Journal*, describing the *Barracuda* and giving the price.

"How much?" Ronnie had asked.

Jack, a gigantic young man of twenty-eight, especially liked Ronnie, who crewed for him so vigorously during the summer races—twice in the afternoon on Wednesdays, Saturdays, and Sundays. The races were for Ronnie not only the high points of the week, but, it sometimes seemed, the only points of the week; and when it was not his turn to crew, he would teach his charges how to swim, or how to make clay pots, or whatever, but always keeping his eyes on the six little sailboats maneuvering for one more point toward their own America's Cup, a twelve-dollar trophy donated by the Community Chest of Salisbury, to be held by the winner of that year's two-month regatta and kept for one year, until placed back in competition the following summer.

"Why do you ask, Ronnie?" Jack Fisher knew that Ronnie's father was impoverished (everybody knew it).

"Just wondering."

"Well," Jack said, "I'm going to ask $150 for it. But I'd give it to you for $110."

All of this Ronnie spilled out breathlessly, leaving his steak untouched.

"How would you raise the balance?" Hal Partridge, pouring himself a fresh glass of whiskey and water, asked his son.

"I have—lined up fifteen dollars."

"How is that possible when your whole summer pay is only ten dollars?"

Mrs. Partridge caught the furtive glance her son shot at Sally, and guessed correctly: Sally had contributed her savings to the pool. Faith Partridge was an ascetic woman, in part by nature, in part by necessity; she needed to hold together a household headed by a free-lance writer whose work was mostly rejected, which rejections drove him to despondent drink, even as his occasional acceptances drove him to festive drink. His erratic income required him to spend two or three days a week writing local news stories for the *Lakeville Journal*, at five dollars per story.

But Faith Partridge's husbandry did not make her lose all perspective. She had a sense for truly important psychological moments, and she knew that this was one. She turned to her husband. "I can get an advance from Indian Mountain. They are used to the faculty asking for an advance toward the end of summer. I can handle it."

With a howl of delight, Ronnie ran out of the cottage. He bicycled the four miles to Salisbury, to Jack's house, to give him the news that his boat was sold, that he must be sure to withdraw the ad from the *Journal*. Jack shook the boy's hand in a formal manner, then, laughing, gave him a fatherly hug. "I'll write out the transfer papers tomorrow, and the *Barracuda* is yours."

Two days later, Hal put up the last twenty-five dollars left over from the *Reader's Digest* check and the mother came up with seventy dollars, plus Ronnie's fifteen. The money was breathlessly counted by Ronnie, and deposited in an envelope.

The money in the envelope, Ronnie said with some formality that he would be returning not on his bicycle, as usual, but on his boat. Indeed, from now on he would commute to work on his boat. Hal and Faith exchanged a smile. After the little boys went home in the bus (4 P.M.), Ronnie sailed the *Barracuda* in a light following wind to the makeshift buoy he had moored in front of his house. He swam in to the beach. Sally was waiting for him.

"Did you do what I told you?"

"Yes" she said, pointing to the tin bucket. "It's all in there."

"Did you tell Mum?"

"Yes. And Dad's away. All she said was, Be careful."

In their old wooden rowboat, they paddled out to the buoy. Sally made the rowboat fast to the buoy and climbed onto the little sloop. Her brother was already at the tiller. He told her to pull up the jib halyard. "I'll handle the main. I can do that *and* steer at the same time."

Sally didn't doubt it for a minute. "Where are we going?"

"That depends," said Captain Partridge, with some deliberation, "on the wind."

The farthest point they could go on Lake Wononskopomuc was just under one mile, diagonally across, to Hotchkiss School. It was there that they beached and had their picnic, and Ronnie told Sally about great ocean passages. She knew about Columbus and Magellan, but not about Captain Cook, or Joshua Slocum, and she listened admiringly, and then Ronnie said that he would be entering the Navy "in a little while"—in a little while, Sally calculated, would mean at least four years from then.

In less than a little while, however, Ronnie did enter the Navy when, after Pearl Harbor, the age requirements for service were reduced to seventeen, parents' consent required. And, a very little while after that, Ronnie's destroyer was torpedoed, sinking off Guadalcanal.

Faith Partridge was alone when the telegram came. Hal had taken a job as communications clerk at Bradley Field near Hartford, coming home only on weekends. Sally was finishing her senior year at the Housatonic Valley High School. Faith Partridge read the telegram, wept for her son convulsively but briefly; she had cultivated stoical reserves on which she now drew heavily. When Hal had given permission for Ronnie to go to sea, she knew that the war would be long, and that her boy might not return. Now she wept quietly, not for her son, safely in God's hands, but for Sally. Faith Partridge had lived tense moments in a hard life, but none so tense as these, waiting for Sally to come home on the bus, to learn about her Ronnie.

SALLY WAS EASILY the leading student in her high school class and was accepted immediately by Vassar which, adjusting its academic calendar to the rhythm of the war, scheduled three semesters during the calendar year, so that Sally could expect to graduate in 1947. Hal Partridge, attending AA, was now earning a regular salary. Faith continued to teach, and Sally worked at Vassar ten hours every week as a bursary student. Her scholarship and her bursary work plus two hundred dollars per year saw her through college.

She moved, for the first year or so, palpably under a shadow and it wasn't until the end of the spring term that her irrepressibly buoyant roommate, M'Lou Weeks, unearthed the cause of Sally's melancholy and set out, with missionary zeal, to do something about it.

M'Lou could always make Sally laugh—that had never been a problem. Sally reacted instantly to humor, as to piquancy. Though there were the exceptions, when she was suffering one of her bouts of melancholy, and when she was reading—Was anyone, M'Lou wondered, a more concentrated reader than Sally? Book after book, notebook after notebook, day after day, month after month . . . It wasn't so much that Sally didn't like, when reading, to be interrupted, it was that she could *not be* interrupted, and it did not matter what M'Lou was chattering about, or how amusing that evening's reflections on the news, national, international, and local—Sally would simply not hear it.

M'Lou, an accomplished mimic, would regularly improvise, at eight in the evening, surrounded by classmates from the adjacent rooms, a version of Gabriel Heatter doing the evening radio news at nine, which few of the girls at Jocelyn House bothered to tune in on. This became a standing social event at Jocelyn, and finally Sally made it a point to suspend her reading in order to listen in on the revelry.

"I address you, mothers and fathers of America"—M'Lou was now Franklin Delano Roosevelt, giving a Fireside Chat, "with the good news, that we shall nevah surrender. If the Axis Powers succeed in killing *every one* of our boys, why, we are a great nation. We will simply have *more* boys, and ultimately, we will triumph! There is nothing to fear but fear itself." Sally had winced, but M'Lou's wholesomeness overcame all, and gradually, under repeated transfusions of gaiety, Sally came up through the dark cloud, and though her mourning for Ronnie would be forever, she could now package it as yesterday's travail—awful forever, but yesterday's.

She had always been naturally beautiful, but it was a kind of hayseed beauty one had to stare at for a while, fully to recognize its completeness. M'Lou, with time to stare, introduced her to just a touch of lipstick and powder and perfume. M'Lou personally, with the aid of her forbidden electrical contrivance, a hair curler, put a little shape at the end of Sally's hair. She introduced Sally, on her birthday, to the pearl necklace, bought at Woolworth's, a progressively authentic version of which, in the years ahead, she always wore.

It was toward the end of her sophomore year that her mother called on the phone, a rare event. Her voice was totally controlled—Faith Partridge would never permit herself to break down again as she had in giving Sally the news about Ronnie. She spoke almost as though she were a Western Union operator reading a telegram. Sally's father had had a relapse (these happened two or three times every year) and had been told by his boss in Hartford that unless he went that very night to a meeting of Alcoholics Anonymous, he would be fired. He had set out remorsefully to do this but had stopped en route at a pub which he left three hours later, proceeding in the direction of the church in whose basement the AA meetings were held, evidently forgetting that the meeting had ended an hour earlier. He did not reach the church, crashing over a steel car railing at the curve of the road near Simsbury. "His neck was broken. He died instantly. I have scheduled the funeral for Saturday at noon, since your train only arrives at 11:05." Sally was sobbing, but kept her hand over the phone so that her mother would not hear her. Sally didn't want to puncture the self-hypnotic efficiency by which her mother seemed to be sublimating her grief. Sally managed merely to reply, "Yes, Mother."

During the next six months or so Sally doubled the frequency of her visits to Lakeville, spending every second or third weekend with her mother, who though not yet forty-five had aged greatly, and was reading extensively in Christian Science. Sally kept bringing her books from her own reading at Vassar, but her mother was not easily distracted from her special interests, which were spiritual, though she did not talk to Sally about them. Sally, at nineteen, began to realize that her mother and she had only one thing in common: They loved each other. Nothing else.

By the time senior year came the war was over, and for the first time there was social traffic with the men's colleges. Sally had been elected to the Daisy Chain, an honor accorded by popular vote to the twenty fairest sophomores. She had a few dates, mostly with West Pointers during her junior year, and, in her last year, mostly double dates with M'Lou and M'Lou's boyfriend's friend. Sally enjoyed herself: they would dance at the college, or meet in New York, go to a nightclub or a concert or both, returning by the late train, sometimes staying over at the highly chaperoned Hotel Thayer. She enjoyed the masculine company but, unlike M'Lou, was not dependent on it. What she was now dependent on was word from Yale. She wanted the advanced degree. Yes, she would settle for nothing less than a Ph.D., and she knew what she wished most to study—that extraordinary, reclusive, modest, infinitely disarming and complex literary genius Jane Austen. At Yale she could study with distinguished men of letters, giants like Wimsatt and Brooks and Mack.

The elm trees were budding on Vassar's great green campus in the squalid city on the day the envelope arrived. Miss Sally Partridge had not only been accepted, but had won a full scholarship. She would break the news personally to her mother, instead of telephoning her. She hurried to catch the bus to Pawling. There she had fifteen minutes to wait for the Harlem Valley Line train. She called the Indian Mountain School to leave a message for her mother giving the time of her arrival at the railroad station in nearby Millerton.

Miss D'Arcy, the school secretary who had been at Indian Mountain since Sally was a girl, answered Sally's greeting with unconcealed dismay. She blurted it out. "Darling Sally, your mother had a stroke last night. She was found this morning and taken to the Sharon Hospital. But it was—too late. We couldn't reach you. Darling Sally, I am so sorry. I will see that someone meets you. No, I will meet you myself. I will help you with—the arrangements."

THAT MADE THREE times in four years that Sally had stood in the front pew of the Methodist Church in Lakeville, hearing now pretty much the same words from Dr. Lerner she had heard before. She felt a knot of resentment, until she doused it with reason: What else should she expect, custom-made prayers over every coffin? There were many more people in attendance this time; practically the whole of Indian Mountain School was there, a number of villagers, and even a handful of Hotchkiss students who had studied under Faith Partridge at Indian Mountain. M'Lou had rushed up from Poughkeepsie, and Miss D'Arcy had organized a little post-funeral reception at the school, with sandwiches, soft drinks, and coffee. M'Lou had borrowed a car at Vassar, and as she drove Sally from the school to her lakeside cottage, she asked frankly whether Sally wished her to stay, or to return to Vassar.

Sally smiled her gratitude at M'Lou's utterly reliable disposition to go along with what Sally needed, which now was privacy. She reached over and gratefully clutched her hand. M'Lou understood.

The following morning, after calling him on the telephone, she visited with Campbell Beckett, who had attended to the sparse legal affairs of the Partridge family. He was ready for her.

The house still had a mortgage against it of about seven thousand dollars, she learned. Her father had died both intestate and penniless, but "your mother made out a will the week after your father's death." He gave Sally an envelope. "You will not be surprised that you are the sole beneficiary. The principal liquid asset is the ten thousand dollars paid by the government when your brother was killed. Faith—your mother —managed to get your father's signature on that check"—Cam Beckett was a family friend as well as attorney, and Sally did not resent his idiomatic references to the family situation— "and she gave it to me to invest. I bought a government bond, and its value is now just over eleven thousand dollars. You can hang on to it if you want, or cash it in. My advice would be to cash it in. We are going to have even more inflation. I would advise you to let the Phoenix Bank invest it for you. In any event, Sally, when you decide, let me know if I can be of any help.

"Now your house is worth—I got an estimate yesterday from Mel Powell—about twenty thousand dollars, and could probably be sold, with summer coming, within a few months. If you decide to put the house on the market through Mr. Powell, he will make all the arrangements concerning furniture, that kind of thing. He would only need your instructions. Or you may want to keep the house and live in it during your vacations. After mortgages, commissions, taxes, funeral expenses"—he handed her a sheet of paper, with his neatly penciled figures— "you would be left with about twenty-four thousand dollars."

Sally leaned over and studied the notations.

"There is nothing there for what I—for what the estate— owes you."

"I don't charge war victims. I think of you as one."

Sally said only, "Thank you, Mr. Beckett."

She got up, and he also did. "I hear you have made a marvelous record at Vassar and that you are going to Yale."

She nodded.

"I was Class of 1918." He smiled his warm, avuncular smile. "It's hard for old fogies like me to think of women at Yale, though I know they've always been in the graduate school, but there are a lot of changes ahead, a lot of changes ahead." At the door he leaned down and kissed her lightly on the forehead.

That afternoon, sitting in the living room in the chair her mother had usually occupied, Sally looked out on the lake. It was mid-April and the green was coming, coming all about her. She could see it in the surrounding trees, and the shrubs, and the little lawn. The water was choppy with the spring puffs. Ronnie's buoy was still there, eight years after he had planted it so excitedly. The *Barracuda* was now hers, she realized: Her father had turned it over to Hopp Rudd, the owner of the little camp, on the condition that he should maintain it, in return for the use of it. She made a note to give the boat to Hopp Rudd, on the condition that it be renamed *Ronnie*. She found herself walking through the rooms, one by one. Her father's possessions were long since gone, as were Ronnie's. There was, really, nothing except her mother's exiguous wardrobe, the paraphernalia of a not very modern kitchen, the radio, the books, the carpets, family photographs, a few framed color prints, and the rudimentary furniture for a family of four. She began to make a list of items she would like to be put into one of those large cardboard containers she had several times seen in connection with household moves. Everything else was to be given away to the church, after Miss D'Arcy had been invited to remove anything she wanted. Mr. Powell would look after all that—in the morning she would call him, and from Vassar she would send out typewritten instructions.

Sally Partridge was twenty years old. And, two months later, she was worth $24,275, had a year's lease on her own apartment on St. Ronan Street in New Haven, at fifty-five dollars per month for the bedroom, living room-study-dining room, kitchenette, and bathroom. Her nearest relative was an aunt of her mother's, who lived in England. Somewhere in England. The following week, the summer semester would begin.

12

Art Shaeffer wore a raccoon coat—he was one of those. When teased, as from time to time he was teased about it, he would say that it was his father's, and he might as well wear it rather than let it rot away in the closet. But the real reason Art Shaeffer wore it was that he was that way, especially about intercollegiate football. His enthusiasm for the home team was so genuine, so robust, it was infectious, and Sally found herself cheering for the Yale team in the game against Dartmouth as exuberantly as though her date was with Herman Hickman, coach of the Yale football team, instead of Art Shaeffer, second-year law student. Yale's loss by ten points put Shaeffer in a very blue mood, and when he drove Sally to fraternity row for drinks and dinner he was depressed. Sally had experienced this before in Art, whom she liked—"a bright, hulking, fifteen-year-old boy" was how she described him in a letter to M'Lou, though Shaeffer was twenty-five, had been discharged from the Marines as a first lieutenant, and was thought of as anything but a boy by his classmates, or for that matter by the Marine platoon he had led in three bloody Pacific operations.

But on entering the robustly Victorian Fence Club, to which he had been elected as an undergraduate at about the time of Pearl Harbor, Art's spirits quickly revived. He took Sally's coat and pointed the way to the ladies' room. It was crowded in the hallway, so he told her her to come down to the bar when ready. "What shall I order for you?" Sally said she would have a Manhattan.

She found him fervently instructing three undergraduates at the end of the long, crowded bar on what, obviously, the tactics of the Yale team should have been after Dartmouth had scored its second touchdown. It didn't surprise Sally that Art was talking not to old friends, putatively interested in Art Shaeffer, football tactician, but to undergraduates he had never met before. This became evident when she arrived, as he had to ask them their names before he could introduce them to Sally. The first student was called Lindsay Bradford, and Sally marveled that anyone so young could actually be in college. The slender seventeen-year-old was not, manifestly, a veteran of the war, and was only problematically a veteran of his first shave. Then there was Richie O'Neill, a tall, vivacious, handsome Irishman who took Sally's outstretched hand and gave her a warm handshake. The third young man gave his name as Blackford Oakes.

"Black What?" Art Shaeffer asked, rising his voice to be heard over the din from surrounding voices.

"Black *Ford*. As in Ford V-8." He turned to greet Sally. She saw a man perhaps twenty-two, strikingly handsome, only an inch or so shorter than Richie O'Neill, his faded blond hair framing a sensitive and expressive face. He had on a fraternity tie, a blazer, and gray flannel pants, as did the majority of the students in the room. He looked at Sally and stretched out his hand. He leaned over to her, "Your escort has just told us how Yale really won the game, even though we didn't."

Art Shaeffer, thrusting a Manhattan at Sally and quaffing his own scotch and soda, turned to Blackford. "You making fun of me? You don't think it would have worked?"

"No," Blackford said, laughing. "I don't."

"Why not?"

"Because Dartmouth's team is better than ours."

Art Shaeffer put down his glass on the bar and stood up, ramrod-straight. "Whatchou say?"

Blackford looked up at him and smiled. "My father was an Indian. I always root for Dartmouth."

The others laughed. Sally said, "Come on, Art. There are other things than football."

But Art Shaeffer, whose glass had been refilled by the attentive bartender, was aroused. "There *aren't* any other things on Saturday afternoons during the season."

Richie O'Neill, in genial diplomatic manner, turned to Shaeffer and said, "Art, explain that move to me again. I used to play football at Hotchkiss . . ."

As he spoke, Richie moved toward him, cutting his provocative roommate off from Art Shaeffer. Lindsay Bradford was now engaged in conversation with a contiguous beer drinker. Sally whispered, "Art gets carried away." Blackford replied, "So would I be."

Sally wrinkled her face as if to say, "Don't get it." Blackford stared at her, her head slightly tilted, her pearls touching the light gray tweed of her soft suit. Her eyes, in the light, were a piercing, intelligent green. She sipped her Manhattan.

"Are you here from—Smith? Vassar?"

"No," Sally answered. "I'm in the graduate school."

"Where?"

"Yale graduate school."

"You *are?* What are you studying? Nursing?"

Sally gave her most feminine smile, but the kind that also bared true grit. "No," she said. "Marine biology."

Blackford looked at her. One end of his mouth winked, the other was professionally solemn. "Oh, that's good. I have been worried about the declining population of whales. Do you intend to do something about that?"

"Yes," Sally said. "I'm going to give up whale meat."

But Art Shaeffer was back, and his enthusiasm was again serene. Richie nodded at Blackford: All's well.

"C'mon, pussycat," Art said to Sally, grabbing her by the arm. "We'll get another drink at the table. But we'd better sit down, it'll be crowded." He nodded to Blackford and Richie, "See you."

Blackford put down his own drink, unfinished. He said to Richie, "Did you ever know her, I mean, see her before? She's *here.*"

"Law School?" Richie asked.

"I don't know. In graduate school. The only thing I'm sure she isn't studying is marine biology. Rich, I'll see you later, okay?"

"Aren't you going to eat?"

"Later." He waved, and made his resolute way through the crowd upstairs to where his coat hung. He put it on and walked down the street to Davenport College, entered the gate and then the portal to his room, climbing the single flight of stairs. He threw off his coat and reached in the bottom drawer where he kept catalogues and directories. He flipped open the Student Directory. Partell, Partissel—Partridge, Sally. "240 St. Ronan Street, Apartment 4." Strange, Blackford thought. No home town given. Partissel, Dino, was listed as from Toledo, Ohio, Partell, Jonathan, from Naples, Florida. Yes, everyone had a home town. Except Sally. Could she be *from* New Haven? It sounded as though her apartment was also her home.

He opened the door on his steel desk, and the typewriter sprang up, mounted on the metal tray. He typed quickly, pulled out the paper, signed it, put it in an envelope. Leaving his overcoat on the chair he pulled a parka from his closet. Downstairs he unlocked his bicycle and headed in the light snow toward Prospect Street, past the Science Building, right at Edwards Street, turning left at St. Ronan. Number 240 obviously at one time had been a large single-family residence, but now was made over into apartments. He walked up the stone steps and looked at the mailboxes. She used only the name Partridge. He stuffed the note into her box and all the next morning, except for the hour's religious service at Dwight Hall, he waited for the phone to ring. At five, he rang her.

"Yes?"—her voice was at once withdrawn and inquisitive.

"This is Blackford. Blackford Oakes. We met— Did you get my note?"

He heard her laugh, but it was not a derisive laugh. "Oh. Black Ford V-8. Hello. Yes, I got it. I meant to answer it. I will answer it."

"Why didn't you just—call? I left my number."

"You are very impatient."

"I'm only impatient to see you again. I've got to ask you a couple of questions. About what kind of crustaceans you can safely eat and what kind you can't eat. Are you free for dinner?"

"No, I'm not."

No explanation; Blackford frowned. "How about a late drink?"

"I don't drink late," she said, inoffensively.

"Do you ever have a hamburger late? Or is there whale meat in hamburgers?"

They agreed to meet at eleven, at George & Harry's, fairly easy walking distance for both. Blackford was waiting for her in a corner booth. She wore a sweater under her dark red windbreaker and a yellow scarf around her neck. They both ordered a hamburger and a beer.

Blackford didn't know what had got into him, but soon he was talking, talking almost without pause. He had no idea, the following day, what he had talked about, but it must have been after midnight before he consciously arrested his flow. But she wanted more. About his father, in the airplane business, or, more properly, "Dad is in the business of selling airplanes as an excuse to keep flying them." About his divorced mother, "She's a sweetheart. Now 'Lady Sharkey,' no less, lives in London." About his stepfather, Sir Alec Sharkey, who had taken Blackford on at age sixteen and sent him to an English public school, Greyburn College. "Awful place." About coming back to America after Pearl Harbor, about the Air Force, and a combat career aborted by hepatitis, "though I did shoot down a couple of Messerschmitts before I got sick." Then there was the German surrender—and now Yale.

He insisted on walking her home, and the snow had begun again, heavy enough now to diffuse the mellow street lights. Tomorrow night, he said, *she* must do all the talking. She smiled and said, "No, not tomorrow night."

"Tuesday, then?"

"No. I don't go out on weekdays. I work. You should know, Blackford, that I am very serious about my work. The nineteenth century was a stretch of copious productivity in the English novel. In the next three years I shall have read practically all of them. I mean, most of them. Maybe five hundred novels."

"Oh," he said, fatalistically. "I understand." Then: "Friday doesn't count as a weekday, really. Let's make it an outing. Go to New York. Do you want to go to the opera, or a concert, a play—what would you like?"

She paused. "I have only been to the opera—twice," she said apologetically. And, accelerating her speech, "I'd like to go to the Met, whatever is playing," suddenly grabbing him by the arm as they crossed the icy street.

"Leave it to me, Sally Partridge. I am majoring in Entertainment, did I tell you? I am taking a course this semester, Escort Servicing 105. Just leave everything to me, but be prepared to catch the four o'clock train. I'll pick you up here at three-thirty, probably in a taxi."

They parted outside her door, and he made no effort to kiss her, but they looked at each other a long moment before she turned her key.

Blackford slept very little that night, and the days until Friday were endless. But his plans were elaborately made, and required borrowing Richie's car and driving to New York. They dined at Schrafft's, and then to the Metropolitan, where *Lucia de Lammermoor* was sung by Lily Pons. Then he drove her to Nick's in Greenwich Village, Blackford's favorite jazz bar. There was a Dixieland band, and, in the fairly long intervals in between, the thin, colored, smiling pianist whose improvisations on popular tunes always excited Blackford and, he now learned, excited Sally equally. They reached New Haven at 3:30 in the morning, and during the slow drive back Blackford became the first person to hear from Sally all about Ronnie, her brother, and how she had adored him.

Blackford proposed that one day in the spring they drive to Lakeville, so that he might see the lake she described, and perhaps even call on the Landons, who had bought her old cottage, and on Hopp Rudd, maybe even have a sail on the *Ronnie*. When they reached the door Blackford said, "And where would you like to have dinner tomorrow?"

As she coaxed sleep, turning in her bed, the dawn already insinuating its way through the curtain cracks, she couldn't actually believe what she had said. It was totally unlike her. What had got into her?

She had said, "Let's eat here. I'll cook." And then the daemon moved her. She heard herself saying, "Dress lightly."

Sally knew that at this time the next day she would no longer be a virgin.

AT THE SAME hour the next night, Blackford was back in his room, having just arrived. It had not been his initial experience, but he had never before deflowered, and when he discovered that this was in process he had felt a kind of tender concern which, together with his compulsive desire, emerged as an act of convulsive and transcendent love. She had showered and returned to him, and whispered that the pain was already gone, and that she knew her beautiful Blacky was unique, and they covered each other in caresses as, with infinite caution, he approached her again, feeling now the return of his passion, and the tenderness. He had sustained it this time a full half hour— or was it only five minutes? He didn't know, knew only that his transporting pleasure had in some measure been shared by her.

Attempting to be quiet while reaching for his pajamas, he knocked over the standing lamp. Richie woke. "What in the hell are you doing up at this hour?"

"Up?"—Blackford could not make any sense of it all.

"Yes, dammit, up."

Blackford paused. "I've been with the girl I'm going to marry."

Richie told him to shut up and go to sleep.

·Book III·

13

Blackford and Rufus were in the private office of the Attorney General. The limber, inquisitive, vibrant young man hadn't shaved that morning, his sleeves were rolled up just short of his elbows, and he wore no tie. It was late Saturday afternoon and the office was officially closed. The Attorney General, his feet on the desk, laughed. "Wants it from *me* directly, that *you*, Oakes, aren't a double agent playing Castro's game at the same time!" He laughed again. "Well, you're not, *are* you?"

Blackford was amused. Rufus less so.

"But what does the sonofabitch want me to do, ride in a motorcade with you? Be photographed giving you a medal? I mean—"

"Something less than that," Blackford said. "This guy is playing with his life, Mr. Attorney General. Miami is full of our people, but it's also full of their people. He doesn't know the story of our work last year in the missile crisis, and obviously I'm not going to tell him that your brother, that the President, asked me personally to represent him in the negotiations with Che. But I have a feeling that no phony formality will satisfy him, and Pano is our primary link with AM/LASH. He won't even mention LASH's name, and of course we won't either. But he has total confidence in you, and if you tell him to go ahead and cooperate with me on the LASH business, then he's going to do it."

"Well, do you have a procedure in mind?"

"Yes, actually."

Robert Kennedy shot up from his chair and leaned back on the bookcase. "Tell me," he nodded to Blackford.

"Okay. We specify a time. For the hell of it, let's say it will be 11:35 next Tuesday. Pano's in the room with me at my hotel in Miami and I tell him to pick up the telephone and ask the operator for Washington information. I tell him then to ask for the number of the Department of Justice. I tell him to dial that number and to ask for 'Pearl' in your office—whatever name you give me, of your private secretary. If the operator asks, 'Who is calling?' Pano will say, 'Pearl's brother-in-law, John Guzmán.' Your operator has been told, and she flashes him to your secretary, who has also been warned, and you're standing by—"

Robert Kennedy managed to look distracted.

"Don't worry. What I'm talking about won't take three minutes, soup to nuts. The secretary buzzes you, tells you this is the 11:35 call you've been expecting. You pick up, and say, 'Pano? This is Robert Kennedy.' Your voice is pretty recognizable. 'We're counting on you to work with Blackford Oakes. I know all about him, and he's one hundred percent.' Something like that," Blackford concluded.

"Hmm. Sure you don't want me to give him a little of your bio? What sports you played at school?"

But the Attorney General was smiling. He seemed to be ratifying the idea as workable. At that moment his red telephone rang. He picked it up. "Yeah, hi, Jack." He motioned to Rufus, pointing to an anteroom. Rufus and Blackford had already got up; they walked into the room and closed the door. After a few minutes the door reopened, with that decisive slam with which the Attorney General tended to open, and close, doors.

He went to his desk and sat down again, motioning his guests to reoccupy their chairs. "First, on the Pano business. Okay." He leaned over and made a notation on his calendar "for this coming Tuesday, April 2, for 11:35. My secretary's name, the one he's to ask for, is Angie. Now, I just talked with the President, told him I was meeting here with you and Rufus. And damned if he doesn't want to see you both." He got up and strode toward the window . . . The problems of the younger brother, seeking at once to execute his brother's will and to defend him against any unnecessary exposure . . . He shrugged his shoulders.

"Well, he's the boss. We're to drive up to the southwest gate and—hell, just follow me." He walked over to a closet and pulled out a jacket and tie.

At the southwest gate of the White House the guard, spotting the Attorney General, immediately waved the limousine on. The AG bounded out of the car, motioning Rufus and Blackford to follow him. The guard at the door opened it, they walked into the basement floor, up the staircase to the marbled floor behind the main entrance, up another flight of stairs to the family quarters, left and then right, into the Lincoln Bedroom, a large bedroom with chairs and a coffee table opposite the fireplace. "Sit down. I'll tell him you're here."

RUFUS AND BLACKFORD drove the twenty miles to Rufus's house in the country and settled down with a drink in the living room, so familiar to Blackford.

"Goddammit, Rufus, you are amazing. You just sit there and tell the President of the United States yes to this, no to that—maybe the most powerful man in the world, and certainly the most magnetic; I don't deny it. When he looks at you, cocks his head a little, and says something in that Boston drawl, you get the feeling, at least I do, that there's something very special there, maybe unique. He's so—well, so utterly appealing. Did you notice, when I tried to thank him for personally interceding with Castro for me, what he said was, 'I think, Black, you'd do the same to save my life.' Goddamn right I'd do the same, but I'm not the President. He is—well, he gives you the impression that he is really an anointed leader—"

Rufus raised his hand. "Nothing I said, Blackford, contradicts anything you've just said."

"What you said, Rufus, was that you would go along with one and only one aspect of Mongoose: the political coup, and that you acknowledged that as things stood, assassination was necessary for any successful coup against Castro. But then, when Bobby came in with the business about the girl, and the poison, and how he had been assured by Hicock it was going to work, you said, 'Hicock's division and mine are different.' Sounded like a bishop. You're your own moral boss, Rufus, and you've made your position clear from the beginning. You'll help expedite an assassination if it's clearly based on political realities, the classical struggle to replace the tyrant—but you won't involve yourself in plots to have Castro killed by an exploding cigar."

"There is a distinction."

"I'll give you that, Rufus, but it isn't one hundred percent clear to me what the distinction is. If Spartacus had risen against the Roman tyrant with only a poisoned wet suit at his disposal, I don't see how the moral case for or against him would have been affected. I do think you're absolutely right, it's critical that the operation be a Cuban operation, but the girl Bobby was talking about *is* a Cuban girl, so I don't see how that changes things." Blackford thought back on the scene, the Attorney General beginning to look just a little bit affronted. "He came close, I think, to telling you that Mongoose was after all one operation, not bits and pieces of several operations. But then did you notice how JFK handled it?" Blackford sipped his drink with admiration. "Just raised his hand, real gentle-like"—Blackford imitated the motion—"and Bobby shut up. All the President said was, 'We have to respect your distinctions, Rufus. But Mongoose has also got to work.'"

Suddenly Blackford laughed. "I wonder if there is another possible comment to make other than the one you then made!"

Rufus half-smiled. "No, I don't think so. I've used it maybe twenty times in my life. No, there isn't a substitute for it: 'I'll do my best.'"

Blackford lifted his glass. He felt elated. He had found something truly to preoccupy him. And his mission also served the purposes of the statesman he most admired. He was pleased that Rufus was ready to let the distinctions sleep. Or else coexist. "Your best is awful good, Rufus. Now, shall we get into the AM/LASH business?"

AS BLACKFORD AND Rufus talked the President was, once again, alone on his rocking chair for the precious moments between the departure of the last visitor and the inevitable summons to social duties. He had come down to do some paperwork after the departure of Bobby and the two spooks, as Bobby regularly referred to any covert agent of the CIA.

A good combination, Rufus, Oakes. The Castro business is one hell of a mess. What are we going to tell the Soviet ambassador on Monday? It isn't all that simple just to tell him we had nothing to do with the Cuban exiles' raid on the Soviet ship coming out of Havana Harbor. The Balu, Baku, *whatever it was called.* He got up, walked over to his desk, and picked up the memorandum he had just read. The report, quoting the AP, gave the text of the official Soviet note: "By offering Cuban counterrevolutionaries its territory and material needs for organization of piratical attacks against Cuba, the U.S. is actually bringing about the dangerous aggravation of the situation in the Caribbean and throughout the world. Without the material support of the U.S. and without the supplying of American weapons and ships, the traitors to the Cuban people sheltering on U.S. territory would not be able to undertake these kinds of provocation."

He returned to his chair. *The trouble is, they're exactly right. That's why the other thing has got to move, and move fast, goddammit. Hmm. If Hicock can get that operation with the girl moving, that sounds good. Bobby tells me she is absolutely ready to go. Did a fuck-scene at a nightclub at age eighteen and Castro saw it. Practically the first thing he did after reentering Havana five years later was have her looked up, and screwed her, but this time she wasn't paid for it.*

God, it really can be useful to be a dictator.—Though I'm not a dictator, and I don't exactly . . . starve to death. But of course that whole plan depends on whether the girl, back in Havana after one year in Miami, can make it back into Castro's bed. Hicock tells Bobby no sweat, Castro adores her. Maybe it's a good thing Blackford isn't in on the Hicock part of Mongoose. She might see him and figure the hell with Castro. He's got it, all right. Bet he has to fight 'em off. I'm glad I was able to spring him last October. Nice guy. Bright.

But what are we going to tell the Russians on Monday about the Cuban exile raids? Actually, dammit, it doesn't matter so much what we tell the Soviets, or what we tell them up at the U.N., it's one of those situations in which they know that we know and we know that they know that we know, and we just come up with boilerplate lies. We can't possibly police all the activities of Chiquita Banana, every Cuban exile, and probably they're getting money and help from inside Cuba. That kind of thing works in the diplomatic world, thank God.

But it doesn't work in my press conferences. "Yes, Mr. Smith?" "Ah, Mr. Smith," you say, "can I expect you to believe me when I say that the government is completely unaware of the activities of four different exile groups that have violated Cuban territory and inflicted damage on a Soviet troopship? Well, Merriman"—that's a good technique, you start off calling them Mr. Snickers, and Mrs. Mars Bar, and then you slip, er, unconsciously, into calling them by their first names. God, they all love it. "Well, Merriman, there are five hundred thousand Cuban refugees, and they all want to hurt Castro and restore freedom to their country. Now that's more people than we can conceivably keep track of. Yes, Sam?" Go quickly to Sam. He usually overstates his questions, and the sympathy flows quickly to me.

Well, all of that isn't till Monday. Between now and then all I have to think about is the crazy Vietnam situation. One more monk burns himself up, we're going to have to ship more fuel to that country. Wish Diem would get his act together, which reminds me, I wish McNamara and McCone could get their acts together. McNamara testifies that Castro isn't exporting Communism to Latin America, McCone testifies that he is, same fucking committee. Maybe the Secretary of Defense could one day talk to the Director of the Central Intelligence Agency and coordinate their testimony.

He smiled. *Fun idea!* He walked over to his desk, flipped up his telephone book, and scratched out two cards, one for his Secretary of Defense, confiding to him the telephone number of the Director of Central Intelligence Agency, the second to the Director of the Central Intelligence Agency, giving the telephone number of the Secretary of Defense. He placed them in envelopes and sealed them. He pushed a button at the side of his desk. An aide entered: "Yes sir?"

"Get these delivered, Joe."

"Yes sir."

"And watch they don't shoot the messenger."

"Sir?"

JFK smiled. "Never mind. Thanks."

The President walked out of his office toward the family quarters, still smiling.

14

It was after midnight when the Commando L raider zoomed in on the *Baku* as it was leaving Caibarién with a shipment of Cuban sugar bound for Leningrad; the raider set fire to much of it before powering back toward Florida. It hadn't been necessary for Armed Forces Chief Raúl Castro to awaken his brother: Fidel was never asleep at midnight. He received the news and told Raúl to come to his house, together with Ramiro Valdés and Osvaldo Dorticós, at ten in the morning.

They were all there, looking grim. Dorticós had already been in communication with the Kremlin and now advised Fidel that both at the United Nations and in Moscow the Soviets would be protesting vigorously. He had taken the liberty, he said, of advising Raúl Roa, the Foreign Minister, to prepare a statement accusing the United States of violating the Neutrality Act, "etc. etc."

Castro nodded. "All right."

"But it is time," he said with some gravity, "to execute our plan for Miami." He turned to his brother, Raúl. "Have plans been made?"

"Yes, Fidel. We have just been awaiting your word."

"Well," Castro said, taking a deep puff from his cigar, "you now *have* my word. If the Americans want to play, we can show them a trick or two. Eh?"

There was general acquiescence that they could show the United States a thing or two in the dirty tricks department. It was instantly apparent to his three close associates that Fidel's anger had risen now and had launched him, as it often did—as it increasingly did—onto one of his high-energy plateaus. It was from these that he tended to act most decisively. And it was clear that he took great pleasure in what he considered the special ingenuity of the revenge he would take. He knew it would hurt John F. Kennedy personally, and that, exactly, was what he wished to do: to hurt John F. Kennedy personally.

THAT NIGHT AT exactly six, in the bedroom of his little house in southwest Miami, the Cuban they called "Alejandro" was, as always, alone with his shortwave listening set and his tape recorder. He pulled out the notebook, the decoder, from behind the bookcase and sat down to listen. The alert, which always came within the first two minutes of Radio Havana's news broadcast, was a slip-of-the-tongue mention of the wrong month. *"Hoy, el día viente y seis de abril—el día viente y seis de marzo"* meant that there would be instructions during the weather broadcast, which generally came between five and seven minutes after the hour began.

The news started off with a declamatory quote from Fidel Castro denouncing American complicity in the illegal raid on the merchant vessel *Baku,* carrying a Soviet flag and Cuban sugar. A sharp protest would be filed with the United Nations "tomorrow, April 27th—tomorrow, March 27th."

Alerted, Alejandro connected his tape recorder. When the time came for the weather, the recorder was on and he listened for the activating phrase. It came. "There is the possibility of rain over Oriente Province tonight and tomorrow." Yes. *The possibility of . . .*

He jotted down down the key words and turned the radio off. The announcer had spoken very fast, and so he wound back his tape and listened again, intently. The key words were 1) "Oriente," 2) "tonight," and 3) "tomorrow." He looked into his codebook. "Execute Operation Oakes."

The basic plan had been made, but there were arrangements that had to be left until the last minute. The airplane ticket, the fake passport, the alert given to Cuban assets in Mexico. And, of course, the timing of the flight, as also of the reception in Mexico, depended on the unwitting cooperation of the target. A log had been kept on his habits and Alejandro was moderately confident the plan would meet with success. The selected executioner was well trained, and his equipment modern.

On March 27 in Miami the sun sets at 6:26.

Fifteen minutes after that time, Blackford got up from his work table to turn on the overhead lights in his living room-study and the floor lamp over the round table on which his papers lay. At his side, also in shirt sleeves, Pano was writing.

There was in hand a communication from LASH. It was the second that had come in directly to Blackford. The first, via Rufus, was a testimonial. *"You can trust Pano,"* was all it said.

LASH had surveyed all the possibilities. He was ready to make final plans to "execute"—LASH was very fussy about the use of that term, having coldly reproached the first user of the word "assassinate"—Fidel Castro. He was ready, he had said, to "execute" Castro for violating so grossly so many provisions of the Cuban Constitution. The only way to carry out the execution, short of committing suicide ("I would not mind sacrificing my own life, but it would hardly be a successful coup d'état if I were not there to assume or to pass on the leadership. There would hardly be any point in executing Fidel in order to turn Cuba over to Raúl"), was to use a sniper's rifle, and in Cuba there was none suitable for his purposes that he could lay his hands on. He needed a true sportsman's rifle, with a telescopic sight. He had exactly the model in mind, a Model 70 Winchester.

At their meeting the day before, when Pano had brought LASH's message in, Blackford had said: "No. No U.S. equipment."

There would have to be other ordnance. He would, by the following day, have in hand an inventory of foreign-made equipment as close as possible to the specifications of what LASH was asking for. "Some of this stuff we have up in Langley," Blackford said, staring at the catalogue listing, "but not all. Let's see in any case. Come around at five, and I think I'll have the information."

Now Pano was taking notes while Blackford, going through the papers, dictated. "There is the Russian Mosin-Nagant or the Dragunov or the German Mauser. The Mosin-Nagant rifle comes with scope sight, 7.62 by 54R caliber." Blackford looked down at a footnote, which advised that the rifle was being discontinued at the end of 1962. Blackford turned his head sharply to retract his dictated notation. At that moment the bullet whizzed through the window.

Both men dropped to the floor. His heart pounding, Blackford crawled to the window and, with hand stretched up, pulled down the curtain. He crawled to the light switches. First he turned off the wall switch. The standing lamp he disconnected by pulling out its plug at the baseboard. Only then did he stand up and feel his way into the bedroom to the dresser. Opening the top drawer, he found his flashlight. Back in the living room he approached the window cautiously and rotated the brass rod that brought in the louvered shutters, so that no light could penetrate. He turned the lights back on.

"Jee-*zus*, Pano, have a look." They talked to each other in soft hisses. Blackford had lowered his head to the level of the bullet hole and was looking back at the table where he had been sitting.

"No, don't. Sit where I was sitting." Pano did so. "I'm about four inches taller than you are. Raise your butt about four inches." He focused sharply on the line of sight, then stood up.

"Never thought a damned footnote would save my life."

He sat down in his armchair. The two men stared at each other in silence. After a minute Blackford said, speaking for the first time in a normal tone of voice, "You in any position to find out who did it?"

"It would not have been done without orders from Havana. No *posibilidad*. Every week a Cuban is rubbed off here, but never an American. Standing orders from Havana. You are the first one. A radical change in policy." Pano paused. "Why you, Blackforrd?"

"That's exactly the question. If they know what we are up to, Mongoose is in trouble. If on the other hand—" Blackford reflected for a moment, and he began again. "They know who I am. You may as well know it too, Pano. When I left Cuba in October, I was under sentence of death by the military court. The question is: Why should they choose this moment to—well, catch up—on neglected business?"

"It could be the *Baku*."

Blackford reflected. "Yes. Yes. I see your point. The United States makes subversive attempts against Castro, Castro makes subversive attempts against known U.S. agents, in particular *this* known U.S. agent. Tit for tat. I wonder how many tons of sugar in the *Baku* were ruined by the fire?" He looked up and smiled. "That would be the free-market price for my life . . .

"Well, compañero, things are going to have to proceed very differently from now on. Don't much like the alternative way of life, but I've done it before. I'll need to get an address from Washington. I'll call you at the usual number tomorrow. We don't want to lose any time in getting back to LASH. But somehow I'm not in the mood to continue operations tonight."

"I will stay with you and help you get safely to your new quarters."

"No," Blackford said. "The guy who shot at me—he obviously shot from a hotel room across the way—must have had a pretty good look at *you* through the glasses. And if they've been checking on me"—Blackford looked at his watch—"at about seven P.M. every day, they've seen you with me more than once. You'd better make your own arrangements."

"I have made my own *arreglos*, Blackforrd."

Blackford was direct. "You use disguise?"

"Yes. A different man steps out of the elevator downstairs. You have never followed me out at any of our six meetings."

"Good. I've had some experience with that sort of thing. But I need a kit. Tell you what. Get a couple of your guys to sweep the front drive between ten and ten-thirty, okay? Then, in your disguise, drive up to the entrance at seven minutes after ten. Tape the headline from the *Miami Herald* onto your left rear window so I'll know it's the right car. I'll steam right out with a bag and a briefcase into the back seat, and you drive off. By that time I'll have the address. And, Pano, I don't know for sure what I'll look like, but don't let anything surprise you."

Pano nodded, went for his own briefcase in the closet, and stepped into the washroom. He was gone not more than a couple of minutes. What emerged was a refugee from a rodeo. Light buckskin coat, Western boots, blue jeans, a long head of hair coming down to his shoulders, a Buffalo Bill mustache, a gold ring on one ear. The briefcase was transformed into a rucksack.

"Goddamn. You're in practice, Pano."

"Who's that Pano, man? Mah name is Jefferson Jackson Coo-lich."

"Coo-*lijjj*, Pano, not Coo-*litch*. But well done, well done."

"Thank you, *compadre*. I will be seeing you, 10:07."

Pano walked to the door, pronouncing, "Coo-leech," "Coo-leech," "Coo-leech."

Blackford waited five minutes. His hand on the trigger of the Luger in his pocket, he walked out of his suite to the emergency staircase. Up two flights, he turned to Room 1407. The key was ready in his left hand. The empty room had a telephone that did not go through the switchboard.

He reached Rufus.

"It's Black. Our friends moved against me just now. Rifle shot from across the hotel. Damned near got me. Pano says I'm the only American they've ever gone after, so it looks like made-in-Havana."

"You all right?"

"Yes, sir. And I need a new address. Unless you tell me different, I'm being picked up here in a couple of hours, and I'll need to go somewhere."

"Any problem in staying where you are for a few minutes?"

"None."

Rufus hung up.

Blackford waited. In ten minutes the telephone rang. He lifted the receiver and gave an identifying code number. He listened, and put down the receiver. He had memorized the address of the safe house. His new quarters, until Mongoose was done.

15

When Fidel Castro strode into Havana on January 8, 1959, as conquering hero, he took the first of many occasions to give a speech. He spoke, more or less endlessly, for the next three months. Castro announced the dreams Cuba would realize under his leadership, but warned there was much work to be done—many "administrative" and "regulatory" actions to be taken, and yes, some disciplinary actions too. In January, one of the activities against which the revolutionary regime would wage relentless war was announced: prostitution and pimping.

After the closing of Santos Trafficante's nightclub, María Raja lived with a succession of lovers in some comfort, in a spacious apartment on Calle Reina. But when word reached her that, the week before, four pimps had been executed (she did not herself use one) and six prostitutes arrested and sent out to a rehabilitation camp, she decided it was time to change not only her profession but her living quarters, and to reclaim her name, María Arguilla. There would be too many former luminaries of the Batista period who would have her telephone number, and perhaps even her address written down in little notebooks that would be perused now with avidity by Fidel's newly constituted vice squad.

Among other assets, María Raja had a second passport. Her mother, a refugee from Hitler's Hungary, was above all things fastidious about security arrangements. It was only because she had had the cunning even as a teenager to make contingent arrangements that María so much as existed. As a girl, her mother had become friendly with a patrolman on the Drava River in southwestern Hungary. When the anti-Semitic williwaw of the mid-thirties suddenly threatened to grow to Typhonic force, young Astra, age seventeen, led her widowed mother to meet her river friend, the elderly policeman with a fondness for the children who played along the river's verdant banks during the summer. He had befriended Astra when, at age seven, she was first taken there to play, and every summer that friendship was renewed.

He quietly—asking no questions—rowed Astra and her mother, with two laundry bags of clothes and toiletries, in the darkness across the border, letting them out in Yugoslavia. It was two years before they landed in Cuba, where Astra had a bachelor uncle who spared no pains to move them, as it were by remote control, what seemed inch by inch, from Yugoslavia and then to Egypt and finally aboard a freighter to Havana, where they arrived in 1941. Astra, a girl of striking beauty, then married a dashing young Cuban in disgrace with his aristocratic family, whose conventions he regularly dishonored, not least, now, by marrying a Jewish refugee from Hungary whose uncle was a jeweler in the commercial district.

But the young couple lived happily during the first two years of the world war, and Astra bore María. It all ended on that gruesome day in which the dashing, stupid young Cuban insisted on responding to a challenge to a duel, and was dead five seconds after his adversary drew his pistol. In return for a very satisfactory settlement, María's paternal grandparents persuaded the widow to adopt her uncle's name of Arguilla, and to bring up her little baby without giving her any knowledge of who her father had been, leaving no clues as to how she might trace her grandparents, if ever curiosity seized her.

Astra had been true to her promise, and María did not know her grandparents. But everything else she did know: that her father had been killed in a duel, and that arrangements had been made with his parents to guard their anonymity. She learned from her mother the need always to give personal security a high priority.

When Astra died (she was run down by a drunken truck driver) María was only fifteen, and she lived then for two years with her uncle, who died leaving María a jewelry store heavily in debt from years of casual credit practices. Her uncle's accountant urged María simply to make her own arrangements with whatever money she had left over from her mother's little bank account, which was less than a thousand pesos. Looking for theatrical opportunities (she had inherited her mother's beauty), María wandered over to the entertainment district and was not entirely surprised—María, like her mother, was born worldly—to find herself talking with a raffish man, Señor Trafficante, who in his plushly upholstered office looked at her carefully, asked her matter-of-factly to disrobe, examined her again, focused lights on her from various angles, and agreed to employ her.

At first it was a fairly conventional skin show, but as the competition increased and María's allure won discreet renown, Trafficante found himself going further and further, and always there were rich tourists, predominantly American, willing to patronize his post-midnight, high-dollar act, and the further the act went, the better they liked it. He evolved, finally, the program that was eventually closed down, though not before young Fidel Castro, seeking relaxation only a few nights before he left to attack, on July 26, the Moncada Barracks, had stopped in and marveled at what he saw.

MARÍA HAD DISTRIBUTED her substantial savings with some diligence in various banks, and when she moved from the apartment, she selected and paid for in cash a small house in the middle-class neighborhood of Santos Suárez, and, at age twenty-six, gave her profession to her neighbors as a drama teacher who until recently had taught in a private school. (She had, of course, a "letter" from the Mother Superior of that private school, regretting that budget problems made it necessary to let Maria go.) She was looking for another position, and meanwhile was happy to be able to live comfortably on a modest inheritance from her mother.

She was befriended by her neighbors, most warmly by Señora Leonarda Sori-Marín, the proud but widowed and lonely mother of Humberto Sori-Marín, one of the closest comrades-in-arms of Fidel Castro. Her son Humberto had written the Agrarian Reform Law, promulgated by Castro as one of his most profound social achievements, and there was great excitement in the neighborhood one Sunday morning. The rumor was that he was coming again. And, soon after one, María saw the little motorcade drive up and stop next door. Out of it stepped Fidel Castro, Humberto Sori-Marín, and two or three companions, to have Sunday lunch with Humberto's mother.

It was on the next such visit—Castro & Co. were comfortable there—that Leonarda Sori-Marín told her son and his friends that her new neighbor, María Arguilla, was among the most beautiful young women she had ever laid eyes on and that in the three months they had known each other, Doña Leonarda had come to look upon María as her own daughter, and then, turning to her honored guest, asked might she, dear Comandante, invite her over to meet the great leader of the Cuban people? Fidel, in animated conversation with his friends, nodded his head vaguely between puffs of his cigar. Delighted, Señora Sori-Marín went to the telephone, rang her neighbor, and told her to come quickly to meet Comandante Castro, Primer Ministro de la República de Cuba. María answered that she would need a few minutes to make herself presentable, and Doña Leonarda said to hurry, hurry, and then went to the front door to tell the guards that she had permission to bring over for a visit the young lady next door.

María arrived and was presented. She bowed in the courtly Spanish manner. Fidel Castro looked at her, pleasantly at first, and then inquisitively. He engaged in routine chatter, with just that touch of *gallant* that he used in the company of beautiful young women, and, for that matter, in the company of old hags whom he desired, back when his word was less than law, to attract to his movement. An hour later Fidel left, bowing in turn to Señora Sori-Marín and to her neighbor, María Arguilla.

At ten that evening, an officer drove up to María's door and knocked.

María, dressed casually in a skirt and blouse—she had been watching television—opened the door, leaving the door chain in place.

"Yes?" she said. "Who is it?"

"I am Captain Gustavo Durango, *a sus órdenes.* I am from the personal guard of Prime Minister Castro. He desires to visit with you." He squeezed his identification card through the crack in the door.

María looked at the card with the photograph of the bearded young captain, and then looked him full in the face; she was experienced in these matters. She withdrew the chain and opened the door.

"I am honored. For when is the Comandante's invitation?"

"For tonight, señorita."

She thought quickly. There was little point in declining to go. She said, "I shall have to prepare myself." She motioned to a chair. "Can I bring you something while I am getting dressed?"

"A beer," said Captain Durango, "would be just fine. It is warm tonight."

In her room, María made herself up with professional skill. She dressed smartly, in soft-colored silk with pastel shades, and the discreetly applied perfume.

The captain insisted that she ride in the back seat of the 1958 Buick sedan. Their conversation was mostly about the weather, though Captain Durango twice remarked the mounting hostility of President Kennedy, notwithstanding his humiliation early that year with the attempted invasion at the Bay of Pigs, and dwelt on the eternal hostility of the imperialists to the Comandante. They reached a house on a street María could not, passing the street sign at night, make out. A sturdy three-story house surrounded by a picturesque brick wall. The captain marched past a detachment of six guards and knocked on the door. Fidel Castro opened it and bowed to María, his right arm extended. He wiggled his index finger at Captain Durango, who, withdrawing, reacted dutifully: "I shall be on watch, Comandante."

How pleased he was to see her, he said, taking her by the hand up the stairs to the central living room, and indicating a couch. "I shall have a rum and pineapple myself. Will you join me?"

She nodded. Castro, the two drinks in hand, sat down beside her. He smiled, and there was glitter and a leer in his eyes. "María, my dear, you know that I have seen you before."

"Of course," she said, sipping. "At Humberto's mother's house. Today."

Castro chuckled. "I mean, *before.* I have seen you before today. Indeed, I have seen all of you. Indeed, a month has not passed since that day almost eight years ago, in July—at La

Gallinera—when I fail to experience jealousy. A jealousy I felt in those days only for the authority of the Batista impostor government."

María permitted her hand to be drawn by his to his crotch. "If that night my fairy godmother had said, What would you most like to be this minute? I'd have said, the liberator of Cuba. If she had said, What is your second choice? I'd have said—" Castro stretched out his hand and pointed, his head turned up as if at a stage, "that man there—the man, María, who was making love to you on the stage."

María was accustomed to sexual overtures of a great variety, and in any event saw no purpose in being demure with a man who had seen her publicly perform her act when she was only eighteen.

She said, soothingly and ardently, "And I, Fidel, wish that I might satisfy the greatest man to be born in this hemisphere in this century."

Fidel took the two glasses with them into the bedroom.

A FEW MONTHS later, walking from the bus stop to her house, María came on Doña Leonarda rushing out of her house toward a waiting taxi. María, by now virtually a member of the household, hailed her. "Where are you going, Leonarda?"

She turned and shouted out, "I will come to your house as soon as I get back. Before dinner, for sure." Her eyes were wet. She had obviously been weeping.

Without knocking, just before seven Doña Leonarda came into María's house and collapsed on the couch, exhausted and breathing deeply. María went wordlessly to the cupboard, poured a glass of sherry, and turned on the stove to heat some tea. She walked over to her slender neighbor, whose lined face suggested an age greater than the sixty-one she acknowledged when making one of her frequent references to the precocity of her important son. She was dressed in black and wore a mantilla. She took the glass of sherry, but set it down on the coffee table.

"I have been to see Fidel," she said, her voice trembling. "He admitted me. I had to wait only a half hour, maybe less. I pleaded with him, on my knees—"

"Leonarda, Leonarda, pleaded for *what*? What is the matter?"

"Humberto. Yesterday he was arrested and charged with complicity in treasonable activity. Of course it is not true, not one word of it. It is the action of an anonymous informant, someone who wants his job. But the charge carries the death penalty, and he is to be tried this very afternoon."

She stopped for a moment, unable to go on.

"Before I went in to see Fidel, I knew I could not go too far, I could not beg him to withdraw the charges against Humberto completely. That will come later. All I could safely do," she began to sob, but there was a triumphant smile through the sobbing, "all I could safely do was to ask him to commute the sentence of death if it is meted out by the court."

She sat back in the chair, and her pose now was regal. "And, María, my pleading prevailed. He took his big hand and stroked my head, over the mantilla. And he said, 'Don't worry. Nothing will happen to Humberto. I promise you, Doña Leonarda.' " Her smile was beatific, and now she took the glass of sherry, but before she had finished it, her eyes closed. María took it from her hand, and Doña Leonarda slept.

Much later, after giving her some soup, María walked Doña Leonarda back to her own house. The following morning María flicked on the radio to hear the news. There was more of the same about the disposition of the survivors of the attempted invasion at the Bay of Pigs. The next item was that Humberto Sori-Marín, having been found guilty of treasonable complicity against the regime, had been executed by firing squad the night before at La Cabaña prison.

María later realized that she reached maturity only that day, at that moment: she felt a concern entirely extrinsic to her own interests. She had not yet learned to love, but she had learned to hate, and, in doing so, felt ready for love.

Two weeks later, Doña Leonarda having been sent off to live with her sister in Sagua La Grande, María's plans were completed. They were drawn from the deep archives of contingency she had taken care to prepare. For this one, she had secured the cooperation of her old employer, Santos Trafficante, based now in Miami. Trafficante, six months before, had agreed, via one of the several agents who remained in Havana, to help her in the event María wished to leave. The plan was this: her grandfather, who fled Cuba when Castro arrived, had died, and in his will had repentantly specified a considerable bequest to his granddaughter, whose identity and whereabouts the grandfather did not know at the time he made out the document. He did not even know the name under which she went. But the estate's executor, using the old family lawyer in Havana (also Trafficante's), had developed leads that suggested that María Arguilla was indeed the heiress. She would need to satisfy an American probate court of her identity, and this would require that she go to Miami and be prepared to stay there for as long as six months, permitting the court independently to verify her representations. Worth the effort, however, since the bequest would amount to "at least one hundred thousand dollars."

María wrote Trafficante, and one week later received from a lawyer in Miami a letter detailing the fictitious situation and requesting that she travel to Miami.

She had been seeing Fidel every week, though at irregular intervals. Always it was Captain Durango who would drive up. Sometimes his knocking at the door would wake her at midnight, and even later: Fidel worked, and fornicated, into the early hours of the day. When Captain Durango summoned her next, she brought with her the letter from Miami.

She had pondered whether to make her request before or after he led her into the bedroom. She was experienced in male moods, and decided that Castro was better approached before than after, when his ardor was dissipated and instinctive suspicion coursed through his brain.

It hadn't, in fact, been difficult. Fidel was in an expansive mood. But he told her that he did not want her away from him for six months.

In that event, she said, she would endeavor to schedule her meetings with the court over convenient intervals. There was the logistical problem. She could only go to Miami via Mexico, commercial traffic of course having long since been terminated between Cuba and the United States. No matter: Money, Fidel replied, was not an obstacle. She could go, stay a week or two, and come back via Mexico—he reached into a drawer and handed her a packet of bills, one thousand pesos. "That will do for several trips, Havana-Mexico-Miami-Mexico-Havana." There would be no problem in getting a Mexican visa (he took out his notepad and scratched out a reminder on which he would act the following morning). She was to write him, telling him what progress she was making. He pulled a sheet of paper from his notepad, scribbled on it, and gave it to her. "That is a private post office number and an assumed name. Use them when you write to me."

"And now," he said, smiling, "there is one condition."

"Yes?" she smiled, as he fondled her.

"The movie. The movie you told me about. The movie Trafficante made of you at La Gallinera. I must have it. I wish to see again what I remember so vividly that evening before Moncada. We will watch it together, and then reenact the scene. You must find Trafficante. That will not be difficult. He is with the Mafia in Miami, and I am sure he will welcome revisiting his great star of yesterday. My star of today!" he added amorously.

She promised to make every effort to secure the film. "If it exists, Fidel."

"It exists," he said confidently. "People like Trafficante never destroy things like that. They are little capitalists, little hoarders. You will see." He led her into the bedroom.

THREE DAYS LATER, María had landed in Miami. Three days after that, she accepted the job as manager of La Bruja Vieja.

16

Major Rolando Cubela sometimes wondered ironically, as he sat at his desk at INRA—the Instituto Nacional de Reforma Agraria, the ganglion of Fidel Castro's administrative apparatus—whether if his neighbor at the adjacent desk cut his finger, Dr. Cubela would remember how to minister to him. For a year after Castro took power—eighteen months after Rolando Cubela had joined forces with him in the mountains, acting first as medical doctor but gradually more and more as aide—Cubela had thought from time to time of pulling up stakes and moving elsewhere to practice medicine. He enjoyed his frequent encounters with Che Guevara who, like Cubela, was a licensed medical doctor. Sometimes they would get away from the hectic demands of revolutionary thought, late in the afternoon, before an official function would absorb them both, to reminisce, or speculate, about one or another aspect of the practice of medicine.

Che Guevara's concern with medicine, however, was by now almost totally ideologized. He cared less how to cure someone suffering from a burst appendix than that the treatment should be the responsibility of the state; that no doctor should become wealthy by "the exploitation of human suffering." Feeling argumentative one day, Rolando said to him, "Che, when is the Revolution going to get around to nationalizing the morticians? Don't they also exploit human suffering?"

Che had puffed on his cigar, a half smile on his face, looking like Cantinflas pondering a question by David Niven on the problem of getting around the world in eighty days. Eventually he answered, "You have something there, Rolando. I must think about that. Yes. I must think about nationalizing the undertakers. Quite right. They exploit human suffering."

But when he looked up at Rolando he knew that his fellow medical doctor was making sport of the whole question, and Che Guevara went on to deliver a diatribe against the American Medical Association which, he said, was notoriously reactionary.

To husband his options, Rolando Cubela had kept free of enduring romantic alliances, which had been especially hard for him after he came to know Felipa Ojedra, the soft-spoken, modest, doe-eyed receptionist at INRA, who clearly welcomed Cubela's advances but was just as clearly determined to let Major Cubela take all the initiatives. It was not in Felipa's nature to act the vamp. But they kept company, frequently taking a quick lunch in the cafeteria and occasionally going out at night to a modest restaurant. On these occasions they never talked about the regime, and Rolando didn't know whether Felipa was an enthusiast for the Revolution. Perhaps she was simply doing a job, a job that not only paid well but gave her important perquisites in Castro's Cuba—access, for instance, to the Diplotiendas, where the select few could buy coffee and extra-conventional luxuries, such as a bar of scented soap imported from Canada, or a chocolate bar.

During the last three months of 1960, Rolando Cubela had thought most seriously about devising means of leaving the country with Felipa, always assuming she was prepared to take the risk, and he felt certain she was. Going then perhaps to Mexico, perhaps to Colombia or even Chile, associating himself with a hospital for a year or so, so to speak relearning his profession; raising a family and forgetting all about politics; in particular, forgetting about Fidel Castro.

Cubela suffered still from the memory of his assassination of Blanco Rico, and back in 1957, although a whole year had passed since he had done the deed, he had so worked himself up over his deed that he reported himself sick at an asylum that gave psychiatric care. Fidel, only recently arrived at the Sierra Maestra to wage his long and successful guerrilla campaign that ended with his arrival in Havana in January 1959, was especially distressed to learn about Cubela's incapacitation, relying on him as he did to minister medically to the 26th of July guerrillas but also to continue his work as one of the leaders of the Students' Revolutionary Directorate, to which position Cubela had been appointed after he had proved himself a true soldier of the revolution by carrying out his assignment on that bloody Sunday.

But Fidel had been reassured by Ramiro Valdés. Valdés reminded Fidel that Cubela was a young doctor, accustomed to hospital and city life. He had been moved to the mountains where he faced extreme physical hardships—traveling every day in jungle heat and freezing at night from the mountain cold, protecting himself and others from snakebite and maneuvering with Castro's guerrillas to evade what so often threatened them, a terminal campaign against the Castro insurgents. You cannot, he lectured his comrade-in-arms, expect an essentially clerical man to get used to such a life automatically.

Before going off to Sierra Maestra to fight with Castro, Cubela had, of course, taken great pains to hide his double life. As far as the hospital was concerned, with which now as a full-fledged doctor he had affiliated himself, he was simply Dr. Rolando Cubela, a private practitioner who was often away on extensive visits to Oriente Province where—who knows, he had other medical patients, family, a sweetheart, whatever; no one pried, and Rolando Cubela had no regular social contacts and no intimates. When he reported himself to the private clinic he was sympathetically and discreetly received, as all doctors suffering from mental stress were received, and ninety days later he was discharged, at his own request.

During those ninety days he came to terms with himself. He decided that he could not expiate the sin he had committed against an innocent man until he had undertaken a great and heroic task of redemption. What this would be, he did not know. Meanwhile, although he would never condone Fidel Castro's perverse decision to assassinate Blanco Rico, the job at hand was to depose Fulgencio Batista, and to give Fidel Castro an opportunity to rebuild Cuba.

By the fall of 1958 there were fewer and fewer references, in Castro's camp, to "Dr." Cubela, more and more to Major Cubela. He was an important aide to Castro, especially in his role as principal in charge of the pro-Castro student movement. He communicated with covert student revolutionary leaders mostly through intermediaries, but occasionally he would depart the mountains and meet with them personally. He was known to them only as *Padrino*, Godfather. Padrino had organized the students for a major strike early in January 1959. It proved not necessary: On January 1, 1959, Batista fled Cuba.

Rolando's job became now not the organization of an insurgent student movement, but the coordination and direction of an organization of student leaders explicitly and in most cases devoutly pro-Castro. His technical superior was Haydée Santamaría, sister of the brave man tortured to death during the Moncada fiasco of 1953, when Castro led the quixotic charge against the well-fortified barracks at Santiago de Cuba, at the time co-leader, with Castro, of the anti-Batista movement. But mostly Rolando Cubela was whatever Fidel Castro wished him to be, doing whatever Fidel wished him to do at an administrative level. He was widely envied as one of the true intimates of the supreme leader.

And one of Castro's requests—it came in the spring of 1962—was that Cubela go to the penal colony on the Isla de Pinos, 100 miles south of central Havana, to talk with Cubela's old medical tutor, Alvaro Nueces. Dr. Nueces had turned against Castro in 1960, protesting the communization of the 26th of July Movement. He had narrowly escaped the firing squad at La Cabaña, and was sentenced instead to thirty years' imprisonment. Alvaro Nueces had been recognized as the leading administrative pharmacologist in Cuba. During the late fifties he had devoted himself to the task of accurately estimating Cuba's need for special drugs and accumulating inventories sufficient to cope with any national emergency that might arise. It was Dr. Nueces who had begun to organize, through a data processing system, tables of reserves, not only of drugs but also of blood. His card system permitted the flow of drugs to go as required from hospital to hospital, always making him aware where and by what amount reserves could be tapped.

With his imprisonment this system had collapsed, refusing to respond to unfamiliar, let alone inept, hands. The ensuing shortage of critical drugs had become not merely acute but the cause of festering public dissatisfaction as, day after day, Cubans died for want of drugs prescribed for their care. Haydée Santamaría, who regarded the people's medical care as a primary revolutionary portfolio, the responsibility of the entire Cabinet, finally went to Fidel. She had known him longer than anyone in his entourage save his brother, had sheltered him in her house before the Moncada affair, and always spoke to him forthrightly.

Her message was that they needed the cooperation of Alvaro Nueces, and that the likeliest person to get it was Rolando Cubela, who not only had known and studied under Nueces, but had indeed entered the revolutionary movement in part under Nueces's sponsorship. Above all, she emphasized, they needed Nueces now. It had been decided, in an early negotiation with the American lawyer James Donovan, that the ransom Cuba would demand in return for the liberation of the Bay of Pigs prisoners was a large shipment of drugs in scarce supply in Cuba. It was exceedingly important that the drugs be intelligently selected, with reference, for instance, to what could not readily be gotten from the Soviet Union or from other countries with which Cuba continued to trade. Nobody knew the field like Nueces.

So, at ten one morning, Rolando Cubela was aboard one of the biweekly transport planes to the Isla de Pinos carrying supplies, as well as forty guards sent to relieve counterparts.

It was a very hot day and the ocean wind blew sand into their faces as they drove from the apron at the little airport at Nueva Gerona to the great iron gates leading into the circular prison. Cubela shielded himself with a handkerchief. With his right hand he lowered the visor on his military cap.

Entering the headquarters building of the prison with the returning guards, he indicated to the official at the desk that he had a message for the prison's commandant, Major Almandriz. He displayed his credentials.

The commandant's office was twenty degrees cooler than the suffocating temperature within the prison. Rolando Cubela gulped the cool air greedily, taking off his hat and wiping the sweat from his face. The commandant crossed the room to extend a limp hand. He was short as a gnome, dark-skinned and bleary-eyed. He indicated a chair and rang a bell at the side of his desk. An attendant in stiff white jacket appeared. "You will have coffee, Major Cubela?" Cubela nodded. Almandriz raised two fingers. Coffee for two. The attendant nodded his head and withdrew.

"I am here on orders from the Revolutionary Government to interview the prisoner Dr. Alvaro Nueces. The Government desires him to cooperate on an important medical problem. I have been deputized to attempt to secure that cooperation in return for a conditional pardon."

"May I, Major, examine your papers?"

"Of course." Cubela handed the letter from Haydée Santamaría, stamped with the approval of Interior Minister Ramiro Valdés, among other things, superintendent of the prison system.

Major Almandriz was clearly disturbed. He cleared his throat protractedly, as if accumulating phlegm to expel. He said nothing, but pulled open a deep drawer in his desk, flicked through the contents, withdrawing a sheet of paper which he studied. While reading he said only, "The main files on the prisoners are kept . . . elsewhere. I have here only the . . . well, bare outlines.

"I am afraid," he said, clearing his throat, "that you cannot see the prisoner Nueces today. He is sick. You should have given me a few days' notice."

Rolando Cubela stood up. He hadn't liked his host from the moment he set eyes on him. "I do not give a shit what you say Dr. Nueces is suffering from. I am not here to discuss your convenience in this or in any other matter. Take me directly to Nueces or put in a call in my name to the Minister of the Interior."

Almandriz bit his lips, said nothing. There was a moment's silence. Then he depressed a buzzer on his desk and a sergeant, first knocking lightly on the door, entered the room.

"Sir?"

"Take our guest to the prisoner Alvaro Nueces. He is"— Almandriz looked down again at his paper—"in Galera sixteen."

Cubela gave a slight nod of the head and followed the sergeant, who had to dodge the steward coming in with the tray of coffee.

They walked down iron grate steps two flights, then through a long, dank corridor. To the right and left were cell doors with small apertures at eye level. The only sounds were occasional moans and what sounded like somnambulists' soliloquies. Cubela looked directly ahead, concentrating on the sergeant's methodical movement toward his destination.

They turned a corner into a similar corridor, again with cells at either end. The lighting from bare electric light bulbs every twenty or thirty feet was dimness itself, but there was enough light to illuminate the number 16. The sergeant signaled to a guard sitting at a table under one of the lights, and motioned to the door. "Open it."

The door to number 16 was unlocked.

The sergeant called out: "Prisoner Nueces, present yourself."

A voice frail of sound but resonant of purpose came from the black void.

"Whoever wants to see me can see me here."

The sergeant said, "Prisoner Nueces, there is an official visitor to see you. Come out immediately or I shall need to have the guards escort you out."

The voice said, "Do as you like. My visitor can see me here or not at all."

Rolando Cubela at that point yanked the flashlight from the sergeant's belt, switched it on, and walked into the cell. He stepped into a mound of human feces. He could barely discern the bodies, to his right and to his left, lying, crowded, on wooden shelves, it seemed. There were others on the floor, some lying, some squatting. He ran the light around the bearded faces that peered blinkingly back at him—there was no light in the Galera save a shaft that came in obliquely from a small circular opening, high above, illuminating a bucket-sized circle at one end of the cell.

Cubela called out hoarsely. "Alvaro, it's me, Rolando Cubela."

A hand directly on his right reached out, touching him on the sleeve. "Rolando."

Cubela reached down and circled his arms under the shoulders of the prisoner and strained to raise him to his feet. He half-pulled, half-dragged him toward the door. Reaching the corridor, he snapped to the sergeant. "Get a stretcher. Quick!" The sergeant relayed the order to the guard, and presently two men appeared with the stretcher. Nueces was placed on it.

"Take us to the clinic," Cubela said. Obediently, they marched off. During the walk Nueces said nothing. Turning a corner, a guard opened a door with the key and entered what seemed a floodlit room. A medical dispensary. Nueces was placed on an examining table. Cubela looked down and examined his old proctor for the first time. He took a deep breath.

At once, Rolando Cubela was an intern again. He put on a lab coat, took bandage scissors, and slowly cut off the patient's sweat- and mud-stained prison uniform with the black "P" on the back, the designation reserved for political prisoners. He ordered warm water and soap. A half hour later, after washing and cleaning the naked body from head to toe, he ordered a straight razor and shaving soap. He then took the pulse beat, listened to his heart and lungs with a stethoscope, and looked into Alvaro's eyes.

He eased the older man off the examining table on which he had been deposited and sat him down in the only armchair in the room. There were now five people in attendance, including the prison doctor, who had at last appeared. They followed Cubela's orders. Early on he had grunted, "I am, in addition to a major attached to the Directorate, a medical doctor." He ordered a blood workup and chest X ray and electrocardiogram. He then told a nurse to bring hot soup and bread.

Nueces was conscious throughout the hour but said nothing. When the tray was brought in, Cubela addressed the prison doctor. "Take us into a private room."

"You may use my own office, Major."

"Thank you."

They sat there together behind the closed door for two hours.

A knock on the door by the second-in-command of Los Pinos finally interrupted them. "Major Cubela, you must come. The aircraft is due to leave in twenty minutes."

Rolando Cubela emerged from the doctor's office. He was pale. The prison doctor was hovering outside.

"What is your name, Doctor?"

"Angel Salvador, *a sus órdenes*, Major."

"I hold you personally responsible, Dr. Salvador, for the return of Dr. Alvaro Nueces to good health. You will be hearing from me. Or from Ministro Ramiro Valdés."

Without further word he walked out.

Three hours later he stormed into the office of Haydée Santamaría. He spoke angrily. "First," he said, "let me tell you what Nueces said in response to our request. What he said was that he would not cooperate with—with Castro's regime in *any* way, at *any* time, under *any* circumstances."

Haydée Santamaría said nothing. "That's all there is to report, Rolando?"

"No, that isn't all there is to report. What there is to report beyond that I am going to report to Fidel. What there is to report is that Pinos is a disgrace, a hideous scar on the integrity of our movement. The comandante—Almandriz—should be executed. A new set of guards should be sent there with explicit instructions."

"You must calm yourself, Rolando," Haydée said, herself attempting calm. "Of course, you have a point. Why don't you write a careful report—a *careful* report." She repeated and caressed the word. "Go ahead, do it now. There is a typewriter in the room you can use. Then we will concentrate on the problem. It is very disappointing news that Nueces will not cooperate, very disappointing news."

Cubela was about to say that he could hardly blame Dr. Nueces, but suddenly he stopped. It was as though that shaft of prison light had reached him here. Here, after all, in the office of the ministry directly in charge of all the prisons in Cuba, it was hardly conceivable that Haydée Santamaría was entirely ignorant of what life was like at the Isla de Pinos.

He sat down methodically to write out the report he had officially commissioned. As he tapped out his message, the epiphany crystallized. He found himself using now the detached clinical vocabulary of the pathologist, rather than expressing the rage of the reformer. As he progressed, a great clarity came. He found himself taking grim satisfaction in the words he was now composing. He typed as if his fingers were ice picks. "My conclusions are that there is only one way in which to deal with the prisoner Nueces, who has refused to come to the aid of his country in these critical circumstances. I recommend that he be tried, and forthwith executed." He had done it to Blanco Rico and now he had done it to Alvaro Nueces. But it was the kindest deed he could perform for his old, sick, tormented professor: give him peace. And Rolando Cubela was guided by a single light. His redemptive mission was incandescently clear. He, Rolando Cubela, would kill Fidel Castro.

17

Castro, returned from Moscow, gave his political intimates, on the night after his arrival, an account of his trip. He preceded it with the exhibit of a 16-millimeter film assembled by his hosts, a roundup of The Fidel Castro Visit. There were scenes of Fidel arriving at the airport at Murmansk, of Fidel riding in a motorcade side by side with Khrushchev, right into the sacred, mysterious walls of the Kremlin; scenes of Fidel standing between Khrushchev and Malinovsky in the most honored spot, atop the Lenin Monument, surveying the May Day Parade, mile after mile of Soviet military strength parading before the camera's adoring eyes; scenes of Fidel visiting the great Space Center, of Fidel peering into the prototype of the Sputnik that first circled the globe that electric day in 1957; scenes of Fidel visiting happy Communist communes in the Ukraine, factory workers in Kiev, schoolchildren in Leningrad; scenes, finally, of Fidel at the airport, toasting to the success of the Soviet revolution, "a revolution which, like that of Mao Tse-tung, will inspire others for years, for centuries ahead."

There was scattered applause among the dozen intimates Fidel had invited to his personal screening of a documentary that in a matter of hours would flood Cuban television. The following morning he would give a major speech on continued Soviet-Cuban amity, and Castro had alerted Radio Havana to set aside three hours, as he "would have a good deal to say."

It was Che Guevara who asked the first question. "How did Khrushchev react to your mention of Mao Tse-tung?"

Fidel was delighted. "Ah, Che, you have, as always, the keenest political ear. It was, of course, my—Cuba's—declaration of independence. Five weeks of intensive wooing of Castro by Khrushchev, and then—that! In all the sessions we had together, no direct allusions were made to our overtures to China. But I thought all along that if I merely *mentioned* China—merely made a single tribute to the noble socialist experiments of Mao—I would make my point, my point being"—Fidel Castro had clutched his speech into oratorical gear. It might as well have been tomorrow, speaking to the thousands of Cubans packed into the Plaza de la Revolución—"that the Cuba of Fidel Castro honors the great socialist endeavors not only of the Soviet Union, but also of the People's Republic of China."

He paused now, and his voice lowered. "Of course, we need to be aware of the continuing special contributions by the Soviet Union to Cuba. In private conversations I did not disguise this. To Khrushchev I said that the embargo by the United States needed to be compensated for, so that Soviet purchases of Cuban sugar, at an . . . agreeable . . . price were very welcome, as also, of course, continued Soviet investments in defensive weapons."

Che interrupted him. "Did you get into the subject of Khrushchev's unilateral actions last October on the missiles?"

Castro was now Professor of International Diplomacy, conducting a seminar for graduate students. "No, Che. After all, the invitation issued to me to go to Moscow came after the publication of my interview with *Le Monde*, and that interview was, to use a popular American legal expression, a 'brooding omnipresence' during my visit. Khrushchev knew that he had behaved without fraternal concern for Cuba's independence when, without consulting with us, he agreed to withdraw the missiles. He knew that I disapproved of that action, knew that I would always disapprove of that action. So what, really, was there to discuss? I mean, why suddenly appear in Moscow and repeat what I had publicly stated?

"But my genial reference at the airport to the work of Mao Tse-tung made my point as distinctly as it could ever be made. What my speech at the airport said was: Khrushchev, we are admiring of the Soviet Union, we are grateful for the aid you are giving us to realize our own socialist revolution, but we cannot be conscripted into the ranks of your sectarian wars against Mao. I think"—Castro spoke at this moment in his self-effacing mode, into which he infrequently lapsed, though never without full confidence that the full significance of his political artistry would be appreciated by his audience—"I think that I accomplished both purposes in my trip: proper credit to the Soviet Union, together with a subtle reminder that Cuba is an independent socialist entity."

The effect of this peroration was slightly marred by Che's aside, directed not so much at Castro directly as to the assembly. "Well, our independence would perhaps be more convincing if we relied less completely than we are forced to do on Soviet economic and military favors."

Castro ignored this, and informed his guests that he would need to spend a little time preparing his speech for the next day, and therefore he wished them to stay a half hour to partake of the refreshments ready for them next door in the dining room, after which he would need to excuse himself, which was Fidel's way of announcing that in one-half hour, they should all be gone.

They ate heartily, drank moderately, and departed promptly. A few minutes after they were gone, Castro's telephone rang. It was the lieutenant at the gate of INRA. "Comandante, I have here Captain Ingenio Tamayo, who says you have requested his visit."

"Yes," Castro said. "I neglected to advise you to expect him. Escort him to my quarters."

Castro was sitting at his desk when Tamayo came in. He did not stand up, acknowledging Tamayo's greeting only with a nod of his head and a gesture beckoning him to sit down on a chair opposite.

He opened the folder on his desk. Saying nothing, he reread the sections he had marked up that morning, after a few hours' sleep recovering from his nonstop trip, Murmansk-Havana, in Aeroflot's TU-114 turboprop.

"Ah, Ingenio, I have been catching up on American anti-Castro activity during my absence. A fat portfolio, you can imagine."

Tamayo laughed, as he was expected to do.

Castro puffed on his cigar. "Yes, they do not let a week go by, do they?

"But this item is of unusual interest," he said. "And for

reasons that will be obvious, I intend that the matter should be *entirely* confidential. That is why I called you."

Tamayo accepted his cue. He said, "I will never betray your confidence, Comandante. You can bank your life on that."

"I will bank my life on nothing, my dear Tamayo, not even on my mother's word. But I trust you, and you have undertaken delicate missions for me in the past."

"I am always at your orders, Comandante."

"You are aware of Senator Kenneth Keating, the imperialist senator from New York State?"

"Yes, Comandante. I am aware of his anti-Cuban record."

"I have noted here," Castro looked down at his folder, "that Senator Keating has raised the question—no. Not *raised* the question. He has *flatly alleged* that the Soviet Union did not in fact withdraw all their missiles last October. He said, in a speech to the U.S. Senate, that there was evidence that there was a missile left. He did not, of course, give out the name of his informant. But we must bear in mind that he has informants of demonstrated reliability. It was this Keating, this warmonger, who, a month before their official discovery last October by the American U-2's, insisted that the Soviet Union had planted several batteries of missiles in Cuba. He was of course correct, but we never discovered who his informants were.

"Now, one month ago, I learn from this material, a certain Ramón Luminante, a Cuban traitor who fled to Miami, alleged at a counterrevolutionary rally in Miami that he had personally *seen* a medium-range ballistic missile. The question of this Cuban's allegation was apparently raised at a hearing of a U.S. Senate subcommittee, and Secretary McNamara has said that the allegation was completely unwarranted, and evidently his word was accepted because, so far as I can see," Castro's eyes wandered once again over the material in his folder, "there has been no follow-up to that charge. The Senate subcommittee was evidently satisfied that they were merely looking at one more of the hysterical charges of the Cuban traitors against our regime.

"But now, one," Castro put on his glasses and checked the date on two of the papers on his desk, "one whole month later, along comes Senator Keating making his speech, reiterating that charge. You will have guessed, I can safely assume, Ingenio, what it is that I have called on you to look into?"

"Yes, Comandante. You wish a search for a hypothetical Soviet missile to be discreetly conducted. Are there any clues? Did the traitor in the first instance detail where he said he saw such a missile?"

"No. But between this morning and tonight, I ordered our Intelligence—and I did this without consulting Valdés; I wish to maintain total confidentiality in this affair—to inform me on where the traitor Luminante was stationed during the period when he was in the Army. He was trained at Campamento Militar de Columbia, he then had a tour of duty at San Cristóbal. He then was transferred to Bahía Honda. Now neither Campamento Columbia nor Bahía Honda was ever a site for the Soviet missiles. On the other hand, San Cristóbal was."

"You wish me to conduct an inspection at San Cristóbal?"

"Yes, I do. But I regret your using that word. You must bear in mind that we have in Cuba right now twenty thousand Soviet military technicians. They are indispensable to our defense. They are engaged in receiving Soviet matériel, assembling it, conveying it to various locations, some of them secret, some of them not secret, and training our personnel in the use of it. In the hidden locations—for instance within certain caves, and there is a very large cave at San Cristóbal—they maintain our MIG fighters, our tanks, our anti-aircraft missiles. They are indispensable to the national effort. For that reason, you cannot simply go to San Cristóbal and announce that you are there on my orders to conduct, so to speak, a body search of the military base to establish whether there is, hidden underground, a remaining missile or missiles, which, I should add, I very much doubt that there is, because the Americans conducted a very strict aerial surveillance of the Soviet retreat, and because it is inconceivable that Khrushchev should have authorized any such subterfuge without—well, without *my* authorization."

Tamayo permitted himself a laugh. "I remember, Comandante, when President Kennedy said in his speech that he would demand a personal inspection of the missile sites to satisfy himself that they had been removed, you delivered that glorious riposte."

Castro smiled, puffing on his cigar. "Yes," he said, "the only satisfaction I had during that unpleasant week was saying no American would be permitted within the boundaries of Cuba to inspect the empty missile sites, 'except Mrs. Kennedy, who is always welcome.'"

Tamayo laughed heartily. "That was a fine moment, Comandante."

"Well, it worked. The inspection point was never pressed. The Americans relied on their U-2 planes to count, one by one, the repatriation of forty-two missiles. And the question, of course, is: Did they miscount? Did the Soviets withdraw not forty-two, but perhaps forty-one missiles? Or forty? Or thirty-nine? Or: Did they in fact plant within Cuba *more* than the forty-two missiles they spoke to me about? And if so, where are those that remain in Cuba? Needless to say, this was not a question I asked Khrushchev during our recent . . . amenities."

"But San Cristóbal is your principal suspicion, Comandante?"

"I have no 'principal suspicion,' Ingenio. At this moment I do not personally believe that there are any missiles left in Cuba. But I would be derelict if I did not inquire into the charge made by this Keating who—no disputing this—has very effective informants. His charge, combined with that of the traitor Luminante, suggests that San Cristóbal is the place to begin looking. If you find nothing there, you must go also to Guanajay, Sagua la Grande, and Remedios. Now, when you arrive at San Cristóbal, be aware that there are several hundred Soviet technicians there, doing very useful work. There were two kinds of missiles planned for us in October, the SANDAL, whose range is a mere eleven hundred miles, and the SKEAN, whose range is twenty-two hundred miles. Both missiles," Castro handed Tamayo a separate folder, "are for all intents and purposes the same size. The SKEAN is," Castro peeked at the memo, "to be sure, 2.5 meters in diameter, compared to 1.6 meters for the SANDAL. But a hidden SANDAL would present pretty much the same problems as would confront a hidden SKEAN." Castro laughed. He pointed to his cigar. "If this cigar were twenty-one meters long, and if it needed, in order to be activated, a transfusion of energy in the form of liquid oxygen and whatever else is needed to launch it, then it too would require a commodious underground berth. It is alleged, in effect, that there are one or more Soviet missiles lodged beneath the storage level of the missiles we became familiar with last year. If there is a hidden missile, it must sit underneath the level at which the other missiles were berthed. In order to be effective, such a missile would need to lie in a cradle that would be elevated to a surface firing posture. That means," Castro said, using his cigar as an academic pointer and looking up as though to a blackboard, "that the accompanying features of a missile ready or near-ready to function would need to be nearby."

"The accompanying features?" Tamayo asked.

"Both the SANDAL and the SKEAN, before they could fire, would need an ingestion of LOX. This is not on the order of injecting them with a hypodermic needle. We are talking about tons of liquid oxygen energy, which is a highly volatile substance, and also tons of special kerosene. At least four technicians would be involved in such an operation alone. My immediate point is that not only the underground hidden missile is involved, but also accompaniments: the staff, and the men to fuel, service, arm, and aim it. What, exactly, they look like, I do not know, but you may need to make it your business to find out. This is not by any means an easy job. There is so much ordnance at each one of our great cave sites, sheltering planes, tanks, artillery, that one truck containing the liquid oxygen would not by any means stand out, especially if it were camouflaged so as to make it apparently useful to serve other purposes. If indeed the senator, Keating, and the traitor Luminante are correct, we must assume that all the auxiliary apparatus is well concealed, which makes your investigation more difficult."

Castro put down his cigar and fixed his eyes now directly on Tamayo's. "Here, Ingenio, is where you must use extra care. On no account can you raise any suspicion whatever as to the purpose of your visit to San Cristóbal. If it turns out by any chance that there is such a missile, Fidel Castro desires two things: one, to know where it is; and two, that the Soviet Union and the United States not know that I know that it exists. If it—they—exist, then I will make my plans. But until then, nothing—*nothing*—is to reach Soviet ears, especially anything that suggests any Cuban curiosity on the subject.

"You will go to San Cristóbal as a military officer whose mission it is to coordinate with other military centers the timetable for the assembly of the airplanes, tanks, and anti-aircraft pieces. You will proceed not with direct orders from me—that would lay the grounds for suspicion. You will have routine orders from Comandante Raúl Castro. But those orders will give you the run of the base. I do not desire to inform my brother about your mission, and accordingly I shall arrange for appropriate papers to be issued tomorrow of a kind that might routinely go out without his knowing about them. Major Rolando Cubela, well known to you, who attends to much of my confidential work, will see to it that those papers exist by Wednesday morning. Your job is to don your old uniform, promote yourself to major, pick up the papers from Major Cubela, who knows about our collaboration but not its purpose, and be off."

Major Tamayo professed his most effusive thanks for his promotion, so casually tendered.

Castro reached into his desk. "There will be incidental expenses, and perhaps some special expenses: the Russian military are not by any means insensible to the uses of cash money."

Fidel opened the bottom drawer and came up with two bundles of money. "Here are one thousand Cuban pesos, and one thousand American dollars. They may prove useful. Here"—Castro scratched out a number on a sheet of paper—"is a telephone number through which you can reach me. Do not use it except as an emergency. You know how to reach me for purposes of making an appointment. *Vaya con Dios.*"

Fidel Castro had never succeeded in expunging from his own or others' use the traditional Cuban valedictory that one should go forward with God.

18

Larry Fillmore would never say about Wild Bill Hicock that his failures owing to a Technicolored imagination were traceable to carelessness in respect of detail. Larry was himself Mr. Discretion professionally, but early on in his dealings with the Agency he had decided that he would permit himself—that he *must* permit himself—that single exception to The Rules, rules which he fervently believed in and devoutly practiced. The rule in question was, simply put, that in covert action, no one who did not need to know could be permitted to know.

But when Larry Fillmore was recruited for service in the Agency at age twenty-four he was freshly married, and Ruth—to use his own words, uttered during their honeymoon—continued to be "my wife, my mistress, and my confidante."

She was a tall, redheaded, sun-kissed, energetic wife, mother, lover, and administrator. Ruth had been a student at the Wharton Business School when they first met. She often made fun of the protocols of corporate detail and organization, in which she was instructed and in which courses she distinguished herself; she was, however lightheartedly, amused by what she called the "mystique of capitalist organization." Nevertheless she understood the discipline and the reasons for it. When Larry proposed marriage, she found herself, Wharton-style, writing down the affirmatives and the negatives of marriage to Larry Fillmore. Although she knew that, whatever the table's bottom line recommended as the prudent option, she was going to marry Larry Fillmore and that she would do so with the passionate conviction that that was what she wanted to do, she would still write out the table, like a dutiful soldier of organizational fortune.

The affirmatives were pretty routine. Yes, she wanted to marry. Yes, she wished to have a family. Yes, Larry Fillmore had all the qualifications of the man she desired to marry: He was attractive romantically (he was alluring and handsome) and professionally (he was in the Foreign Service, was obviously upwardly mobile); he spoke French and German, he was bright and studious, he was lively and imaginative, he was by nature a monogamous type. Sure, Larry had "known" other women, as the biblical idiom so chastely put it. But she knew that when, of all places on the subway in New York, bound for Fifty-seventh Street to hear Rosalyn Tureck play the Goldberg Variations at Carnegie Hall, he stuttered out his proposal of marriage, he had not made such a proposal before to any other woman. She pressed his free hand with hers while they stood, each with one hand on the aluminum stanchions they relied on to maintain their balance. She knew instantly what her answer would be. Even so, at her little apartment, shared with a fellow graduate of Wharton, that night she would write out the table of Advantages/Disadvantages and force herself to reflect on them. The following morning, interviewed by General Electric for a junior executive position to which she aspired, she found herself answering, in reply to the question, Was she prepared to think of General Electric as her true vocation in life? "Well, sir, that in fact depends. Because if I get married, I will need to decide whether the plans General Electric has formed are compatible with those my husband has in mind." She might as well have said to her interviewer that her loyalty to General Electric would depend on Westinghouse's convenience. The official looked at her with bewilderment and disapproval deep-frozen in his face. He paused, and concluded the interview by telling her that she would hear in due course whether she was "quite what General Electric has in mind" for the job.

She entered that datum in her Negative/Affirmative table that night, and when she was done, the Negatives quite overwhelmed the Positives. She laughed, tore the table up, called Larry on the telephone, and said, Yes, she would marry him.

When Larry Fillmore told his superior in the Agency that he had become engaged, he was told that on no account could he reveal to his fiancée what his actual affiliation was, that he must continue to affect to be a Foreign Service trainee. The instructions he was receiving in safe houses in New York, to be followed by instructions in Washington, were to be held strictly confidential.

"How long before I can tell my fiancée what my work actually is?"

"The answer to that is simple: Never. You will be permitted to tell her that you are associated with the Agency, but only after we have done a clearance on her."

When, Larry had asked, might that be?

The bureaucratic burden of the work that needed to be done (was the answer) would take a good while, because there was a considerable backlog, and there would need to be an FBI check of some detail on his wife. "And since you are a deep-cover agent, the questions that need to be asked are necessarily more difficult to pose. I mean, we can't very well go to her college roommate and say, 'Is Ruth Williams a loyal American?' We need to go about these matters in an . . . oblique way."

"Well, how long will it take?"

"About a year."

That night, 364 days in advance of her projected clearance, Larry told Ruth that he was a deep-cover agent of the Central Intelligence Agency. Did that, he asked, make a critical difference in her decision to marry him?

No, she had answered promptly. "But it would make a deep difference to me if, in our married life, I am not permitted to know what you are doing, what your problems are, and what is concerning you."

Larry found himself replying without any misgivings: "You will always know—everything."

He had entered only the single unspoken qualification: *Anything except that which, by your knowing it, would put you in danger.* She sensed that he had made a mental reservation. And she added, "What might endanger me is what I would especially insist on knowing."

Only then had there been obvious hesitation. But he yielded, maintaining within himself the single qualification that he would not *unnecessarily* expose her to danger. They were married the following month.

Ruth Williams, as far as her family and friends were concerned, was marrying a Foreign Service trainee, at this point in his career, leaving New York for Washington.

Eight years later, Larry was discussing with Ruth the pains Wild Bill was taking to ensure the security of arrangements involving the return of María Arguilla to Havana. More particularly, to her precise destination—the bed of Fidel Castro. Wild Bill had spent the better part of the week canvassing every contingency. Sitting at the kitchen table as Ruth served the TV dinner, together with fresh fruit and an ingeniously selected inexpensive wine, Larry outlined the details to Ruth.

"Most important," Larry said, "is sustaining the plausibility of the original deception: Why she went to Miami. Remember: When María went to Miami, all she knew was that she couldn't stand *him* any longer, and that, to avenge her friend Doña Leonarda, if she could, she would kill him herself. She wanted, needed to be, out of town. She was ripe, from our point of view: the right person, all set, who just needed recruiting. Our people picked up the scent. Our guy—Pano—got to her, and from there on it was only a question of: How do we do it?

"She's a hell of a bright lady, and nothing WB proposed was okayed without her closest attention. The one thing we had to go on was her assurance that Fidel wanted her back, and would tolerate unanticipated delays in her getting back. The problem always was the plausibility of her prolonged absence. WB has done a pretty good job here, as far as I can see. María has a folder full of legal documents, records of appearances before the probate judge (who is one of ours). Letters written to her asking for birth certificates, asking for every conceivable detail about her mother, where she was married, hospital records, baptismal records. Then there are copies of letters written by María to her lawyer in Havana (also one of ours), copies of that lawyer's answers—all of this consuming a hell of a lot of time, all of it strung out with fierce-sounding judicial deadlines for answers that would have made it impossible for María to return to Havana for an extended visit.

"Then there are intentionally obscure notes in the folder— when exactly she wrote her little love notes to Castro about the reasons for her protracted absence. Inscrutable to anyone reading the file who was unaware of the context of those notes. But just the kind of thing that would pass inspection if any of Castro's agents, or even Castro himself, was examining the file to see if everything fitted. For instance, María wrote to Castro on March 30, 1962, saying that the unexpected judicial delay necessitated her taking a job, since she couldn't afford to just sit in Miami and wait for lawyers in Havana to answer letters providing the information the probate people in Miami were insisting on.

"It's been over a year since she left Havana, and she's heard personally from Castro a total of three times. Twice was indirectly, by telephone. A Castro agent in Miami called María and said that he had a message from 'your friend.' These messages didn't amount to much. All he said was that his 'client' hoped all was going well, and did she need any help in order to get passage back to Havana? She did get one letter from Castro. She has that, and it isn't a part of the file she is keeping, but she has that letter, and it is—I haven't actually seen the letter, nor has WB, but he told us María reported it was just a 'routine love letter.' But in the letter he reiterated his ardent desire that when she returns, she bring 'your little secret film.'

"She answered that letter by saying that Trafficante had promised her that if she finished the year as the manager of his restaurant, he would give her the film. She promised that just as soon as she completed the legal formalities in Miami, she would have the film and would be free to return to Havana."

"What about the money? The money she is supposed to inherit? Is WB planning to give her the money, or will the story be that the probate court wasn't satisfied with her identity?"

"Wild Bill wrestled with that one with the people upstairs. He was resolute on the point—that the money must *actually* be turned over to her. Makes the whole enterprise *feel* legitimate. The Agency wasn't all that happy about putting that kind of dough in her private account, but WB insisted. And after all, if there is a happy ending to all of this, she is expected to give the money back. WB managed to get from her a will—he has the only copy—leaving the money, in case of her death, to a gentleman called Ulysses Sameron, a.k.a. Uncle Sam.

"Anyway, next week, April twenty-ninth, the probate is scheduled to rule in her favor, and ninety-five thousand eight hundred dollars will be deposited in her account at the Barnett

Bank. She will of course have a record of that deposit, and a copy of her letter to the bank instructing it to buy U.S. bonds. That's when she writes Castro and says: 'Hooray hooray, the First of May/ Outdoor fucking begins today!' Then she drops just a little hint of Do-you-really-want-me? dear, as I am so anxious to see you, but you are so busy with world affairs. I mean, I know all about your visit to Moscow and everything that must have piled up for you. . . .

"The scenario obviously calls for him telling her, either in a personal letter or through his telephone spook, 'Yes, *darling María*, I want you back in my bed not because you are now worth one hundred thousand dollars more, or because you have a 16-millimeter film of wonderful home entertainment, but because I desire you almost as much as I desire the nationalization of Havana's kiosks.' What we assume will happen then is that she will make reservations to go back to Havana, that she will get the visa in Mexico City—yes, returning Cubans actually need a visa to go to Cuba. At some point she is likely to be put through the grill, we figure. I doubt it will be in Miami, though God knows Castro has enough people there to do it, but obviously it's harder there. They *may* do it in Miami just the same, on the grounds that it would be easier to check the American end of her story: easier to check the bank account, the probate judge, etc. Or they may do it in Mexico—in which case there would be a delay while she cooled her heels there while they checked. Or? They may wait until she gets to Havana, do the check there. We don't know. But it shouldn't make any difference."

"Is it your guess," Ruth probed, "that Castro would shrug his shoulders if she got miffed? Suppose she got through to him and said, 'If you don't trust me, to hell with you. And you'll never get to see my movie, or to play the part of Romeo.' "

"María is a professional. I mean, nobody since Nana has had more experience than she at knowing just what she can say to a lover: when and exactly what. WB thinks it best to leave that to her instincts. What we worry about—what *I* worry about (Wild Bill doesn't worry about anything except maybe a total eclipse when he's about to shoot a hole in one)—is just that one thing."

"The cold cream?"

"The cold cream. And what's in the cold cream."

Ruth paused. "I know you say WB has told you the pills are guaranteed to work. Tasteless. Dead-four-hours-after-swallowing-them, yet no-sensation-of-any-kind-for-three-hours. But what else is involved? I mean, she's in that suite of his, she arrived with her little packet of toiletries. No surprise there; she's been doing that every time since her first visit. So he isn't surprised. So they go to the bedroom and do it. So then she goes to the bathroom and pulls out the Big Pill. So what's she actually supposed to say then? 'Fidel, darling, you sound hoarse. You've been giving too many speeches. Here are some wonderful pills they've invented in Miami for people who give three-hour speeches'?"

Larry smiled, not without a trace of anxiety. "María tells us that after lovemaking he inevitably drinks something. Sometimes it's a shot of rum and Coca-Cola, sometimes it's plain Coca-Cola—which by the way was becoming pretty scarce at the time María left Havana, she told us, but Castro had his own private supply and presumably it's inexhaustible. Sometimes he drinks just plain water. And sometimes he rings for hot coffee. Still other times he reaches into the little refrigerator that sits in the dressing room and grabs a cold beer."

"That doesn't sound good, if sometimes he fends for himself."

"María has a plan. At the appropriate moment she says, 'Fidel, I feel like a cold beer, a beautiful Havana beer. I haven't had one in almost a full year. Can I have one, and get you one while I'm at it?' Her guess is he'll say sure—Yes, the power of suggestion. She will go into the bathroom, where she's headed anyway, grab the pills out of the cold cream jar, wash them off, pour a little hot water into a glass, stick the pills in until they melt—less than fifteen seconds, TSD promises; then pour Castro's beer into the glass, pour herself a glass, and go back into the bedroom. The whole operation has been carefully timed. It doesn't take more than a minute and a half, and normally she is in the bathroom for a couple of minutes."

"Is Castro a Byzantine type who might suggest exchanging glasses?"

"No, he's never done that. But if he did, she would drink his beer, and within five minutes go back into the bathroom and take a solution which will be in her toilet bag. As long as it's taken within fifteen minutes, the poison will—what's the right word for it, Ruthie?"

"Abort?"

"No, not quite right—"

"Neutralize?"

"Yes. It would neutralize the poison."

□19□

Rolando Cubela had had enough experience with Fidel to put great store by the leader's sixth sense, an intangible about which Fidel was never willing to speculate; maybe the only subject he did not enjoy discoursing on, with the possible exception of Mirta, his former wife, about whom nothing—ever—was said.

Cubela remembered the day in the Sierra Maestra after a long, zigzag retreat from persistent Batista military mountaineers egged on by the huge bounty put on Castro's corpse. At eleven in the evening, exhausted, the tattered band of fewer than thirty guerrillas put down under a jagged rocky overhang that provided shelter something like a grotto, especially welcome in the sultry rain.

They had eaten—no fires permitted, no smoking even, and all conversation was whispered and exclusively utilitarian ("More bread, please." "I need at least one .32 cartridge for my pistol. Am completely out." "We must get some penicillin"). After their cold gruel and bread the men began to stretch out, covering their heads with whatever scrap of clothing they could dig up from their field packs.

Suddenly the word was whispered about.

"Fidel says assemble."

There were the low moans, the soldier's special tender, but never any thought of recalcitrance.

The narrow mountain path guided them around the mountain hollow and two hours and twenty minutes later they were settled opposite their old grotto, one mile away as the crow flies. They were numb with fatigue. At two-thirty they were awak-

ened by the sound of machine-gun fire—they could see the
tracer bullets from three sides firing into their camping ground
of a few hours ago. If they hadn't decamped, there'd have been
no survivors.

How had Castro known?

He gave no explanation. And after several other such es-
capes, no one asked anymore. "It would be bad luck to ask,"
Raúl Castro had said to Valdés. "But it's been that way with
Fidel since he was a boy." Back when Raúl was a boy, he'd have
explained it as his mother was given to explaining the phenome-
non, that Fidel's guardian angel was looking after him. But of
course there being no such thing as guardian angels in the July
26th crusade, Raúl had now to say only that it was mere "luck."
He had for a while, en route from the guardian angel to luck,
dabbled with the term "sixth sense," but gave it up after being
informed by a schooled Marxist that sixth senses were a bour-
geois neuro-biological superstition.

So that when Rolando Cubela concluded that he had the mandate—to execute Fidel Castro—he was prepared to be ever so
cautious in his plans. Nothing reckless. Nothing that would
heedlessly challenge the fabled Castro luck. He was profoundly
respectful, never mind Marxist dogma, of Fidel's guardian
angel and his protective ways. The desirable end was obvious:
There was first the end, second the appropriate sequence of
events leading to its realization. After a month's deliberation,
Cubela had it down on paper—in his mind:

1) Castro's death—it must be absolutely assured.

2) A plausible new Cuban government—instantly promulgated.

3) A leader of that government put forward with an unassail-
able record as an opponent of Batista; indeed, he should at one
point have been a close confederate of Castro, against whom
Castro had turned because he had objected to the suppression
of freedom in Cuba. Cubela having disqualified himself other
than as a broker, there were several candidates for the position
of the Leader. Huber Matos or Commander Guillermo Morales
would each qualify. Both of them were in prison. Both had
fought with Castro at Sierra Maestra.

4) Indispensable to the successful political outcome of the
coup would be instantaneous recognition of the new govern-

ment by foreign governments. Best not to begin with the United States, else it would appear that the United States was the new regime's procreator. The best place to look for immediate recognition, Cubela reasoned, was Venezuela. Rómulo Betancourt was the key—the adamant socialist who had opposed Batista so vigorously. He, along with Costa Rica's José Figueres, was a grand figure of Latin American democracy. Betancourt, who (like most people) had early on sided enthusiastically with Castro and his insurgency, was by now volubly disgusted with what Castro had done to his country. As President, his influence with the ruling party, Acción Democrática, was definitive. And if Venezuela moved to recognize the new Cuban government, so, almost reflexively, would Costa Rica. The two should act within hours of the assassination. Only after that should the United States move.

5) The cooperation of the United States, Cubela mournfully acknowledged, was quite simply indispensable. Perhaps even to consummate the deed itself—the execution, as he persisted in thinking of it. The United States would need to be involved, however, surreptitiously. And the U.S. would need to provide channels for timely exchanges with Betancourt and Figueres.

6) Although Cubela was prepared to act alone on the execution, he would need to establish lines of communication with the anti-Castro resistance forces, estimated at about two thousand strong.

They were centered in Camagüey, and were fast dwindling in size, owing to Raúl Castro's successful campaign against them. Cubela would need, acting through a cutout, as the spy people call agents not identifiable as such by either of the participating adversaries, to be in touch with Jesús Ferrer, the young anti-Castro rebel leader. The rebels' job would be to effect the immediate execution of Raúl Castro, Ramiro Valdés, Osvaldo Dorticós, and Che Guevara.

With those four figures gone, Cubela reasoned, Castro's cadre would be thrown into anarchy. Of almost equal importance would be the takeover of La Cabaña prison where at least one of the prospective successors to Castro was imprisoned. To storm La Cabaña would be time-consuming, bloody, and possibly lethal to the chosen successors.

No, the Commandant of La Cabaña—the gruesome American, Captain Herman Marks—must surrender. This would most likely be effected by radio communication offering him amnesty *provided* he opened the gates of La Cabaña and turned himself in within thirty minutes, and provided no prisoner under his command was harmed. In return he would have safe passage to Miami. Otherwise, he would be shot that same day.

And—Cubela asked himself, bluntly—what if it does not work? He subdivided that question into two parts. The first supposed that he would succeed in killing Castro but the revolution against Castro's regime would not succeed: that, twenty-four hours later, Raúl Castro would be as firmly in charge of Cuba as his brother had been twenty-four hours earlier.

But even if that were the result, Cubela consoled himself, the enterprise would by no means have been a failure. His personal commitment, made that night when he left the Isla de Pinos, was relatively modest. *He must kill Fidel Castro.* The rest— the liberation of Cuba from Castroism—was greatly desirable, but it was not the primal imperative that drove him.

And what if he failed in his attempt to kill Castro?

Either way, he would need to make provisions for his own survival. Rolando Cubela, naturally introspective and studiously so since his month with the psychiatrists, knew himself well and was not reluctant to acknowledge that his resolve to assassinate Castro was not to be confused with a presumptive indifference to his own life. Rolando wanted to live a long, full life, with Felipa (preferably) at his side and, eventually, with grandchildren, whose tonsils he would come out of medical retirement personally to remove.

So?

He would need to arrange for his own escape from Cuba. But, also, he would need to arrange for his mobility—his independence—on arriving elsewhere. He had no appetite for the prospect of landing, via a fast speedboat, in Miami, being awarded some secret medal or other by the CIA, speaking at a testimonial dinner in his honor by the Cuban liberation group Alpha 66—and finding himself without the means to pay a hotel bill, let alone the means necessary to establish himself in Colombia or Peru, to resume his career as a practicing medical doctor.

One trouble with the anti-Castro underground was that one

never knew what was, and what was not, accurate. One began by assuming that most of what one heard was inaccurate. And what one heard was by no means limited to rumor propagated by the resistance. Quite the contrary, the regime was far gone in paranoia. And the resistance aimed for implantation of their rumors (many of them made up out of whole cloth) in the mind of the highest levels of Castro's government. This was done by various means.

The most audacious had been the five-minute broadcast on Havana Radio by Jesús Ferrer. Cubela was not listening to the radio when it happened, and the daily press made no mention of the momentous incident, but everyone knew about it, and everyone spoke of it. It was especially dramatic because the young rebel Ferrer had begun his broadcast—the regular announcer was sitting three feet away in the studio, tied to a chair, gagged, a pistol aimed at his head—by saying that exactly ten years ago, at this very spot, young Fidel Castro had seized this very microphone, occupying this identical studio, and had spoken for ten minutes before fleeing the lowering policemen of Batista. Quite remarkably, Ferrer had managed to dig up a recording of Fidel Castro's broadcast on that memorable day in the spring of 1953. "The voice you will now hear," Ferrer had said to the radio audience, "is easily recognized by you. It is the voice of Fidel. Of Fidel Castro. Here is what he said ten years ago from this studio."

There was a little static, and then the unmistakable voice. "*I am Fidel Castro. I am a Cuban patriot. I am a soldier of freedom. I am dedicated, together with my loyal and patriotic companions, to liberating Cuba from the oppressive forces of the illegal government of Fulgencio Batista. I pledge you, when we come to power: freedom, democracy, liberation from all forms of oppression and imperialism.*"

Ferrer then spoke fervently and quickly for the few minutes he calculated he had before Castro's police descended on him, to ask whether Fidel Castro had delivered on his promises.

That episode had electrified Cuba. It made no difference that it was greeted by the official silence of the press, radio, and television. Radio Havana, an hour or two after Ferrer had fled and regular programming had resumed, made reference to an escaped lunatic who had been subdued, given sedatives, and returned to the hospital where he was, of course, receiving free medical attention under the revolutionary government.

There were other attention-getting episodes of the kind, though none quite so dramatic. But there was rumor, rumor, rumor . . . Castro suffered from an incurable cancer and would be dead within thirty days . . . Che Guevara was disillusioned and was returning to Argentina to initiate a true Marxist democratic revolution there . . . The United States was planning a major military operation against Cuba which would be launched not later than July 4, America's Independence Day.

These were what Cubela thought of as Operation Rumors. Open-curtain-quick-close-curtain rumors; exit Castro.

But there were rumors of an entirely different quality. Sotto voce rumors, Cubela called them. "Did you hear," Ingenio Tamayo might say to him at lunch, without any sense of guilt for passing such a rumor along, "that the CIA is planning to paralyze all our electrical systems? They have apparently developed some satellite that has that capacity: actually to shoot down a laser beam and immobilize all our electrical generators! It's a rumor, of course, Rolando, but not something we can afford entirely to ignore. I reported it to Fidel himself yesterday, when we met—we see each other," Tamayo said casually, flicking his cigarette ash into the tray, "quite regularly. Of course, I know that you, Rolando, as one of his special intimates, see him all the time. Anyway, I thought I should pass the rumor along."

And there was the rumor—this one persistent, varying only on the question of the size of the bounty—that the CIA was offering one million, two million, three million, five million dollars for Castro's head. That was the rumor that caught Cubela's special attention and that led, after two months' excruciatingly attenuated probing of contacts, to the first communication, through Pano Iglesias, between Rolando Cubela and Rufus.

20

Ingenio Tamayo was a mean-spirited man—who very much
enjoyed performing Fidel Castro's highly surreptitious commissions primarily because, as often as not, they called for the
discreet elimination of someone Castro did not wish officially to
detain and execute. Tamayo greatly enjoyed the art of contriv-
ing accidental causes of death, as he had with almost all of the
men (and, yes, one woman) Castro had dispatched him to kill.
It hadn't been possible in every case, but when he could accurately report to Castro a success, it would follow a formula. "I
am deeply disappointed" (he *always* used this device) "to have
to bring you ill tidings, Comandante. José González last night,
while attempting to repair the fuse box in his apartment, was
electrocuted. Attempts to revive him were unsuccessful."

And Fidel would always act out his part. "Ah! How sad,
Ingenio, how sad! José González was such a good, fine, patriotic
man!"

Usually the two men were alone when Tamayo reported that
his commission had been completed. When that was so, they
would both break out into raucous laughter after their histrionic exchange. When, as sometimes happened, there was someone else in the room on unrelated business, Castro and Tamayo
would satisfy themselves, after the moribund dialogue, with an
oblique cross-glance, an exchanged wink.

But Tamayo was a *balanced* mean-spirited man. He knew,
for instance, that his current assignment would require him to
be ingratiating. And much else. To begin with, there was the
professional preparation to be done. He had taken a full four
days to read the files on the Soviet missiles, and as he drew on

his cigarette after painstakingly going through the material, he amused himself with the thought that perhaps he should spend another four days learning how a) to curb his temper; b) to appear to be interested in what other people were saying; c) to express concern for others' concerns, whatever these were; and d) to conceal his contempt for his intellectual inferiors, which—Ingenio Tamayo paused deliberatively—meant, well, just about everybody. Though Che Guevara was a very learned man; and no one had quicker insights than Fidel.

He let his thumb brush over the spine of the Top Secret folder, leaned back in his chair, and concentrated on the question: Just exactly how should he proceed?

The file was thick, but almost diligently incomplete. Much of it had been assembled by Castro's own intelligence personnel, some of whom had observed the super-secret arrival of the missile tankers, followed their transportation to the preselected sites, at night, in the long trailers, and witnessed their placement in the hidden silos.

Along with the missiles came heavy launching bases, designed to support and aim the missiles at their predesignated targets. As these launching bases were progressively installed, their compass bearing gave some clue to targets lying downrange. It was not specified, in his material, what were the targets the individual missiles were aimed at, but it was general knowledge that each missile had its programmed destination, selected in Moscow. The idea had been—had the grand operation worked—suddenly to confront the United States with the news that practically every major city in the country lay at the receiving end of the trajectory of forty-two missiles sitting in Cuba.

Great stuff! Tamayo thought. *God,* what a wonderful spectacle it would have been—if they had all been fired, and nothing even worth looting was left in the major American cities! That would show the gringos! A beautiful thought, Tamayo sighed.

Was there then a missile, or even more than one missile, still left in Cuba? Left, if the traitor Luminante was to be believed, in San Cristóbal?

Tamayo had deduced that if indeed the missile was in San Cristóbal, then it would have been one of the medium-range ballistic missiles (SANDALs), not one of the bigger, longer-range intermediate-range ballistic missiles (SKEANs). These last, which had a range of 2,200 miles, had all been destined, according to Cuban Intelligence—and as much was confirmed by Soviet sources—for Guanajay and Remedios. In San Cristóbal (and in Sagua la Grande), the smaller SANDALs had been emplaced, with a range of 1,100 miles. The Soviets, he noted, called them simply SS-4's, but there were numerous notices in his folder—a good many of them in English, taken from trade and technical journals published during the past few months in North America; there had been extensive coverage in particular in *Life* magazine—that referred to them as SANDAL missiles, the name by which they were known in NATO.

Very well, SANDAL it will be, Tamayo thought. I am looking for a SANDAL. He poured himself a glass of rum, and began to sing. *"O SANDAL mío, O SANDAL mío, sta'n fronte ate, sta'n fronte ate. . . ."*

He rehearsed his knowledge of SANDAL. Length: 68 feet (he had got that from the *Air Force* magazine. The equivalent was 21 meters, just under). Diameter: 63 inches, or 1.6 meters. Weight: 60,000 pounds—i.e., 27,000 kilos, approximately.

He stared at a picture of it. According to *Life* magazine, a picture taken on November 7, 1962, in the Red Square parade . . . Graceful bastard, Tamayo thought. It looked like a sharpened, round pencil. Very pointed. At the base it had a flared skirt, was without tail fins, using instead what looked like delicate control vanes. In order to launch, he had learned, the SANDAL needed a transfusion of liquid fuel. Such fuel, according to one article in *Air Force* magazine, was highly volatile and would need to be banked in a large tank. From there it would be hosed in at huge pressure into a trailer tank. Upon ignition, a mix of some kind was induced, kerosene combined with liquid oxygen, within the combustion chamber. The trailer, of which a photograph was shown taken by a U-2 flight, was unfortunately not distinctive. Long, yes, but so were some army trucks long. And the height of the tank-trailer was no more than that of a conventional Army 2 1/2-ton truck.

So Ingenio Tamayo simply needed to look for a hidden 21-meter missile not too far separated from a tank of appropriate size, and a trailer. He had been to the huge military facility at San Cristóbal only once, but he dimly remembered that there were fuel tanks all over the place, and, for that matter, trucks and trailers all over the place.

He finished his drink. Ah well, he thought, he might as well spend his last evening in Havana for a fortnight or so with La Huerita, "Little Blondie." She never dared to charge Ingenio, damn right. He had got her out of one of the prostitute rehabilitation camps, and she was now well sheltered in an apartment, as what little blondie would not be well sheltered who granted her favors, among others, to Raúl Castro?

He depressed a button which signaled to the drivers' pool in the garage that Major Ingenio Tamayo would be downstairs within five minutes, and if his car and driver were not there waiting for him, prepare to die.

His story was entirely plausible, and as he handed his papers to Major Gutiérrez at the headquarters of Camp San Cristóbal, Gutiérrez merely sighed (one more piece of visiting brass) and pressed a button for an orderly, to whom he gave instructions to come up with field-grade officer's quarters that were empty and clean. To Tamayo he said that he, Gutiérrez, could very well understand the need for coordination, "with all those Russians running all over the place—if you threatened to shoot me dead, I wouldn't be able right now to give you a count on how many of them are here, *right now*, within—twenty. Every day I ask Colonel Bilensky how many men he has here, and I have the impression he uses any pleasant figure that comes to mind to satisfy me. Sometimes he says two hundred and twenty, sometimes two hundred and seventy, sometimes one hundred and seventy. He seems to like round numbers. Of course, they live in their segregated section, they have their own mess hall, their own officers' quarters. But—let us face it—every few days"— Major Gutiérrez pointed through the window at what looked, a kilometer away, like the mouth of an assembly plant on the distant plain, sheltered by a monstrous cave—"down from there, every few days, comes something for us. A truck. A tank. A fighter. An anti-aircraft battery. We mustn't complain."

Tamayo spoke cautiously now. "But surely, Major, you have your own men inside the Soviet compound?"

"Yes, yes, of course. It isn't as it was during the days of the missiles. Last year, between mid-August and the crisis in October, no Cuban was permitted"—he stood, pointed again out the window, squinted, and finally sat down.

"No use. You can't see it from here. But half a kilometer *behind* the assembly plant is a second one of those caves that abound in San Cristóbal. It was actually cordoned off with barbed wire while the missiles were here. And the understanding with Castro was that only Soviet technicians would be permitted in the area.

"But that is changed, now that the missiles are gone. Among other things, we provide the sentries at the gate. And then we have twenty, thirty men, officers and technicians, who are inside most of the time. They come back to their own quarters only to eat and sleep. Their job is to observe the assembly of the Soviet hardware and to learn. They will be the principal teachers of our own maintenance men. They are among our best men, many of them graduates of the engineering school at the University of Havana."

The orderly came back with a key and a voucher, which Ingenio Tamayo signed, reminding himself to say "Thank you" first to the orderly, then to the Comandante.

TAMAYO PAID SPECIAL attention to how the Cubans within the Soviet compound were dressed. Almost all of them wore fatigues, with their insignia of rank pinned onto floppy cotton epaulettes, their last names stenciled above the left chest pocket. Sometimes, especially among those who worked outdoors, the top half of the fatigue costume lay on the ground, and these men wore only T-shirts, making it impossible to know their names or their rank.

Tamayo's initial visit was short. A half hour later he was back, this time wearing fatigues. He had got the orderly to stencil his name on a pair while he waited. Impatiently. He took from his briefcase a clipboard. It held down a thick pad of yellow-paper forms. These he had personally devised and had printed. Across the top was listed the camps within which Soviet ordnance was being assembled—Guanajay, Remedios, Sagua la Grande, and San Cristóbal. He circled the first three of these, to give the impression that this was the fourth assembly plant he was inspecting. The pad was sprinkled with questions that permitted him a full range of official curiosity. Were there strategic reserves of fuel? Sufficient faucets to supply drinking water? Sufficient reserves of truck tires? Of Sizes X, Y, Z, A-prime? Much of that and, on the other side of the sheet of paper, such questions as: Were the living quarters satisfactory? Was the food well cooked? Plentiful? Was the 16-millimeter movie projector in good working order? And then a large space, headed by the universal question: "Other?"

The Cuban lieutenant in charge of the native detachment was one Junio Barrios. Tamayo asked a Cuban soldier peering at two Soviet technicians engaged in operating a crane which was gently lowering an airplane wing onto an IL-28 bomber where he could find Lieutenant Barrios. The soldier pointed sulkily in the general direction of the cave and then spotted the major's oak leaf, drew himself to attention, and asked did the major wish him to take him to the lieutenant? Tamayo nodded curtly and followed the soldier into the great cave, bustling with activity around a half-dozen huge crates, the first one being disassembled by what looked like fifty Lilliputians.

They approached a young mulatto with a halfhearted beard on his chin. The soldier saluted and went back to his airplane wing. Tamayo introduced himself and sketched his mission. Lieutenant Barrios apologized and said that his orders required him to ask the major to show his credentials. Tamayo did so casually, lighting a cigarette.

"Oh sir, I'm sorry. Absolutely no smoking. Soviet regulations."

Tamayo nodded and ground his cigarette under his heel, after taking a deep drag.

He asked some questions, scribbling away on his pad, and then requested to be presented to the Soviet official in charge. Colonel Bilensky, Barrios said, was away in Havana, leaving his deputy in charge. Tamayo was introduced to a Major Kirov. Tamayo saluted, took a deep breath, and launched into Operation Ingratiation. Within a half hour Major Kirov had invited the newly jovial, congenial Tamayo to join him for dinner at the officers' mess. Tamayo smiled his acceptance and said he would be delighted to do so. Meanwhile, he would proceed on his rounds.

Tamayo had a practiced eye.

There was nothing in the cave itself that could conceivably shield a 21-meter missile. The natural cave was over a hundred meters long, and half that in width. There were assorted trailers and trucks within the cave and outside it. There were six big tanks outside the cave, two within it, the latter with sentries seated at wooden desks alongside. Yet it was as easy as this: If there was a missile, it had to lie beneath the steel flooring. If there was a missile, then its liquid oxygen was contained in one of the two tanks. Tamayo's job would be to ascertain whether the rectangular steel sections making up the flooring were large enough to permit a crane to lift out a 21-meter missile 1.6 meters in diameter. A missile below the ground would need fairly regular maintenance, primarily the regulation of humidity, but also—Tamayo congratulated himself on the patience with which he had read the technical information in *Air Force* magazine on the care and feeding of missiles— careful attention to the electrical jungle within each missile, including the all-important batteries necessary for in-flight guidance.

If there was a SANDAL down there, there had to be a manhole somewhere.

21

An elderly man, using a cane and favoring a stiff leg, stepped down from the bus on Flagler Street in Miami, two blocks away from the apartment house toward which he walked, slowly but steadily, the straw hat on his head tilted, when he rounded the corner, to protect his face from the sun. Underneath the rear of the hat, a tuft of white hair projected. The old man wore a weary white linen jacket, without a tie, and workmen's coveralls with shoulder straps. From the deep left pocket of his work pants a folded copy of *Life* magazine protruded. His right pocket was also weighted down: perhaps a tool of his trade, a passerby would conjecture. He walked into the apartment house, took the elevator to the ninth floor, then to Apartment D. He entered the apartment, closed and double-locked the door, went into the hanging closet, full of an assortment of workmen's clothes, removed a towel hanging from a hook at the back of the closet and, with a second key, swung open a panel at the back of the closet. Closing it from the other side, he flicked on a switch. It gave him, from a monitor placed above the hidden closet door, a television view of the hallway and the entrance hall into 9-D.

He was now in a two-room suite with an opening only to a fire escape, none to the hallway. One room was a bedroom, the other a studio-dining room. In between were a kitchen and bathroom.

Blackford Oakes removed the magazine from his left pocket and the .32 automatic from the right pocket and took off his hat and trousers, hanging them on a hook. He replaced them with a pair of khaki pants and a cotton sports shirt. He looked at his watch. His session downtown, at which he and two other agents were briefed by the commander of Alpha 66 on the raids planned for the following week, had consumed, in all, almost three hours. Pano would arrive within fifteen minutes, with the promised word from AM/LASH, he hoped. And Rufus would arrive before five, assuming that his flight from Washington was on time.

Pano hove in. Blackford was always faintly alarmed when he had a scheduled visit with Pano because the man whose entrance he surveilled through the television monitor, first coming into Apartment 9-D, then into the closet, and now into the studio, was never recognizable as the Pano he had last seen. This time Pano was—of all things—a monk, including tonsure and shuffle. Blackford smiled, and without being asked went into the kitchen to come back with a cold beer, by which time all traces of the cleric had disappeared.

"I hope while you were a monk you prayed for me," Blackford said to Pano, seated comfortably at one end of the couch, fanning himself with Blackford's issue of *Life*.

"The monk needs to pray for you, Blackforrd, but mostly for the whole situation. It is a most awful *desarreglo*."

"Yes," Blackford said, picking up the morning paper from the coffee table. "Do you know José Miró Cardona personally?"

"I know everyone personally."

"Do you know the Pope personally?"

"Ah, dear Pope John. Of course I know him. In fact, he baptized me. He was for many years my mother's lover."

"I thought J. Edgar Hoover was your mother's lover?"

"That was, uh, pre-Pope. No, post-Pope. No, anti-Pope."

"Shall we cut the *mierda*?"

"We shall cut out the *mierda*, if you wish, Blackforrd."

Rufus, Blackford said, would be with them within the hour. The events of the past two days, Blackford wanted reassurance, had not shaken the determination of AM/LASH.

"It does not help very much, Blackforrd, to have Fidel Castro give a speech to one hundred thousand Cubans on the second anniversary of the Bay of Pigs and quote Miró Cardona, until two days ago the president of the Cuban Revolutionary Council in Miami—quote from Miró Cardona's ten-thousand-word statement saying that President Kennedy promised a second invasion of Cuba and has betrayed that promise—and then hear from Kennedy at a press conference that although the United States cannot coexist with a Soviet state in this hemisphere, he does not plan to let the exiled Cubans make U.S. foreign policy from the state of Florida. And what does Castro then say to the roaring crowd? *That although Kennedy has given up the idea of invading Cuba, he is working hard to assassinate Cuban officials!*"

"And, of course, this has been denied."

"Yes, of course it has been denied. But it also happens to be true. Now AM/LASH must assume even tighter security arrangements around Castro."

"You say LASH 'must assume.' But you must know. I mean, you have been in touch, right?"

"Yes. But 'in touch' with LASH is not exactly the way to put it. He is profoundly determined and faithful. But he is also supremely cautious—"

A faint noise from the monitor arrested their attention.

It was one of Rufus's wonderful endowments that he had no singular feature of any kind. Even his clothes were, somehow, unnoticeable. He wore no disguise; but, on ringing the door, he twice adjusted his fedora. Rufus's identification signal.

Pano went through the closet to 9-D and led him in. Blackford reached out intending to take Rufus's jacket, but Rufus shook his head, then his hand. Rufus did not take off his jacket, Blackford reminded himself, except—presumably—when going to bed, or working in his rose garden. He accepted the Pepsi Blackford handed him.

From the straight-back chair in the dining room, he began to speak. He had been that afternoon with the Attorney General, who was "raging mad" at Castro for his speech, "raging mad" at Miró Cardona for releasing his ten-thousand-word allegation against the President, and only a "little less mad at Mongoose for the failure to get the job done." Bobby Kennedy had warned that Castro's charge that the U.S. Government was plotting his assassination made any contemplated arrangement even more precarious than anything heretofore attempted.

Rufus looked at Blackford and managed to communicate that on this particular point he would elaborate when they were alone. "But the Attorney General's final words were, 'For Chrissake, you and Hicock should get on with it.'

"I reminded him that I was not involved in the Hicock operation, did not desire to be, and did not wish to know any details about it." Blackford knew better than to remonstrate on the theme of the Elusive Distinction.

"But I am here to listen, with Blackford, to you, Pano," Rufus said. "You know the specific plans of AM/LASH? Tell us."

Pano took the rest of his beer slowly. All the usual jocularity had faded from his face.

"LASH declined to confide the details to me."

There was silence.

Blackford spoke. "To whom does he intend, then, to talk?"

"He will talk either with you, or with Rufus."

Pano paused. "In Mexico."

"In Mexico?" Rufus frowned. "Does LASH get to travel about at will throughout Latin America?"

"It is more complicated than that, Rufus. The meeting is to take place in Mexico. His demands will be made known in Mexico, and the details of his operation will be made known in Mexico. But not by LASH."

Blackford's impatience showed. But Rufus was merely reflective. He was presumptively understanding of anyone else's concern for security.

He asked, "With whom are we to speak in Mexico?"

"I have a name—'Consuelo'—and a telephone number. That is all I could get. And, Señor Rufus, there is no such thing as bargaining with LASH. He moves at his own speed, makes his own demands—I have up to now found them reasonable—and determines his own movements."

Rufus looked again at Blackford. Pano understood. He got up and went to the closet for his monk's cowl and the hairpiece.

"That is all that I can do for you, gentlemen. Blackforrd will let me know your decision?"

He shook hands with them both, and was let out of the safe house.

They sat over a chicken-and-rice TV dinner and a bottle of wine. The two electric fans in corners of the room worked well, and from the fire escape window cool air entered into the bathroom and flowed into the living quarters. Although they discussed the situation in general for several hours, with speculation as to the internal meaning for Cuba of the bellicose exchanges of the past few days between Kennedy and Castro, on specific matters in hand there was, really, only the single question before the house: Which one of them would go to Mexico?

Rufus finally addressed the question. "I think you had better go, Blackford. I'm getting regular reports from Anthony Trust and others on related matters, communications that sometimes require a quick response. And then there is the Attorney General. When he desires to see me, he desires to see me right away."

"Okay. The other approaches I've been working on are pretty attenuated compared to LASH, and I'm briefed already on what the Cubans are planning for the next few days. I'll get in touch with Pano and go to Mexico tomorrow."

CONSUELO, AS HE was known in this operation, stood by the window of his office in downtown Mexico City after receiving the cryptic telegram from Miami. In fifteen years of professional life Consuelo had engaged in interesting, even engrossing enterprises, most of them concerning Mexicans, often Mexicans seeking ways, legal and penumbral, of taking out of Mexico sums of money accumulated by political activity Consuelo never inquired into. But the assignment he had from Rolando Cubela was, to say the least, startling, and Consuelo had done heavy-duty reflection before, finally, agreeing to cooperate. As a professional, he decided, he had little practical choice: he could hardly turn to someone else and say, "Would you be good enough to cooperate with a friend of mine in Cuba who seeks help in arranging the assassination of Fidel Castro?"

And—Consuelo did not disguise it—he thought the idea of replacing the aggressive, atheist, murderous regime in Cuba greatly overdue. It was providential, Consuelo thought, looking out of his office window, from which he could see the entrance to the grand Palacio de Bellas Artes, that Rolando Cubela should find himself in such intimate circumstances with Castro.

He remembered making that appointment to meet with Fausto Cubela, Rolando's father, years ago. It was three months after the accident. Cubela had left the hospital in Mexico City after six weeks, and had been flown to Havana in a stretcher aboard the plane. He was back at his farm but needed, in his semiparalyzed condition, day and night care. The little ranch had been put up for sale, Consuelo had found out, but as a farm it had never been more, really, than something from which the bullfighter eked out his spartan income. And now Fausto Cubela would never again be able to work on his farm, let alone resume his profession as a picador.

What had happened one Sunday, three months earlier, was, as the taurino press called it, "a true tragedy." The picador will normally gore three times before closing out that episode in the three-act drama of a bullfight.

But there are variables. The matador, fearing a particular bull, may stand by uncomplainingly during three lances visibly enfeebling. Or the crowd may roar its disapproval of the damage being done to the bull after the very first lancing. The matador has the option of appealing to La Presidencia to abort the procedure. If he agrees, the president will fling a white handkerchief over the front of his box, a signal to the trumpeters to sound the advent of the next episode with the banderilleros. Some bulls, as they charge into the ring, unscathed and ferocious, catch the special fancy of the crowd, as "Estrellito" had done (all bulls are given names; everything in Latin America is given an individual name). Here was a proud bull indeed, weighing over 400 kilos, every ounce of which was mobilized to kill. The crowd cheered him on as he dauntlessly charged the peones, who performed their graceful but cautious passes, permitting the matador to observe the bull's mannerisms. And then the matador himself had had a triumphant series of *verónicas*, urging a great *faena*, the final spectacle at which the matador would first lead Estrellito through the dangerous, exhilarating paces showing off the matador's special skills, and, finally, thrust the fatal sword into the same spot the picador had softened.

Fausto Cubela had entered his long lance a second time at exactly the correct point in the bull, and Estrellito charged mightily against his attacker, pushing Cubela and his horse back several meters. Cubela continued with all his might leaning into the lance. The crowd began to howl. A huge cataclysmic roar of disapproval at the excessive damage being done to the bull, whose fighting spirit might extinguish under such heavy punishment. Why didn't the stupid president order the fornicating trumpet to sound!

Still nothing from the presidential box.

At this point the matador dashed from his observation post into the ring, to join the protest of the crowd—psychologically important, lest he give the impression that he desired the picador to disable the bull, or dispirit it. The matador gesticulated wildly at Cubela to back away with his pic. Cubela, desperate under the conflicting pressures—obey the judge, or the crowd and the matador—twisted on his waist to look at the matador. At that moment three things happened: The trumpet finally sounded; the bull suddenly withdrew from the picador, who had been standing up in his stirrups leaning to one side far out over his horse with all his strength; and Cubela, unbalanced, his eyes turned elsewhere than on the bull, fell head forward from his mount. The bull charged him.

It was only five, perhaps eight seconds before the matador succeeded in distracting Estrellito, causing the bull to charge him and leave the gored Cubela lying on the ground. But it was time enough for the horn to sever the spinal cord in Cubela's neck, and although at the hospital they were able to control the bleeding, Cubela could not move his head, or his left arm and leg. He was paralyzed for life.

The insurance company gave him a lump sum of one thousand pesos, and he would not qualify for his Cuban Social Security for another fifteen years. The payments necessary to keep his son Rolando in medical school were now a financial burden quite simply out of the question.

All of this Consuelo knew when he arrived in Havana on a sticky day in August. The following morning, the appointment having been made with Señor Cubela via his wife, he drove to the little finca. Fausto's son, Rolando, opened the door. Consuelo introduced himself and asked whether it would pain the younger man's father if Consuelo were to speak to him directly. Rolando turned to his mother to permit her to reply to the question.

"Mejor, señor, hablar entre nosotros."

Better to do his business with mother and son: Fausto had not yet got used to company, and it embarrassed him to speak without control of his lips.

They sat down and Consuelo opened his briefcase, withdrawing two envelopes. The first—he counted out the bills—contained ten thousand pesos, more money than the entire finca was being offered for. The second envelope contained a check. "This will be deposited at the Trust Company Bank in Havana. The trustee of this account has been instructed to pay all tuition, medical, and incidental expenses of Rolando Cubela until he receives his medical license."

Rolando and his mother stared at the young visitor, open-mouthed.

"Sir, to whom do we owe this—this salvation?" Rolando asked.

"My client," said their guest, "is Luís Miguel Dominguín. He feels responsible for having distracted the attention of Señor Cubela from his duties at the fight in February."

Señora Cubela begged him to stay and eat something, quietly convinced that so distinguished a visitor would not share a meal in such indigent surroundings. She and her son were surprised when he replied that he would be honored to stay for lunch. He was there for two hours.

When finally he rose to go, Rolando asked for the address of Señor Dominguín. The lawyer raised his hand and said that the matador's express wish was that no member of the family should write to thank him.

"He considers it his own delinquency in the bullring, and does not wish to be reminded of it."

Rolando asked if he might have the lawyer's address. Opening his wallet, Consuelo handed him a card with his office address.

STANDING IN HIS office, Consuelo reflected that that meeting had taken place in 1956. In seven years, he had not heard the name of Rolando Cubela. But, arriving in Mexico a week ago with a delegation of Cubans to attend a Pan-American Marxist congress, Rolando Cubela had pleaded Mexican dysentery.

After his colleagues had trooped off to the auditorium, he slipped away from his hotel room and was waiting in the office at Cinco de Mayo to meet with Consuelo. Consuelo had recognized the young medical student, though he looked now fifteen years older. He greeted him warmly and brought him into his office.

That was at ten. After a few minutes, other appointments were canceled. Lunch was brought in at one. No calls were taken. At six, Cubela left the office. Consuelo felt a great weight.

But he had said yes.

Yes, under the name of "Consuelo," he would agree to meet with a high executive of the CIA; yes, he would reveal the plans his client "AM/LASH" had made to proceed with the assassination of a chief of government; and yes, he would specify exactly what AM/LASH expected of the American government.

The telephoned telegram from Miami had informed Consuelo that he would be meeting with "Bledsoe"—as AM/LASH knew Blackford Oakes—who would leave word at what hotel and in which room Bledsoe could be reached. It would be up to Consuelo to dial the hotel and ask for the room number.

With a deep sense of an irreversible engagement in an enterprise that could haunt him for the balance of his life, Consuelo turned from the window, went to his telephone, dialed the number of the Hotel Geneve, and asked for Room 322.

22

On the second evening of his state visit in Moscow, Fidel Castro had been carried way by an oleaginous toast in his honor delivered by Soviet President Leonid Brezhnev. He had begun by replying in kind with ardent generalities about the wisdom, courage, compassion, and vision of his hosts. He went on. And suddenly Colonel Yitzkah, who as Chief of Protocol was in charge of Castro's hour-by-hour schedule, found himself half-listening to a florid invitation by Castro to "all the relatives of all the Soviet patriots now in Cuba helping us with our revolution: I wish to meet you all, and shake your hands on behalf of the people of Cuba."

All the relatives of all the Soviet patriots helping Cuba with their revolution! Colonel Yitzkah's reaction was: The dumb sonofabitch is talking about—well, maybe ten thousand people! There were—the colonel didn't know the figure exactly—somewhere between six and eight thousand Soviet technicians still in Cuba, even after the return of eight thousand with the missiles evacuated in the October fiasco. Figure half of them bachelors, that still makes—he calculated as Fidel Castro rhapsodized on the theme of his and his country's debt to these "great masters of their defensive craft"—that makes, half, say, of eight thousand; that makes four thousand married. That madman has just managed to issue a public invitation to *four thousand Russians* to come and greet him! Come greet him in *my* country! Castro has just invited us to put on, with a couple of days' notice, a reception larger than the diplomatic party we give on May Day! Does this dumb bearded bastard know what he is doing?

Yitzkah hoped Castro would simply forget about the whole idea, after his windy expansiveness wore down. But a half hour later Castro, still talking, stressed again that he could not return to Cuba without making this "gesture."

"*Some gesture,*" Yitzkah thought: It will only tie up my office night and day and cost maybe a hundred thousand rubles.

At the exclusive reception after the banquet, Castro, from the center of the knot of officials and celebrities surrounding him, motioned to Colonel Yitzkah to approach him. Kindly arrange matters so that he could do as he had promised, he said matter-of-factly.

Colonel Yitzkah replied that his job was to do *anything* His Excellency desired, but that it would be *extremely* difficult, on such *short* notice, to round up *anything like* all the relatives of all Soviet personnel in Cuba.

Castro stared at him as though he had not heard him. Imperial gestures are not the subject of cost accounting, his stare seemed to be saying. Then Castro said, "When?"

Colonel Yitzkah bowed and left Castro, who resumed his animated talk to aides and Soviet officials. The interpreters labored impatiently so that Malinovsky and Gromyko could understand and react appropriately. Colonel Yitzkah moved to another little knot of Russian luminaries, standing by the bar, bowed his head deferentially and asked Nikita Khrushchev if he might have a word with him. Khrushchev drew away from his entourage.

"What is it, Yitzkah?"

"You heard Premier Castro, about the relatives of Soviet personnel in Cuba?"

"I wasn't listening, to tell the truth. Long day. Our . . . guest speaks at endless length. What did he say?"

"Well, Comrade Khrushchev, he said he wished to 'greet' *personally* relatives of all Soviet personnel working in Cuba."

"He said *what*?"

"Just that, Comrade. I calculate roughly that would mean sending out about four thousand invitations. And the worst of it is that everyone living within Moscow would almost certainly come, and that probably would mean—oh, one, maybe two thousand people."

"He'll forget about it in the morning."

"I am afraid not, Comrade Khrushchev. He just this minute asked me when exactly the event could be scheduled. What am I to do, Comrade?"

Khrushchev thought, downing his drink. "Tell him at noon tomorrow that you have been through the files, and that there are only about two or three hundred relatives of our technicians living in Moscow. Set up a tea, get thirty or forty of them to come."

"Whom do you wish invited from—from our government?"

"Keep it small. The ambassador to Havana, obviously, a few East European representatives, and oh, a half-dozen others, I don't care. I won't be there. Tell the members of the Politburo I don't want them there. Goddamn bore."

"Yes, Comrade Khrushchev."

THE RECEPTION WAS held the following Friday afternoon, after Castro had come back from his tour of Industrial Russia. Entering Georgievsky Hall at the Kremlin, he was greeted with heated applause by the hundred attendants. En route to the microphone, he turned and whispered to Colonel Yitzkah that he was surprised that there were so few guests present.

The colonel replied that it had not been possible to do more in just three days.

Castro reacted by proclaiming that, given how small the assembly was, he would greet each Russian individually.

A line was formed, and the guests began to file by. Castro asked everyone questions. The same questions. The colonel, looking at his watch, calculated despondently that, at this rate, the reception would last two hours.

About halfway through the line's passage, following established procedure, Castro was introduced to the next person in line. The officiating protocol officer said, "Mr. Prime Minister, I present Mrs. Olga Kirov."

She was a slight, fair woman in her thirties, a tiny piece of fur choked tightly around her slender neck, her light brown hair carefully coiffed. Her woolen suit was worn, but neatly fitted.

"And where is your husband stationed, Madame Kirov?" Castro routinely asked.

"At San Cristóbal," Olga Kirov answered, smiling.

And then she said it, in bold and resonant accents: "I do wish, Comrade Castro, that you would persuade our government to permit us to go and live with our husbands while they are in Cuba."

The translator had no option than to transcribe the statement exactly: there were too many people in the room who spoke both languages.

Castro listened intently, smiled warmly, motioned to an aide to take a note of Mme. Kirov's request and to remind him to raise the subject with the General Secretary. Olga Kirov smiled exuberantly, bowed her thanks, and, a half hour later, was drinking tea with one of the Cuban interpreters, a woman who was an official in Cuba's Foreign Office. She told Olga Kirov, in answer to her question, that she had learned Russian as a child, when her father had been the Cuban military attaché in Moscow. She continued, she said, to conduct classes in Russian at the University of Havana. "But most of the time, I work in the Foreign Office."

Olga Kirov was elated by her personal communion with the high and the mighty; such a change from life in the one-room apartment she shared with Zinka Petrov, a spirited artist (she sang in the Bolshoi Opera chorus)—another wife whose husband was stationed in Cuba. Though even that small apartment was agreeable shelter from the drab office in which, six days every week, she worked as a file clerk.

"Your husband is at San Cristóbal," the interpreter said, a smile obtruding her creased face.

"Yes, yes. Do you know San Cristóbal?"

"I was born and raised in San Cristóbal. My mother lives there, and I visit her every other weekend. It may even be that I have met your husband, at one of the parties occasionally given by Colonel Gutiérrez for the Soviet contingent. I am always invited, because I can interpret."

Olga was carried away by it all. Soon she found herself blurting out, "Would you, dear Señorita, do me the favor of mailing a letter to my husband on your return? It takes such ages and ages to go by regular mail, sometimes as much as two months."

"Of course, with the greatest pleasure."

Arrangements were made. Olga would deliver the letter to

the Cuban Embassy, marked "Personal," and Señorita Evita Rincona would mail it in Cuba. "I might even arrange to hand it personally to your husband next weekend, when I plan to be in San Cristóbal."

The following day Olga Kirov took the bus to the center of Moscow, walked into the Cuban Embassy, explained that Señorita Rincona was expecting her, and was admitted into the special reception area, heavily manned because of the manifold requirements associated with Fidel Castro's visit. Olga explained herself to a Russian-speaking Cuban sitting at one end of the reception table who said, "Of course," reached for the letter, attached a label to it, and put it in her Out basket. Olga gave profuse thanks.

Three days later, at one in the morning, there was a loud knock on the door of her apartment.

It was all as of ten years before, in the days of Stalin. Such knocks, at such hours, were not commonplace anymore, but neither were they isolated. Olga Kirov was in due course driven to Lubyanka Prison, booked, and placed in a solitary cell.

It had been surprising to Major Rostropov when the orders had come in to prepare for the prisoner Olga Kirov at such an hour, and surprising to him, on examining the orders from the high command, that the detachment of three KGB agents sent to bring her in had been instructed to search every cubic inch of the woman's apartment. That hadn't taken so long, though it would have taken less long if Olga's roommate, Zinka, had screamed and yelled a little less—she had, finally, to be taken out and locked in the police van until the KGB were done, the report read.

But the orders respecting Olga Kirov had come down straight from Vladimir Yefimovich Semichastny, Chairman of the KGB. The charges against her, Major Rostropov reflected, were serious, but hardly *that* unusual. She had evidently attempted to evade routine censorship by giving an envelope to a member of Castro's Cuban entourage. When the Cuban interpreter, one Evita Rincona, had mentioned to her Soviet counterpart this trivial favor she was so gladly doing for the wife of one of the Soviet technicians, the Soviet interpreter had sternly objected that the accommodation was in violation of Soviet rules, that she must have the letter, get it photographed, and

only then return it to Evita Rincona for delivery in San Cristóbal.

A few days later, on the eve of the departure of Castro and
his party, Señorita Rincona reminded the Soviet interpreter, at
the final Soviet-Cuban social affair, that she had not yet returned Mrs. Kirov's letter. Evita Rincona got only the brusque
reply: "It has been confiscated."

Adding, after a pause, "I am sorry."

THE SOVIET BUREAUCRACY tends to move slowly, but it can,
under certain kinds of pressure, move with great speed. In the
computer files on Soviet personnel serving in Cuba, only six
technicians—out of eight thousand—had a special marking attached to their names. This signified that they and their activities were to be supervised directly by Semichastny—that is, by
the head of the KGB. All letters mailed to these six technicians
were to be read with special care, as also mail from them. A
letter that appeared in any way unusual was to be brought to
Semichastny for his personal scrutiny. When the censor, at the
special request of the Russian-Cuban interpreter, promised a
quick reading of the letter to Major Kirov from his wife, he
checked his files routinely, and spotted the monitory marking.
Accordingly he read the letter attentively. Even if he had not
been warned about the especially sensitive aspect of the Kirov
correspondence, he'd have reported the letter to Special Branch
KGB because, in that letter, Olga innocently mentioned to her
husband that she had asked Fidel Castro himself please to
invite the wives of Soviet technicians to visit in Cuba. And—the
censor's eyes stared with dumb astonishment at what followed—she, Olga, thought that once she got to Cuba, she and
Anatoly should consider taking out Cuban citizenship, since
Anatoly had written so many enthusiastic letters about Cuba,
its climate, the friendliness of the people. They were childless,
Olga wrote ruefully, and had, really, no ties to the Soviet Union.
Why not go to live in another socialist country, where life was,
apparently, so much more pleasant?

Twelve hours later, the fate of Olga Kirov and her husband
was being discussed by, no less, Nikita Khrushchev, Malinovsky, and Semichastny.

They arrived quickly at priorities. The first was: What did Olga Kirov know, if anything, about the nature of Anatoly Kirov's assignment in Cuba? To get this information was of primary importance. If it developed that she knew anything at all about the hidden missile, Olga Kirov would need to be silenced, permanently. Moreover, only the most trusted "examiners" must be allowed to question her. And the questioning must be done with Semichastny physically present, to interpret knowingly her replies, which might be inscrutable to examiners unaware of the august secret of the hidden missile.

Number Two: The KGB agent at San Cristóbal—Lieutenant Vassilov—should be instructed to keep a special watch on Major Kirov and report every week on his every activity.

Number Three: As soon as practicable, Major Kirov would be recalled (they could call it "home leave," even though he was not due to return to Moscow for another nine months). A suitable replacement would be dispatched to relieve him. A suitable replacement, Malinovsky said, looking into a folder, had been singled out several months ago. Captain Nicolai Pushkin had been trained in the maintenance of the larger missile, the SS-5, SKEAN, and it would take only a few weeks to familiarize him with the differences in the two missiles, as also, of course, to acquaint him with the super-secret nature of the operation. "He has all the general technical qualifications of Kirov, and was in charge of preparing for the emplacement of a missile battery of SS-5's at Remedios during September and October, and he is a bachelor."

Khrushchev was satisfied.

No ONE HAD counted on Olga's fragility. Her examiners, in one of the soundproof rooms reserved for that purpose, had proceeded according to routine, even as the head of the KGB himself observed the proceedings from his chair, through the frequently used peephole, wearing headphones so that he could not only see but hear what was going on. Later, he swore to Khrushchev that a thirty-year-old man would "hardly have noticed" what the examiners had done. Her head could not have been held under the water in the huge sink longer than "oh, believe me, Nikita Sergeyevich, not longer than—twenty seconds." However many seconds it was, Olga Kirov had died. The examiners at first thought it merely a matter of water in the lungs, and the doctor was quickly summoned. But she did not respond. The water in her lungs had brought on a fatal heart attack.

There were formalities to worry about. The official story would be that Olga Kirov was summoned by the police because there had been a report—utterly false, as it turned out (obviously the work of a Cuban *agent provocateur*)—that her husband, Major Kirov, had been wounded by a sniper at San Cristóbal. They wished to break the news to her gently, and give her such medical care as she might need. But even before the report came in that it was a false alarm, she had suffered a heart attack and died. Major Kirov would be given home leave at the end of the month.

There was the problem of Zinka Petrov. She was told the identical story that would be given the following day in the coded telegram to Kirov; and no doubt she would understand the causes of the tragic end of her roommate's life.

But they were very wrong about Zinka Petrov. Zinka was a close friend of a fellow singer in the Bolshoi Opera chorus who, two years before, had entertained, lavishly, a visiting Cuban tenor with whom she had established a special line of communication, courtesy of the Union of Artists. Zinka had no difficulty in asking her friend to convey a message to her Cuban tenor, written in the florid language of separated lovers. That message, appropriately disguised, read: *Contact Major Kirov* (she gave his telephone number at the officers' quarters at San Cristóbal). Zinka's message to her dead roommate's husband was straightforward: *Olga was killed by the KGB last night. Nothing else you hear is true.*

23

San Angel Inn is the name by which a barrio in the southern part of Mexico City is still known by most of its residents, notwithstanding that its official name is Villa Obregón, named after the dictator assassinated there in 1928, whose embalmed hand still reposes in a statue dedicated to him on the spot of his assassination. It was judged doubly appropriate by his court at once to honor the fallen leader and to pursue his campaign of official anticlericalism. One less "Saint" as a geographical location, plus the nice blasphemy of assigning, in its place, the name of the dead religious persecutor.

And within the barrio called San Angel Inn stands an old inn, called, however confusingly, San Angel Inn. This hostelry was not renamed Obregón Inn. At one time, when Mexico City was a tidy, manageable city of 500,000 residents, San Angel Inn was a two-hour carriage drive from the center of town, down Calle Insurgentes, in the direction of Cuernavaca and Taxco. Now the Inn was surrounded by fashionable residences, yet managed to retain a detached remoteness, with its large garden, fit for promenading, and its distinctive internal arrangements: it comprised a dozen old, Spanish-dimensioned suites, to one of which Consuelo directed "Bledsoe." He gave eleven the following morning as the meet-time.

Blackford smiled inwardly. Clearly he was not meeting with a trained intelligence agent, else the appointed time would not have been given in round numbers. If the initiative had been Blackford's, he'd have specified a rendezvous at 11:03. He made it a point, of course, to arrive at exactly eleven, having asked at the desk directions for "Suite Calero." A bellboy led him there, Blackford knocked, and the door was opened.

A handsome man, about Blackford's age, smiled and extended his hand. "Señor Bledsoe, I am Consuelo, at your service."

Blackford was instantly taken by the manner of his host, assured, soft-spoken, animated. He was two or three inches shorter than Blackford, and his face showed just that trace of color that suggested somewhere along the line—perhaps a hundred, two hundred years ago?—a rivulet of Indian blood into the Castilian mainstream. His features were fine, his skin without trace of a beard. The eyes were a soft brown, his lips austere yet full-blooded, his teeth faintly uneven, as if he had been tended by an orthodontist who permitted the survival of dental character. He was wearing a finely fitted light-gray suit ("English public-school gray," Blackford once called that special shade, because it always reminded him of the uniform he had worn at Greyburn). Consuelo's tie was dark red, with diagonal lines of bright red spaced three or four inches apart. His shirt was light blue, the collar buttoned down.

The host motioned Blackford to an armchair, whose back abutted a long, windowed door that opened to San Angel Inn's garden. Consuelo sat on the sofa to Blackford's left, and between them was the coffee table with, fittingly, a pot of fresh coffee, from which Consuelo began to pour.

"Sugar?"

"No thanks. Black."

Consuelo poured two cups, brought out a silver cigarette case, obviously antique, and offered a cigarette to Blackford, who declined. He was glad that his permission ("Do you mind if I smoke?") had not been asked. Blackford had long since acknowledged that cigarette smokers are uncomfortable if they cannot smoke their cigarettes, and shouldn't feel they need to ask permission to be comfortable. He had made a passing effort to detoxify Sally during senior year at Yale, but hadn't since hectored her (or anybody else) on the subject of smoking.

In his twelve years with the Agency, Blackford had met with myriad men and women under circumstances not generically different from those that today brought him, using a pseudonym, to deal with someone, himself using a pseudonym, to further a common purpose. On some occasions it became important—in some even imperative—subsequently to undertake inquiries after such a meeting as to the true identity of the other party. Whether that would be necessary this time around, Blackford would decide later.

And, at such meetings, the business at hand was, usually, quickly brought up. Consuelo, being Latin, could not proceed without at least one amenity, and so he asked whether this was Bledsoe's first trip to Mexico. Blackford answered that no, he had in fact been several times in Mexico—indeed, he had once before dined at San Angel Inn.

He did not reveal that when he had done so, he was staying only one street away, at Calero, with an American expatriate family and his—friend. Blackford no longer permitted himself to think of Sally as his former "girlfriend." He had never particularly liked the term, and in any case it was with greater and greater frequency being used to describe exactly the relationship he had had with Sally, though to be sure they had thought of themselves as affianced.

He repaid the opening amenity by remarking that it was obvious, from Consuelo's fluency in the language, that he had spent a great deal of time in the States. Yes, Consuelo said, in fact that was so, he had been schooled there. He did not say where, and Blackford was not able to guess, from his unaccented English, where.

"Of a personal nature, Señor Bledsoe, I desire you to know only this, that I am not a Mexican intelligence agent, and that I have not traveled to Cuba since Castro took power. I am professionally engaged by my client, whom we both designate as 'LASH,' or 'AM/LASH.' I agreed to act as intermediary because I sympathize with my client's desire to liberate the Cuban people. It is, really, that—that uncomplicated."

Blackford bowed his head in acknowledgment of the information, but did not reciprocate by giving Consuelo any information about his own background, or profession, or motives. He hoped that Consuelo would in due course conclude that Blackford had not risen through the ranks as a Mafia executioner. His silence prompted Consuelo to proceed.

He told Blackford that LASH had confided to him what he

expected from—he had begun to use another word, stopped, and substituted, "your Agency." Blackford quickly concluded that Consuelo thought it vaguely wrong to use "your government" in connection with a plot to assassinate the leader of a foreign country. Before presenting Bledsoe with the details planned by LASH for the project, he would need to dwell on the reassurances, "indirect and direct," that LASH required.

To begin with the former, he said, LASH assumed that the assassination would be instantly followed by the designation of a new leader of the Cuban people, pending national democratic elections. LASH concluded that such a leader necessarily—he emphasized the word *necessarily*—would be a former associate of Castro's in order to stress that the assassination and ascendancy of a new leader was not an act of counterrevolution sponsored by Batista.

Blackford nodded his head. "Does he have someone in mind?"

Consuelo said that two people would qualify. They were Huber Matos and Guillermo Morales. The first was in prison at Isla de Pinos, the other at La Cabaña.

"Has LASH specific plans for yanking one of these from prison after the assassination?"

Consuelo responded that much thought had been given to this, that LASH had the idea that an ultimatum delivered by radio to the commander of one or both of the prisons would have the desired effect. He detailed LASH's thinking on the subject.

Blackford got up, loosened his tie distractedly, and then said, "No. In my judgment it will not work. There simply won't be time. Assume—let's talk hypothetically—that Castro is shot at noon. Unless LASH has in mind an explosion that would simultaneously take out Raúl, Valdés, Guevara, and Dorticós, one of these is going to have the police, the army, and the reserves alerted by twelve-fifteen to batten down the hatches. Martial law will be declared. And as a matter of fact, Señor Consuelo, since my mind is roaming now on the proposal, it isn't entirely inconceivable that Matos and Morales will be ordered executed immediately after Castro falls as putative threats to the post-Castro Communist government." Blackford looked out the window, pausing for only a moment . . .

"No. Although . . . we would be delighted if the train of

events you describe were to take place, it simply isn't going to happen. Either Matos or Morales has to be lifted out of the prison before the assassination, or you're going to need to get somebody who is free, around whom what we hope will be an exuberantly increased resistance can instantly gather. And even then it's likely there will be civil war, and it's by no means predictable that the resistance would win it."

Consuelo interjected that corollary plans made by LASH would call for instant diplomatic recognition given to the deputized successor. The effect of this would legitimize the assassination, increasing the possibility of a recognizable, genuine, traditional coup.

Blackford spoke cautiously. "We have not been idle these past six months. Highly discreet inquiries have been made, the pressure points identified. Within twenty-four hours of the death of Castro, we would anticipate diplomatic recognition of the new government by four Latin American states"—he smiled—"unhappily not including your own. And, at a discreet but by no means remote interval, diplomatic recognition by my government."

They dwelt on the subject of recognition at some length, but Blackford returned to the question of the deputized successor and asked whether LASH had considered "something a little more like the July 20 affair in 1944—aimed not only at Hitler, but at his entire high command."

He had considered it, Consuelo replied, and ruled it out as simply unworkable. LASH did not have the resources, nor would he find the opportunity to undertake tyrannicide on such a scale.

"In that case, Consuelo"—both men were now dropping the "Señor" when using each other's name—"there is no way to avoid a civil-war phase in this operation. But the leader of the anti-Castro forces has got to be free and mobile. What's the matter with Jesús Ferrer? God knows he was never associated with Batista. He's only twenty-eight, although well prepared, and during the last two years of Batista's government he was a graduate student at Oxford."

Yes, Consuelo agreed, but Ferrer did not have the advantage of having worked with Castro, though their families had ties—and this advantage LASH set high store by. Blackford countered that Ferrer could proceed to name to a new council recognized leaders who had been betrayed by Castro, including the imprisoned persons. "But obviously, for the sake of their safety, a direct assault would need to be planned on the prisons. I am going to have to ask a very direct question, Consuelo: Is LASH in touch with the resistance? I mean, in touch with Ferrer?"

Yes, Consuelo said; but only through a trusted intermediary. "Ferrer has no idea of the identity of LASH."

"Well, has LASH asked the obvious question: How much firepower could Ferrer bring to bear immediately on the situation? For instance, could he take Pinos? That's quite a fortress there."

Consuelo replied that LASH was counting heavily on a sense of liberation that would be experienced by the Cuban people. "That, plus the electrical effect of the death of someone whose invincibility is now taken almost for granted by the Cuban people. The fact that Castro proved mortal would have convulsive effects on Cuba."

"God, you don't have to convince me of that, Consuelo. I mean, we're willing to go with just the elimination of Castro, on the grounds that his successor isn't going to come in with the special charisma of that bastard. But since you asked to talk about succeeding events, we have to have plausible answers to the kind of questions I'm asking."

Consuelo paused to light another cigarette, inhaled it deeply, and said with a look of concern on his face that clearly reflected his own misgivings about the enterprise: "LASH does not believe that he can engineer what you call so aptly a 'July 20' assassination attempt. But this does not mean that he has necessarily neglected the possibility of other . . . events quickly succeeding the . . . main event."

Blackford nodded. He did not need to ask for more specific details. It could be that LASH knew that, with Castro dead, others would rise quickly against Castro's closest associates.

Consuelo raised his hand. "I have ordered our lunch. Are you ready for it?" Blackford nodded. Consuelo picked up the telephone and, in authoritative, direct, but genial Spanish, relayed his instructions.

Blackford picked up the conversation. "It comes down to this.

We will come through with the diplomatic business, but there has got to be a plausible government to recognize. And until you free one of those birdies from prison, I can't see that you can do better than Jesús Ferrer. But you and LASH can ponder that one, only for God's sake do it quickly."

"It is not impossible to communicate with LASH, but it is not easy, and communications are not in the form of free discussions of the kind we are now having."

"Okay, do it with reference to your own schedule. But let me tell you about my Agency's schedule. It is: *Get on with this*. It is getting harder all the time. I don't know whether you have seen or spoken with LASH since Castro's speech Saturday about how we are all trying to assassinate him. But that speech has got to suggest heightened security—"

Concerning the problem of heightened security, Consuelo had up-to-date information. He relayed it to Blackford, describing some of the added precautions that had been taken to guard above all Castro himself, but also others . . .

They were interrupted by a knock on the door. A trolley of hot food was wheeled in. Both men were silent until the waiters had left. Consuelo broke in: "Please. We have been talking over two hours. Let us take thirty minutes to eat."

Blackford said, sure, his mind exploring the ramifications of what Consuelo had said.

During the meal, Consuelo engaged in general conversation having to do with the plight of Cuba, the "incredible" crisis involving the missiles of the preceding October. "I assume," Consuelo smiled, slicing the chicken breast, "that you will not take offense if I give you my own view of the matter, which is that your government should have taken the initiative in October to—blast the hell out of Castro's government?"

"There would have been a lot of dead people."

"How many dead people are there going to be if there is civil war? I will give you a figure you are perhaps not acquainted with. Our own civil war in Mexico began with the overthrow of Porfirio Díaz in 1910, and it did not really end until Obregón. During that ten-year interval, two million Mexicans were killed."

Blackford was familiar with the statistic, but pretended not to be. Better manners that way. He said, "I happen to be a deeply convinced personal admirer of President Kennedy. I do not deny that he has made mistakes. Certainly we would agree that his failure to provide air cover for the 1961 invasion was a mistake. Whether he could have handled the business last October any better, I just don't know, and you may be right. But just don't *underestimate* John F. Kennedy. He's got guts, he's smart as a pistol, he's a captivating human being—"

He stopped abruptly. He had committed a cardinal sin. Consuelo now knew that Blackford had been personally exposed to Kennedy.

Blackford both admired and appreciated the professionalism of Consuelo's handling of the problem—as if Consuelo had not made the obvious inference.

"Yes," he said, "all of us feel the same way. I feel myself that I know the President, from all the exposure he has gotten, from his speeches, his wonderfully adroit press conferences . . ." He picked up the telephone again, and without delay the two waiters reappeared, removing the lunch and leaving a new pot of coffee.

When they had closed the door, Blackford spoke. "Look, we have to get down to very concrete details at this point. My— group has two interests. One, the assassination must be consummated. Two, there can be no involvement traceable to our government—"

"I know, I know, I know. LASH has made that abundantly clear to me. So let me tell you now what he has planned. Nobody knows this except LASH himself, me, and now you."

He outlined the details of the planned assassination.

Blackford reflected on them. He asked, "Is LASH an expert rifleman?"

"He is a very expert rifleman."

"We have, as you must know, had several transactions through his representative in Miami on the matter of the rifle. We are ready to situate, at a designated spot on an accessible part of the coast of Cuba, a Russian-made sharpshooter's rifle with a scope sight—specifically, a Mosin-Nagant, model 93/38. The instrument has been thoroughly tested. The scope is set for one hundred meters. It is readily adjustable for the distance you have in mind. Strapped to the rifle, in Spanish, will be instructions on how to make that adjustment for each ten-meter distance. Thirty-six rounds of ammunition, obviously more than is necessary—for the primary task—will be in the same waterproof container. What else?"

Consuelo took a draught from his cigarette.

"LASH does not intend, so to speak, to commit a kamikaze attack. He accepts the fact that you cannot safely arrange for his escape. He has made his own arrangements, and they are satisfactory. He will direct a motor vessel to Jamaica. He will be out of Cuba—whatever happens—after the assassination. But he needs one thing more."

"What?"

"One hundred and fifty thousand dollars in cash. He requires . . . professional mobility after the event."

Blackford wondered at the figure. It was exactly the sum that had been guaranteed by Mongoose, before the October crisis, to the Mafia, in return for Castro, dead.

"There is no point in arguing about the sum of money. Where is it to be deposited?"

"It is to be given, in cash, to me."

Blackford paused. For the first time his mind returned to the opening formality, the generic question whether Consuelo's identity would need to be probed. Consuelo instantly read his mind.

"You must know, Bledsoe, that you have no alternative than to trust me completely. Any attempt to get between me and LASH will abort the operation."

"I understand," Blackford said, slowly, deliberately. "When? The money?"

"At our next meeting."

"Why can't the money come in to you from another . . . agent?"

"That arrangement will not be acceptable." This was said with a finality Blackford did not even consider challenging.

"When?" he repeated.

"I will be in touch with you, through the same channel we have used. You will then return to Mexico. I will have answers to questions you have raised that can be answered. At that meeting, I will give you the date of the—execution. It will be not more than seven days after our meeting."

There was nothing more to discuss. Blackford found himself

saying, as he got up, "If it matters to you, Consuelo, I do trust you. I am very glad that LASH selected you to represent him."

Consuelo had risen. He gave a tiny bow, Mexican style. "And," he said, "I trust you. Let us pray that LASH's mission will prove to be a July 20."

"With different results."

"With different results."

Suddenly Blackford broke out into a wide smile. "Better watch our metaphors, Consuelo, or we may end up talking about Nuremberg."

Consuelo returned the smile. And said, " 'Sic semper tyrannis' aren't the words—or the deeds—of war criminals."

They shook hands, and Blackford left the Calero Suite.

24

María Arguilla received an answer to her letter, and it was written in Castro's own hand. He was "mad with desire" to have her return. She must do so *"prontísimo."* Merely fly to Mexico City, go to the Cuban Embassy, ask for a visa (the Embassy would be instructed to expedite her travel), and before the end of the week "we will lie together, and perhaps be entertained by a first-rate movie!"

María looked into the mirror on the dressing table of her apartment on Fifteenth Avenue. Trafficante had consented to her continuing to occupy the restaurant's apartment during the two or three months required to find and train her successor.

She took a deep breath. This was her final opportunity to pull out. She closed her eyes: but what she saw, her eyes once closed, she read as nothing less than a mandate. What she always saw was the face of Doña Leonarda on the morning María had walked across the little lawn to give her the news of her son's execution. María opened her eyes, and her resolution was now set. She reached out for the jar of cold cream, unscrewed the lid, and inserted her thumb and second finger an inch below the surface.

They closed on the two capsules. She pulled them out and stared at them. Would these little concentrates, each not much larger than an aspirin, actually prove to be the instruments by which the Cuban people would be liberated? And—she found herself saying the words out loud—serve a small, but critical subsidiary purpose: Doña Leonarda avenged?

Her meeting on Monday with Mr. Hicock and his aide had, really, taught her nothing she had not already been advised of.

On all points, Mr. Hicock was wonderfully, cheerfully reassuring. No, there was no *possibility* of the pills' decomposing in the face cream. No, there was no *possibility*, once melted in hot water, that they would not instantly diffuse through *any* surrounding liquid, hot or cold, that Castro might choose to drink. No, there was no *possibility* that he would feel any pain whatever for three hours. No, there was no *possibility*, after he *did* feel pain, that the poison could be extruded from his system in time to save his life. No, there was *no doubt* that, if such an emergency arose as to require María herself to swallow the pills, the neutralizer she now had would work (she passed her eye over the conventional-sized bottle with the yellow liquid labeled "Mild laxative. As required, two ounces at bedtime"— signed by a doctor in Miami, dated two months earlier). No, an autopsy would *not* identify the poison as available only in the United States.

She was given a telephone number and an address in Havana where she could get emergency help. The slip of paper with the information was held in front of her until she had memorized it; then Mr. Hicock ceremoniously burned it. If she telephoned that number, she must ask for "Fidelito." ("I *like* that," Mr. Hicock had laughed joyously.) She would need to be guided by her own judgment: If she decided to hide, "Fidelito" could *easily* arrange to bring her back to Miami. "As you know, there are more than a hundred escapees every day by boat. And U.S. naval vessels are patrolling the waters more rigorously than ever, so that it is only a question of getting twelve miles out from Cuba, and 'Freedom of the Seas takes over!' " Wild Bill Hicock said excitedly, with the same pride he'd have shown if Freedom of the Seas had been his firstborn son.

María Arguilla was careful to pack commodiously. It would not do to return "permanently" to Havana after an entire year in Miami without a considerable wardrobe, especially now that she was formally affluent. Accordingly, she bought six large suitcases, had them stenciled with her initials, stuffed them full with everything she owned, plus some secondhand clothes bought cheaply, and bought a first-class ticket to Mexico City on the following morning's Eastern Airlines flight.

She was surprised when, at the airport in Mexico, a middle-aged man, portly and officious (he bellowed out instructions to the porter who accompanied him), approached her at the gate of her flight, his diplomatic badge, pinned conspicuously above his breast pocket, permitting him into the inspection compound. María had spotted a large cardboard rectangular sign on which was written, "ARGUILLA." She approached him and he bowed, asking if he had the honor of addressing Señorita María Arguilla.

She nodded, more inquisitive than apprehensive.

"I am Gustavo Esteban Quijano, assistant consular officer at the Embassy of the Republic of Cuba. My superior, Señor Alessandro, has instructions from Havana to expedite your arrangements. I telephoned to the number given to me in Miami, but you had already left. I was given your flight number, and am happy to have found you in order to help in any way I can."

María Arguilla was shepherded through Immigration and Customs, Quijano talking without cease about such subjects as the difference in temperature between Miami and Mexico City, the subtle differences between the temperature in Miami and in Havana, all on account of the Gulf Stream, and his painful absence from Havana for six long months, but all the news was wonderfully reassuring about the great economic and social progress being made back home under Comandante Fidel.

Her bags identified, passed, and placed by the porter on a long trolley, Quijano asked whether María had reservations. Yes, she said, she was staying at the Hotel del Prado, and had planned to go that very afternoon to the Cuban Embassy to apply for a visa. He tut-tutted her about this entirely unnecessary inconvenience, asked her for her passport, and said that he would make all the necessary arrangements.

Might she, María asked, be able to count on taking the flight to Havana the following day? "If I miss that flight, I shall have to wait until Thursday."

Quijano said that the three-times-per-week flights to Havana were heavily booked but—he winked—he would see to it that she was seated aboard the plane before the other passengers. "And if that means one passenger has to delay his passage— why, that is a pity, no?" He chuckled.

"After all, it's *our* airline, is it not? And *our* revolution!"

María smiled, appreciatively.

They had certainly got the word in Mexico, María reflected,

sinking down into the couch of the flower-filled suite into which the Cuban Embassy had upgraded her. No questions. No nothing. But perhaps all that would happen in Havana?

Indeed it did, although the auspices were unexpected.

On the airplane the next day she had written out a note on Compañía Cubana de Aviación stationery. She wrote simply:

Dear F. I am here, longing to see you.

Love,

M.

Waiting for her bags at Customs in Havana, she was about to drop the envelope with the international postage stamp into the postal box when a hand reached up and firmly arrested hers, the fingers gripping her envelope, drawing it back from the postal slot.

She looked up at a young, bearded man who, extruding the envelope from her hand, said to her politely but firmly, *"Seguridad, Señorita."*

He asked her to accompany him. They walked into a bare room with a desk, two chairs, and a large picture of Fidel Castro.

"I regret very much, Señorita Arguilla, but I must look at this letter."

It was addressed: "Sr. J. J. Martí, Apartado de Correo 2008, Oficios y Teniente Rey, La Habana."

Maria said nothing. Her interrogator did not open the envelope at once. He picked up his telephone and dialed a number. He spoke in whispers, but what he said was audible to anyone sitting a few feet opposite.

"Yes, Bracero here. Airport—in re Arguilla."

He did not have to wait long. He was put through to the security operative. He reported studiously into the telephone, "An envelope. Addressed to 'Sr. J. J. Martí, Apartado de Correo 2008, Oficios y Teniente Rey, La Habana."

Again he waited, tapping his finger impatiently on the desk. When the earphone was active again, he sat up, and let his hand slowly idle on the table as his eyes widened.

"Sí, Capitán. Sí, Capitán. Entendido, Capitán. Entendido, Capitán."

He put down the receiver, and returned the envelope to María Arguilla.

"A thousand pardons, Señorita. You need not fear that anyone will hear of this."

María thought it time to retaliate. "I cannot give you the same guarantee, señor—what is your name?—"

"Hernando Bracero Delavera, *a sus órdenes.*"

"—that no one will hear about this."

Without another word, Bracero opened the door and, silently, escorted her through the Customs formalities. There was general consternation about the checked baggage. María's was among those that did not materialize in the off-loading station. Bracero told her he would personally see to it that her baggage would arrive at her destination—he would deliver it himself. She must not submit to any foolish delays, he said self-consciously. He took her vouchers and she thanked him, her curtness gone.

She drove in a shopworn 1958 Ford taxi to her little house in Santos Suárez, noticing, en route, only what seemed a uniform deterioration. The shops more threadbare, the trees and shrubs sparer, the buildings and houses more dilapidated. She was tired, and progressively irritated that her luggage hadn't come. Finally—two hours later—the bags arrived, with apologetic explanations from Bracero for the bureaucratic tangle at the airport.

Although she wished ardently to be done with her mission, she rather hoped that Captain Durango, if he was still acting as Fidel's procurer-escort, would not come to fetch her that night. She assumed that the letter she had finally succeeded in posting would not be seen by Castro until the following day, perhaps even the day after. Meanwhile she would put the house in order, get some rest, listen to the radio, watch television, and buy magazines and newspapers from the store at the corner, catching up on the local scene.

At ten o'clock, there was a knock on the door. María groaned. She had not even made herself up. But it wasn't Captain Durango. It was two men, both dressed in fatigues, the senior clean-shaven, the junior with so much beard María wondered for a moment exactly where his mouth was. They were, of course, "Security," and they dutifully exhibited their documents.

She invited them into her living room while feeling an explosive resentment not so much that there should be a security check on Cubans returning to Havana as that they should present themselves at such an unpardonable hour. She considered telling them to go away and to return in the morning, but reasoned that anything that would cause any blip in her security file was to be avoided.

Captain Herrera explained that such interrogations as he and Lieutenant Ramos—Ramos bowed his head slightly—conducted were routine, and that since Señorita Arguilla had been absent from Cuba for over a year, she must understand the lengths to which the imperialists were going in order to attempt to subvert the Revolution. The political overture continued for almost ten minutes, during which María felt a fearful urge to drop off to sleep; but, eventually, Captain Herrera began his questioning. Lieutenant Ramos took notes.

She wondered whether the name of Fidel Castro would come up. She was determined not to use it except as absolutely necessary.

Why had she left?

Why had she stayed so long?

Whom had she been in touch with?

How did she live?

How did she pay her bills?

Who were her lawyers in Havana?

On and on it went. When asked for one document or another she feigned a feminized absentmindedness, ransacking one suitcase and then another before coming up with the relevant document. She did not want to appear conspicuously prepared for such questions as they asked, however practiced she was. She stated her objections only when, after midnight, Captain Herrera said that he would need to take four of her documents with him, which of course he would return to her, probably by the end of the week. She insisted that he give her a receipt for these documents, and that each one be described in detail.

Finally, they left.

María went to her bed. She found herself, half asleep, wondering whether such an interrogation had in fact been entirely routine. Or—and this was the likeliest explanation—were they agents, so to speak, of the royal guard? Perhaps their superior took special pains to examine anyone who would be in personal contact with Fidel Castro; and, she sighed, there was no question that she would, very soon, be in very close personal contact with Fidel Castro.

Finally, she fell asleep. And the next night, at ten, Captain Durango came for her, exactly as of old.

The only item she carried in her little overnight bag that she hadn't always brought with her on her previous trysts with Castro was a can of 16-millimeter film. It suddenly occurred to her, as she was being driven to Fidel's house in Cojímar, that she had never taken pains to view the film, even though the facilities for viewing 16-millimeter films, in one of the back rooms at Trafficante's nightclub, were there. She wondered suddenly if, in the ten years since it had been taken, the film had gone bad? If so, would this cause Fidel to be disappointed? To pout? To be enraged? He had made so many references to the film and his desire to evoke the vicarious ecstasy he had experienced in 1953 ... Well, she thought, if the film was not good, there was nothing she could do about it now.

Fidel's greeting was quite simply overwhelming. He embraced her as though she were the Revolution's only child. The familiar sitting room was unchanged, but instead of the smattering of hors d'oeuvres and the few bottles of this and that at the bar, there was champagne and caviar, and foie gras, and fruits, and vodka.

"This is not just a routine day, this is a celebration!" Fidel said, seizing a bit of everything and stuffing it all onto María's plate, and then helping himself. The champagne in the ice cooler had been opened, and he poured and drank deeply. "It"—he held up the champagne glass—"is one of the few pleasant things I can think of now being produced by De Gaulle's France," he commented, as ever inclined to political orientation. He plied María with questions about her life in Miami and rejoiced over her ultimate success in getting "your little capitalist nest egg." ("You must remind me not to confiscate it!")

But all of this—food, wine, conversation—was progressively irrelevant as he became amorous. Suddenly he was on his feet. For a fearful moment María thought a professional would appear to handle the projector; but no, Castro removed a drape behind the couch, revealing the machine at the ready, and, María's reel of film in hand, he began threading it.

"I took a refresher lesson in the operation of this machine this afternoon. I did not intend to take any chances! I was the projector operator at my preparatory school. Every Friday night we would show a movie based on the latest miracle at Fatima, or something like that"—he was bent over the machine. He reached now to the wall and turned off the overhead lights. He flicked a switch on the projector and a beam illuminated the portable screen situated ten feet in front of the couch. The *whhrrr* of the home movie filled the room. María braced herself for what was to come.

It was all there, in shots long and embarrassingly tight. Trafficante had synced in some exaggeratedly voluptuarian music, a pulsating, "Bolero"-type non-stopper that sought rough emotional congruity with the events depicted on the screen. Halfway through the showing, Fidel began to disrobe and motioned to María to do the same. He wished, he whispered to her, to replicate the movements of her young screen lover, and she was to do exactly as she had done at La Gallinera. When, ten minutes later, the film reached its climax, so did Fidel Castro, who disengaged himself only to rush back, reverse the film, and begin it again.

At its end, Fidel smiled, his eyes half closed.

Maria rose and said she would go to the bathroom. "I am thirsty for a beer." Could she bring him one? Yes, he said dreamily, he would have a beer. Maria reached into her bag for her robe, went into the dressing room with her toilet kit, and closed the door.

She took from the little refrigerator two beers, and from the cupboard two glasses. She quickly doused herself with perfume. Her heart was pounding so violently she had to pause before she could control her fingers to turn the lid on the jar she withdrew from her bag. Finally she opened it and let her trembling fingers descend into the cold cream.

Her heart stopped beating.

The capsules were not there.

She began hysterically to dig out the contents of the jar, kneading the cream between her fingers, incredulous. She reached the bottom of the jar, and the door behind her opened. She wheeled about.

He was loomingly there, in his bathrobe, a leer on his face. He extended his arm out toward her, palm open.

"Is this what you are looking for?" He held the two capsules in the palm of his hand.

Two uniformed men, one of them with pistol drawn, entered the bathroom. María had no feeling in her legs as they dragged her out.

25

At the Soviet officers' club in the San Cristóbal compound vodka was inexpensive, and its enthusiastic consumption was certainly one of the causes of the general merriment before the dinner hour. Ingenio Tamayo, greeted at the door by his host, Major Kirov, soon noticed that Kirov was anxious to detach himself from his compatriots in every way. It went so far—or had Kirov *always* preferred rum?—as asking the Cuban bartender, after ascertaining that his guest wanted a beer, not for a vodka straight up, or for that matter a vodka anything, but for rum and Coca-Cola—*doble*. Kirov then drew Tamayo to a corner of the large lounge where over a hundred Soviet officers were gathered, drinking and gabbing, some of them filing by the bar to give their orders. Almost all were dressed in light cotton khaki trousers (a few wore dress whites). The club's weekday regulations specified "optional dress," and this translated into a variety of sports shirts. There was no other Cuban present, so far as Tamayo could see.

They spoke to each other in English, in which Kirov was competent, Tamayo fluent. To Tamayo's surprise, Kirov was yearning to talk, indeed to talk about matters normally thought to be too ideologically risqué to discuss, in particular between strangers—although Anatoly Kirov did not let Tamayo feel for very long that he was a stranger.

Kirov plied Tamayo with questions of theoretical concern to students of Marxism-Leninism and, patently, of immediate concern to him. Had Tamayo studied Marx at college? Had he read Lenin? Had he read the text of the 20th Congress speech, February 1956, in which Khrushchev had outlined the brutalities of

Stalin? Did Tamayo believe that the faults in leadership identified by Khrushchev had in fact been eliminated in the Soviet Union?—If not, did Tamayo believe, as many imperialist scholars insisted, that such faults as Stalin was so blatantly guilty of inhered in the system? Or was there a special Russian component that had caused the evolution of Communism, over a period of forty-six years, to take the particular direction it was taking in Russia?

Tamayo, altogether taken aback by the behavior of his host—he acted almost as if he were on drugs of some sort that induced this intimate torrent of questions—answered cautiously. But he wished above all to get close to Kirov and so, however ambiguous his answers, they never had the effect of dampening the conversation. On the contrary, Tamayo managed to be a kind of enthralled listening post. He concluded that indeed it had been established that Stalin was a "very cruel" leader, but, to be sure, Stalin had had singular historical problems to confront, from the internecine question of the succession after the death of Lenin, to the dogged resistance of the kulak class, to the war by Hitler, to the atomic monopoly by the American imperialists—

Wait! Kirov said.

He wished to fetch another drink. Would Tamayo have the same?

He was back quickly; the line had thinned out, and most of the officers had passed into the cafeteria. Kirov plunked down the two glasses on the little round table and resumed talking. "What," he said with some solemnity, "about Castro? Is *he* different?"

Time for *extreme* caution, Tamayo thought.

"Different from what?"

"Well, different from *Stalin*?—I mean, obviously Castro is different from Stalin, but is he different from the *kind* of man Stalin was?"

Above all Tamayo wished to come up with the answer Kirov wanted. He decided, on this question, to act decisively. "Yes. Castro is *very* different. He has no taste for human suffering. He is resolute when he needs to be resolute, but always he acts in the interest of the Cuban people and of the Revolution. Yes, he is *very* different."

Kirov drew his chair closer. He was speaking now within six inches of Tamayo's ear. "Do you *know* Fidel Castro?"

Again Tamayo gambled. "Yes. I know him *very well.* I was an early recruit in the movement, and he has honored me with special assignments. I report directly to Fidel Castro."

Kirov's eyes opened wide in a combination of curiosity and awe.

"Let us," he said, "go in and have something to eat, and then I do hope to resume the discussion—provided you are willing to do so, Major Tamayo?"

"My friends call me Ingenio."

"I am Anatoly. Let us eat our dinner and then drive to San Cristóbal and have a drink. Do you have a car? Because if not, I can requisition a jeep." Tamayo said no no, by all means he had a car, parked right at the Administration Building. During the meal they were crowded around by young Soviet officers speaking in Russian. Kirov said very little, and nothing of any interest.

He is waiting, Tamayo guessed, for an opportunity to move the conversation in a discreet direction.

A half hour later they were at El Burrito de San Cristóbal, at the quiet southern edge of the town. Other customers that night were mostly natives, though two Russian lieutenants and two Cuban girls made up a rowdy table at one end, struggling to communicate with each other in pidgin Spanish.

"What I want you to know, Ingenio," Major Kirov bent over the little round bar table in the corner of the saloon, "is that I am a profound believer in Marxist destiny. We . . . specialists . . . are very carefully picked by our superiors and they correctly concluded that my belief in the philosophy of socialism is very . . . deep . . . profound. I am also enough a man of this world to accept that difficult social developments sometimes need . . . forceful . . . heavy"—Kirov struggled for the English word—"help from"—he snapped his fingers this time, searching for the word he wanted—"from critically—located human beings. But a true Marxist-Leninist must distinguish between necessary and unnecessary force and violence. Would Castro agree with that?"

"Devoutly," said Ingenio Tamayo. He took great comfort at this moment in his atheism. If there were a God, he told himself,

Ingenio Tamayo would just now have been hit by a bolt of lightning.

Kirov was drinking heavily. Tamayo ordered a glass of beer every time Kirov ordered a double rum and Coca-Cola. And suddenly it flashed before him! *Tamayo might be given an opening to construe a conversational jog in an unexpected way.* Dangerous, but with the possibility then of spectacularly profitable results . . .

Tamayo was in the men's room. *What,* Tamayo's mind was racing feverishly, *What would he stand to lose by simply coming up with it?* Whatever Kirov's reaction, given his volatile mood his face would register vital information. And, if total ignorance were unconvincingly professed, Tamayo could, if he chose, simply ignore it, and proceed methodically with his investigation. *But just conceivably—*

Tamayo sat down, and put his hand around his glass. Kirov said, "Let me tell you something, Ingenio, that I have not told any of my friends."

"You mean, that you have not told any of your *other* friends, Anatoly."

"Yes," Anatoly Kirov smiled, wanly. "Yes. You are my friend. I know that. Well, it is this. On Wednesday I receive a telegram that my wife, my wonderful wife, Olga, was suddenly dead of a heart attack in Moscow." Tears began to well up in his eyes. "And then, yesterday, I get a message from a Cuban—never mind who, Ingenio; there is no need to go into that—a message from a Cuban who has access to a wire. He gave me a message from Olga's roommate. A *wonderful* woman, a singer with the Bolshoi Opera chorus. Zinka Petrov reports quite bluntly. Here—here are her words exactly. She said by wire: OLGA WAS KILLED BY THE KGB LAST NIGHT. NOTHING ELSE YOU HEAR IS TRUE. Those were her words.

"Now, just understand that my wife Olga did *not* die of a heart attack at age thirty-four. Her roommate—Zinka—would not make up so serious a charge. Why, then, did they kill her? I have thinked of nothing else for thirty hours now. I have not slept. I reread every letter I have receive from her since coming in August. More than one hundred letters. I do not keep a copy of my letters, but reading her letters I can tell what I wrote about, and what I did say in several letters was that life in Cuba under the excited leadership of Fidel Castro seems a—better life than in the Soviet Union.

"There is, I remember in one of the letters I write, the question of the climate. It gets *very* cold, for *very* long periods, Ingenio, in Russia. And a true socialist man will attempt to further the Revolution from whatever country he lives in. I did say to her, I *now* recall it, in one letter, maybe in two or three, that perhaps we consider a permanent home here in Cuba, helping Fidel Castro to commit the Revolution. Is it her receipt of such a letter? Our mail is always being read, you know, Ingenio. Did you meet Lieutenant Vassilov today? Well, he is the KGB—the principal KGB—in the camp: It happens that I know *certain* things *others* do not know, or *need* to know . . ." Kirov was rambling now a little, Tamayo noticed, and by no means would Tamayo discourage him from doing so. On the contrary, he encouraged his own plastic facial muscles to move with appropriate reactions to everything Kirov was saying: surprise, indignation, grief, shock, curiosity. Tamayo was pleased with his running accompaniments, and was ready at any moment to strike.

"Yes, perhaps it was that letter," Kirov was going on, beginning a fresh drink, "because although the official—philosophy of the Kremlin is that what matters most is that someone is a Communist, not that he is Ethiopian, or Cuban, or Russian, or anything else, in fact—and here, Ingenio, is another great abuse of Marxist principle—in fact, we Russians are especially nationalistic. But why will they actually *kill* my wife because *I* express such thinking? Well," he said, looking sternly down at the floor, "they will be sorry, they will truly be sorry."

Ingenio moved closer to Kirov, and to the question he was edging toward.

"It is a terrible, terrible story, Anatoly, one of the worst I have *ever* heard. And," he spoke with great concentration given to every syllable, "although the Soviet leaders have been in some respects very generous—after all"—Tamayo pointed vaguely in the direction of the San Cristóbal military compound—"that is why you are here, that is why most of you are here, to help us with problems of basic ordnance. But it is also regrettably true that the Soviet Union is capable of letting down its allies. That certainly was the case during the great crisis in October."

Kirov looked up at Tamayo. He began to speak, but stopped and, instead, drank again from his glass.

Tamayo decided to fire. *"And then, Anatoly, they leave one missile underground here and do not tell us."*

Kirov's face turned red.

"Who told you that?" His voice was suddenly at Present Arms.

"We have our sources, Anatoly. You do not disbelieve Zinka about what the KGB has done, Fidel does not disbelieve his informant about what the Soviet Union has done." *Now, now, now it will come,* Tamayo thought, staring hard at his new friend.

Finally Kirov spoke. He was no longer touching his glass. He said softly, "Ingenio, we must meet again, and soon. But we must take extra-special cautions. We are permitted every other weekend to go to Havana for recreation. Tell me—I will remember—the number to reach you this Saturday morning."

"The number, Anatoly, is 65-0886. I will repeat that: 65-0886."

"What you tell me about Fidel Castro is very very important news for me. I will see you again in two days. Now I think we must separate ourselves. I know," he nodded discreetly in the direction of the bar, "the Soviet captain who just entered and is standing at the bar. You leave, and I will return to the camp with him, and go now and drink with him. It is this simple, Ingenio—only from now on it will be 'Major Tamayo'—I ask you as a hospitality to dine with me at the officers' club, and you reciprocate by asking me to drink with you at the Burrito. You pay the bill. We spoke of matters of common interest having to do with logistical necessities of the Cuban Army. As they say here, *Buenas noches*—Major Tamayo."

"Buenas noches, Major Kirov."

HE DROVE BACK to the compound. Ingenio Tamayo was elated. It was as good as an execution. He would not wait. He drove into the headquarters building. Entering the fluorescent-lighted little outer office, he showed his identification to the duty officer and said he required a private telephone line on which to call "headquarters." He was shown to an adjacent office, and the duty officer depressed an outside line button and left the room. Reaching the operator, Tamayo identified himself and gave the name of the person he wished to speak to.

A second operator asked where he was calling from. Tamayo peered down to the telephone's base and gave the number. He said, not without drama, that his call was urgent.

"Just a minute, please."

In a moment or two, the Comandante's voice sounded.

"Yes, Ingenio?"

Tamayo's heavy breathing was audible at the other end of the line. "Comandante. *It is true.* That is all for now."

Tamayo hung up the telephone, dizzy with self-satisfaction.

26

Aboard the Eastern airliner to Mexico City, Blackford wore a disguise (he was a Hasidic rabbi, wearing a black frock coat, a beard, and yarmulke under a black felt hat). When lunch was served, rather than commit any inadvertent dietary solecism, he ate nothing, and so emerged from the plane, with his false passport, hungry. Blackford thought Rufus overcautious, but—true—he had not worn a disguise to the San Angel Inn meeting, and Rufus had got word from counterintelligence in Mexico that one of the many Cuban agents sheltered in the Cuban Embassy had logged Blackford's arrival in Mexico City.

A great deal had been done in the fortnight since the meeting with Consuelo. Contacts with the resistance inside Cuba had been invigorated, and the seed had been planted in the ear of Jesús Ferrer that local "dissatisfaction" with Castro in Havana could result in "definitive action" being taken against him, perhaps by an outraged Cuban citizen at a public rally. The bluster by Castro about assassinations, the word went out, "planned by the United States Government," had simply been a cover to disguise Castro's own frailty at home.

Ferrer received this news gladly, Rufus had hardly been surprised to learn. Ferrer was not easy to contact, but it never took more than a couple of days to get a message to him. This was accomplished through the use of a resistance radio (moved every two or three days to a different transmission site) within Cuba. The radio could reach Ferrer in his nomadic base in the Sierra Maestra Mountains. And Ferrer traveled every ten days or so to one or another of several addresses in Havana where he was well sheltered and from which he could coordinate, or attempt to do so, the activities of the resistance working out of Miami.

At one of these meetings he was told that in the event Castro were assassinated, Jesús Ferrer should instantly declare himself president of the Provisional Government of Cuba pending, in six months, national elections. His Cuban adviser in Miami, a member of Alpha 66, told him that there was every reason to believe that anti-Castro Latin American governments would come through with quick diplomatic recognition, but that it was exceedingly important that he should move quickly. Above all it was imperative that he should broadcast on national radio. A resistance unit operating within Havana would give this enterprise top priority. Ferrer, who thought and acted decisively, suggested that at the next meeting within Havana he record a tape which could be played over the radio wherever he himself happened to be. His idea was greeted enthusiastically.

Ferrer, back in the mountains, worked carefully on three scripts.

The first would confine itself to the fact of the "death" of Castro, announcing the new government, declaring amnesty for all former members of Castro's government who "disarmed within four hours" of this announcement. (Ferrer would have preferred to say "before six o'clock this afternoon," or "before midnight tonight," but he could not anticipate the time of day at which the announcement would be made.)

The second script, unlike the first, which lasted only one minute, lasted approximately five. It called on the "democracies" in the world to recognize the Provisional Government and welcome the return of democracy to Cuba.

The third script was a spirited twenty-minute indictment of Castro. A recitation of former friends, and even family, he had executed, imprisoned, tortured, or exiled. There were economic figures to give out which, Ferrer knew, would not be challenged by Cubans who had suffered almost five years of Castro's communization and its economic consequences. Then Ferrer spoke warmly of former companions-at-arms of Fidel Castro who had been betrayed by him. Ferrer would, at this point, dub in excerpts from Fidel's broadcast promises of 1953 and 1959, as had been done so successfully when Ferrer had taken over the radio station briefly.

These scripts he brought to Redondo Street, to the self-effacing house of retired diplomats Ernesto and Teresa Lascasas. Ferrer recorded the scripts on an old but serviceable German tape recorder. The old diplomat, his wife, and two young Cubans—one operated within the city, the second had come in two nights earlier on one of the speedboats from Miami, depositing a cache of arms at Nuevitas in Camagüey—listened to the eerie sounds of the new young leader announcing the "death of Fidel Castro." When the three tapes were over, Doña Teresa said that it was the most musical half hour she had ever heard.

Rufus, meanwhile, had devoted many hours to the New Direction. Anthony Trust traveled from Latin American capital to capital, giving word—discreetly, dramatically, enticingly—of the new young leader in Cuba who was attempting to do what Fidel Castro had promised but failed to do. No account of Ferrer's background, from that point on, failed to stress the family ties of the Ferrer and Castro families.

Young Jesús Ferrer, with his cosmopolitan background, his derring-do in the mountains, gradually limned into the consciousness of the press. His name became, gradually, conspicuous—for if It was to happen, Jesús Ferrer must not be a stranger.

The job of canonizing him within Miami, Blackford decided, was better not attempted. There were at least four figures in Miami who thought themselves the logical—indeed the indisputable—leaders of post-Castro Cuba. To impose over them a twenty-eight-year-old virtual unknown would simply generate sibling jealousy, already so rife in Miami as to make Blackford despair of a united effort against Castro.

Let it happen elsewhere, and let the diplomatic initiatives, planned by Mongoose, effect the anointing of Jesús Ferrer. Better that than Blackford attempting, from a hidden apartment, wearing idiot disguises every time he left, trying to bring about a diplomatic consensus among the expatriate groups. Pano thoroughly agreed. "There is no purpose *at all* in doing the one before the other. *Esperamos*, let us hope."

Much but not all of this had been relayed to LASH through the Miami-Havana contact. What Blackford didn't know was how much of it had, in turn, been relayed to Consuelo by LASH. Would it transpire, at their meeting tomorrow, that Consuelo was wholly ignorant of the political plans that had been made? These, after all, had replaced those LASH had begun by insisting on—namely, that the head of the Provisional Government be an ex-Castroite, scooped out of prison to serve as the president of the Provisional Government. Blackford would of course report to Consuelo that the rifle had been delivered, together with the appurtenances, at the designated spot in Luyano near Havana. And—Blackford found his eyes turning down to his traveling briefcase stowed under the seat in front—he had the money. One thousand, five hundred one-hundred-dollar bills. Odd how little room they occupied, Blackford thought. He could have squeezed a million dollars into that briefcase, though not that much in the special compartment in which the money was hidden.

Blackford found himself looking forward to his meeting with Consuelo. This had nothing to do with the justifiable relief he would feel at no longer carrying around a hundred and fifty thousand in cash. It was that he had found, in the aristocratic, earnest, nimble Mexican, an affinity of spirit and temperament. Blackford was reading, on the airplane, the book of letters from Whittaker Chambers to William F. Buckley, Jr. He had marked a particular passage. Buckley had taken a friend to visit Chambers, and of the experience Chambers had written him, "I liked Galbraith at sight. This happens so seldom with me that I wondered why it happened. As I listened to him laugh, watched him study the titles of my books, watched his mind fasten on one or two points of no great importance in themselves, but somewhat as an ant, at touch, clamps on the rib of a leaf that may be littering its path, I liked him better. I decided that what I liked was a kind of energy, what kind scarcely mattered. One of our generals was once being ho-ho-hearty with the ranks, as I understand generals are sometimes, especially if newsmen are present. He asked a paratrooper, 'Why do you like to do an insane thing like jumping out of airplanes?' The paratrooper answered, 'I don't like to, sir; I just like to be around the kind of people who like to jump out of airplanes.' I felt something like the paratrooper about Galbraith." Blackford knew instantly that such had been the effect on him of his three hours with Consuelo.

An hour later, at the airport, he casually opened his briefcase for inspection by Customs. The inspector was evidently himself Jewish, because he gave an extra-courtly bow, waving the rabbi on. Blackford hoped he would not be accosted by another rabbi, anxious to talk shop. But in the event, he was prepared. (He was in Mexico to see his sick mother, who had emigrated to Mexico after the war, leaving her son to pursue his rabbinical studies in Cleveland, Ohio. Just enough chatter to permit non-abrupt conversational disengagement.)

The taxi driver he addressed in Spanish, and asked to be taken to the Hotel Geneve where, checked into his bedroom, first he ordered from room service a *carne asada* with frijoles and guacamole and a beer. Only then did he dial the number he had memorized. He had, in any event, been asked to dial that number between seven and nine.

"I was expecting you, Bledsoe," he heard the calm, musical, authoritative voice of Consuelo.

"Everything okay?"

"Yes and no. I did have this telephone checked, and unless there is something wrong at your end, we are all right. I have no reason to be suspicious of anything at all, but the last communication from LASH asked that I take special precautions. Reason not given. So—tomorrow we will not meet at San Angel Inn. How well do you know the environs of Mexico?"

"Well, I've been around a little. Where do you want to meet?"

"Do you know where Tres Marías is?"

"Yes, I do as a matter of fact. That's where you bumped off the last genyooine competitor for the presidency of the republic who wasn't a member of PRI." Blackford's reference was to the assassination of General Francisco Serrano, in 1927, before the Partido Revolucionario Institucional became the single-party political boss of Mexico. "You're talking about Tres Marías on the road to Cuernavaca?"

"Exactly. And no more wisecracks about *our* assassinations, or I'll give you some comparative figures," Consuelo commented playfully. "There is a little huddle of open-air tortilla and beer stands. Are you familiar with them?"

"I have twice stopped and snacked there."

"I propose that you park before the first stand, I'll park beyond the third, this side of the gas station. I will arrive at exactly noon and order two lunches. I'll take them across the road to where the wooden picnic tables are—it is a state park. You arrive at twelve-fifteen. You will see me beginning to eat. Sit down opposite me unless, directly behind me, on the ground, you see the morning newspaper. If you see that, it means that I have spotted something—anomalous. In that case, return to your car, and call me again tomorrow evening."

Blackford said fine, he would pick up a car first thing in the morning. "Don't be surprised, Consuelo, when you look for me. I hope you won't see me, in fact. I'll be the guy behind the beard."

"Beard? Isn't that what you call a little bit corny?"

"Not corny among the Orthodox, Consuelo. And I am very orthodox. At least on this trip."

Ramon laughed. "*Hasta luego*, Bledsoe."

IT WAS AN unusual day, a raw October day, in a city renowned for its cool and sunny fall climate. And, as Blackford drove past University City to the beginning of the old mountain road—the government was busy building a three- and four-lane highway that would shorten the hour's drive to Cuernavaca—he felt the unusual chill. As the car began to climb toward the high point in the mountain range, ten thousand feet above the level of the sea, two thousand feet higher than Mexico City, five thousand higher than Cuernavaca, the fog and wet were dispiriting. Blackford wondered why Consuelo hadn't chosen almost any other site, in the comfortable capital city. Oh well. An outdoor lunch in this weather would surely discourage counterintelligence; he made himself smile.

There were only two other cars parked in the Tres Marías area. Tourists, seeking a little sustenance. It was exactly 12:15 when Blackford took the key from the ignition. Wearing a black frock coat under his raincoat, his briefcase in his left hand, he crossed the road and walked toward the picnic area. There was only the one dauntless picnicker, his back to the road. Blackford approached him. The morning *Excelsior* rested reassuringly on top of the picnic table, secured from the wind by the bottle of beer placed on top of it. Blackford greeted Consuelo and sat down opposite. Blackford had the view of the road, Consuelo of the park.

"Any problems?" Blackford asked.

"No problems," Consuelo answered. "Do you intend, rabbi, to bless the meal before eating it? It is good and hot, by the way."

Blackford laughed. "I take it you have never submitted to the disciplines of the covert agent."

"That is quite correct, Bledsoe. And I never propose to do this kind of thing again, once I have taken care of LASH. I felt embarrassed, talking to you last night, because of all things my wife entered my study while I was using my private, unlisted telephone. I didn't see her. And there I was, with talk fit for a twelve-year-old. By a twelve-year-old. Secret assignations, disguises—the whole thing." Both men, while conversing, were eating their enchiladas and tacos and guacamole, downing them with cold Carta Blanca beer.

"Hilarious. What did she say?"

"She is—" Consuelo began to speak but restrained himself. Privacy privacy privacy, he said to himself. Never mind the utter confidence you repose in the man you are talking to.

"You will understand, Bledsoe, I must back up. No details. She *was* very understanding. She said she knew 'a certain amount about that kind of thing.' But to return to the original subject, she too made me swear to make this my last operation. She did not need to persuade me. But—the clock is ticking. What do you have to report?"

Blackford told him that the decision had been made to push Jesús Ferrer as first President; that no one had devised any plausible means of getting any of Fidel's old confederates out of prison. "Are you aware of that decision?"

"I am aware of it. LASH has approved the plan. It may be too late—next Saturday is the day, Bledsoe; Saturday, November ninth. The great moment. Now, if it is not too late, Jesús Ferrer should be counseled to appeal as openly as he can to Matos and Gutiérrez Menoyo—to declare them national heroes, to promise not only their immediate release from prison, but prominent portfolios in the Provisional Government. Every step in that direction discourages rampant civil war—that is what I fear most. And what about—the other things?"

"The shipment at Luyano has been made. Day before yesterday. No problem. LASH should have the material in hand. Or perhaps he elects to leave it hidden for a few days. That's his business, provided he doesn't get caught. The money is in my briefcase, six inches from my left foot. Take the whole briefcase. Below the magazines and paperbacks—and the Talmud—is a hidden compartment. Simple. Two plastic screws at the rear. Loosen them. With a nail file, coax the hinged folder up. It's in hundred-dollar bills, unmarked."

There was never any question of opening the case and counting the money.

They had finished eating. Consuelo spoke. "You leave here first; I will wait a few minutes, read the paper, and go with your briefcase to my own car."

"How soon will you give LASH the word?"

"What word? I told you, the operation is scheduled for Saturday."

"I mean, the word about our meeting. Hell, confirmation about your getting the money."

"I will not be communicating again with LASH. It was left that I would call only if—"

"Get down!" Blackford screamed, diving under the table.

The shot from the rifle hit Consuelo. Blackford drew his automatic from his coat pocket, and with the other hand yanked at Consuelo's jacket. Consuelo slumped off the bench to the ground, giving Blackford extra cover. Blackford peered out from under the bench Consuelo had been sitting on. There, on the road in front of the tortilla stand, was a green Chevy and, in the back seat, the rifleman. A second shot exploded, ripping from Blackford's hand his wristwatch, an inch from Blackford's head. Blackford released the safety notch and fired four times into the car, thirty yards distant. He peered out again. The driver of the car was no longer visible. Blackford had evidently hit him. The rifleman was now out of the car, wrestling to open the door to the driver's seat. Blackford took careful aim and fired again. The rifleman fell to the ground.

Blackford yelled out to the provisioners in the tortilla stands. *"Come! Come quickly! Help!"*

He ran up, crossed the road, and directed two old men and a teenage boy to Consuelo. He shouted at them in Spanish to pick him up and get him into the kitchen, sprinted then to the green Chevrolet sedan. The rifleman was dead, the driver still alive, but lying inert on the floor. He looked back. Consuelo was now being carried across the road. Blackford asked a dazed woman who had stood by her brazier where the nearest telephone was. Only one, she said, pointing to the gas station fifty meters down the road. The gas station attendant was running toward the excitement. Blackford stopped him: "Where do you call for the police?"

To Mexico City or to Cuernavaca, either one, was the answer.

He rushed back into the kitchen where Consuelo had been laid down on the large wooden table.

He needed only that one, quick look . . . The bullet had entered Consuelo's head at the back, and come out just under his nose. Blackford closed his eyes, and found himself saying, *"Oh my God, why?"*

He slipped his hand into Consuelo's back pocket and brought out his wallet. Empty of any identification. Consuelo carried nothing in any other pocket. There was only a Hertz Rent-a-Car voucher, dated that day, stamped a few minutes after ten in the morning. It was made out to "Carlos Gómez." That, Blackford reflected in an odd moment, is their way of saying John Smith. He looked at the voucher for credit numbers. There were none. There had been a cash deposit of five thousand pesos. About six hundred dollars. It had clearly been an all-cash transaction. Like his own.

Blackford thought quickly. To the older man, clearly in charge of the little kiosk, he said, "My dear friend is not dead. I must take him quickly to the hospital in Mexico City. There may still be a chance. I will bring my car right here in front of the store and we will put him in the back seat."

To the gasoline attendant who, with the others, crowded around the kitchen, he said imperatively: "Go immediately and telephone to the police in Cuernavaca. Tell them to bring an ambulance. I shall drive from the hospital, where I will leave my friend, to the police station in Mexico, and we will get to to the bottom of this terrible thing. I am Rabbi Horshowitz from

America." Blackford ran to his car and, a moment later, the engine running, stopped it directly outside the stand.

Three men began tenderly lifting Consuelo into the back seat. The old man said to Blackford, "I fear he is dead, rabbi."

"Do not say that. I have had medical training. It is wonderful what they can do in a proper hospital. We must hope—and pray." The old man, tucking Consuelo's legs into the back of the car, blessed himself. Blackford gave him a pat on the back, went quickly to the driver's seat, executed a quick U-turn, and roared off through the fog.

His mind floated up through the maelstrom. The things that needed doing . . .

He strove to put them in order. They began to take form.

He would stop at a gas station, at the outskirts of Mexico City. His raincoat would conceal the body, which had slumped forward and lay now on the floor of the rear compartment. He would look in the telephone book for a mortuary. There was bound to be one on Insurgentes. He did. And indeed it was there, and called Mortuorio Insurgentes. There he would sound the alarm and deposit the corpse . . . He had come across the body on the rainy road, back only ten kilometers.

The two strong-armed men dispatched to the car with their stretcher were accustomed to handling inanimate hulks. They spent their days going out and collecting them. The mortician wanted to know where the señor rabbi lived. Blackford was grateful that, as a rabbi, he was accepted with uniform deference. When, consulting the yellow pages at the gas station looking for a mortuary, he had also taken care to memorize the name, address, and telephone number of what seemed, given the boldface type in the directory, a substantial synagogue. He rattled in Spanish that he was an American, assisting at the Beth Israel Synagogue on Chapultepec Avenue—"Here," he said, "give me that piece of paper. I will write down my address and telephone number." He did this quickly, without losing his control of the situation: "Now I leave it to you to report immediately to the police. My duty is to report this event to the chief rabbi. The police can reach me, and if I have not heard from you within the hour, I shall call you. Give me your card," he demanded imperiously. The mortician instantly handed him one. "Thank you, Señor Rabbi."

Blackford left.

It was out of the question—he was driving in the direction of the Hotel Geneve—to return the bloodied car to Hertz. He would call from the airport the next day to say it had been stolen, and then he would write to the Hertz agency at the Prado from America, giving the name to which his deposit should be sent after the car was found.

He drove to a garage near his hotel, entered it, drove the car into the indicated berth, locked it, took his voucher, and walked out, tipping the attendant.

In his hotel room, Blackford collapsed. He permitted himself ten minutes, sprawled out on the couch. Lying there he stared at his soiled, bloody, damp rabbinical clothes, and allowed himself to weep quietly for a man he had only twice been with. Never again, Consuelo had said, would he engage in such work. Never again, Blackford closed his eyes, would he, indeed. He prayed for his departed friend, and for his family.

He undressed now, put the soiled clothes in a laundry bag, showered, dressed in slacks and a light sweater, and sat down to think.

Only LASH knew the identity of Consuelo.

No one in Miami or Washington knew it. CIA personnel and CIA assets in Mexico had been rigorously warned against any sleuthing. Consuelo had made it clear: LASH would disengage if anyone interfered with arrangements respecting his security.

All there was was that telephone number.

And now Blackford knew that it rang in Consuelo's house. To his private study. He could, of course, simply forget the corpse at the Mortuorio Insurgentes. At some point, he thought bitterly, the Bureau of Found Corpses would meet up with the Bureau of Missing Persons. But that might take a week. In Mexico, longer perhaps.

No. He must ring the number, and announce that—that something had happened—

To whom?

He could give no name. He would say—he found himself rehearsing the Spanish: *"Su patrón está muerto. Se encuentra en el Mortuorio Insurgentes, Calle Insurgentes 1238."*

Or he could take a path a little more cowardly, a little more appealing, not say that the man was dead. He could say to whoever answered—most likely it would be his wife, Blackford thought, and probably he would need to ring insistently to draw her to the study—*"El patrón quiere que Ud. le llame por teléfono, Número, etc." The head of the house—patrón* does not translate, Blackford took refuge in mechanical observations—*"the head of the house desires that you should telephone him at"* he looked down at the mortuary card, *"327-38-88."*

But the mortician would answer the telephone, and nothing coherent would likely ensue.

"This is the Mortuorio Insurgentes, at your orders."

"I am calling for Señor X."

"There is no Señor X here, señora."

"But I was told to call this number by someone who said my husband wished me to call him here."

"You must have the wrong telephone, señora. This is a mortuary. And there is no Mr. X here."

Blackford began to sweat. Yes, it was always possible that the mortician might say, "Is this related to the unidentified corpse brought in here by a rabbi a couple of hours ago?" But then the—widow would need to show a complementary ingenuity before they could put two and two together, causing the anonymous message to translate to: *The corpse of Mr. X is lying in the Insurgentes Mortuary.*

No, Blackford.

Still, perhaps he could say—

Impulsively, he grabbed the telephone and dialed the number.

It rang—and rang and rang. Eight, ten, twelve times, fourteen—someone picked it up. He heard a woman's clear, lilting voice. *"¿Bueno?"*

He said in Spanish, *"¿Está la señora?"*

There was a slight pause on the other end of the line. She had detected the accent. She spoke now in English. "This is Mrs. Morales," she said. "Sally Morales. Who is it?"

Blackford held the telephone in his hand, paralyzed. He could not put it down, and could not speak. He heard her say, "Hello? Hello? Hello?" And then here was a pause. "Blacky? It's you. Oh—oh, Blacky, has something happened? To Tony?"

He could not go through with it. He managed to hang up the

phone. He rang for the bellman, who came quickly. Blackford pulled out a one-hundred-peso bill and said to him brusquely: "I am going to dial a telephone number. A lady will answer. Tell her you have been instructed to say that the gentleman she is looking for can be found at the"—he shoved the card at him—"this address."

The message was transmitted.

27

Rolando Cubela doubted if more thought had ever been given to planning an assassination. During the six months since his return from Pinos he had contemplated what he saw as the four generic situations in which Castro became exposed. The first he called *The Public Castro*.

He gave very serious thought to these, including speeches and such, concluding that it would require him to pose as a photographer with a very long telephoto lens. His advantage, in these as in other situations, was that there was no pass he was not in a position to secure: He was, in the eyes of Castro's headquarters, quite simply an integral part of the headquarters; that, together with the advantage of being one of Fidel's confidants. But even if he used the most sensitive, effective silencer, eyes immediately surrounding would turn to the photographer, never mind the large, distracting photographer's protective hood that would give him a few moments' camouflage. He could probably time his shot to coincide with a wild burst of applause, since these were frequent at Castro rallies. That would help. And he could situate the camera, and might plausibly choose to do so for purely professional reasons, near one of the exits to those huge stadiums Castro preferred for his speeches. He would pull the trigger, and then bound down the concrete stairway to the stadium's approaches, walk slowly to the exit at the wire fence, and there his confederate from the resistance forces could speed him off. He went several times to the stadium where Fidel spoke most frequently, located himself near one of the entrances—there were such at intervals of about twenty yards. The most appropriate one, approximately one hundred yards from where the stage was traditionally set up, was ideal.

And although he calculated that he could disassemble and then reassemble the rifle under the protection of the photographer's hood, bringing in the units in one of those photographer's carryalls, still, there was something about it he did not like. One never knew, just for instance, the exact location of individual security guards. What if one stationed himself in the identical aperture Cubela wished to occupy? What if a general alarm caused the closing of all the exits at the surrounding gates?

Then there was what Cubela called *Castro At Play*. This meant Castro on horseback (infrequent), Castro eating (unpredictable locations), Castro having sex (frequent, but not readily accessible), and Castro scuba-diving. This last was the most attractive of the *At Play* possibilities. Castro liked it when his intimates joined him in exploring the multifarious reefs around Cuba, and there was one reef in nearby Havana, off the Rosita de Hornedo Hotel, that he returned to frequently enough to make it possible to explore just how an assassin might do his work on or around that reef. Six months ago it would have been gratifyingly easy to nab Castro underwater. Swim up behind him, which Rolando Cubela and others in the entourage often did, wait for an occasion when it was just him and Castro; approach the madman, plunge his ocean knife into the back of his neck—exactly where, Dr. Cubela knew confidently—swim away underwater, and surface a kilometer or two down the beach, as far as his tank and the current would take him.

But ever since April, when Castro charged that he was the ongoing target of U.S. assassination attempts, he was never in the water without two Cuban frogmen armed with dynamite spear guns at his side; and the launch that hovered over him had two guards, one with a machine gun.

Cubela considered doing it from the beach. Hiding the rifle in one of the dressing cabins (there were a dozen of these, built when the reef had been an attraction for hotel guests), and drilling a hole at eye level. There were two special difficulties. The first was that in order to accommodate the telescopic sight, there would need to be a second hole, two inches above the first. And to use both—one for the bullet, the other to spot the target—would impose a rigidity in the rifle's arc inconsistent with the kind of lateral mobility a rifle required, tracking an active swimmer and prepared to fire the moment the head bobbed above the water. Carving in the old wood, something on the order of a half-moon to allow the rifle sufficient compass, might attract attention.

And, then, the dressing cabin was not deep. He could saw the rifle stock down to minimum length and thus attempt to maneuver behind the half-moon opening without the rifle protruding. Yes, but there would be some noise from the rifle crack, even through the silencer, and any guards in the area would descend on him quickly. He considered sawing the back of the bathing cabin so as to construct a swinging door, allowing him to escape from the rear. But there would still be a stretch of beach before reaching his car. He abandoned it.

Still another possibility was: *Castro in a Motorcade*. Rolando Cubela had been almost set on this plan when—once again—he ran into April 1963, the assassination speech. The Security Office at that point decreed: No more motorcades in open cars. A flat prohibition. Castro acquiesced, upsetting weeks of work by Rolando Cubela.

The fourth situation was—*Castro At Work*. Cubela had constant access to Castro in the three offices he mostly used. Two of these would not permit a view of him from anything like the distance Cubela needed in order to effect a getaway.

The third did. The office on Cuba Street in Old Havana. It was an old monastery, a square building constructed around a courtyard, the cloistered garden where monks once strolled and said their offices. There were still benches to sit on. And tables had been placed about. When the weather was good, some of the staff would elect to take their trays outside to eat lunch.

The room across the courtyard from the entrance, on the second floor, above what used to be the chapel and was now the printing office from which Castro's instructions flowed out to his subjects, had been the monks' refectory. It was a large room in which one supposed that eight or ten tables, each feeding a dozen monks, once stood. Now it housed one large rectangular table, long enough for twenty to sit around, and straight-backed chairs placed side by side against the wall. The beauty of it, from Cubela's point of view, was that although the old refectory windows were of old glass, one could discern through them, especially with the aid of a telescopic lens, the features of the men and women seated around the table.

Directly opposite, on the other side of the courtyard, was the office of the chief guard, familiarly referred to as "the cockpit." Rolando Cubela had cultivated a friendship with Tati Gaspar, the master sergeant who regularly presided over the one-man cockpit, HQ for the guards. Tati moonlighted as a gunsmith. He loved to look at, and assemble and disassemble, firearms of every kind: to fix this bolt, adjust that trigger, polish a dried-up stock. Rolando Cubela feigned an identical interest in guns, but modestly laid claim to none of the skills of a gunsmith such as Tati. At one point, to establish a precedent and test the waters, he brought in a rusty rifle from his father's collection. It dated back to the 1898 war with Spain and the United States. "Just think, Tati, this gun could have fired at Theodore Roosevelt!"

"I'd like to lay my hands on the rifleman who missed him. Not, Captain, your father, I assume? Grandfather?"

"I honestly don't know. My father never spoke of it when I was young, and now, with his stroke, he cannot speak at all."

Tati laid the rifle on his desk, which served him also as a workbench. He picked it up, snuggled the stock to his shoulder, and looked down the barrel, out the window of the cockpit, across to the Cabinet Room. Tati could look directly out over the courtyard. To his right was a microphone through which Tati might, if he wished, bellow orders to the courtyard or to the barracks—a device he never used, preferring to walk down the stairs and over to the guards' barracks room to the left, where he would give orders calmly and succinctly.

Most Saturdays, at about ten in the morning, Castro met in the grand hall, the old rectory, a kind of sub-Cabinet Room, with a dozen subordinates always including Rolando Cubela. Castro's place was at the center of the table, Last Supperwise, facing the courtyard. The old glass windows were almost always open to let in air. From the cockpit, directly opposite, he could be seen clearly. A schedule of meetings for the next few weeks was regularly issued by Castro's adjutant.

There would be such a meeting at ten o'clock on Saturday, November 9. On that day, and in that way, Cubela would execute Fidel Castro.

CUBELA HAD IMPROVISED nothing. On his way to the Saturday meeting, at fifteen minutes before ten, he brought the Russian Mosin-Nagant, appropriately muddied and in disrepair. He carried it in his right hand, as a hunter might carry a shotgun returning from the field, without any attempt at disguise. "I'm taking this to Tati to fix," he told the guard, who would in any case have admitted Captain Rolando Cubela if he had been carrying a machine gun.

Cubela walked up the flight of stairs. Tati was seated, reading a newspaper and sipping from a cup of coffee.

"I've really got something for you, Tati. I bought it yesterday from a soldier just back from a campaign at Escambray. He picked it up after a firefight with the guerrillas. It's probably Czech." Tati had stood, and was examining it. "The scope sight is missing and also the bolt, and God knows what caliber it is: I can't read it off the barrel. Could you look at it while we're having our meeting?"

Tati was ecstatic. He said he had never seen that model, but that it wasn't Czech, it was a Russian Mosin-Nagant.

There was the single hazard—that Castro would unaccountably leave between 11:30 and 12. At over thirty such meetings Cubela had attended, he never had. Nor had Tati ever failed, at exactly 11:30, to go down to the mess hall for the early lunch served to the cadre of the *cuartel general:* others ate at 12. When Tati went down, he was regularly relieved by Staff Sergeant Manzi, who had often seen Tati and Major Cubela together engaged in informal conversation, and so was never surprised when Cubela walked into the cockpit.

During the preceding week, Rolando Cubela practiced doing three things, one after the other. The first was slipping into place the rifle's telescope. He had, with a chisel, made reciprocating little nipples and indentations so that, blindfolded, he could insert the scope, turn by hand the wing nut he had made to replace the regular screw, and tighten it instantly in place.

He practiced with his eyes closed. At first the operation took him thirty seconds. By the end of the day he could do it in less than five.

Then there was the silencer. In less than four seconds, it could be screwed on.

After that, the "missing" bolt. Again he practiced with his eyes shut. Removing it from his pocket, he probed with his thumb the breech into which it should slide and snapped shut the hinged bevel that kept it in place. Then he inserted the cartridge clip and, with a thrust of the bolt, slid a 7.62 x 54R cartridge into the chamber. He had not been able to better sixteen seconds for the entire operation; but on the other hand, he had done it in sixteen seconds sixteen times, with his eyes closed.

How long to line up Castro? The scope was set exactly to the right distance—48 meters, across the courtyard, between the cockpit and the Cabinet table. To sight Castro, thirty seconds; conceivably one minute.

The deed done, he would let the rifle down, open the door, walk down the stairs and out the main entrance. His confederate, in the car, would be waiting for him.

At 11:35, Cubela would inconspicuously leave the meeting. His seat was fairly near the door, and from time to time, especially when meetings would go on for several hours, as they frequently did, there were such departures—the washrooms were nearby. He would walk past the men's room, down the staircase, cross the courtyard, climb up the stairs, and open the door to the cockpit. No knock on the door—in his case—would be needed.

Time? One minute forty-five seconds. He would say to Sergeant Manzi that Manzi was wanted by Lieutenant Gallardo, and that he, Major Cubela—since his presence was no longer needed at the meeting—would gladly sit in Manzi's seat until he returned, or until Tati did. Lieutenant Gallardo was in charge of the little coterie of bodyguards that surrounded Castro wherever he went. He would be stationed outside the Cabinet Room at his desk in the corridor, with two guards standing, or sitting, by him. A summons by Lieutenant Gallardo would be obeyed unblinkingly.

Rolando Cubela would then take the rifle. It would probably be lying on the workbench, though possibly Tati would have put it in the rifle locker alongside. And proceed.

Had he left anything out?

Yes. Because Tati had itchy fingers, Cubela had to tell him please just to study the rifle, but not to disassemble or fiddle with it. The soldier from whom Cubela had bought it confessed he had saved a pile of "bits and pieces" he had picked up in the little tent that had evidently served the guerrilleros as a spare parts armory, and would bring them to Cubela that very night. "Conceivably, our missing parts are there. So let's wait before we try to improvise anything."

Tati had nodded his head, adding only that there was no reason, was there, not to go ahead and clean and oil the rifle?

"None."—Cubela smiled, in acknowledgment of Tati's obliging offer.

IT WAS 10 A.M. Saturday, November 9, and they were all at their stations. Castro was late. But then Castro was always late. The only question was whether he would be ten minutes late or one hour late. For Rolando Cubela it did not matter, so long as he wasn't two hours late, moving into the cockpit's lunch schedule.

He was surprised by his relative calm. He put it down to the long training he had at hospital operating tables, where blood was simply another commodity. That, together with his hardened resolve ever since leaving the Isle of Pines. And then, always, there was the face of Blanco Rico. First that surprise. Then the horror. Then the insensate look . . . Castro's tutelage of seven years ago was paying off.

Castro appeared at 10:20. Everyone stood. He motioned them to sit down, put on eyeglasses, lit a cigar, and pulled toward him the typewritten sheet with that day's agenda.

At 11:24, to Cubela's relief, Castro was engaged in a discussion with a representative from the Ministry of Agriculture. Castro was being sarcastic. He wished to know how physically it could happen that coffee would become scarce on the island of Cuba. "If I were to empty my pockets in a field, in a month it would be a coffee farm . . ." This would go on for a time.

Rolando Cubela got up and walked quietly out. He did not

turn his face as he passed Castro, following the protocol of inconspicuousness, as was natural when someone needed to go to the bathroom.

Now his heart did begin to pound. But he did not allow his pace, setting out to cross the courtyard, to quicken. One step at a time, he repeated to himself, one-step-at-a-time. In one minute and fifteen seconds he had crossed it, and now he walked toward the staircase, passing by the mess hall, whose door was open. He climbed the twelve stairs and opened the door. Sergeant Manzi was leaning back in his chair, his legs on a crossbeam underneath the workbench. He quickly stood up.

"At ease, Sergeant. Lieutenant Gallardo spotted me coming this way—my part of the agenda is finished, and I want to confer with Tati. Anyway, he asked me to summon you. He is at his regular station. I'll wait here until you get back. In fact, I'll be here until Tati gets back."

Sergeant Manzi nodded. "*Sí, mi mayor.*"

He made a gesture to comb his hair with his fingers and walked out of the room.

Cubela moved quickly. The rifle, cleaned and oiled, was there on the workbench as anticipated. He lifted it and very nearly shut his eyes out of habit, simulating three days' practice. Eyes open, he inserted the telescopic sight he had pulled out of his deep jacket pocket and tightened the wing nut. From another pocket, he took the silencer and screwed it on. Then, from a hind pocket, the bolt, clamping down the lock. Now the cartridge clip, snapped in.

For the first time, he stole a look across the yard. Not easy to make out human figures at this distance. But in a moment he was examining the scene through his perfectly focused telescopic sight. His left elbow on the desk, he lowered his right elbow and eased the rifle down until he saw the crystal window frames. He was viewing the left end of the table, staring at Ingenio Tamayo. Ease it to the right, just a little.

He was staring now at the face of Fidel Castro, who was talking animatedly. Cubela lowered the cross hair. It was now squarely in the middle of Castro's forehead. His right finger began to tighten, ready to squeeze slowly—

The door flung open. A glance. Tati. Cubela, shaken, pulled the trigger. There was the *Whsst* of a shot fired through a silencer. Tati stared at him. For just a moment. A second later his pistol was drawn and he fired into Cubela's left arm. Cubela fell forward. Tati seized the microphone and bellowed out a general alarm. Already Castro was surrounded by his associates and bodyguards. The bullet had knocked the cigar from his hand, as he was bringing it to his mouth. Three guards, summoned by Tati, rushed up to the cockpit.

Tati nodded toward Cubela. "Handcuff him." Only when they had done so did he let down his pistol. He went to the telephone and dialed a number, quickly related what had happened, and asked for instructions. Within a few minutes, Rolando Cubela was in the back of a police van; destination, La Cabaña.

In the crowded cockpit, something like a summary court-martial was going on. Why had Cubela been there alone? Tati explained—Sergeant Manzi had filled him in on the details. What had brought Tati up to the guardroom? "I saw Captain Cubela walk past the mess room, so I gulped down my soup to go tell him that I knew where I would locate the right bolt for his rifle. I discovered that during the morning. He left the rifle with me."

Raúl Castro had materialized, breathing heavily after running up the stairs. He heard the last part of the exchange. He was pale. Everyone became silent in his presence.

"*I do not believe it!* The assassin leaves his rifle to be looked after by the sergeant of the guard!"

"Comandante . . . I know . . . there are irregularities. But, sir, I saved his life."

"Perhaps he will save yours. I doubt it." Raúl motioned to the guards to take him away.

In minutes, Tati was directly behind Rolando Cubela in the processing room at La Cabaña.

28

Che Guevara, Raúl, and Ramiro Valdés had seen Fidel Castro confront danger. Twice, Che recalled while sitting in the large living room in Fidel's suite in the Habana-Libre-Hilton where Fidel worked and slept two, sometimes three nights a week, Castro had very nearly been killed by Batista's army, once at an ambush from which he narrowly escaped. His stamina and resilience were legendary. After intuiting the ambush that prompted Castro to lead his men around Pico Turquino in the Sierra Maestra, a perfectly calm Castro had begun, at three in the morning, in the wet, bleak, cold air, to reminisce, of all goddamn things, about his school days. It was a good deal safer, in those days, to say, "For God's sake, Fidel, would you please shut up and let us get maybe one hour's sleep before we're next shot at?" The official Castro of tonight, Che reflected, bore little resemblance to the imperturbable private Castro of Sierra Maestra.

Fidel Castro was raging mad.

"*I know*," he said, "*I know* the operation was American! Where would Cubela have got a Russian sharpshooter's rifle?— just to begin with?" Che observed that the existence of that rifle was hardly conclusive proof of U.S. involvement, that after all there was a flow into Cuba of myriad Soviet and East Bloc ordnance—

Castro simply glared at Che, spit into the wastebasket, and walked toward the door. He turned: "What in the name of God can be delaying them at Cabaña? Tamayo is there to supervise the interrogation. That ought to be enough. It is"—he looked at his watch, and was disgusted at having to use a bandaged right hand to move up his left sleeve so that he could see it—"eight forty-three. They began to go to work on him at three. He is either dead, or he has talked. There is no other possibility. Not when Ingenio Tamayo is in charge. I am going upstairs to eat. I wish to eat alone. Raúl," he nodded at his brother, "get food for"—he pointed vaguely at the three men. "I wish you all to wait."

He slammed the door shut.

Che, smoking one of his little cheroots, began to wheeze. An asthma attack. They were all familiar with the symptoms. He gulped down two of his pills, walked into a deep closet, and there, from a standby tank, inhaled some oxygen. The asthma had been especially bad during the last three months, so he kept tanks not only in his own office and house, but also in the three offices most often used by Fidel. He emerged, in a minute or two, visibly better. He lit another cigar and told the steward who had come in to take orders that he would have soup and a ginger ale. Raúl said simply, "Steak and beer. And a daiquiri now." Valdés nodded: he would have the same.

They found conversation difficult. Valdés spoke: "Fidel wants action."

"It didn't help," Che said, "that our people missed my old friend Oakes in Miami."

"And again in Mexico," Raúl added. "Killed the wrong man. I say the wrong man, but that lawyer was not out on that mountain range talking to Oakes about how to make tamales."

"No," Valdés, to whom the Cuban Embassy had reported, said: "—the lawyer, Morales, was obviously up to something, and most probably up to something involving Cuba. But what it was we're not going to know. The driver has recovered and the police have worked on him. He refused to talk, demanding to be taken to the Cuban Embassy. He's not there yet, but my guess is the Mexicans will just deport him back here. After all, *he* didn't shoot anybody.

"Morales turns out to have been a big-timer in Mexican social circles. Huge funeral. Married to an American only a few months ago. Old Spanish family. But nobody, not anybody, is able to find out what in the hell he was doing with Blackford Oakes. We only discovered Oakes by tracking Morales. The driver talked privately in the hospital room with our consul, told him the hit man was convinced it was really Oakes after observing them with binoculars during their picnic lunch. The rabbi getup didn't fool him. He had looked hard and long at Oakes during the earlier San Angel Inn meeting with Morales. It was after that we told him to fire away if Oakes was spotted back in Mexico. And Morales led them to Oakes." He paused. "Oakes is a pretty sharp shooter, Che. Too bad you didn't succeed in converting him last year."

"Or in executing him." Raúl was salting an old sore. And succeeded in drawing pain.

"What are you going to do, Raúl, when we run out of people to execute?" Che asked. "Move to another country with a fresh population?"

Fidel burst in. Tamayo was with him. Che thought him appropriately dressed. All black, like an executioner. An executioner who had had a long day.

Castro said to Tamayo, "Tell them."

Tamayo bowed his head to the Armed Forces Minister, the Minister of Industry, and the Minister of the Interior.

"Gentlemen. Well—" Castro was pacing the floor behind him. The others sat in armchairs behind their trays. Tamayo wondered whether to continue standing or to sit. Castro gave no directions, so he continued to stand, as though addressing a seminar.

"—the prisoner was very, very tough. But finally we moved him. A telephone stuck by his ear, his mother at the other end, under—persuasion—"

"We don't need those details, Tamayo," Che Guevara interrupted. Everyone in the room knew about Tamayo's special skills.

Tamayo went on. "It was indeed an American operation. Of course, Cubela is a traitor. One cannot blame that on the CIA. But we have the whole story. The rifle was delivered from Miami to a pickup point. We know exactly where. Also, of course, the ammunition. Cubela was to be taken from the offices on Cuba Street by car—one of Jesús Ferrer's men, and we do not know his name, though we have the telephone contact number, and Security is taking appropriate measures there. Security has also gone to the dock at Luz where a speedboat was waiting for Cubela—a Miami-based boat. He knew only the dock number, and that the boat is called *La Vallarta*. It was prepared to take him to Jamaica. From there he planned to go to Mexico. Someone called Antonio Morales was prepared to give him one hundred and fifty thousand dollars—a gift of the American Government!" Tamayo concluded triumphantly.

Raúl looked up sharply at Fidel. Evidently Fidel had elected not to tell Tamayo what they knew about Morales. Accordingly Che and Valdés were silent.

Tamayo remained standing. It was up to Castro to decide whether he should continue in their august company.

Castro was deep in thought, and no one spoke. Suddenly he turned to Tamayo. "Ingenio, go upstairs to my library. Order whatever you want. I will call you."

"*A sus órdenes*, Comandante."

He left the room.

Castro turned to his three closest confederates.

"This does it. Last week, they send a whore to try to poison me. Today, a rifleman. In my own headquarters. There have been raids all along the coastline. In Matanzas we captured three guerrilleros, all U.S.-supplied. I warned Kennedy. I said in my April speech, I said, *those who practice subversion against other countries must expect like treatment. Those who attempt assassination need to know it goes both ways.*

"Six months ago"—he turned to face Raúl—"you wanted me to order the execution of the Mayor of Miami, and I said no, that would be a meaningless act. I do not intend now a meaningless act.

"I intend to bring about the assassination of the President of the United States."

There was silence. Che Guevara, the closest student of Fidel's character, knew the profundity of Fidel's outrage. It was now all-consuming. Something like the passion that had sustained Castro from 1953, when he launched his puerile attack against the Moncada Barracks, to the triumphant January day six years later when, entering Havana, he found not only Cuba, but the world at his feet. It was the single-purposed Castro he was hearing now.

And yet: was there something *besides* the assassination attempt that was driving him? He supposed that there was. Could it be the fact of Rolando Cubela, a close confederate for so long, turning traitor? But Fidel had experienced that before, comrades-in-arms who had turned against him. True, none had tried to kill him. *Their* "treason" was ideological; better, it was disloyalty. Some, Castro had had shot; others he sent to Cabaña and to Piños. Was it a special feeling he had for Cubela? They had been close, but not quite in the category of blood brothers. Was it something else? Something Che didn't know about? Another traitor, maybe?

He looked about the room.

Raúl? Inconceivable.

Valdés? Preposterous—though Ramiro was less enthusiastically pro-Soviet than Fidel. On the other hand, Fidel's own feelings about the Soviet Union were affected by events. All Fidel could talk about between the October crisis and the mollifying visit to Moscow was the disloyalty of Khrushchev during the missile episode. Could it be President Osvaldo Dorticós? Augusto Martínez, at the Labor Ministry? Carlos Rafael Rodríguez?

Or was it something entirely different?

Castro pointed to Valdés. "Just last week—maybe it was more than a week ago, I forget—you told me that Perjuez in Mexico reported that an American veteran, married to a Russian and living in Texas, had approached him about assassinating Kennedy in Dallas—"

"I told Perjuez," Valdés replied, "to show the American veteran the door and to speak to no one, not even to his wife, about the conversation. The American got in to see him only because he had a letter from our Fair Play for Cuba Committee, making the special request—"

"Did Perjuez keep his name and address?"

"I can only assume so, Fidel."

"The first thing tomorrow, Ramiro, get in touch with Perjuez. Tell him if there is any leak, I myself will tear out his throat. He is to locate the American. Have him come to Mexico again, as a tourist. Tell Perjuez to arrange a meeting and ascertain what specific plans he had in mind. I cannot imagine that he would need direct help from us, except perhaps to make an escape—"

Raúl interrupted. "Fidel. We would not want the assassin of an American President to make an escape."

"Let alone an escape expedited by the government of Cuba," Che added.

Fidel bellowed. *"Of course I am not going to implicate Cuba! But I am going to see Kennedy dead! On my sacred honor, I mean to avenge what he has tried to do to me!"* Che was startled. He had never heard Fidel Castro so angry.

Castro paused for a moment. "Kennedy over there"—he pointed in one direction—"and Khrushchev over there." He pointed in the opposite direction.

Khrushchev? Has he gone mad? Che wondered.

Suddenly Castro's voice quieted. He walked over to the desk and pressed a button. Instantly an aide opened the door. "Get Tamayo. He is in my library."

Tamayo came in.

Castro sat down. He motioned Tamayo to sit and pointed to a straight-backed chair, facing the semicircle of armchairs and sofas.

"Compañeros," Castro said grandly, "Khrushchev left a medium-range ballistic missile in Cuba. It is underground at San Cristóbal. The chief Soviet technician has defected. The missile has a range of eleven hundred miles. It is pretargeted, as all the Soviet missiles were pretargeted. The missile's control settings, with the launch properly oriented, will guide the missile to Dallas, Texas—eleven hundred miles. Khrushchev has engaged in the deception of Cuba on a grand scale.

"Tell them the story, Tamayo."

29

Fidel Castro had got out of the habit of furtive midnight meetings, far removed from the handy personal and political apparatus he had got so used to which, with the push of a button, would get him a world leader on the telephone, a woman on his couch, or a French, Chinese, Mexican, or even Cuban meal. It was only five years since he had eaten and slept in the Sierra Maestra, but now he was used to different arrangements. Still, he bowed to Raúl's plans, Raúl having taken over the planning for the critical visit with Kirov and with the ballistic missile, the SANDAL.

"I rather wish we could junk Tamayo," Fidel said to his brother as, in Castro's spacious office at the INRA, they discussed arrangements, early in the afternoon of the evening designated for the meeting. "But for some reason that useful reptile seems to have got this Major Kirov hooked, and I suppose we'd better not take any chances."

"There's something else, Fidel. Kirov doesn't know Spanish, and we don't know English. We hardly want a conventional interpreter on this one. Kirov and Tamayo both speak English. And Kirov's cooperation depends—explicitly—on his meeting with *you*."

Fidel nodded, and dragged again on his cigar. Raúl gave him yet another lecture on the responses Fidel *absolutely* needed to make in the event Kirov began "what Tamayo calls his 'Marxist seminar.' You are to agree with everything he says." Raúl found himself smiling. "It will be good for you, Fidel. Just remember: We can destroy the missile, knowing where we now know it is. But we can't *use* it, in any sense, without Kirov's help."

Fidel spat out a bit of tobacco.

The historic introduction of the most important defector in Soviet history and the most glamorous young Communist leader in the world was to be held in a Cuban military armory, only a few hundred yards from the San Cristóbal cave. Appropriate orders had gone out. The camp commander, Major Gutierrez, had been told by the office of Armed Forces Minister Raúl Castro to place guards around the armory's entrance and also the entry to the cave because he, Comandante Raúl, and two "guests from the Soviet Union" would be conferring in the armory, and after that inspecting the matériel in the cave. No one, Raúl specified, was to be admitted into the area after sundown, and, after sundown, only a single military truck. The driver of the truck would be Major Ingenio Tamayo (whom the camp commander had a few days earlier met); seated on his right would be Comandante Raúl himself. In brief, only the vehicle with the Armed Forces chief in it could be admitted.

The arrangements were concluded, and on the pretext that he was leaving to have dinner, as from time to time he did at the house of a friend, Castro and his personal guards would leave INRA. Arriving at a point on the outskirts of Havana near the Guanajay military installation, Castro's sedan would stop. Waiting for him at the gates of the installation would be the army truck. In the back, Ramiro Valdés. Castro would tell the guards to return with their jeep to Havana, that he desired no accompaniment where he was going. Tamayo would get into the driver's seat, Raúl into the seat next to him, and off they would go, unescorted, the eighty kilometers to San Cristóbal.

RAÚL TELEPHONED FIDEL from the main entrance. "Are you ready?"

"I have decided not to go."

"You *what*?"

"Come upstairs."

Raúl found his brother spread out on a couch, cigar in hand, a copy of *Revolución* on his lap. Raúl recognized the set expression on his face.

"What's going on? You approved all of the plans."

"The plans were made on the assumption that I needed to lay eyes on the SANDAL missile. But you tell me that Tamayo has seen the missile, and indeed Tamayo told me he had seen the missile even before you knew about it. It occurs to me that there is no need for me to see another missile. I have seen a great many. I have all the information I need. Instead of you, me, Valdés, and Tamayo going to San Cristóbal, bring 'Tolstoi,' as we are agreed to call him, here."

In fact there was sense in what Fidel said, though Raúl was humiliated at having to cancel plans so elaborately made. And he did not know—this he would need to check with Tamayo— how easy it was for Kirov—for "Tolstoi"—to depart the camp unobserved. The possibility of his arriving that very night, to discharge the pledge of a personal meeting with Fidel, seemed to him offhand, remote. He said as much to Fidel.

Fidel answered that in that event, Tolstoi could come "tomorrow. Or, for that matter, on Saturday. We know what we want, but what we want we don't need to have tomorrow or the day after. Let's not get carried away. And don't take the opportunity to suggest to me that it is *I* who have been carried away: I know what I am doing. Every hour it becomes clearer to me what I am doing."

Raúl left the room. In his own office, he made three telephone calls. The fourth was to Tamayo to whom he explained that existing plans had been canceled. "Our friend Tolstoi is to come here."

"I am not sure how easy that is to arrange."

"Your job is to arrange things whether they are easy or whether they are not easy. You have only to concern yourself with security. If Tolstoi cannot come to Havana tonight, call me back and tell me when next he can get to Havana."

In forty minutes Tamayo was back on the phone, very pleased with himself. "It has been arranged. The gentlemen Tolstoi needs especially to worry about is away. The—head man pays no attention to senior—people coming and going to spend the night hours in two or three especially attractive places in town. Tolstoi will go to one of those places, make necessary arrangements, come out the back door, and drive to Havana. I will meet him at eleven-fifteen at a particular spot. We should be with you twenty minutes after that."

Raúl relayed the word, first to Valdés, then to Che Guevara, and only then—he was still miffed—to his brother, who received the news as he might have received news that the day after Wednesday would be Thursday.

Because Fidel Castro was thinking about Dallas. He had not worked out a suitable revenge to take against Khrushchev. But he contemplated with dizzying satisfaction the "divine boomerang"—the phrase he was turning over and over in his mind. The Americans still thought him a banana republic caudillo, didn't they? Someone they could dust off, as Trujillo had been dusted off? Well, their gringo government would discover that things were very different. No, Fidel had no intention of suggesting by the least inflection that he was in any way connected with the idea—and, indeed, it had not even been his idea. He was not proposing to Perjuez that Cuba provide any technical aid for the American veteran. He just wanted to know that the desired end would be accomplished. What worried Fidel, in his single-minded desire to see Kennedy dead, was what, exactly, he would do if the American veteran changed his mind. Or, for that matter, if he fired and missed. Would he, Castro, then need to become active in pursuit of Kennedy, as the CIA had been active in pursuit of him? His mind was floating from one to another approach, from hypothetical plan B, to plan C, to plan . . .

And, he gritted his teeth, he did have a nuclear missile. Preset for Dallas.

At 11:30, Raúl was called to the telephone. It was Tamayo. "Comandante, Tolstoi has said that in no circumstance does he agree to go to—to any place where—where your brother regularly works. He says he simply will not take that risk."

"Can't you satisfy him that we can arrange to bring him in unseen?"

"I have tried that. I have tried even suggesting he come in disguised. He says, simply, *No.*"

"What would he find suitable?"

"He says a small private house, with not more than two bedrooms. He thinks that would pose the least hazard to him."

Raúl was gritting his teeth. If the engagement were for the next day there would be no difficulty. But at 11:30 P.M.? Suddenly he thought to ask, "Where do you live, Ingenio?"

"In an apartment."

"Are you married?"

"No, Comandante."

"Where is your apartment?"

"Avenida Quinta A, #8602 in Miramar. It is very humble, Comandante."

"What floor is it on?"

"Five-B."

"Ask him, right now while I am on the telephone, if he would agree to meeting there. I can't guarantee it will work with the Comandante, but tell me what he says."

Tamayo was back on the phone. "He says yes!" he almost shouted his relief. Then, more soberly, "Tolstoi says yes."

Raúl drew a deep breath. "Are you at a telephone where I can call you?"

"Not easily."

"Very well, call me. Call me in *five* minutes. If I decline to take the call, call me in *ten* minutes. Keep doing that until we speak again."

Fidel was astonished by the development. All 220 pounds of Fidel Castro Ruz wanted to say, Fuck Tolstoi. But—of course, of course. The strategist was thinking now. In fact, there was hardly any demand made by Tolstoi that Fidel would not honor. There was no man in Cuba more important to him than Tolstoi . . . at this hour. Castro knew how to control himself, when controlling himself was necessary to the advancement of an objective. All this took fifteen seconds. He said to Raúl. "Very well. Take me to wherever it is you intend to take me."

BUT THE CONFRONTATION turned out to be very gratifying to Fidel. When he walked into the little flat, Tolstoi stood at attention. Then he knelt on one knee, and bowed his head.

"This," he said in English, while Tamayo stuttered out the Spanish translation, referring to his prostration, "is still in my blood, as a Russian. It is the veneration we felt in our blood for our sovereign. You, Comandante Fidel Castro, are my sovereign. You are the carrier of the flame of Marxism-Leninism. You, by your example in Cuba, will illuminate the Marxist movement throughout the world, and perhaps even expunge the cruel and barbaric Marxism being practiced in the homeland of Lenin."

It was quite a show, and the histrionic element in Castro, always easily aroused, was instantly alight. He found himself stretching out his hands as a czar might have done in conferring blessings on a postulant. His hands over the bent head of Kirov, Castro said, "Rise, Major. You do honor to me, and to your sacred convictions. Indeed, we are all gathered here to pursue the word of Marx and of Lenin."

Raúl could hardly stand it. *The goddamn Pope couldn't have done it better,"* he whispered to Ramiro Valdés, who gave a furtive, understanding wink.

Tamayo was beside himself with pleasure. He had delivered the greatest catch to Fidel in the history of espionage. And ninety-nine percent of the power of Cuba, plus a man with a nuclear missile at his disposal, were all here, in apartment 5-B, Avenida Quinta A, home of Ingenio Tamayo. *A sus órdenes.*

Castro broke the spell by saying, "Let's sit down."

Tamayo immediately assembled four chairs and pushed his little dining-room table to the center, moving a standing lamp.

Kirov said he assumed that the Comandante would want to know the relevant details of the SS-4, and he was prepared to give these. But he felt he should first communicate the contents of a telex message that had come in from Moscow that very day.

He pulled a stretch of fan-fold paper from his pocket, reached over to focus the standing lamp on it, and began to read. He himself had to translate the Russian into English, which Tamayo then translated into Spanish, so that the operation was slow. But then, the message wasn't long.

He would skip over, Kirov said, the "language when it is just official." His eyes on the block-letter Russian, he began to purr . . .

"MAJOR ANATOLY KIROV ATTENTION . . . YOU ARE ORDERED RETURN TO MOSCOW ACCOUNT UNFORTUNATE WIFE . . . ACCIDENT . . . YOUR REPLACEMENT CAPTAIN NICOLAI PUSHKIN WILL . . . DISEMBARK HAVANA

NOVEMBER 12 . . . ON BOARD . . . VIA . . . AEROFLOT SPECIAL FLIGHT . . . REASON FLIGHT TO BRING CULTURAL MINISTER FURTSEVA . . . TO DISCUSS . . . CULTURAL EXCHANGES WITH . . . CASTRO ETC. ON NO . . . POSSIBILITY . . . ON NO CIRCUMSTANCE . . . INFORM CUBANS OF THIS EXCHANGE . . . PUSHKIN WILL ARRIVE AS CONSULTANT ON BALLET TO MINISTER FURTSEVA . . . PUSHKIN FULLY BRIEFED . . . YOU WILL FOLLOW HIS INSTRUCTIONS . . . PREPARE LEAVE . . . DEPART . . . EMBARK RETURN FLIGHT SAME AEROFLOT FOLLOWING DAY. . . . MALINOVSKY."

Kirov looked up from his paper, and over to Fidel Castro. He no longer looked like His Imperial Highness, the Czar of International Marxism. He looked, Kirov thought, as Ivan the Terrible must have looked. His face was seized with fury at one more sign of Khrushchev's disdain of Cuban sovereignty.

It was a very long session. Kirov arrived back at the brothel barely in time to change into his fatigues and show up for Soviet reveille at Camp Cristóbal at 7:45 in the morning.

30

After Kirov left and Fidel Castro returned to INRA, he did not sleep. And he knew that he would not sleep until a final plan of action formulated in his mind. He knew, also, that he would be restless until he had word from Perjuez in Mexico.

At eight in the morning he ordered his day's appointments canceled. He told his valet-aide, Enrico, that he would go scuba-diving. He should summon the helicopter, as Castro would travel to the reef at Jibacoa.

It lay off La Urbita, an old seaside villa confiscated several years before from the Manzanilla family, used now primarily by Castro, and occasionally for high-level visitors—Jean-Paul Sartre had stayed there, and Aleksei Adzhubei, Khrushchev's son-in-law. Today it was empty, and Fidel told Enrico that after he swam he would take his lunch there.

"How many will you be, Comandante?"

"One," Castro said.

Frogmen at his side, Fidel dove the tank's full half hour, at a depth of over a hundred feet. He liked to swim on his back, slithering over the coral and gazing way above him, on the silver of the water's surface. A pargo and a cherna swam just over his head, at a synchronized rate of speed. Castro reached up lazily as if to fondle the cherna, which of course slid out of his grasp. It occurred to Castro that he was like the fish, always sliding out of the grasp of Kennedy and of Khrushchev, both of whom thought to use him . . . but things would now change, he thought . . . things would not again be as they were, he said to himself. He turned lazily around and checked the time meter on his wrist. Five minutes of air left. His guards did not like it when he postponed his ascent beyond the seven-minute point. And sure enough, there was Gerardo, gesturing to him to surface, his thumb pointing up. Castro wished he could smile through his mouthpiece—the only facility denied him in this wonderful wet suit brought him by the American negotiator, Mr. Donovan. He waved complaisantly, began his exhale and rose twenty feet; stopped, inhaled, began another exhale, rose another twenty feet. Three more of these and he was on the surface. He felt tired, and a little hungry, as he was dragged onto the launch, which soon zoomed in to the dock.

From his shower he emerged into the patio naked, and sat in the sun wearing only dark glasses. He had brought neither a book nor a newspaper. He simply sat and stared, halfway between the horizon and the sun. A tray was brought to him. Fresh seafood, pineapple juice, a bolillo toasted and buttered. What he had asked for. Yes, he was used to getting what he had asked for. He ate, at first listlessly, then voraciously.

Now, he said, *now* he would sleep. He walked back into the house, into the bedroom, onto the turned-down sheets.

It was after five in the afternoon before he woke. He dressed in slacks and a sports shirt and walked out into the terrace. "I am ready," was all he needed to say.

At the east end of the large lawn, the rotors began to turn. Fidel climbed into the helicopter with Enrico and his personal doctor and eighteen minutes later landed at the beach near his house at Cojímar.

Inside, Raúl was waiting for him. Castro sat down.

"Well, Raúl. What is it?"

"Perjuez called just after you went diving. He would talk only to you or to me. I took the call. He spoke very guardedly, but it was plain what his message is. The American veteran is planning to go through with it."

Castro perked up.

"Any details?"

"He said he had the details, but would not communicate them other than personally, and did I want him to come to Havana? I thought you would say yes, so I said yes. He had made a contingent reservation on our afternoon flight. He will be here within the hour."

Suddenly Castro was animated. His eyes flashed. He stood,

flicked down the lever on the telephone intercom: "A Coca-Cola." He looked up inquiringly at Raúl, who nodded. He depressed the lever again. "Two Coca-Colas." He slapped his hands together.

"We are beginning to move, Raúl, beginning to move. Have Perjuez brought here directly. He is to speak to no one except to you and me. In fact, he may dine with us. About nine, you say?"

Raúl nodded.

Castro went to his desk, piled high with paperwork. For the first time since the meeting at which the cigar had been shot from his hand by a bullet, he attacked his work with gusto. He did not yet know fully what it was, but a plan was crystallizing in his mind. And when this happened, he knew that the gestation would take its own course, and when it all came together, he would enjoy post-partum exhilaration.

OLIVER ALEJANDRO PERJUEZ was an old diplomatic hand who had taken early retirement to protest the coup that brought Batista back into power in 1952. He elected to live in Mexico and when, in 1956, Fidel Castro and his company of eighty-one guerrillas set out from Mexico on his historic voyage to Oriente on the *Granma*, Perjuez, however discreetly, was there to see them off, after devoting a full month to helping them secure the equipment they needed. He even managed to whisper to Castro that he wished he might be one of them, but that at age sixty, with a wife in ill health, he could not go. Castro remembered all of this, and three years later Perjuez was pressed back into duty by Castro's President Osvaldo Dorticós, the objective being a professionally equipped diplomatic corps—loyal to Castro.

Excepting only the Soviet Union's, Mexico's was the most important Cuban diplomatic embassy. The government of Mexico had hailed Castro when he came to power, and unlike so many Latin American countries ultimately disillusioned by Castro's behavior—some even closing down their embassies in Havana—Mexico, under President López Mateos, had remained hospitable to Castro and Castroism and pointedly voted, in international assemblies, against the United States on any issue in which Castro's Cuba was involved. It was important to place in charge of such an embassy someone with the greatest experience and demonstrated loyalty.

Ambassador Perjuez, who looked like an academic—a man of amorphous figure and shriveled countenance designed to bloom only in library stacks—was a man of formal habits, and when he entered Castro's private living room-office, bowed. Fidel walked up to him, slapped him on the back, and said, *"Bienvenido, compañero."*

The steward served drinks to the three men. Raúl told the servant to stay out of the room until he was summoned.

Perjuez then began, without delay. He told them about the American veteran—he so described him, he said, because although a civilian he wore military dress, however informally—whom he had listened to under the most discreet circumstances. The meeting, said Perjuez, was remarkable primarily because the American, while anxious to communicate his intentions to a representative of a government the American deeply admired, hadn't asked for anything. *"Nothing,* Comandante. He did not ask for logistical help, he did not ask for money, he did not ask for sanctuary. He simply wanted to talk to me."

"Does he know who he was talking to?" Raúl asked.

"He does not. He was told merely that he would be talking to 'a man of authority.' True, I must guess that he suspects who I am, though we did not meet in my office."

"What do you make of him?"

"I knew you would ask the question, as I asked it of myself. First, of course, there was the obvious danger, that he was an *agent provocateur.* I will tell you how I handled that in just a moment, but first: What impression did he give? That he is not, well, one hundred percent 'upstairs.' But a limited intelligence is not necessarily an encumbrance in such a mission as he has in mind. He is an enthusiastic Communist, married to a Russian woman, as you know, and it was several months ago in New Orleans that he took up our cause, working for the Fair Play for Cuba Committee."

"Raúl, remind me. Which one of our operations is that one?" Castro broke in.

"That's the one designed to get support from the—naturally simpáticos: cosmopolitan New York literary types. You remember—1959—the meeting with Comrade Slansky? You should, Fidel, since we were with him two whole days when he described the great success of the Soviet operation in England in the thirties—getting the very important Cambridge students, aiming at the middle class, cultivating the idealism of the intelligentsia—this is part of our operation, though it has suffered since the missile crisis. Anyway, its most prominent supporters include Truman Capote, a figure of significant cultural importance in New York; and, as you would expect, Fidel, Jean-Paul Sartre, Simone de Beauvoir; and Herman Mailer—he is a big star in the American literary world who keeps saying he wishes to be 'president,' by which he means the leading American literary figure. He adores Hemingway, which has helped us. Raúl Roa takes care of the financial problems of the Fair Play Committee."

"Yes. Now I remember. Go on, *Señor Embajador.*"

"The veteran has a job now in a book warehouse in Dallas. The presidential motorcade is scheduled to travel past it, right under his window."

"Did he tell you what kind of weapon he was planning to use?"

"He tried to. I stopped him. Yes, I stopped him. I said that the official position of the Cuban Government is as it has been stated by Premier Castro: There is no doubt that President Kennedy is an imperialist who has subsidized and continues to subsidize aggressive espionage and even assassination attempts, and although Prime Minister Castro has warned that aggression begets counteraggression, in fact the Cuban Government has yet to sponsor assassinations. I said 'assassinations'—I conveniently swept over the incident in Miami last spring, the attempt on the CIA agent, but that did not make the papers—and said I had no knowledge that any such were being planned. I reminded him that he was an American citizen with his own views and that—I said the following, Comandante, with *great* care, because I thought I knew the response it would elicit from him—I said, 'Besides which, although I honor your grievances against the foreign policy of your country, you must forgive me if I confess that I doubt very much that you plan to do as you say. Such ventures involve a great deal of risk, and the chances against their succeeding are overwhelming!' "

"How did he respond?" Fidel asked, leaning forward, anxious.

"As I hoped. His lips tightened and he said with great determination, as if I had made light of his machismo, '*You doubt me?* You will see, señor, you will see.' Then he added, 'I have not asked you for one thing. And I repeat, I do not wish one thing from you. But perhaps in the days to come you will honor me, whatever becomes of me. My plan is a good one. In one week you will see.'

"I greeted his reaffirmation kindly, with a trace of condescension. I then said that *if I truly believed him,* I would report directly to you, and probably you would pass along the word to Washington, such being your respect for international conventions on assassinations of heads of state, whatever the violations of those conventions by President Kennedy."

Fidel could not contain his glee. He stood up and slapped Perjuez on the back. "*Hijo mío,* well done! Ah, well done! I wish I had a recording of that conversation."

"You do, Comandante." Oliver Alejandro Perjuez reached into his pocket, pulled out a tape, and dropped it on Fidel Castro's desk.

LATE THAT NIGHT, long after the others had gone, Castro sat staring through the window up over the roof at the descending moon. He had done so for over two hours. Castro had a feeling. One of those feelings that marked him as a man of special destiny, because always such feelings had led him toward his objectives. He had a sense that when the moon totally disappeared from view, his mind would finally fasten on his Plan (he now capitalized the word in his mind). He did not wish to cheat, and so he kept his head absolutely rigid on the pillow. Otherwise, by raising it an inch, he could prolong his view of the moon another ten minutes . . . another inch, another ten minutes—no. No cheating. He lay absolutely still, and when the moon was gone completely, under the rooftop at eye level, it came to him.

31

When the commandingly elegant Yekaterina Alekseevna Furtseva, Minister of Culture, arrived in Havana to spend two weeks discussing a full program of Cuban-Soviet artistic exchanges, she was greeted at the airport by Armando Hart Dávalos, the Education Minister, under whose portfolio all artistic activity went forward. She came with a substantial retinue, including a young Soviet pianist (a man) and a violinist (a woman) who were prepared to give a few unscheduled recitals, courtesy of the Soviet Ministry of Culture. A bespectacled man wearing a double-breasted gray suit of the kind that could not have been made elsewhere than in Moscow descended the ramp, and was introduced as deputy to the minister, in charge of ballet. If one followed his movements, as Ingenio Tamayo studiously did from his position at the edge of the Cuban entourage, one would have the impression that his duties were largely clerical. He was carrying his own and his minister's briefcase, and was fussing over the baggage, indicating which went here, which there. A low-level bureaucrat was the impression he gave, which impression was the impression Nicolai Pushkin sought to give.

Tamayo had commissioned two highly trusted men from the Security Section. They were told to keep Tamayo in radio contact, advising him of the movements of the man in the double-breasted gray suit traveling under the name of "Oskar Marchenko." Their responsibility went beyond merely keeping their eyes on Marchenko. When Tamayo gave the word, the two security men were to detain Mr. Marchenko, taking great care to separate him from his briefcase, handcuff him, and—without hurting him—put him in their car and drive to Barracks C at San Cristóbal. If he was noisy, they were to gag him. One of the security men spoke enough English to communicate to the Russian, and if Marchenko-Pushkin knew neither English nor Spanish, he would need to be instructed by hand signals.

Tamayo did not wish Marchenko detained until he was well away from Havana. His ostensible superior, preoccupied with ballet, had obviously been informed that Marchenko was to acquiesce in covert arrangements involving his superior's "aide." So that when Marchenko left the city of Havana, the ballet master should not expect to hear from him again.

And Marchenko, Tamayo suspected, would, most surely, leave Havana, since his destination was San Cristóbal to relieve Tolstoi-Kirov. The detention would take place, on the assumption that Marchenko-Pushkin's plan was to drive to San Cristóbal, about a half hour before he arrived there. Tamayo did not know whether Pushkin would make independent arrangements to arrive at San Cristóbal or whether he would telephone Tolstoi-Kirov to ask that a car be sent to fetch him. In the latter event, he would most likely call Kirov directly, who would, by prearrangement, volunteer to fetch Pushkin himself. In that event a second squad car, also armed with two Security officials, would come along to do to Kirov exactly what was being done to Pushkin. Captain Pushkin, in detention, would understand that he and Major Kirov were undergoing identical experiences, identical detention.

Pushkin, as it turned out, wasted no time. He did not even appear at the initial luncheon for the Soviet delegation. There were no place cards, so he was not missed. In his hotel room, shortly after arriving, he read a telephone number from his notebook to the operator. Pushkin was pleased finally to be using the Spanish he had labored so hard to learn on his last visit in Cuba. He had arrived with one of the earliest missiles in August only to leave so ignominiously three months later. During the tumultuous month since being told he would be returning to Cuba on an important mission, he had been given intensive training. But he had found time to pursue his Spanish studies. And then had come the epochal briefing the day before his departure, delivered by Malinovsky himself.

"Está en la línea," the operator said. Pushkin was connected

to the Soviet Command Center at San Cristóbal. He asked for Major Kirov. An orderly said that Major Kirov had been expecting a call and had left word where he would be. If the caller would leave his number, the orderly would have Major Kirov return the call.

All this was done.

Kirov said on the phone that he would be happy to go to Havana to pick Pushkin up, the only alternative being that Pushkin take a bus. *Bus?* Pushkin said evenly that he would prefer to go by car, which in any event would give them an opportunity to get acquainted.

Kirov told him that in approximately two hours he would be at the hotel and would call up to Pushkin's room.

"I will be ready."

Kirov was left with a problem—the usual one of leaving the camp at San Cristóbal on days and hours other than those specified for leaves. But he had thought the problem through. Tamayo was conscripted to send him a telex, datelined Moscow, with all the appropriate coding. (Indeed, the wording had been written out by Kirov himself.) The cable said that Comrade Eska Chodopov, the deputy ballet assistant arriving on Aeroflot's cultural exchange flight on November 12 at José Martí Airport, was a special friend of Major Kirov's late wife and had attended to her during her last hours. She would be happy to have the opportunity to talk with the widower. Kirov took the telegram and showed it to the adjutant, asking permission to leave the camp. "She just called me. She says she's going to be pretty busy beginning tomorrow, but could see me this afternoon." The adjutant nodded understandingly, and assigned Kirov a pool car.

PUSHKIN'S BAGGAGE INCLUDED a heavy metal suitcase, presumably containing refinements, and even spare parts, for the missile, Kirov thought. He helped to load it into the trunk, together with the two large heavy-canvas suitcases. Pushkin kept his briefcase on his lap and the two men drove off.

There was the kind of chatter Soviet citizens exchange when one has just come in from Moscow and finds himself talking to someone who has been many months away from Moscow. But after about fifteen minutes of this, Kirov got the impression that Pushkin was delaying any talk of a professional nature. Now he was reminiscing about his own stay in Cuba. He had been in charge of a battery of three—anticipated—SKEANs in Sagua la Grande. Pushkin then began analyzing the dramatic events of the preceding October, as they bounced along the neglected highway into the heat of the sugar country. The dogged conversation about events a year old was approaching the point of strain. Kirov was enormously relieved, notwithstanding the surprise written on his face, when they heard a sound behind them. A police siren.

Kirov braked his car to a stop.

There were two unmarked cars, in a moment clearly recognizable as police cars. One car pulled ahead of them and stopped. The second stopped behind. A total of four men, two with pistols drawn, approached from the two cars. The leader said only, "We have orders to detain you."

Both men, in three languages, protested vigorously. Pushkin was led into the rear car, a handcuff already on his left wrist. In the car, the loose handcuff was slipped through an iron eye hook, and then onto his right wrist. As the rear car drew forward, Pushkin could see that Kirov was in the back seat of the forward car, similarly tied down. One of the four men took over the car Kirov had been driving. For a few kilometers they drove as in a caravan. But at the fork entering San Cristóbal, Pushkin's car went in one direction, the car with Kirov, followed by the Soviet pool car, in the other—with the luggage.

And Pushkin's briefcase.

32

The following morning, Major Kirov paid the first of his twice-daily visits to the Soviet communications center. Only he was permitted to use the Command Center's communications center, for traffic directed to his particular detachment; and only he possessed the code that unlocked the meaning of messages dispatched from Section G/L, Armed Services CC, the Kremlin. He was left entirely alone during this operation, and that isolation was centrally convenient to the Plan.

Because orders he would be "receiving" from the Kremlin were actually being transmitted by Kirov to Kirov, an operation easy enough, with a little technological sophistication, to effect on the telex satellite: San Cristóbal to Soviet satellite to San Cristóbal. The text Kirov had carefully rehearsed in his quarters, on a typewriter, so that he could fastidiously replicate the signals, dates, times, and code numbers associated with Kremlin-cabled traffic to San Cristóbal.

Fifteen minutes later, Kirov emerged and walked to the adjutant's office next door, nodded, and leaned over to use the telephone. He told the operator to give him the commandant. On reaching Colonel Bilensky, he identified himself and said he needed to speak with him. He was given an appointment immediately, and five minutes later sat opposite the Soviet commandant, who proceeded to read not once but twice the cable allegedly sent by General Malinovsky.

"I wonder whether we shouldn't ask for confirmation, Kirov?"

"Yes, you are right. I did just that, Colonel. Look down at the bottom of the fold." The general lowered his eyes, and there it

was. "OUR CABLE INSTRUCTIONS 111532ZA KKSC KIROV CON-
FIRMED."

"Well," the colonel said, "that would appear to be that. We must discuss details now."

Colonel Bilensky knew about the SS-4 hidden under the steel flooring inside the cave. But only he and Kirov and Kirov's six technicians did. The two guarded tanks deep within the cave that husbanded the liquid oxygen (LOX) and the kerosene were off limits except to Kirov and his men. The original detachment of Soviet workers who had placed the SANDAL underground had done so during the hectic weeks of September when all forty-two missiles were being deployed. The crew engaged in the excavation necessary to conceal Petrouchka, as the missile had been named (Soviet missiles, no less than Soviet submarines, are all given a name, usually feminine), had long since departed Cuba. And the Soviet crew engaged in pulling out and retransporting to Soviet ships the missiles being evacuated were not aware that, under the flooring, lay Petrouchka. Personnel rotation had effectively taken from San Cristóbal anyone engaged in the original interment of Petrouchka.

The colonel thought out loud. The instructions from Malinovsky were explicit: the missile was to be pulled out of the ground, installed on its assembled launcher, and the supporting equipment was to be prepared in such a way as to permit a missile firing within six hours of word from Moscow.

"Where, Major Kirov, is Petrouchka programmed to land?"

"I am sorry, Colonel. I am not permitted to answer that question."

"Yes, yes."

It had been made clear to Colonel Bilensky that Kirov was in absolute command of the missile and that the colonel's orders were to expedite any arrangements dictated by Moscow to Kirov.

"But—if I may ask this—do you have the equipment here to reprogram the target?"

Kirov paused, as if giving thought to whether he could conscientiously answer that question.

"I do not mind your knowing this, Colonel, but let us keep it to ourselves. The answer is no. To ordain a different destination would require a programmer to come from Moscow. It is a very delicate business, radio-inertial guidance. What we can do very easily is abort the targeted instructions, which is in effect an abort procedure. That would cause Petrouchka simply to drop into the ocean. And, of course, it is within my power to disarm the missile, transforming it simply into a heavy piece of metal."

The colonel greatly wished to speculate on the motives for the Kremlin's orders, but was being careful not to give to Kirov, who was after all twice a day in touch with his command post in the Kremlin, any grounds for suspecting that his curiosity was inordinate. Kirov spotted this, and made it easier for Bilensky by engaging in speculation of his own.

"I can only assume, Colonel, that the plans are to dispose of Petrouchka, which is fine by me—I would be glad to return to Moscow, even though it would involve a painful visit to my late wife's grave ... Perhaps Moscow plans something in connection with a peace offensive, and Petrouchka is to be one of the exhibits in that offensive."

The colonel seized on that explanation. "Of course! Of course! Undoubtedly that is what it is to be."

Kirov interrupted him. "But on practical matters, Colonel, you will note that the cable specified that under no circumstances are the Cubans to be permitted to know about the missile, and this poses a problem. There are Cubans working in front of the cave every day, and also inside the cave. We will need the large crane to lift the missile. We will then lay it on the launcher. Then we will need to move it toward the mouth of the cave. Now, the height of the mouth of the cave is not sufficient to permit the designated launch angle for Petrouchka. This angle, as also the azimuth toward which the missile must point, needs to be accurate within one degree as to both height and azimuth. It is one thing to close off the mouth of the cave— that could be done in a few hours with cloth strung from the top, as with a curtain. The interior of the cave would then be off visual limits. We would of course need to pull out the ordnance that stands now in the way of the missile coming up through the flooring when the steel plates have been unbolted and set aside. But when the missile actually needs to protrude: How are you going to camouflage it?"

Colonel Bilensky was pleased by the question. Because in the last year of the great war, serving as a captain on the Eastern Front, he had been designated (without a single hour of formal training in the field) camouflage officer for the Soviet 51st Division, and he had had to camouflage the huge repositories of fuel and the tank-repair center from the German bombers. He had learned a great deal about camouflage.

He explained to Kirov that he should visualize a cave that grew higher and higher. "I give you a hypothetical example. Suppose that you needed an elevation—how long is the missile?"

"Twenty and seven-tenths meters."

"And how high off the ground does the lowest part of the missile stand?"

"One and six-tenths meters."

"What will be the height from the floor to the top of the missile when it is properly postured?"

"I would need to consult my papers—"

"Very well, but let us take a hypothetical number. Suppose that you need a total elevation of eighteen meters—just suppose. Now, the height of the entrance of the cave is what?"

"Fourteen meters."

"So. The principle of camouflage is natural projections. Since the cave's height diminishes as you proceed toward its base, we have an angle. For the sake of argument, we'll call it an angle of fifty degrees. The well-trained camouflager would 'extend' the cave at an angle of fifty degrees until its new mouth is eighteen meters above the ground. With wooden scaffolding"— Colonel Bilensky took a sheet of paper from his desk and a heavy black pencil and drew a rectangle—"we create a Bigger Cave. And the same material we use at the existing mouth of the cave, we use to cover the new mouth, adding material at either end. Like a bathtub screen that pulls out from the wall, over the length of the tub, then forward back to the wall." Colonel Bilensky was pleased.

"Now here, Colonel, is an operational detail you may not be aware of. It is this, that when the SANDAL is fired, the blast is, as you may imagine, appropriate to sending a thirty-ton weight eleven hundred miles. The blast is huge and of course lethal.

"Now, normally, a safe few minutes before a missile is fired ground personnel are ordered off to occupy a bunker, or more than one bunker, in an adjacent area. The engineers who designed the missile operation of last fall did not specify the construction of bunkers for one good reason, namely that the caves themselves were the best natural bunkers.

"But in order to utilize the caves as bunkers, the missile will need, shortly before its firing, to be moved." Kirov traced the movement with a series of dots on a legal pad, having first sketched in the mouth of the cave. "The missile, let us say an hour before its anticipated launch—remember that we are now going to operate without effective camouflage—is—see here? brought out through the mouth of the cave. Then it makes a sharp right turn (or left turn, it does not matter) for a hundred meters. It then is made to recede, from the level of the cave entrance, oh, another hundred meters. So that when the moment comes to fire, the missile launcher and the missile are actually parallel to the long axis of the cave. What this means is that the missile controls can remain within the safety of the cave. Indeed, however many ground personnel are involved, they can safely reside within the cave during the actual launch."

"How do you plan to move the missile and its launcher?"

"Precisely the right question to ask. What we will need to do—there are other ways of handling this problem, but this I think is the simplest—is to construct railroad tracks that describe the passage I have just drawn here. Not only the missile, then, but also the two tanks are at the appropriate moment hauled along the tracks. You will note that the tracks here"— he pointed to the sharp V he had drawn—"have to take into account turning the missile around. Otherwise, the missile would be pointing in the opposite direction. So the missile will, having made its right turn, swerve first left, and then back up into its rest position. There, the angle of the missile will need to be rechecked, and of course the azimuth at which it is designed to head."

"Very well. A couple of hundred meters of railroad track don't take long to lay. Is it your recommendation that work on this should be simultaneous with work inside the cave?"

"It is. There is no security reason to disguise a railroad track, which is useful for many conventional operations. And there is no reason to delay getting the missile ready, as the Kremlin has ordered, 'as quickly as possible' for that reason. So kindly add that to your list of things that need to be done by your detachments."

"I understand."

"Very well, Colonel. I leave it to you to organize a Soviet detachment to help me and my team with the extraction. The first job is the removal of the flooring. We shall be busy with a thousand details. We check the humidity every week, of course, and the batteries. But we will be well occupied. How long do you estimate at your end, so I can tell Moscow when we will be ready?"

The colonel frowned. He was wondering whether it should be organized as a day-and-night operation. The more people involved, the greater the risk of exposure. He sketched for a moment on his pad. "Our end of the operation should be completed in four working days. If Moscow needs quicker action than that, we can do it in two and a half days. I leave it to you to communicate with Moscow on the matter. As for the Cubans, we will simply tell them that an anti-aircraft gun of an experimental nature is being assembled, and that Moscow has decreed that this be done under security. That's all they need to know. That's all, come to think of it, that anybody needs to know." Kirov too was taking notes.

"Yes, Colonel. I will get the answer to the day-and-night shift question in my communication at fourteen hundred. I shall summon my men and tell them to prepare for our operation. As soon as you have installed the camouflage on the existing opening of the cave, we will remove the manhole cover and, little by little, the surrounding plates. And, Colonel, I shall need to consult with my people on a very private basis and more frequently than under existing arrangements. I shall need private quarters nearby. I notice that Barracks L on the south side of the cave has not been used for a few weeks. Could I install myself there?"

The colonel pulled out a map and studied it. He picked up the telephone and called the quartermaster. Was he planning anything for Barracks L? "A what? A special clinic for venereal disease treatment? Well, postpone that until further notice, and mark down that Barracks L is for the exclusive use of Major Kirov and his Special/Tec detachment."

"Thank you, Colonel."

HE GOT THE key to Barracks L, which in anticipation of its use by the medical unit was spotlessly clean, with utilitarian furniture, a few beds, and even a precious air conditioner in the principal office. He dispatched one of his assistants to make a copy of the main key.

After a hastily eaten dinner at the officers' mess, Kirov went to the barracks building and turned on the little radio transmitter he had put on the top rack of the coat closet that afternoon. Tamayo was waiting at the hotel for his signal.

"All clear. I'll be waiting for you."

Tamayo drove through the gate, showed his identification, and walked over to Barracks L, carrying the briefcase of Captain Pushkin.

Its lock was strong, and Kirov looked about for something to serve as a crowbar.

"Permit me, Anatoly," Ingenio Tamayo said. He bent over the case, after pulling a small leather pouch from his pocket, about the size one would require for a set of reading glasses. The tools of one of his trades were there and in a minute or two with the keys he snapped open the latches.

Kirov lifted out a batch of papers.

He read them with avid interest. Tamayo was quiet, suppressing his impatience by scanning a copy of *Playboy* he had got from the black market.

He stole a glance at Kirov, whose expressive face was contorted. Finally Kirov put the papers down.

"Tell me," Tamayo said. "Anything special? Routine stuff?"

"Much of it is routine. Instructions for some technical improvements, using the material in that aluminum suitcase, probably: longer-lasting batteries; fresh fuses, that kind of thing. Two or three manuals governing care of the electrical system. How to use a new meter to check on the internal guidance points X and Y."

"That all?"

"No. There is a secret letter to Colonel Bilensky. It instructs him to wait until midnight tonight when the camp is quiet. He is then to send two guards to my quarters to bring me to the colonel. The colonel is to advise me that I am charged with treason and that for reasons of national security he is there and then conducting a summary court-martial. He is to find me guilty as charged, and to order my execution. Before dawn tomorrow. That all of this has been done is to be confirmed by Captain Pushkin at the regular ten o'clock broadcast tomorrow morning."

They were silent.

Kirov was reflective. "Whatever it was that caused them to kill Olga now makes it necessary to kill me."

Another moment or two of silence. And then Tamayo:

"Does Pushkin have a fresh code?"

"Yes. But thank God, it too is here. Tomorrow, when radioing Moscow, I am Captain Pushkin. There is one thing I worry about."

"What is it? Anything we can do to help?"

"I worry about Lieutenant Vassilov, the KGB officer here. I wonder if Moscow will advise him separately of my execution."

"Does he know about Pushkin coming over as replacement?"

"Not that I am aware. If he does know, then we can expect fireworks very soon, when Pushkin fails to materialize while I am still around."

"Would we be safer if Lieutenant Vassilov met with a fatal accident? It is one of my . . . specialties."

"Let me answer that tomorrow, after I have spent time at the communications center. I think I may be able to tell by playing with the radio logs whether he has had any independent messages."

"And if he has?"

"If he has, I think you had better be ready with a plan."

"That will hardly be easy, within the Soviet detachment."

"He travels about. I will also give it some thought. It occurs to me that perhaps I should not sleep in my quarters tonight. If there were a knock on the door I would suffer a heart attack."

"Do you have alternative quarters other than right here, where they would also come looking for you if they got the word?"

"Yes. The quarters I have in mind specify double occupancy of a single bed. But come to think of it, I am in extreme need of distraction."

They shook hands.

Anatoly Kirov sat down. He took a matchbox from the corner of the table and burned the papers ordering his execution.

33

Blackford Oakes left the apartment a few moments after ten P.M. The night was moonless, as he knew it would be. He wore a bright yellow suit and a fedora, and he carried a walking stick and a small canvas duffel bag. His face, neck, and hands were blackened. He was a dude, heading out for a night on the town. Three blocks away a car, having made the signal, slowed. The door opened. Blackford stepped in.

Pano gave instructions in Spanish to the man in the driver's seat. They drove south, to Marathon, in the midsection of the Florida Keys. The powerboat was waiting.

At the dock, Blackford undressed, keeping the blackening on his skin, and put on a wet suit. The snorkel and fins were in the boat. The passage to Punta 32, as the rendezvous had been designated, would be less than two hours, traveling at full speed. If the two Cubans handling the boat thought it wise to slow down before reaching Cuban waters, it would take longer. A half a kilometer from land, by low-powered radio, the boat would signal the resistance guerrillas at Punta 32 that the swimmers were descending into the water. Blackford and Pano would slip into the water and swim toward a light that would shine every four or five minutes, dimly. The boat would retreat at slow speed for twelve miles, then, at full speed, return to Marathon.

Blackford thought back on his last passage by boat in these waters. Only, he had been headed in the other direction . . . and had not made it. He allowed himself, however briefly, to ponder how pleasant the sensation might be if a Coast

Guard vessel were suddenly to heave by and prevent him from going in the direction he was now headed. *Let this cup pass from me, Lord.*

As they began to rev up to full speed, Blackford stared at the dull white-green luminosity of the wake being made by this powerful Elco. It was pleasant to reflect that nothing illegal was happening, or would happen, for the first thirty-eight miles of this crossing. Freedom of the seas! But the last twelve miles . . .

The communications system among the guerrillas was operative, indeed in some respects highly refined. If Cuban radar picked them up, dispatching a patrol vessel toward the projected point of entry into Cuban waters, the little radar set at Punta 32 would in turn pick up the vessel and an abort signal would go forward, followed in the Elco by a quick U-turn and 40 mph speed back toward Florida. But the Cubans didn't have the resources to insulate the whole of their vast coastline. Night after night, a resistance boat traveled to the island with supplies, with men, or with men and dynamite, for a quickie hit-and-run.

There were no problems tonight, and shortly after one in the morning they went into the water, and waited for the shaft of light. It came almost instantly. They waved at their escorts and began noiselessly to swim in the direction of the light. The water, Blackford thought, was just the right temperature. Cool enough to refresh him, warm enough to permit him to save energy.

On landing at the beach they were met, an identifying signal exchanged with Pano. They took off their fins, put on their wet sneakers, and walked for a half hour in the direction of a village, a few of whose lights were still shining.

They stopped outside the village at a little farmhouse almost hidden by the surrounding sugarcane. It was a resistance outpost. Blackford ("Joe") and Pano ("Bolero") were introduced to "Miguel," the largest Cuban Blackford had ever seen, and to "Mico," who could not have been twenty years old. Both men were dressed in the *campesino* garb of sugarcane workers. They brought out heavy dark bread, fish, and warm beer. The following morning they would hear directly from "Nena." She would report on security arrangements at San Cristóbal.

Blackford was shown his cot, in the single bedroom in the cabin. He lay back and tried to piece it together. He wrestled with it all, unsuccessfully.

THE CALL HAD come that morning, from Rufus. By code, Blackford was given a number. A second code gave him the auspices under which he was to make the call, namely, from a random pay telephone. This meant, under the vexing and arduous circumstances of his life in Miami, donning a disguise. He had a dozen in the closet and elected the easiest, the beach bum with the straggly beard.

From the phone booth outside a busy McDonald's he listened . . .

A U-2 flight, doing its twice-a-week run over Cuba, had yielded an anomalous picture taken over San Cristóbal. The picture was of one of the great caves that, a year earlier, had housed the Soviet missiles. Six experts had pored over the picture of the thousand-square-foot area designated the year before as SCS12 (for "San Cristóbal Site #12"). An anomaly no expert could explain was that, measured against other pictures, the cave's mouth appeared to have increased in size. Indeed it looked, as one cryptoanalyst put it, "as though the cave had simply grown. Goddamndest thing. But the proportions of what could be glimpsed at the cave's mouth hadn't altered." A quick intelligence analysis meeting had been called, Rufus presiding. There was no question that an elaborate camouflage effort had been undertaken. There was visible what was shaped exactly like the nose of an SS-4 missile. Painted black-brown, but its sharp profile unmistakable.

Could it be?

"Inconceivable," one expert had, mistakenly, commented.

"The last time I heard that word spoken," Rufus said icily, "was on October 15, 1962." That was the day the photographs were developed revealing the massive Soviet missile emplacement: the beginning of the Missile Crisis.

THREE HOURS LATER, the CIA task force concluded that they must mount a "ground operation." And the obvious man to put in charge was Blackford Oakes. With his aide, Pano, he would need to go to San Cristóbal and have a look. Their mission would be expedited by the resistance, with which Pano was in close touch. Rufus spoke to Blackford about the range of possibilities opened up by the emergency expedition.

When Blackford returned to the safe house, Pano was waiting for him. He brought two letters. Twice a week, Pano, on his rounds, was handed letters addressed to Blackford and mailed in care of the Fontainebleau Hotel. Before breaking the big news to Pano, Blackford excused himself to open his mail, so welcome in his solitary circumstances in that wretched safe house.

The first was from his mother in London. She chatted with him about this and that, about his stepfather's declining health—"though you are not to worry, my darling Blacky. The doctor says it is only a matter of a strict diet, and more of those pills." She hadn't said what kind of pills. Lady Carol Sharkey didn't distinguish between aspirin and insulin, and probably, bless her heart, didn't know the difference between them. "When will I see you again, my beloved, beautiful" (Blackford winced) "Blacky?"

The second letter, he recognized from the coded return address in Mexico, would be from Anthony Trust. He opened it, expecting the usual political clippings. Inside it was a sealed envelope. Blackford's heart began to pound. On the envelope was written, *For Blackford Oakes, confidential.*

The handwriting was Sally's.

He excused himself again, and went into the bedroom where he tore open the letter. The message was brief:

Dear Blacky, I know that the fault can't have been yours. The coincidence has been a nightmare, but I am over it. I am pregnant. And I long to see you again. The past is, necessarily, past. You are still my darling Blacky. It was signed, simply, *S.*

He needed a full fifteen minutes before reconciling himself

to it: when next he left the safe house, it would be to go not to Mexico, where his heart yearned to take him, but to Cuba, where his mission, his endless mission, dictated he should go. His hand was trembling, but he knew he had to write to her, and did, before returning to the living room to break the news to Pano about the village where he and Blackford would be spending the night, after the long day that lay ahead of them.

34

T
hat first afternoon, Nicolai Pushkin shouted himself hoarse
and spent himself to the point of exhaustion. He demanded, in
his remarkably fluent Spanish, to see the Soviet commandant.
Then he demanded to see the Soviet Ambassador. Then he
demanded to see the Foreign Minister. Then he demanded to
see Fidel Castro. *Where in the name of God am I!* he shouted
out to the lone guard outside his lone cell. He was not in a
formal prison, but in a single stucco building, obviously used as
prison quarters for a single prisoner. His barred cell looked
directly into the guard's cozy quarters. The thickly built guard
did nothing while Pushkin expostulated, except to read, seated
at his desk, his comic book.

At seven, in response to three steady knocks, the guard
opened the door and took from someone outside a cafeteria tray
of food. Supper. He slid it under the cell bars. Pushkin stopped
talking. He grudgingly lifted the tray onto his desk. The jail cell
was comfortably furnished and included a toilet and shower. He
could not, however, see out the window, which was barred and
eight feet above the floor, a black blind pulled down over it. The
furniture was immovable.

At eight, the first guard was relieved. The night guard was
a young man, perhaps twenty. His hair was longer than conventional in the army, his chin beardless, his features even, his eyes
a searching brown, and he appeared preoccupied. After the first
guard had left, he took up his post, and after a few minutes
approached the prisoner and, at a safe remove from the long
bars, said, "Roberto tells me you speak Spanish. My name is
Leandro. I think we can save a lot of trouble if I tell you that

I have been instructed that no request of yours is to be so much as listened to, let alone honored."

Pushkin was caught by the mandarin Spanish of Leandro, totally free of idiomatic Cuban pockmarks. "Now there is no way in which I can keep from listening to your requests, because I am not deaf. But if you do not make any requests, you will not suffer the frustration of my not heeding them.

"In any other way," Leandro said, pulling the chair up to the desk, "I shall attempt to oblige you. You have water, and up until midnight I can get you bananas, pineapple, coffee, and hot soup. After that, nothing until six in the morning. I am here for twelve hours. I am not permitted to sleep, of course. And the telephone may ring from time to time, as my superiors will wish to know about your—spirits. If you ask me any questions having to do with why you are here, how long you will be here, and what the likely disposition of your case will be, I can answer you with all frankness: I haven't the slightest idea. For all I know, Fidel has declared war on the Soviet Union and you are the first prisoner."

Nicolai Pushkin, for the first time since leaving home, felt that a human being had entered his life. After he had stopped kicking and yelling, so to speak, he had concentrated very hard on the probable reasons for his detention and that of Anatoly Kirov. He began, one by one, to examine every contingency, and explore it.

The loss of his briefcase was not serious in respect of the technical data. The Cubans could not begin to understand what the SS-4 refinements added up to. Nor, he speculated, could they necessarily infer, even from a close reading of the documents, that they had to do with a nuclear missile buried in Cuban soil.

He paused a little over that one. He simply did not know the level of sophistication of Cuban physicists. Perhaps one of them would be drawn in, and the translator would attempt to communicate what was in all those manuals. Perhaps the physicist would then say: "Jesus, Mary, and Joseph"—a favorite Latin American expletive, he had noted—"that can only mean that there is a Soviet missile somewhere in the area."

But he doubted it.

The inflammatory document was the one ordering the execution of Anatoly Kirov. Pushkin hadn't been told what Kirov's crime was, but obviously it was egregious. It would have been logical to transport him back to Moscow, try, convict, and shoot him there, Pushkin thought. Shortly before his plane took off, the KGB had shoved the instructions into his hand, briefly explaining that Kirov was a demonstrated traitor, scheduled for immediate execution. Obviously they feared that conventional detention, followed by a handcuffed trip in a Soviet security van from San Cristóbal right to the apron of the Aeroflot plane, would give the traitor Kirov too great an opportunity for contact with the Cubans.

And that, he reasoned, could mean only one thing: Moscow was taking no chances on Kirov's speaking the single sentence: "There is a nuclear missile buried in the ground in the main cave at San Cristóbal." That's all. Kirov could say that to a Soviet guard, confident that that guard would repeat the statement and, inevitably, that it would be overheard by a Cuban. Whatever his treason then, it obviously did not consist in his having already told the Cuban Government about Petrouchka, else such precautions would be senseless.

Of course, this did not preclude the possibility that, right now, under detention, Kirov was spilling the beans. Pushkin simply could not guess the reason for the harsh treatment.

But what were the Cubans up to?

It seemed to him, as he dwelt on it, that to this there was only the one reasonable answer: They had discovered Petrouchka. Perhaps it was a subordinate technician, a member of the six-man staff, who had tipped off the Cubans. Perhaps it was accidental.

Never mind. Sometime after eleven in the morning, the Kremlin would be aroused. Section G/L would be there, waiting for a message in the new code from Pushkin. No message. They would wait an hour, perhaps two. They would check the equipment and circuits. Then they would telephone Colonel Bilensky and ask, "Where is Pushkin?" To be sure, before asking, "Where is Pushkin?" they would need to inform Bilensky that a replacement officer for Kirov called Pushkin had been dispatched to San Cristóbal without preliminary word being given to the colonel because of the security problem involving Kirov, who was not to know that he was about to be replaced. Which would lead, naturally, to their further question, Oh, you *did* execute Kirov, did you not? Whereupon the colonel would send out the alarm: that no man called Pushkin had arrived, and that Kirov had been missing since the afternoon before.

That would get the Kremlin moving! Chaos at San Cristóbal! Right there alongside their secret SS-4! The Soviets would then move in in force. He smiled a smile of satisfaction. When the Soviets move in in force, they move in in force. It would not be easy to explain to Fidel Castro why he had not been informed of Khrushchev's plan to keep the SS-4 hidden in San Cristóbal. But, Pushkin sighed, these things have a way of working themselves out between Superdictators and Minidictators. Fidel needed the Soviet Union; though to be sure, the Soviet Union was delighted to have Castro.

The reasoning was clear in his head. He calculated that twenty-four hours from now, Colonel Bilensky would have forced Castro's security people to take him to Pushkin, he would dust off his clothes and telecommunicate to General Malinovsky for further orders.

His spirit calmed, and he renewed his interest in Leandro.

The young guard was leaning over his desk, a heavy book on his left, the light focused over it, and, on his right, a notebook. He would read a page or two, and then write down his notes. Pushkin watched him for a half hour.

"What, may I ask, Leandro, are you studying?"

"That question you may ask, Captain. I am studying physics."

Pushkin thought for a moment. No, it didn't matter that Leandro should know this. "I am a physicist."

Leandro looked up. "You are?"

"Yes. Nicolai Pushkin, Doctor of Physics, Leningrad University 1953, *a sus órdenes.*"

Leandro's bright eyes were shining. "What branch of physics?"

Pushkin paused for just a moment. He decided it was best to ask his question first: "What branch of physics are you studying, before I answer you that question?"

"I am studying nuclear physics."

"That is the subject in which I have my doctorate," Pushkin

said, thinking what-the-hell, that doesn't mean I have been sent to Cuba to build a nuclear bomb.

Leandro stood up and drew his chair closer to Pushkin's cell. "Would you mind if I asked you a few questions?"

"Not in the least. I am hardly busy with other pressing engagements."

It became a three-hour seminar. There were some difficulties, mostly revolving about Spanish translations for arcane Russian terminology. Happily, most nuclear language relies heavily on Greek and Latin roots and it never proved impossible finally to communicate everything Pushkin wished to communicate. Leandro was lost in admiration of Pushkin's knowledge. Pushkin, having gone thus far, decided there was no point in concealing that he had been in Cuba last summer ("where I really learned my Spanish, though I had studied it before") in connection with the aborted missile arming of Cuba.

Where had he been stationed?

Sagua la Grande.

Why was he here now, with all his knowledge, merely to superintend the assembly of planes, trucks, tanks, and anti-tank weapons?

Pushkin thought quickly. "This is to be kept between us, Leandro." He recalled his conversation with Kirov in which brief mention was made of security boilerplate. "But the Kremlin is developing a new anti-aircraft weapon which is nuclear-powered. One of my jobs, after receiving instructions, will be to discuss with your military the feasibility of bringing the prototype here and making tests in this area."

Leandro's excitement was manifest and he asked Pushkin if he would like Leandro to bring him a bottle of rum—he knew where he could find a bottle, even at this hour. Pushkin said that would be wonderful. And, when the rum came, he was able to persuade Leandro to take a glass along with him, as a brother physicist.

Pushkin went to sleep an hour later, satisfied that this would be his only night in jail.

TWO DAYS LATER, Pushkin decided he would need to rethink his analysis. There was simply no way to explain his continued isolation given his failure to telecommunicate to Moscow last Wednesday at 1100. Moscow's leverage was simply too great to permit Castro to hold an important Soviet emissary in detention for three days . . .

He lifted his head from the pillow he was lying on at midday, feeling the heat.

Of course. There *was* that possibility. What would flow from it?

The possibility that at 1100 a telecommunication *had* in fact gone to Moscow. *Signed* Pushkin. Using the code detailed in a sheet in his missing briefcase.

But who could do this, and what would the message say? The briefcase was in Cuban hands. And there are Cubans who speak Russian . . . But no Cuban would have access to the Soviet communications center guarded over by Colonel Bilensky. If that message went through, surely it could only have been put through by a Russian with access to his briefcase. Kirov was in detention. Could it be another Soviet officer, not formally a part of the ballistic team?

He reiterated—it had to be a native Soviet. No Cuban, never mind his training in Russian, could master the kind of vernacular the Kremlin would expect to receive in telexes from the field, the bureaucratic accretions, the idiomatic twists and turns. Besides, Moscow might ask a concrete question about the functioning of the new gadgetry. The kind of question no one but a trained missile specialist could hope plausibly to answer.

Why, he kept asking himself, were he and Kirov being detained? One thing was obvious to him. It could only mean that the Cubans had the story, had found out about the missile. Nothing of lesser consequence could justify their detaining someone of his, Pushkin's, importance.

And so: they knew the secret. What were they going to do with it, except rub it into Khrushchev's face that he had deceived them? But why was it necessary, in order to do that, to maintain Pushkin in detention? His brain pulsated with frustration. He counted the hours and the minutes until the dumb clod Roberto was relieved by the bright, engaging, informal Leandro.

Who arrived that night with no fewer than three books he wished to get Pushkin's reaction to. The night before, they had spent most of their time on nuclear physics but also had had some personal, even intimate conversations. Pushkin told the young man that he had been spared service in the war because even at the age of fifteen he had stood out in his work in mathematics, physics, and chemistry. He had been sent to a special school. "I was forever in school," he reminisced. "But I was only twenty-three when I got my doctorate. Surrounded by men as old as thirty-five, and older." He had, he said, gone to work in developmental and experimental laboratories, and during the past year or so had been detailed to field duty, "to get a sense of nuclear front-line work."

He had thought it prudent to animate even more the imagination of young Leandro by telling him that although he had not revealed the fact before, the prototype of the new anti-aircraft atom-powered weapon was already in San Cristóbal, but it could not be used except by Captain Pushkin, who alone knew the relevant firing technology as developed only in the past few months in Soviet laboratories.

In turn, Leandro spoke of his own past. He said that his father had been a "capitalist coffee baron." He had been shot while trying to escape with Leandro—"I was just following my father. I was only sixteen. It never occurred to me to challenge my father's judgment. Mother died when I was ten." Young Leandro had been imprisoned, eventually released on probation, and sent back to complete his training, only in uniform. "I am a full-time soldier, and also a student. I go three days to Havana by bus and take my classes, and get back here in time to take care of you."

"When do you sleep?"

"Oh, on the bus. Here and there." Leandro smiled his engaging young smile.

On night three, Leandro spent the first hour pointing out what he thought were contradictions in a Spanish-language text that was represented as a direct translation from a Soviet text. Leandro said that in several places it seemed to him to make no sense, and he wondered whether the problem was in the translation.

He slipped the book through the bars to Pushkin, who spent time sorting out the problems and complimenting Leandro on spotting the anomalies.

Pushkin edged the conversation over into the nuclear architecture of the new, secret anti-aircraft atom-powered surface-to-air weapon. Did Leandro have access to the cave at San Cristóbal?

Leandro smiled and managed to say, "Leandro has access to pretty much whatever Leandro desires to have access to. I know my way around, and I am friends with everybody."

"You mean, you could actually enter the cave and see the SA-8 anti-aircraft weapon, see whether the SA-8 is actually being assembled?"

"Yes. I could, probably. But why should I, Captain? I mean, there's got to be some reason why you're in here, and though I like you a whole lot and I appreciate your great mind, I don't want to get my ass thrown into the same side of the bars as you're on."

Instant retreat. "Of course. But you will know, when you are more advanced in your studies, and when you have perhaps contributed to the development of a new weapon—or a new anything—something of the excitement one feels at the prospect of seeing it actually assembled, in anticipation of testing it. Pretty much like the kind of excitement *you* experience on finding some of the answers to the questions in these books. Only, you know, more so."

Intentionally, he changed the subject and, in hushed tones, began describing to Leandro some of the great secrets of Soviet nuclear technology. Yes, he was running a risk. But, if it came to that, he could see to it that Leandro was, when the right moment came, so to speak, laundered—he could, after all, be taken to the Soviet Union for advanced training. And there were other possibilities. By now, it was safe to rule out the possibility that the KGB were alert to his situation. Whoever got hold of the radio had succeeded also in intercepting and perhaps doctoring any communication to Lieutenant Vassilov.

Meanwhile he must give Leandro information that would genuinely excite and inspire him. And create a sense of obligation to Pushkin. The need for requital.

On the fifth evening, Leandro himself brought the subject up. "About the cave . . ."

"Yes, Leandro?"

"I made a couple of inquiries. Of a friend on guard duty. We go to Havana in the bus together. He is studying music. We play soccer together. I am on his team. We are very close friends."

"And?"

"And he said yes."

Pushkin kept his voice steady. "Said yes to what?"

"Said yes, he knew I was passionate about physics, so if I wanted to sneak a look at the new anti-aircraft weapon, I could."

Pushkin had to work hard to contain his voice.

"Will you?"

"I did. My friend just gave me one of those guards' identifications, and a submachine gun. I went in behind the curtain, as though I were looking for something. I crossed the cave, and took a small tool chest from a steel cabinet. Made it seem as if I had been sent in by the chief mechanic to bring out his tool chest. I wheeled around to walk back out and I got a good look at it. It is lying on the floor. A big hole at the far end, where it must have been lifted from. About eight Russian technicians running every which way. Major Kirov giving orders from a desk with a light on it—"

Major Kirov! The clouds parted . . .

"—and you know something, Captain? That's no anti-aircraft weapon. That's an SS-4."

35

Blackford woke when he heard voices. He dressed quickly and used the sponge and piece of soap lying by the pail of water.

He and Pano were introduced to Nena, a middle-aged woman without makeup, her gray hair braided and twined about her head. She worked in the clerk's office of the warehouse at San Cristóbal, charged with ordering supplies for the military installation, and selected for that position in part because she spoke Russian, her mother's native language. Thus Nena could translate the demands of the Soviet commissary into Spanish and attempt to locate, and get delivered, the foods and miscellaneous provisions necessary to maintain a detachment of four hundred Russians and two thousand Cubans.

She was a devoted enemy of the regime with an effective cover: Her husband was a colonel in the Cuban Army, traveling around Latin America as a military attaché to Esteban Alemán, an ambassador-at-large whose job it was to improve Castro's relations with Latin American governments. Alemán was specifically in charge of meeting with the Latin American military to emphasize the threat posed by U.S. imperialism. Her husband had been away from Cuba for over three months. Neither he nor Nena regretted their separation. They were estranged, and had been for years, though as with many Latin Americans who had grown apart, they did not press on to divorce.

Nena brought two messages.

The first concerned activity within the cave. She had reports from guards who, the big black curtain notwithstanding, had had glimpses of the principal object of attention of the Soviet technicians working long days on a large new Soviet anti-aircraft weapon. She had got only unverified rumors about it, but it was said to be the very last word in Soviet technology. The reason for the secrecy, she had been satisfied, was that the anti-aircraft weapon would have the capability of knocking the elusive U.S. U-2 spy planes from over the skies of Cuba, and—again, this was the word that had got around—the Soviet Union did not wish the United States to know that the SA-8, as they called it, was being deployed in Cuba until the Kremlin was ready to deal, *mano a mano*, with the U-2's.

Blackford listened carefully and interrupted her before she went on to her second piece of intelligence. Did she know, he asked, the dimensions of the anti-aircraft weapon?

No, she said. I hear it is very big, but not gigantic, I think.

Did she know its diameter?

No. Was she correct in assuming it would be slim, since the pictures of all the anti-aircraft weapons she had ever seen seemed to her to be quite sleek?

Blackford nodded.

Miguel looked up at Blackford: Okay to continue?

Blackford nodded. Nena went on:

"Jesús wishes to meet with—with you, Señor Ohkks. He must know whether you agree to talk with him."

Blackford said Yes. "Where?"

"He believes right here is best. It is secluded, we have friends nearby who would report any movement of Cuban military or police searching the area. And we have here our powerful radio. It can summon an escape boat to the beach, if necessary."

"How often is the radio used?" Blackford wanted to know.

The large, hunky Miguel, it turned out, was by profession a radio technician. He answered the question in detail. The radio was used constantly to receive coded messages from resistance leaders in Miami. It was also used to transmit. Its antenna was especially configured to emit a directional beam that lessened the chances of its being targeted by radio direction finders manned by Cuban intelligence.

"Even so, we never let the radio remain in any one place for more than three days. Tomorrow, during the evening, we will move it to another location."

"How reliable is the transmitting?"

Miguel looked with pride at the machine in the corner, a heavy old RCA which, from its appearance, had clearly had tender—and inventive—loving care. "Pancho," Miguel said, caressing the nickname of his machine, "is wonderfully reliable. The signal is seven megahertz and can be made to go to other high frequency bands. I can regulate its power. Usually it speaks only to Miami, but I can transmit to New York and to Rio if I give it maximum power. But if I did that I would proceed to move it to the next site within an hour. Those heavy, big signals are not easy to beam out of earshot of Cuban radio."

Blackford and Pano accepted the coffee, pineapple, and bread placed in front of them. They sat around the rough wooden dining-room table.

"On the matter of Jesús Ferrer, when can I expect him?"

"He is not far now. Two hours after I leave, he will have your message. Two hours after that you can expect him."

"I do not know what he looks like, Nena."

"That is a very great advantage. There is in circulation only the picture of him at Oxford, and he wasn't wearing a beard. You cannot tell men apart easily when they wear beards."

"Have you seen him?"

"I have seen him," Nena said, her voice reverent.

"All right," Blackford said. "Now here is what we need to know. Do the Soviets plan to test the anti-aircraft weapon? That is one question. The second: Can any of your friends give you exact measurements—not to the centimeter, obviously, but as exact as possible—on the weapon's length? Also, word on its width? And any details about the manner in which the launching platform is designed would be useful. Is the weapon sitting at an angle?" Blackford knew that it was, because the U-2 picture had established this. He didn't wish to pass that information on at the moment. "Are there liquid oxygen facilities within reach of it? We very much need this information."

Nena nodded, putting down her coffee mug. "I will do what I can. I must be getting back. They will expect me not later than ten back at the warehouse, and before that I must get word to Jesús."

They shook hands. "I have heard much about you, Mr. Ohkks."

Blackford nodded. It was never easy to reply to such a gesture. He had become sensible to the problem of acknowledging the gratitude of the proud and warm Cubans he had worked with. "I hope and pray for Cuba," was all he said.

Pano crossed himself.

SOMETIME IN THE early afternoon a man wearing a straw hat and leading a mule, which in turn dragged an open wagon filled with sugarcane, stopped by the little cottage. He wiped his brow with his sleeve and let the reins fall to the dusty ground. He walked slowly to the farmhouse door and knocked.

Miguel opened the door. Blackford, now dressed in peasant garb, the black of the night before gone from his face and replaced with a light brown pigment, sat at the table reading a newspaper, a pistol on his lap. Mico was in the bedroom, its door open only an inch or two. He had a shotgun at the ready. Pano, on the approach of the wagon, slipped out the back door and entered the privy, leaving its door ajar, permitting him to scan the horizon to detect the movement of auxiliaries.

"What can I do for you, compañero?" Miguel said.

The man at the door could be heard through the main room to answer. He said, in a deep, resonant voice, "Do you believe in Jesús?"

Miguel paused. "Which Jesús?"

"Both of them."

No formal identification signals had been arranged. But Miguel needed nothing else. He said gravely:

"Yes. I believe in both of them. Enter, Señor Ferrer."

Miguel swung open the door and Blackford looked at a man of about his own size and trim, the hair black and straight, the face heavy with sweat and grime. Beneath his *campesino* trousers he wore sandals caked with mud and dust. The shoulders were square, the teeth a yellow-white, the nose thin and straight, his expression that of a man accustomed to taking charge, though there was also fear in his eyes, the fear of the hunted.

He let Miguel come to him and embrace him, as also Mico, who came in from the bedroom, shotgun still in his hand. Pano came in from the privy, and was introduced. Miguel turned toward the table. "And, Señor Ferrer, may I present—"

"El señor Ohkks." Jesús Ferrer now broke into the English he had learned and mastered at Oxford. "I am happy to meet you, Mr. Ohkks. I have some knowledge of what you attempted to do for my country a year ago, and the high price you paid."

"Not so high as others paid," Blackford said, taking his hand.

Jesús Ferrer sat down and asked for a glass of water, which was instantly brought to him, followed by a cup of coffee, a plate of fruit, and a chunk from the freshly baked bread Nena had brought with her earlier: cover for her, sustenance for her friends.

Jesús, speaking in Spanish, told Miguel and Mico that he would now be speaking in English with their "guest." It would be wise if they kept their eyes open. Miguel nodded, and beckoned to Mico to follow him out of the cabin. Pano, at an eye signal from Blackford, left with them.

Blackford thought it wise at once to express his enthusiasm for Ferrer's cause but to communicate the limitations the President had placed on U.S. involvement in anti-Castro activity.

"You must know, Señor Ferrer—"

"Jesús." He spoke in English.

"All right. But I cannot bring myself to pronounce it other than as in Spanish," Blackford smiled. "I am a sinful man with much to atone for, but I do not use that word except prayerfully."

"I understand totally. Say it as in Spanish, and it will not offend."

"You must know," Blackford continued, "that our government has said that it will not engage in subversive activity against Fidel Castro." He looked up at Ferrer. His manners were good. He did not smile derisively, and Blackford managed a straight face. "I am here for a single purpose, which is to establish whether the object that protrudes from the cave is a nuclear missile. Specifically, a SANDAL—an SS-4. My chief has examined photographs of it and the visible part of it coincides exactly with the cone of an SS-4. It is highly improbable, we would all agree, that it is in any way menacing, but we need to find out a) whether it is a missile, and, above all, b) what Castro plans to do with it. Perhaps he has in mind some exhibitionistic peace demonstration, we don't know. I know that there isn't anyone better informed than you on the scene, and I'm hoping you can help us."

"I can help you not in answering those questions, but in suggesting means of getting the answers. The top men around Castro are totally inaccessible, ever since last Saturday's attempt on Castro himself. Raúl, Valdés, Dorticós, Che Guevara—one might as well attempt to strike down Khrushchev."

"Jesús, you must know that I am not at liberty to discuss with you any plans for the assassination of Castro."

This time Jesús did smile. There was, suddenly, a wink in his eye: "I shall continue to hold you blameless, Mr. Ohkks, for the attempts made over the past months on Castro's life."

Blackford could not suppress a smile. "Saintly of you, Jesús. But you get my point."

"Of course I do. I look to your government for only one thing. Help in securing diplomatic recognition when that great, that heaven-sent moment comes when the monster is brought down. And if what is brewing now is something that can precipitate a definitive political crisis, then your help will be needed instantly."

"You should know that much work has been done on the matter you touch on, and our friends are at the ready."

"I am confident that is the case. Otherwise, there would be little motive in my seeing you. But now to the business at hand."

He turned to the wooden table and, with a pencil, began to doodle on it. "There is no question that something special is going on. My people keep their eyes on the scene, and the pace of activity in INRA is abnormal. And, of course, there is the commotion within the cave at San Cristóbal. But there is, in the thick of it all, a relatively subordinate character, and he is infinitely accessible, indeed he travels alone by automobile almost every day between Havana and San Cristóbal, where he is ostensibly engaged in some kind of quartermaster's survey. But in Havana, he regularly goes to INRA."

"He is?"

"He is an ogre called Ingenio Tamayo."

"Tell me about him." Blackford suppressed what he had been told by Pano months before about Tamayo.

"Ingenio Tamayo was trained as an officer at Managua Escuela Militar. He is four, five years younger than Fidel, and he is a sadist. While at officers' school it is generally accepted that he was responsible for poisoning a superior officer. He gravitated always toward the underside of military life. He volunteered, just after Castro marched into Havana, to take charge of the day-and-night firing squad at La Cabaña. He always insisted on personally administering the coup de grâce. When Castro has a particularly dirty job to do, he gives it to Tamayo. It was Tamayo who superintended the 'interrogation' of Cubela after he was caught and, before that, María Arguilla."

"What makes him so important to us?"

"Somehow he got mixed up in the operation involving Major Kirov, the Soviet technician in charge of the San Cristóbal project—the new anti-aircraft weapon, I am led to believe. Whatever more there is to it, Tamayo knows. Whatever is intended to be done, Tamayo knows."

"Well," said Blackford, "I take it you can bring him in all right. How do you propose to get the information you want from him?"

"By praying that he is like other sadists—a coward. Did you, at college, read Sandor Rado? He distinguishes between brutal men, who are not necessarily cowards; and sadists, who almost always are. I suppose," Jesús Ferrer looked doleful, "that we will have to have a field test to probe this question."

Blackford's lips tightened. "I don't believe in torture."

"I don't either. But just as I don't always practice what I believe, so sometimes I do not believe in what I sometimes practice."

"When?"

"Tonight."

"And if he breaks, how soon can I hear?"

"Tomorrow morning."

"I shall be here. Or did you plan that I should move?"

"My people are well situated. If you are in serious danger, you will be moved. I do not expect it. Perhaps tomorrow will be a big day."

Blackford said, smiling, "Good, as I shall need to be going home. Tomorrow is November 22, and on November 23 Harvard and Yale meet in football."

"Ah, yes, I understand. And, the same day, Oxford plays rugby against Cambridge."

36

When Leandro told Pushkin, in so many words, that he could recognize an SS-4 when he saw one, their relationship, without another word being spoken, evolved: From that moment on, they were co-conspirators. Leandro found himself resisting analytical implications of his new role. In fact, he was, simply, swept away by a drama to which his prisoner, yes, his *prisoner*, had the key.

The formal arrangements did not alter in any way. Regulations were scrupulously obeyed. Pushkin feared most that Leandro should, for whatever reason, be relieved—replaced by another one of those automatons like Roberto, the daytime guard, who got through one comic book per twelve-hour stretch. He went so far as to suggest to Leandro that they ought not to have their rum nightcap.

"It's against the rules, and abiding by the rules is the prudent thing to do."

Leandro agreed.

"Maybe I should complain about you?" Leandro smiled.

"What would you say?"—Pushkin went along.

"Oh, let me see. I could say that you are really Khrushchev's younger brother and when you get back, you are going to cut off all aid to Cuba."

They spent time in light exchanges, but also in other ways. Pushkin had by now thoroughly acquainted Leandro with what it was like to grow up as a talented young man in the Soviet Union, applauding on the one hand all the opportunities he had been given to advance in his work, but acknowledging that there were many frustrations. And there was the inevitable separation from family life—"by the time I was seventeen, I hardly knew my mother or my father, even though they wrote to me dutifully." Leandro said that in Cuba he had had a most difficult time as he had seen his father's reaction against the regime—toward which, at the outset, he had been well disposed. But his anger had mounted as his freedom to operate his own sugar company was first diminished, then removed altogether. "We were very close after my mother died, and I loved him very much, and always he was trying to protect me. I think if he had been willing to leave Cuba alone, and then make arrangements for me, he'd have got out." Pushkin permitted himself to say that he could understand Leandro's father's devotion—"You are a very special person, Leandro, with very special properties." At this point Leandro asked if Captain Pushkin had a family he had needed to leave in the Soviet Union in order to return to Cuba, and Pushkin said no, that he had been so engrossed in his work, he had not had time to get married and raise a family. But that if he ever had a son, "I would hope he would be a little bit like you." And Leandro had replied that since he no longer had a father, he would gladly accept Captain Pushkin as a godfather, if Captain Pushkin would pay him that honor. Pushkin reached his hand through the bars and placed it on the brown flaxen hair of Leandro, and said, with a hint of mockery in his voice, but with an overriding sense of gravity, "I baptize you Leandro, my son."

But there was much work to do, what amounted now to the daily report.

Leandro, without great difficulty, had managed to get his musical friend to give him a standby guard's pass for the cave, and every day he reported in, as if to regular duty, at 7 P.M., one hour before he would vanish in order to take up his post guarding Pushkin at the isolated special Barracks C, a kilometer down the road, en route to the artillery range. Between six and seven in the evening, Leandro would make the rounds along the perimeter of the curtain, but every day he would find an entirely plausible reason to dip inside. At seven there were not many Soviet technicians still on duty, though Major Kirov was almost always there until after eight. The second night, Leandro entered with four cold beers in a cardboard carton. He went directly to the chief Soviet guard. "You ordered these?"

The guard, in barely manageable Spanish, said, *"Yo . . . no . . . cerveza,"* and Leandro's young face was the picture of confusion.

Major Kirov, from his workbench, observed the sight and laughed. "Over here," he beckoned to Leandro. "Whoever did order them is just plain out of luck, because I am going to take two of them and"—he looked over at the guard, with forlorn countenance—"and Babiski here can have one"—he motioned to Leandro to hand him the bottle—"and you," Major Kirov squinted to read the identifying badge on Leandro's vest pocket, "and you—Leandro Caballo—can have the fourth, in return for your promise not to tell our benefactor what happened to them." He laughed, and returned to his desk.

THAT NIGHT LEANDRO reported that the elevation of the missile had begun. "It is on a launcher, at an angle of about forty-five degrees. There are two tractors in front, and the work on the mouth of the cave seems to have ended—it is out about ten meters farther than it used to be, and a big rectangular security curtain has been built. The two big tanks that used to be in the rear of the cave are now on railroad tracks that stretch right to the mouth of the cave."

Leandro was gratified when Captain Pushkin explained to him exactly what movements were required to situate the missile in a ready-fire position. On the basis of the information Leandro then brought him, Pushkin estimated it would not take more than two days before Petrouchka was ready to go. "One day to finish moving the launcher out and set the angle of elevation and the firing azimuth, and a half day to fill the tanks—a tricky business—with the kerosene and LOX."

"Would they need to fire it right after putting in the fuel?"

"No," Pushkin said. "But within twelve to twenty-four hours. After that there is attrition in the valves, seals, and other control elements, and the missile begins to lose range. Though"—Pushkin was asking himself the question for the hundredth time—"one supposes they might not need the SANDAL's potential range of eleven hundred miles. Hardly, if what the Cubans intend is to fire it into the ocean, which continues to be my conviction. But there is a way of finding this out, and at the right time I will tell you what it is."

"When will the 'right time' be?"

"After they feed the LOX into the missile. At that point they must do something within a day. Of course, they can always let the oxygen out. But I can't imagine, if they go to all the trouble of putting it in, why they would proceed simply to let it out. No; if they put it in, it will be because they intend to fire."

On Thursday, Leandro came in as usual at eight and was visibly distressed that Roberto felt like chatting before leaving the detention building. Was Leandro tiring of his watch duty? Roberto thought it time for a day or two off. Would Leandro accompany him to Major Tamayo to request relief? Leandro stalled, and finally, after about fifteen minutes, Roberto left.

"Captain, Captain! They are going to insert the LOX to-night! Tonight. Beginning at midnight. The whole shift has off between six and midnight, with orders to be back on duty at the cave at midnight. The tanks have been wheeled up alongside the missile." Leandro was excited. But not so excited as Captain Pushkin.

Pushkin went to his desk and on a pad of paper sketched out, with painstaking clarity, a diagram of the inside of the firing cavity. He flipped the sheet over and drew on the two succeeding pages. He returned to the cell bars. "Bring your chair," he said to Leandro, without raising his head.

Leandro brought it up obediently by the cell bars, and sat down.

The teacher, inside the prison cell, explained to his student outside the cell the meaning of the four valve handles in the bottom section of a nuclear missile. He pointed out the innocuous sequence, and the deadly sequence. If the tiny door, the firing door, of the shell's casing was bolted shut with the valve handles in the one sequence—he illustrated—the missile was harmless: the radio detonation signal would then be inoperative.

"But if the valves are in *this* sequence"—he pointed to the second sketch—"the missile is scheduled to explode."

Leandro was silent. So was Pushkin.

"What do you want me to do, Captain?" Leandro's voice was that of a boy asking for direction.

Pushkin paused. Then, "Procedure specifies that the firing door be left open until immediately before a launch, with the valve handles set in the harmless sequence. Then the technician in charge, Major Kirov—theoretically, only after receiving tele-communicated orders from the Kremlin—changes the sequence into the FIRE position. The firing door is bolted shut and the missile is launched. It is off on its lethal course."

"Can anything then be done?"

"Yes. After the launch, the technician sitting at radio control *must* do one of two things. He can push this toggle switch to the right"—Pushkin turned the page to a drawing of the radio panel and pointed—"which is the ARM mode. It activates the radio-controlled arming of the nuclear warhead, but ensures that the nuclear charge cannot explode in less than five minutes. The purpose is to prevent accidental detonation of the missile's warhead over friendly territory."

"And the other toggle?"—Leandro pointed to the second switch on the drawing.

"That is the DESTRUCT button. Flip it, and the missile's nuclear trigger, which is ringed by conventional explosives, is disabled. The missile, without guidance, comes down, in pieces, harmless. That option is conceived as the option the command technician has if, on launch, the missile is clearly defective—if it is wobbling through the sky instead of rising cleanly into its trajectory."

"How long between firing and the option to destruct?"

"A limit of five minutes. After that it is no longer within effective radio-control range."

There was another pause. Until, again, Leandro said, "What do you want me to do?"

"I must think. I must carefully weigh all the alternatives."

Leandro drew a deep breath. "Do you want me to let you out?"

Pushkin thought. "Not now. That might end any possibility of avoiding a catastrophe. I must stay here, and you must report to me, development by development. Everything now depends on you, Leandro"—Pushkin paused again, and then said softly, "Leandro, my son."

37

They came together at Cojímar, in the large living room. Fidel Castro was elated by the drama of which he was the central figure—or at least the central actor. The central figure was the President of the United States.

On Castro's desk was a second telephone, a direct line to the cave. When Castro picked up the line, Kirov would answer it. Castro had already tested it. Kirov had answered sleepily when Castro picked up the phone at eight in the morning.

"This is hardly a day for you to be sleepy, Tolstoi."

"I am sorry, Comandante. I only got to sleep at five. It took that long to do everything."

"Is everything now ready?"

"Everything is now ready."

"I shall now hang up and have my technician bring you in on the radio."

"Very well, Comandante. Over and out."

Castro opened the door to an adjacent office. A radio had been installed there. Castro was not going to take any chances on a failure in communications. "Fetch Cave One," he ordered, stepping into the room. The operator, his dial preset, flipped a switch and a moment later spoke. "Command One calling Cave One, Command One Calling Cave One."

The voice of Kirov shot back. "This is Cave One, this is Cave One. Go ahead, Command."

Castro grabbed the microphone from the operator. "Just checking, Tolstoi. Everything seems all right."

"Yes, Comandante."

"You may go back to sleep. I shall not test again until near zero hour."

"I don't think I can go back to sleep, Comandante. But maybe I'll go get some coffee."

"Over and out, Command One." Castro, who visibly enjoyed the use of instruments that effected his will miles away, gave the microphone back to the operator.

To this meeting, they arrived early. Raúl was there at 11:15, Dorticós was there a moment or two later, followed by Che Guevara and, at 11:25, Ramiro Valdés.

Fidel sat at the head of the dining-room table. In front of him was a Zenith shortwave radio. Next to it an AM radio, tuned to station WQAM in Miami, the Top 40 rock station with the large signal to which much of Havana was regularly tuned in, and which always reported headline news as it happened. The shortwave radio was tuned in to the powerful, clear channel CBS station in Dallas. Every now and then Castro would raise the volume. There was static, but the broadcast was audible. It was a talk show and four guests were discussing whether President John F. Kennedy was doing a good job.

Two Democrats, two Republicans, saying the usual things—Castro could not follow, in English, anything other than simple declarative speech—but it was such speech, after all, he was waiting to hear. Meanwhile Che Guevara and Dorticós could follow the English, and occasionally one or the other of them would translate any comment of particular interest.

Castro kept both sets on, but after a while turned them down. There was the faint monotonic sound of people talking, from the one set and, from the other, the muted beat of the rock music, implacable in its cacophony.

Castro had greeted his ministers, as they came in, with a mere nod of the head as he focused on the broadcasts. At 11:30 he turned the radios down almost to total silence and looked about him.

"Where is Tamayo?"

As tends to happen when such a question is broadly posed, his four ministers began looking around, as if to focus on the member responsible for his absence.

No one spoke.

Castro was annoyed. He flicked on his intercom, behind him on the desk, and said into it, "I want Major Ingenio Tamayo. Look for him. Telephone his home, his office. Report back."

He looked about him. His ministers' faces were uniformly grim. Time, thought Castro, to show the qualities of the leader.

"The world will know—the world will one day know, will soon guess—that attempting to assassinate Fidel Castro is an unprofitable business. Eh, Che?"

"Yes, Fidel. Let's hope that's all the world will learn."

Castro shrugged his shoulders and puffed on his cigar. "If it comes to that, we know what to do. The radio technician is next door. He has three dials preset. The first is to the cave.

"The second is to our elite guard, which is at San Cristóbal at the ready. Their leader, Captain Primero, has his instructions. The third is to Pentagon Radio; they call it"—Castro looked down at his notepad—" 'the Pentagon's Military Affiliate Radio Service.' " He had special trouble rendering "Affiliate" in Spanish.

"I have even written the script." He pulled it out of his pocket.

"Of course," he paused, "even though I have some—reputation—as an extemporaneous speaker, it is important that my message should not sound too—well, too rehearsed. For that reason I have written in one or two—well, verbal clumsinesses, the kind of thing that might be said by someone very excited. And, of course, I shall use the appropriate tone of voice. Are you ready? Where's Tamayo? Goddammit."

Again his hand reached for the intercom—just as its buzzer rang. He listened.

"Not at home? Or in the office? Well, send out a general alarm for him. No. Cancel that." Castro thought, his hand still on the intercom switch. "Cancel that. Forget it. He'll probably come in."

He looked up at his companions. "Damn. Should have put that reptile under guard. Wonder where in the hell he is? Still, there is nothing we can do about it. A general alarm is just what we don't need during this"—he smiled—"sleepy Friday morning . . .

"So, I begin. I imitate exactly the voice I will use when transmitting. Are you ready?"

They all nodded.

"'Attention Pentagon Radio Attention Pentagon Radio Attention Pentagon Radio.'"

Fidel's voice rang out, dramatic, stentorian, *allegro animato*.

"'Extreme emergency! This is Prime Minister Fidel Castro of Cuba speaking. This is Prime Minister Fidel Castro of Cuba speaking! There has been a most terrible, a most horrible accident'*—*you notice," Fidel explained, his voice now conversational, "the repetition? 'A most terrible, a most horrible accident'? As a writer, I would not engage in such crude repetitions. But here, it gives verisimilitude to the heat with which I am speaking. I resume:

"'A nuclear missile has been fired toward the United States. It was fired by a secret Soviet technical detachment. My government had no knowledge of the hidden missile. When we learned only this morning of the imminent launch the Cuban Army did everything—absolutely everything'*—*You see," his voice dropped again, "the sincerity? 'Absolutely everything'—the please believe me, dear-gringos-touch; pretty good, don't you think?" He smiled. "I resume:

"'To prevent launch. Engaged in massive fire fight against Soviet technicians' inexplicable act of aggression. All were killed in Cuban effort to reach firing area in time to abort launch. We do not know if rogue missile'*—*'rogue missile.' Do you think that is too, well, too—fluent? Maybe I should say, 'wild missile.' Yes, that's better, I think."

Castro took out his pencil and wrote over the typewritten sheet. "I resume: 'We do not know if wild missile is an MRBM with range of eleven hundred miles or an IRBM with range of twenty-two hundred miles. The accidental firing was at San Cristóbal where last fall there were only the SS-Four missiles but perhaps there was a hidden SS-Five. Our military were never close enough to missile to identify. There is no way of knowing where missile is heading. But impact time will be ten to twenty minutes. The government of Cuba will welcome a U.N. delegation to explore this, this'*—*Did you notice? 'This, This.' Two 'This'es, hardly the kind of thing you would hear from a finished speaker reading from a text, right? I resume: 'most awful tragedy.'*

"Then," Castro said, puffing again on his cigar, "I will repeat that message. I think I will repeat that message over and over until it—hits."

"How many minutes after the launch do you plan before making the first transmission?" Che Guevara asked.

"Aha, Che. You are shrewd as ever. I was thinking about that. In fact, I discussed it with Tamayo. We must not forget the objective. *The President must die.* It would hardly do for the Pentagon to get word to Dallas and then for Kennedy to dive into some kind of bomb shelter, and we kill—and one million Texans get killed—and the only person we care about survives. So I will delay a few minutes. Raúl, you got from the Special Services people the estimated time of flight for an SS-Four traveling eleven hundred miles. It is ten minutes, right?"

"Right."

"Well, you see, I said we did not know whether it was an SS-Four or an SS-Five—that suggests true ignorance of which of the October missiles it was. Since an SS-Five goes twenty-two hundred miles, I said ten or twenty minutes. That could be general knowledge. After all, we were surrounded by the fucking things only a year ago. It would not surprise that I would remember the length of time the SS-Fours and the SS-Fives took to reach target, right?"

Che nodded his head. "On the other hand—"he began—

"Quiet!" Castro's hand blasted up the volume control on the shortwave signal.

"*. . . There on top of the gangway is President Kennedy. He and Mrs. Kennedy pause and smile. She is holding on to her hat. There is lots of wind out here at Love Field on this warm, humid November day. There's a lot of hands for the President to shake down here before they go off in the motorcade to the luncheon speech . . .*"

Castro turned the radio down, but only for a moment. Only to say, "Now we will all keep quiet and listen." He turned the radio's volume up.

38

Pano tore into the house. "Get out! Get out! Police! Police!"

Blackford grabbed his pistol and headed for the back door. He opened it and began to run into the tall sugarcane when he heard a shout and looked left. It was Miguel waving at him. "Señor Ohkks! Señor Ohkks! It is Jesús! Jesús!"

The speeding car was pulling up in front of the farmhouse; Jesús bounded out, followed by two armed men, all three dressed as *campesinos*. Blackford turned and headed back into the house. Jesús Ferrer was trembling. All seven of them were now in the room.

Ferrer signaled to his two fellow guerrillas. He pointed to a trapdoor in the ceiling. "Get up there. The machine guns are there. Bring them down. That," he said to Blackford, "is why we are here. Without that firepower, we're helpless."

Ferrer walked then to the corner of the room, leaned against the wall, and kept standing while he spoke.

He addressed Oakes in English. "I don't see any sense in maintaining security at this point. We're going to need cooperation from everyone in this room. Urgently. Within the hour. Do you mind if I speak in Spanish?"

"It's your call," Blackford said.

Jesús Ferrer closed his eyes and kept them closed as he spoke. He looked like a drained but resolute prophet, speaking before his execution. He spoke calmly, lucidly, electrically. Everyone remained on his feet.

"Ingenio Tamayo—who is dead now—broke an hour ago.

"Castro is inflexible. He is going to avenge the attempts on his own life by assassinating President Kennedy.

"The Cuban Embassy was approached in Mexico last week by an American veteran who told the ambassador he planned to shoot Kennedy. Castro ordered the embassy to make more specific inquiries. The effort is to be made while President Kennedy drives from his airplane in Dallas to his luncheon speaking engagement. Today. His car is scheduled to pass right by the building where the American veteran works. It is estimated that the motorcade will pass by sometime between thirteen hundred and fifteen hours and thirteen forty-five—I'm using Cuban time.

"Castro and the four ministers who are in on the plan will be listening to the shortwave radio. *If the American veteran succeeds in shooting Kennedy*, Castro will telephone to the cave at San Cristóbal and instruct Kirov first to disarm the SS-Four missile, and then to go ahead and launch it and let it fall into the Straits of Florida—and that way show the Russians he, Castro, and *only* he, is in charge of secret missiles on Cuban soil.

"But if the American veteran misses the President—or if he misses or changes his mind and abandons his plan, and the President arrives safely at his luncheon engagement, *Castro will call the cave and instruct Kirov to arm the missile—and launch it."*

There was a slight pause before Ferrer, who now opened his eyes, finished:

"Five minutes after the launch, Castro will broadcast to Pentagon Radio to warn that a rogue Soviet detachment has fired a missile that the Castro government did not even know existed, that in the attempt to prevent the missile from firing, all the Soviet technicians were killed.

"It is now twelve-thirty. We are fifteen minutes from the entrance to the camp at San Cristóbal, another two or three minutes to the cave."

Blackford stood up. Ferrer continued:

"I have two good, brave men here." He pointed to his companions, descended from the attic, the machine guns cradled in their arms. "It is too late to get Nena to rouse our people in the San Cristóbal area. There is no time for tactical refinements. We must be prepared to drive into the camp in a supply truck, and use it as though it were a tank. There is time to get a truck from Nena, I'm sure—she's surrounded by them. Then we go to the gate. If necessary, we kill the guards—there are only four, routinely. Then as fast as the truck will go. My plan is to ram the missile. It cannot be launched on its side." He stopped suddenly.

"Miguel," he said, "get in touch with Nena. Never mind radio security. Tell her to have a supply truck by the gas station outside. Use Station SC Six. They guard the channel and have access to a telephone. Tell them to telephone to Nena. And if she cannot perform this by thirteen hundred hours, tell Station SC Six to get a covered truck of any sort from anybody and have it there. Extreme emergency."

Jesús Ferrer turned to English. He was speaking now only to Blackford.

"Mr. Oakes, I see that you are ready to move. We cannot predict that we can succeed in aborting that launch. We don't know what kind of protection Castro and Raúl have arranged for the launch site at launch time. *We cannot run any risk of precipitating by our presence an armed launch.* Tamayo did not know whether Castro instructed Kirov to proceed to launch in the event of any outside disturbances at the camp, or whether by radio Castro would order an armed launch if he was told there was shooting at Cristóbal. There is only one way absolutely to guarantee that hundreds of thousands of Texans won't be killed and that a nuclear war won't be set off. And that is, if we stand by . . . until after the President's car has passed the assassin."

Blackford said nothing. He stared dumbly at Ferrer, who could see that Blackford was struggling to assimilate what he had just been told. When Blackford did speak he did so without any clear sense that he had heard. Blackford said simply, with odd lack of conviction, "You're full of shit—"

"*MR. OAKES!* Blackford. Please *wait wait!* Think, *think!* Just to begin with, there is the overwhelming probability that if the assassin proceeds with his plans, he will fail. Presidents of the United States do not go about unprotected. But in any event, the President is going to be just as dead if the SS-4 lands in Dallas as if a sniper hits him. And there is *no doubt* that if the assassin does fail, the missile will go off *unless I—I, Jesús Ferrer, and five or six men—succeed in overwhelming the launch site.*

"Now the chances of our doing that are not very great. But we may succeed, and will give our lives in the attempt to succeed. But we are not going to try to abort a launch, an operation which will mean death for every one of us if the operation is meaningless. *And it will be meaningless if the President has already been shot.*"

Blackford's stare was interrupted. But Ferrer went on—

"Now here, Mr. Oakes, are my plans. I have in that car," he pointed to the car in which he had come in, "a reliable radio receiver and transmitter.

"We will wait in the truck with the radio tuned to Dallas. You will stay here, also tuned in on Dallas. *If* the presidential motorcade arrives at its destination—if it comes *close* to its destination with President Kennedy unhurt—I in my truck with my guerrillas will charge into the launcher at the cave and fight to the death, which as I say is predictable, to disable the launcher.

"But precisely because we *cannot know* that we will succeed, we cannot *under any circumstances* warn President Kennedy."

Ferrer looked Blackford in the eyes, all but abandoning any hope of reaching him. He finished:

"There is not one word I can add to what I have said. And I have not one minute to lose. May the God I was named after look over us during the next hour. It could be the beginning of the end of the world. Goodbye."

Impulsively, Jesús Ferrer gave Blackford a Spanish *abrazo.*

39

On the advice of Captain Pushkin, Leandro attempted sleep shortly before midnight. Leandro had thought up, and was passingly amused by, the contrivance he suggested by which Captain Pushkin could jolt Leandro into life if it should happen that there was a knock on the door. In such an event, there would be a little time to spare: the door was bolted from the inside. Leandro took a ball of waxed string, reposing in the clinical hamper along with bandages, scissors, disposable syringes and needles, and the usual medical-first aid inventory. He gave one end of it to Pushkin and then strung out the roll to his desk chair where, his feet resting on the desk, he proposed with his makeshift pillow to attempt sleep. He tied the second end around his ankle. Pushkin practiced a jerk or two, succeeding in each case in jolting Leandro's ankle sharply enough to awaken him from any prospective slumber.

Leandro made the arrangements notwithstanding his doubts that he would ever succeed in slipping off into sleep, though he recognized that he would need to be alert during the whole of Friday, the following day. Or, more precisely, for as much as the twenty-four hours after the missile was filled with its propulsive energy. That process would take from midnight, when it was scheduled to begin, until about six; which meant that the danger period, according to Pushkin, would be between six A.M. and six the following morning; though, more likely, the missile, if it would be fired, would be fired within the first twelve hours. Between six in the morning and six at night. Leandro would need to be very busy, very alert.

THEY HAD TALKED, as ever with the cell bars between them, for two hours. Pushkin would try out an idea and Leandro would meditate on its strengths and weaknesses. Leandro would then try out an idea, and Pushkin would weigh in with the same critical scrutiny.

They went through a half-dozen scenarios, ranging from the improbable (e.g., with whatever firearms Leandro could assemble and smuggle into the prison barrack, they could emerge and descend like the Light Brigade on the cave; among the weaknesses in this plan was that they were 598 bodies short of the 600), to the super-discreet antipodes (something along the line of putting sleeping potion or poison in Major Kirov's morning Coca-Cola. Where would they get such drugs at midnight?).

Their minds traveled through it all, jettisoning this as impractical, that as too reckless, the other as insufficiently conclusive.

Eventually Pushkin said that the physical objectives of their action needed always to dominate their thinking: What were they after?

"Either the missile must be incapacitated so that it cannot launch, ever. Or, having been launched, it must be disabled." A hypothetical alternative would be, then, to contrive to alter the sequence of the valve handles. From Active, to Inactive.

They agreed that there was no practical way to do this last. The moment at which—if those were Castro's orders—the valves were mortally activated would be highly charged. It was psychologically inconceivable that it would be followed by a relaxed moment or two, let alone a period of five or ten minutes, during which the firing door was left slackly open—leaving time for a Messenger of Peace to alight, unnoticed, and simply disarrange the sequence.

No. If and when the valves are adjusted to the deadly sequence, the very next thing is the bolting of the door. "We will simply eliminate any further consideration of that alternative, Leandro."

Leandro agreed.

What if the valves were innocently configured, and the door then closed? In that event, Pushkin said, there was, quite simply, nothing to worry about. Pushkin could turn his attention to the mundane question of his release from this prison-hole. But in order to know in which order the valves were set, it would be required that someone who knew the difference between the deadly and the innocent configuration should be present at the moment of their setting.

There were eight men in Cuba who knew the difference between the benign and the malign settings. Six of them now were in the cave, under orders from Kirov, who was taking radio orders from Castro. The other two were Pushkin and Leandro. "The other five hundred who know the difference are in the Soviet Union," Pushkin said.

Suppose that the door were to close on the valves without its ever having been possible to know whether the missile was deadly or castrated? "It goes off," Leandro imagined, "and we simply do not know whether it is armed or disarmed. What are the alternatives then?"

"They are, first, to switch the DESTRUCT toggle."

It amused Pushkin that Leandro, his hair over his young but furrowed brow, thumbed through Pushkin's notepad to point to the relevant switch—"That one. We flip it to the right. That, or else, second, we prevent the radio operator from switching the ARM button. Otherwise, the missile will fly off to complete its mission."

"There is a third alternative," Pushkin said.

"Oh?" Leandro looked up.

"A premature launch. If Soviet procedure is followed, the valve sequence will not be ordained until just before the scheduled launch. If the launch were to take place before that was done, the missile would go off, not only with the valve door open—which would almost certainly deflect it from its destined course—but transformed into an innocent piece of steel casing. One more meteoric oddity, landing in the ocean or the desert someplace."

"How do you cause a premature launch?"

"A regular launch is a two-man operation. Actually, a three-man operation. The senior technician acts like an orchestra conductor. One man, when the officer in charge gives the signal, closes and detaches the oxygen pressure valve, and the second pushes the button that electrically ignites the launch trigger."

"To make a premature launch, then, would mean a lot of

friendly people—two, three—acting together in a friendly situation, right, Captain Pushkin?"

They ruled out the premature launch.

And that left them with the DESTRUCT option—unless Leandro was able to establish that the missile was going up with its valves benignly configured.

They ended their discussion shortly before midnight, Leandro visibly straining for sleep, with only three procedural arrangements agreed upon:

1) The clod—the other guard, Roberto—had to be got out of the way. This would be arranged by Leandro's getting from his music student friend at the cave's guard office a written order. He would hand that order to Roberto when he came on duty at eight. It would read, "Order from the Captain of the Cave Guard"—that Roberto Gallos's next tour of duty, from 8 A.M. until 8 P.M. on November 22, would be to render additional assistance to the corps of guardsmen engaged in looking after the security of the cave.

Leandro nodded. He knew where his musical friend was quartered. He would endeavor to get such an order and the accompanying identification pass that night, or at seven the next morning, in time to hand it to Roberto when he arrived at eight to relieve Leandro.

2) At eight in the morning, Leandro would report to the cave with his usual pass and constitute himself de facto commuting steward between the Soviet mess hall, a block or two distant, and the Soviet technicians behind the curtain. They had got used to him, over the past five days, and would not be surprised if he was there at eight with a tray of hot coffee and sweet rolls; again at nine with more of the same; again at ten with whatever he could lay his hands on—Coca-Cola, orangeade, pineapple juice. "Keep it up all morning long. They must get to think of you as a constant presence in the cave."

Leandro nodded. Pushkin paused, and wrote on his notepad in large Cyrillic script in block letters: ATTN MESS HALL: *Private Leandro Caballo will expedite minor refreshments for our detachment working in the cave. Please cooperate.* Pushkin scratched out the initials of the Russian commandant, Colonel Bilensky.

3) Leandro would need to come in with two pistols, one for

his own use, the second for Pushkin, in the event the decision was made that they should both attempt to descend into the cave. Pushkin must be supplied with Cuban-style fatigues and a guardsman's pass.

Leandro hesitated. "Ask for one more pass? I just don't know," he shook his head. "Maybe that would make even my good, reliable friend suspicious." He smiled suddenly. "You could use *my* pass! By the time you come along, I will have been in and out so often with my Coca-Cola and coffee and hot dogs and pineapple, they will not inspect my pass anymore."

Pushkin agreed that that was a reasonable risk.

And they agreed they could go no further.

LEANDRO WENT OUT to find his musical friend. In a half hour, he was back with the pass to use on Roberto in the morning. It was then that he agreed to undertake an hour or two of sleep. Five minutes later, the waxed string attached to his ankle, he was slumbering.

40

Blackford, seated in the stiff-backed chair he had sunk into when Jesús went out, was alone now with Miguel, Mico having been conscripted to go with the assault party. *He needed above all, he told himself, to think.*

But he resisted thought: He was, just now, overcome with the conviction that he had come to the end of the line, and he wondered distractedly whether, in the next world, he would be with Sally. He allowed himself a *Green Pasture* scene, his hand and his lovely Sally's tied together eternally, no squabbles, no interruption, a long melody.

But the reverie was only a matter of moments. He kept hearing, softly at first, but now insistently, the adamant grating of Jesús Ferrer's voice—Jesús telling him that someone would attempt to assassinate the President of the United States in a matter of an hour or two, followed by something very complicated, about how nothing could be done about it.

Cold sweat on his unshaven face, his mind wholly concentrated for the first time on Jesús' words, he thought now only this: that he had to save John F. Kennedy from the potential assassin.

To do this he would need to overpower Miguel.

He slipped his right hand into his pocket and fondled with near-sensuous satisfaction the automatic pistol in his pocket. Miguel—the huge six-foot four-inch Miguel—continued to hover, his back to Blackford, over his beloved RCA, twiddling, as ever, Pancho's dials.

There was no alternative, Blackford reasoned. He would

need quickly to kill Miguel. Too much fuss and time, reasoning with him, disarming him, tying him down, running the risk of failing; there was no time for all that.

Blackford raised his pistol. His trigger finger tightened—and, abruptly, stopped. Jesús Ferrer's analysis exploded in his mind. *The President is going to be just as dead if the SS-4 lands in Dallas as if a sniper hits him.*

He lowered the pistol and eased it back into his pocket.

He was now thinking clearly; finally, he thought, he was thinking again . . .

"For God's sake's, Miguel"—Blackford found that he needed to clear his throat. He did so, and repeated himself. "For God's sake's, Miguel, you've already got the Dallas station, why are you screwing with the dials?"

"Ah yes," Miguel's voice came back proudly, as he bent over his machine. "My Pancho picks up not only the CBS station in Dallas but other stations in Dallas! I am traveling from station to station, to listen to the most coverage of the Kennedy trip. CBS-Dallas is went to a quiz show halfway in the ceremonies at the airport. But now I have found a fine station, KXAS-NBC. Kennedy is still at the Love Field, but he is getting ready to get into his car."

Blackford left his chair and leaned back against the wall. To keep his balance. The pumping of his heart seemed to be tilting him to one side.

Earlier, he had carefully observed the radio while Miguel was operating it. Conventional stuff: *I could operate it in my sleep,* he thought. Radio to CIA; to the Pentagon; to Dallas police—*a matter of minutes. Just say: "Protect President en route Love Field to destination. Assassination plot confirmed."* And—just to save time—sign off, "CIA."

But that fancy was behind him, he reminded himself, impatient.

Miguel had suddenly turned up the sound and Blackford heard the announcer say, *"That's quite some motorcade! The President and Mrs. Kennedy, the stars of the day. Up front with them, Governor John Connally. In the next car, the Secret Service, as usual. The third car is Vice President Lyn-*

don Johnson's car, and he has with him Senator Ralph Yarborough . . ."

And then the icicles, riveting his thought, directing his action: the final words of Jesús Ferrer rang again in his head:

"The President is going to be just as dead if the SS-4 lands in Dallas as if a sniper hits him"—and so would millions of others.

Blackford forced himself to sit down again as the merry commentary from Dallas continued, this time from the press car following the President.

But he remained seated for only a moment.

Blackford said hoarsely to Miguel: "I am going to take the motorcycle in the shed and go to San Cristóbal. Here I can't do anything. There, they will have one more gun."

"But señor," Miguel turned from the radio to confront Blackford, "Mr. Ferrer said you were to stay here."

"I do not work for Mr. Ferrer." Blackford was on his feet. He lifted his pistol from his pocket, as if merely to check the cartridge supply.

Miguel understood. He half nodded, turning back to minister to Pancho.

JESÚS FERRER SAT in the driver's seat of the military supply bus Nena had provided. He had driven to within a few hundred yards of the gate of the San Cristóbal camp. Mico, wearing only a T-shirt above his khaki pants, was ostensibly working with a tire jack on a deflated right front tire. At a voice signal from Ferrer, he would be back in the front passenger seat, his Uzi back on his lap. Jesús Ferrer was listening with ferocious concentration to the shortwave radio. A makeshift antenna had been attached to the bus's regular antenna. The signal was coming in. President Kennedy's car had left Love Field.

LEANDRO COUNTED THE trays he had brought into the cave from the mess hall since, beginning at seven in the morning, he began to act as de facto full-time busboy for the Soviet technicians. He had managed, without any difficulty, to appropriate one of the standby, freshly assembled but untested motorcycles. The Soviets, during the past month, had shipped, assembled, and stocked more than one thousand of them, for use by Cuban military patrolmen. Each was to be tested for a hundred kilometers or so before being sent off to designated Cuban military posts. Leandro happily used his, parked alongside a dozen others on the test racks, to travel every hour to Pushkin, in his little isolated prison one kilometer away.

When Leandro had first got to the cave, after handing Roberto his notice to report for duty in the cave area, he was astonished. The missile was no longer in its customary position. It was situated alongside the cave, a hundred meters away, obviously towed there during the night on the railroad tracks he had observed being laid early in the week. He thought this development worth a special trip back to Pushkin, but then the captain told him that it was not surprising, given their decision to charge the missile the night before. "If you're going to fire the thing, safety requires shelter for ground personnel and for the technicians who actually dictate the detonation. The obvious place for them is within the cave, and, for the missile, outside the cave. But that means, of course, abandoning any thought of camouflage. I don't doubt they are going to fire today, under the circumstances." Pushkin told Leandro he had better return, keep his eyes open, and report back every hour.

There had been nothing of consequence to report at the next three visits, save Leandro's success at circulating, unmolested—like the beer-and-peanuts boy in the bullring—inside the cave.

On the fourth of these trips, just after noon, he was able to report excitedly to Pushkin: "I have seen the firing door cavity. I wandered off with a tray of Cocas and doughnuts to the missile—there are four or five men there—and got a good look at it as I was passing the tray around."

Pushkin reacted with some excitement. "The valve handles?"

"They are in the OFF position."

"They are as I described?"

"Exactly."

"Have you heard anything about a firing time?"

"Only this. Kirov's number-one technician, when I was serving him a hot dog, said to me—in pretty good Spanish—'You'll be bringing us more than this hot dog for lunch, won't you,

Leandro? We won't be taking off the lunch hour. The lunch hour will be our busiest hour of the day.' "

"You don't need anything more than that," Pushkin said. "Have you located the radio command terminal?"

"I know where it is. Deep in the cave, near its base. Major Kirov has a desk just opposite, and there is a telephone on it, and a radio behind. But I have not succeeded in taking a look at it. Every time I approach it, the technician who sits there gets up, moves forward in front of the radio console, takes my Coca-Cola or hot dog, waits for me to go away, and only then goes back to his lair."

"But if you had suddenly to dive in there, you would know instantly, wouldn't you Leandro, which switch you needed to flip? Where each switch is located?"

"Yes, Captain. You don't forget things like that."

Pushkin looked affectionately at his young disciple. He said in soft tones, "No. *You* wouldn't forget things like that." And then, after a moment's thought, he shrugged his shoulders and said:

"Leandro, you may not have a chance to make one more round-trip here before the big event. I think now is the time."

He did not need to say anything more. Leandro walked across the room, took the cell-door keys from the desk drawer, and unlocked the cell.

"The pistol." Pushkin examined it. A Spanish Llama revolver with six shells in its cylinder.

"Do you want more cartridges?"

"I may as well."

Leandro gave him a handful. Pushkin stuffed them into the pocket of the fatigues he was putting on. A plan had slowly crystallized in his mind. But for once he did not share it with Leandro.

CAPTAIN NICOLAI PUSHKIN stepped out of his cell into the sunlight for the first time in ten days.

He was appropriately dressed, in Russian military khakis with a staff sergeant's chevrons and Leandro's pass safety-pinned to his vest pocket. The light was blinding. He lowered his fatigue cap and closed his eyes, then opened them gradually. He said calmly to Leandro, "I shall ride in the back of the motorbike. Go right to the cave."

In less than five minutes they were there. The entrance to the cave area, however makeshift, was formally manned. A half kilometer beyond it, at the entrance to the cave, a semicircle of thirty or forty Cuban infantrymen stood, bayonets on their rifles. Pushkin peered beyond the cave at the tumescent missile, apparently unattended, gray against the sun, the missile poised at an angle of about fifty degrees. He could see no bodies. Evidently the technicians had been ordered into the cave, whose black curtain was now collapsed. The guard lazily motioned Leandro to the barricade. Pushkin, sitting behind on the motorbike, casually exhibited his pass.

The guard looked at it, without actually examining it. He addressed Pushkin in Spanish. "When did you join the guards' detachment?"

Pushkin's Spanish was fluent, but it was not without accent. He replied with a trace of impatience, "I am a Soviet mechanic, assigned to help at the cave."

The guard looked over at his colleague, a wizened staff sergeant. He turned to Leandro: "You vouch for him, Leandro?"

Leandro nodded. "Vouch for Boris? Sure. He's been here for two months. Good man. Don't hurt him. He loses at checkers with me." The sergeant waved the motorbike and its two passengers in.

They parked the bike and walked toward the cave's entrance. Leandro departed for the commissary and in a few minutes was back carrying two trays of Coca-Colas, one on top of the other. He eyed Pushkin to take one of the trays. Both of them, tray in hand at waist level, reached the entrance to the cave. From within the shadow of its lip Pushkin could see, approaching them from the missile itself, a Soviet technician. He carried, loosely in his hand, a wrench. Clearly he had just now bolted shut the firing door. *Oh God*, Pushkin asked himself: Is the missile armed or disarmed? He thought furiously, and by the time the loudspeaker gave out its order, he knew what he had to do, and felt confident that, if he survived, in less than one minute he could explain to Colonel Bilensky the grave deception, the deception that might—that might yet—begin an international nuclear exchange. A world war. The order blared out: *"Stand by for launch. Stand by for launch."*

THERE WAS TOTAL silence at Cojímar. Only Castro counted in that room. And he was, in effect, everywhere, all the time—turning the sound from the radio up, or down; switching from rock music to commentary; making comments.

Just after 1:30, word had come in that the presidential motorcade had started out from Love Field. To Castro's dismay, the broadcasting station then slid into its regular daytime programming. He turned the dial, first with huge decisive movements, this way and that; then slowly, reaching for the four stations whose dial numbers he had been given as likeliest to follow the President's path. He tried the second—and got a program on that day's stock market and farm price movements. The third brought in a money-raising auction for the Dallas Red Cross. The fourth, "cowboy music," as he disdainfully referred to it. He slammed his wrists down on the table when suddenly he stopped—the Miami station, KMAX, had interrupted its rock and roll and was speaking of President Kennedy's trip to Dallas. The announcer was doing a recap of the reception at Love Field and of the important political significance of the trip, given Texas's strategic leverage in the 1964 election, only one year away . . .

Castro muttered. "Why does not the idiot report on what the President is actually doing? Where he is? Che, you understand English. Tell me if I am missing anything."

He did not need to urge Che on. He and Dorticós were listening, heads bowed in concentration.

Suddenly there was verbal confusion. The announcer said that something had gone wrong in Dallas. Stay tuned, he said . . . The sound of a firecracker. But nothing to worry about, he was certain . . .

Castro turned white. "He fired! And obviously he missed! Get me Kirov," he shouted out at the radio operator.

"Kirov here, Cave Station, come in, Command."

"We are going to fire. Arm the missile."

"All right, sir. I am in radio contact with our technician out at Petrouchka. Hold on, Comandante." Castro was not used to being told to wait, but today he did not complain. Within a minute, Kirov's voice was back.

"Got the order through, sir. The missile is armed, and the door is being bolted. Within three minutes, as soon as the technician takes cover, we can be ready to—"

"Fidel!" Che screamed. "Listen! Listen!"

Castro dropped his microphone and leaned over to the radio.

The Miami announcer: "It looks as if somebody shot at the President. The presidential motorcade is speeding away—to a hospital. Come in, Ollie. Ollie, do you hear me, this is Steve in Miami. I can't make you out. What did you say? Is there any further news on the shot at the President?"

Che hissed at Dorticós: "Try Dallas on the other radio." Dorticós bent over the second set and brought in the first station to which they had listened most of the morning. A voice came in clearly.

"—hospital. Parkland Memorial Hospital, apparently, is the closest to the scene. The presidential car should arrive there within a minute or two. One bystander, just a few feet from where the bullet was fired, said to a local broadcaster that he was certain the President had been hit—"

"Give me Kirov back," Castro bellowed out to the radio operator.

IN THE BUS, at 1340, Jesús Ferrer heard the radio bulletin. "*A shot—several shots—have been fired at the President! Repeat, a shot has been fired at President Kennedy. The presidential car is speeding forward, with motorcycles in the lead. Stand by! Stand by! Shots have been fired at the President.*" Jesús Ferrer waited tensely to hear whether the shot was fatal. His men were ready, and Ferrer's eyes were on the missile. There was suddenly the awful question on which he hadn't dwelt. The missile was scheduled to go up no matter what. Go up armed if Kennedy was—was what? Unhurt? Merely wounded? If dead, the missile would be harmless: but how would Castro know? Might Kennedy linger in the hospital? An hour? A week? A month? Meanwhile, what? Jesús Ferrer had no appetite to be killed needlessly. But it would take his bus, charging through the guardpost, a full minute to reach the missile; from fire to take off would require only twenty to thirty seconds. There would be no banging into it if the launch had begun: the bus would not be able to come close to the fiery galaxy. Was he obliged to take no chances, to charge ahead? The radio: "There are only glum faces around Parkland Memorial Hospital, ladies and gentlemen. But no official word. The President is in the operating room—"

From the third seat of the bus, Pano's voice was heard. *"Open the door! Open the door! It is Oakes! Joe! Open it, Jesus, Mary, and Joseph!"* Mico opened the bus door and Blackford climbed up. He had been running. He looked Jesús in the face.

"Quick. Brief me."

"They shot him. We do not know whether he is dead."

Blackford paused. "I say we take out the missile. Can't risk it going off."

"It will not go off—if Kennedy is—if he is—"

"Dead?" Blackford almost shouted. He began to move toward the driver's seat. Jesús Ferrer flashed an order. *"Agárrale."* Two of Ferrer's men rose from the front seat. The first blocked the aisle, his right hand circling one of the bus's aluminum bars, his left another. The second man crouched down in the aisle and leveled his machine gun at Blackford's groin. Ferrer hissed out in English, "Wait, Blackforrd. Wait, wait one moment. Be calm."

But then they heard the roar from the missile. It was too late.

THE SILENT WHITE soapsuds at the missile's base began to accumulate, lazily at first, then, gradually, in torrents; then came the noise that shook the membranes of the inner ear even a hundred yards away, within the safety of the cave, so that when Pushkin brought out his pistol and fired three times at Kirov no one could distinguish the pistol sounds from the great, comprehensive roar, except Leandro at his side. But the Soviet guard opposite saw the action: he saw a man dressed as a Soviet sergeant lift a pistol and aim it at whoever it was, outside the guard's view, at the command-post level of the cave. The guard swiftly raised his rifle and fired at Pushkin, dropping him to the ground with a bullet that only narrowly missed Leandro before reaching the cave's stony wall opposite. Leandro rushed past the body of Kirov to the radio console. He fired his pistol into the head of the technician, swung around, and slammed his wrist triumphantly over the DESTRUCT switch. A fusillade from Soviet guards, opposite, brought Leandro down. He hit the ground as three miles up on its trajectory, Petrouchka exploded in midair.

At that moment, six Cuban Special Service guards—the elite guard deployed for this special mission—opened machine-gun fire on the Soviet personnel, a thousand rounds fired at six Soviet technicians and two dozen Soviet guards.

IN THE BUS, Jesús Ferrer and Blackford were paralyzed by the deafening sound of the missile launch. Blackford stared as it rose into the sky, and, in a few seconds, shattered into fragments, falling in pieces into the ocean.

CASTRO HAD ACTED precipitately? He smiled as he puffed on his cigar and leaned back in his chair. "Fidel knows best," he teased.

But—they were not sure about him—he had fired the missile only a minute or two after news of the shooting. How could he know it was fatal? Maybe it was just a head wound?

The cars had arrived at Parkland Memorial Hospital and it was plain from the tone of voice of the announcer what to expect. At exactly 1400 it was confirmed.

John F. Kennedy was dead.

"You see?" Castro beamed. "You just need to trust me. Eh, Che?

"Osvaldo?

"Ramiro?

"Raúl?

"Let us have a little lunch."

They had had to wait until nearly midnight because the contact was scheduled for 0025, and it was a half hour's walk to the beach, Miguel and Mico serving as guides, Blackford and Pano following behind. Jesús Ferrer had left them just after the sun had set.

It had been very strange. The name of the victim had not once been mentioned, not by Ferrer, nor by any of his men, nor by Nena who came by. They had reached the little farmhouse separately, arriving in three different conveyances. Pano, all but threatening force, persuaded Blackford to abandon his motorbike—Mico mounted it—and ride in the automobile with him, leaving the second car to Ferrer and his three companions. When they arrived, Blackford went into his bedroom and quietly closed the door. At about six, Pano knocked. When told to come in he opened it. Blackford was sitting on the bed, still in his *campesino* clothes. Pano asked if he might bring him something to eat or drink, Blackford thanked him and said no. An hour later, Pano knocked again and said that Jesús Ferrer was about to leave, and would like to say goodbye. Of course, Blackford said, remaining seated on the bed. Pano looked at him inquisitively, and then retreated, and brought Ferrer into the little bedroom with the little cot and the crucifix directly above the slightly stooped head of Blackford.

He moved to be on his feet, but Jesús Ferrer put his hands on Blackford's shoulders. "*Siéntate, compañero.*" Sit down, my friend. "I am only here to say goodbye, though I suppose farewell is the word even Oxford would have authorized on this occasion. I wish to say only this, that although some people forget their debts, some do not, and I am that, perhaps not more than that, one who does not forget, and will not forget, you, and what you have attempted to do."

Blackford looked up and began to speak, but Jesús saw that he was having difficulty, so he placed his hands once again on Blackford's shoulders and whispered the words, "Farewell. *Vaya con Dios.*"

Soon after they set out—stealthily, through the thin little swampy forest between the farmhouse and the beach—Pano became aware that Blackford was walking somnambulistically. At one point where Mico, ahead of him, turned obliquely left, Blackford kept walking forward. Pano had needed to quicken his pace, seize Blackford, a hand on each arm, and gently redirect him to the left, following the trail of their guides. It was so when, reaching the cache behind the beach where the swimsuits had been hidden. Blackford dutifully put his on, including the face mask. Pano whispered, removing Blackford's mask, that it was not necessary to don it until the boat appeared.

It did so at exactly the contracted time, and the exchange of light signals was done. Pano said goodbye to Miguel and Mico, and Blackford said goodbye, and he noticed, vaguely, that they did not look him in the face.

They swam out to the same Elco that had brought them there on Wednesday night. The same two Cuban pilots helped them into the boat, and soon the captain turned on the power and, at moderate speed, moved toward the twelve-mile frontier.

Blackford, lying on the spartan settee, was jolted by the sudden revving of the boat to its furious sixty-knot speed after it had reached open water, the freedom of the seas.

There was no moon, but stars, especially congested, Blackford thought—crowding, perhaps, to ogle the events below— and there was a chill in the air. Blackford wondered if there was a chill in the air in Dallas. He wondered, too, what was the temperature in whatever room Fidel Castro was occupying. For almost eleven hours he had fought the compulsion to visualize the scene but now he couldn't any longer, so he let it happen. The cavalcade of stars. The crowds and the cheering. The photographers and the press. And then—the shot. He closed his eyes.

He had to face the question. Not the question, Could he, Blackford, have prevented it?

He had answered that question to his satisfaction. Yes, he could have prevented death from that bullet; no, not from another cause.

The question that tormented him now was whether he had been, somehow, responsible . . . in some way, indeed, an agent of—*that* bullet?

Operation Mongoose.

Mongoose, R.I.P. The operation as dead now as its godfather. Blackford closed his eyes, and his mind flowed from scene to scene. *The victim on the day of his inauguration. The victim on the day he sat in the Lincoln Bedroom*—quietly, oh so smoothly, quieting his brother.

He saw Consuelo, suddenly dropping below the husky outdoor picnic table at Tres Marías. He had to sit up. He leaned over the side of the speeding boat, and was sick.

Pano sat down on the chair, opposite the settee and, intending relief, said, "In a few minutes we will be there. I will spend the night in your apartment."

Blackford nodded, unsmiling. He was very pale, and Pano insisted that he put on a heavy-weather sweater. Blackford did so.

Fifteen minutes later the boat eased into the slumbering little harbor at Marathon and tied up at its slip. Pano turned his flashlight onto the settee and whispered, "We are ready, Black-forrd."

There was no reply.

He shone the light on Blackford's face, and quickly snapped it shut.

He climbed up to the cockpit.

"*Está durmiendo, nuestro compañero. Déjelo tranquilo.*" Yes, their companion was sleeping, and yes, they would let him rest quietly.

This is a work of fiction.

The most conspicuous historical characters are, obviously, characters in history, and some of the episodes are drawn from official and nonofficial, but creditable, sources.

—Operation Mongoose was the name given by the CIA to the attempt to assassinate Castro, from 1961 to 1962, and to related questions. Previous and subsequent attempts on Castro went under different names (Senate Select Committee to Study Governmental Operations with Respect to Intelligence Activities [hereafter cited as Church Committee], *Interim Report: Alleged Assassination Plots Involving Foreign Leaders*, 94th Congress, 1st Session, 1975, p. 139; Thomas Powers, *The Man Who Kept the Secrets: Richard Helms and the CIA*, Alfred A. Knopf, 1979, p. 129; John Ranelagh, *The Agency: The Rise and Decline of the CIA*, Simon & Schuster, 1986, p. 383; Tad Szulc, *Fidel: A Critical Portrait*, William Morrow and Company, Inc., 1986, p. 573).

—The attempt to assassinate Castro via a wet suit, to be given to Fidel Castro by James Donovan (without his knowledge), was made. Donovan's gift to Castro of a different wet suit is factual (Church Committee, op. cit., pp. 85–86; Powers, op. cit., p. 150; Ranelagh, op. cit., pp. 388–89).

—Allegations to the effect that the Soviet Union had left in hiding in Cuba one or more nuclear missiles were made by Cuban refugee sources and later by Senator Kenneth Keating (January 31, 1963). These charges were denied by Robert McNamara and John McCone on February 6, 1963 (*Facts on File Yearbook*, 1963, pp. 50–51).

—The attempt to poison Castro by poisoned pills through his mistress is factual (e.g., Paul Meskil, "CIA Sent Bedmate to Kill Castro," *New York Daily News*, June 13, 1976).

—The assassination of Blanco Rico by Rolando Cubela in 1956 is factual (George Crile III, "The Riddle of AM LASH," *Washington Post*, May 2, 1976; Powers, op. cit., p. 151; Arthur M. Schlesinger, Jr., *Robert Kennedy and His Times*, Ballantine Books, 1979, p. 589; Hugh Thomas, *Cuba: The Pursuit of Freedom*, Harper & Row, Publishers, 1971, pp. 889–90).

—The attempt to expedite the assassination of Castro by providing Rolando Cubela with an appropriate sniper's rifle is factual (Church Committee, op. cit., p. 89).

—The statement by Castro threatening retaliation against political assassination is factual (Crile, op. cit., "The Riddle of AM LASH").

—The sponsorship of Operation Mongoose by President Kennedy and Attorney General Robert Kennedy is asserted by Thomas Powers (op. cit., p. 155) and John Ranelagh (op. cit., p. 38).

—Although any direct knowledge of the plan to assassinate Castro was denied by CIA Director (1961–65) John McCone (Church Committee, op. cit., p. 99; Powers, op. cit., p. 149; Ranelagh, op. cit., pp. 387–88), it is widely questioned that he was in fact ignorant of the operation (e.g., Powers, op. cit., p. 150). It is not disputed that Operation Mongoose and its successors were administered by a division of the CIA.

ACKNOWLEDGMENTS

I wish to record my gratitude to the legion of friends who helped me with this novel—

Tony Savage typed the drafts with derring-do, using WordStar, Smartkey, and Savage-All. I yield to him the speed record, though with my Kaypro 386 plus all Tony's above, plus PathMinder, plus DesqView, plus SideKick, plus Daniel Shurman of Humanware to make sense of it all, I am, well, something of a dreadnought on a word processor.

Dorothy McCartney was principally in charge of the research, and will soon be offering classes in Cuban history.

Professor Perla Rozencvaig was good enough to supply me with details of Havana, 1963, which I found invaluable.

The manuscript was read by my wife Pat, my sister Priscilla, my brother Reid, my son Christopher, my friends Charles Wallen, Jr., Professor Thomas Wendel, and Sophie Wilkins—to all of them, my thanks.

Frances Bronson, as ever, provided the editorial coordination; invaluable, cheerful, indispensable.

Mrs. Chaucy Bennetts, the copy editor, caught one thousand and one solecisms.

Joseph Isola (he reminds me) has now proofread twenty-two of my books, since that fateful day in the sixties when, after spotting errors in my most recent book, he carelessly volunteered to help me with future books.

Alfred Aya, Jr.—as always—was my technical adviser; ever resourceful, ingenious, knowledgeable, and demanding. If there is a filament out of place in the missile scenes, it is not the fault of Mr. Aya.

Above all, I am indebted to Samuel S. Vaughan of Random House. This is the twelfth manuscript he has edited, and no one could have taken greater pains nor exercised better judgment than he in his recommendations. I am proud of our professional (and personal) association, and take pleasure in dedicating this novel to him.